Angst to the Nth

by
D.C. White

D.C. White

ISBN: 0983735506
ISBN-13: 9780983735502

DEDICATION

To my awesome husband and soul mate. We went over the
rainbow and guess what we found. Dreams do come true. This
has been awesome, sometimes hard and sometimes way to
easy, but all in all a dream come true. Thanks for being you
and making life a lot better for me.

ACKNOWLEDGMENTS

Thanks to our readers. You asked and here it is. I still can't tell you, but I guess you'll find out soon enough. Don't worry, we're not done yet! But soon, very soon, you will know the whole story. Hope you enjoy reading it as much as we did writing it.

Chapter One

"This is Sidney Norwood with breaking news, live from WKTL Channel 7 News, Metro D.C. This is your only full news channel, reporting live outside the Capitol building. This has been a crazy day. Earlier, we reported to you on how the vote passed and the reaction from the citizens, how they feel about the passing of this law. The reaction of the chip has been largely accepted, however, there seems to be quite a bit of anger suddenly surfacing. We are waiting for the . . .

"Sidney, we've lost you, we have no audio or visual, are you there" asks Gerry Partell of World Vision Now from New York. "I can't seem to hear anything, is she able to hear me" he asks his camera man.

"No sir, we seem to have lost her . . . we're trying again, hold on, there's a message coming in for you, can you hear it" . . . yes, Gerry motions with his hand to his ear, acknowledging receipt of the message.

With a horrified look on his face, he motions quickly to his camera men to bring him live. "Are we live" he asks loudly in a shocked voice, and is given the go from his camera man. "This is Gerry Partell with World Vision Now. I've just received a message from a source close to the Capitol building. There's been a large explosion in front of the Capitol building, in the spot that Sidney Norwood was standing, giving her live update. The sidewalk where she was standing is now a twenty foot crater. Anyone near that vicinity is gone" he adds in a shaken voice with tears streaming down his face. "Sidney Norwood was in the spot of the explosion, there's no possible way that she survived, nor did many that were in the vicinity." Gerry motions to cut to commercial and notifies the public that "I'll be right back with more up to the moment news." He grabs his handkerchief and scrubs his face, trying to wipe any sign of emotion from his appearance. "I need a comb" he demands in a shaken voice. "That poor woman" he says to everyone standing around in shock "she was annihilated, along with her team. Let's see if we have anyone near the Capitol building that can get live pictures to us. Someone needs to continue reporting for the public."

"This is Gerry Partell with World Vision Now out of New York. We'll be getting the live video feed any moment now, from Washington D.C. Let's recap what just happened. Sidney Norwood was reporting live outside of the Capitol building, standing on the front sidewalk near the fountain when there was an explosion that left a twenty foot crater in the spot where she was standing. It took out the front steps, and part of the foundation across the front of the U.S. Capitol building."

"It looks like we have a camera back and as you

can see, the smoke and concrete dust is still hanging in the air, making visibility impossible. It looks and sounds like utter chaos is happening. As you can see, people are running and screaming in the streets. If we could find a reporter close to the scene, wait, is that Jim Cochran? See if you can get him to talk to us and let us know what's going on right now."

"Gerry, its Jim, I can hear you, what can I do for you" he asks in his deep voice, shock in every line of his being. "Jim, we just heard what happened, can you verify please."

"Sure Gerry" he begins as the camera crew finally focuses on his face, a face covered with white soot and many smudge marks from him trying to brush it off. "There's been an explosion on the sidewalk in front of the Capitol building, approximately ten minutes ago, in the spot that Sidney Norwood was standing, giving her report."

"So far there is no sign of her or her camera crew. With all the chaos surrounding it, the police and fire departments swarming the scene, it's impossible to distinguish who is where. I refuse to report that she's gone until I've received word from someone of authority. Until then, I'm reporting that the information regarding Sidney Norwood is not official."

"The damage, however, to the Capitol building, looks extensive. There's broken glass, concrete dust, and bricks lying about. The concrete dust has not settled yet, so it's making viewing of the area difficult, at best. There looks to be many people injured by the falling debris. The death count could be in the hundreds since there were so many people witnessing this 'first of its kind of vote for the chip implementation.' Seconds after the tally of the vote was announced, an explosion rocked the area. It happened so fast no-one had a chance to move away.

"So far, we've received no information regarding anyone claiming this act. It's early yet, so the cause of this atrocity still remains unknown. The Capital building has obtained extensive damage, judging by the amount of broken glass, and bricks that are lying everywhere. It's possible the whole building is leaning slightly forward. It's difficult to tell since the sidewalk where the fountain was and a large portion of the foundation area is missing. People are lying on the ground or wandering around looking confused and lost, some injured and all of them looking as if they were in a war zone. It's hard to believe that this happened after we've had only peace and quiet for the past few weeks."

"Why now, what happened that caused this person or group of people to do something like this. Today was just supposed to be a day of celebration. We were being notified of the results for the chip, about the vote and how it went. This was definitely not part of the plans for today. Hopefully, we'll hear something soon about the cause of this tragedy, and how many people this affected.

"As you can hear, it's mass chaos everywhere you look. The noise is tremendous, people are screaming, looking for loved ones, or walking around in a daze while trying to go somewhere, anywhere. The police have converged on the area and now hopefully everyone will be evacuated safely.

"This is 'BREAKING NEWS' the President of the United States, Jane Martin, has declared a federal emergency and called for a police state. There have been explosions in all the major cities of our country, it seems all timed to explode at the same time. A call has gone out for the National Guard. They will be meeting with the Local LEO's and the FEDS to take over all of the public safety measures in every state. We will bring you the most up to date information that we can get, so please stay tuned. This is Jim Cochran of WELT News Channel 3, Washington D.C.

"Oh my God" Kat screams as she watches the utter chaos that surrounds the Capitol Building. "I can't believe this" she yells to Des. "What the hell just happened" she asks while she runs to get to the area of the sidewalk where Sidney was standing. "There's no sidewalk left" she exclaims in disbelief after she wrestles her way to the front of the area of the explosion. Stopping when she gets there, a twenty foot crater in place of where the sidewalk used to be, and where her friend, and reporter, Sidney Norwood was last seen standing, giving a live update. With fear etched in her face, she turns to Des "Damn it, she didn't deserve to be killed, not like this, not like this." Was she the reason, or was it something more. The vote, it had to be the vote. "She never did anything to deserve this" she cries at Des.

"I know Sir, this is terrible. There's nothing left."

"The Capitol, look at the Capitol. Shit, this is not a safe place to be standing" she says as she watches a brick land on the ground not ten feet in front of her.

"Let's move it here Des, watch for falling debris. Go, go" she yells as she takes off for an area that looks relatively clear. Des is following close behind until a brick finds her right shoulder, knocking her to the ground. All the commotion is towards the front of the building, not here at the side. Once she reaches the side of the building, away from the site of the explosion, she turns to yell at Des and finds her lying on the ground about a hundred feet behind her.

"Des" she screams as she runs back to where she's lying on the ground. "Are you alright" she asks breathlessly.

"I'm sorry Lieutenant, but I don't think so. I got hit in the shoulder by a falling brick. I think it's broke."

"Shit, shit, shit" Kat swears as she drops to her knees next to Des, coughing and choking, trying to get air in, instead of concrete dust. Des has a glazed look in her eyes from the pain and is quietly moaning.

"Help, we have an officer down here" she yells between coughs, while frantically searching for a medic. Everyone appears to be busy, so she gently helps Des to sit up, checking her for any open wounds. Des gasps in pain at the sitting position, tears leaving tracks through the dust on her face. "We have to move you" Kat informs her. "This is not a safe place to be, we can't leave you here. Can you walk?" she asks urgently.

"I'm going to try" Des assures her "can you help me up?"

"Yeah, on three" Kat says "one, two and"

"Shit" Des says as the pain nearly takes her back to her knees. "Alright, I'm up, as far up as I'm going to get" she informs Kat.

"Okay, let's try to get over there a little more, out of the falling debris area." After practically carrying her, they get to a somewhat safer area "can you stand here for just a minute while I try to reach someone?" Kat asks her.

"Yeah, just make it fast Lieutenant. I'm not sure how long I can do this" she admits, the pain making her dizzy.

White-faced and shaky, Kat moves away from the building and grabs her phone to call Snake. "Snake, it's bad" she cries. "They just killed Sidney. She's gone, there's nothing left, and Des is hurt. She thinks her shoulder's broke, she got hit by a falling brick" she says, hysteria building.

"Kat, Kat, calm down, take a breath, calm down and tell me what happened again."

"There's been a huge explosion in front of the Capitol building. The sidewalk that was there is now a twenty foot crater. The spot where Sidney Norwood was reporting from is gone. There's nothing left. Des and I were running away from the sight, too much falling debris, but before she got to a safe area, she got hit with a falling brick and thinks it broke her shoulder. She's in a lot of pain, and I can't find anyone to help her."

"Are you all right" Snake demands.

"Yeah, just shaken" she admits, tears streaming down her face, leaving trails in the white dust that covers her from head to toe.

"It's all right Kat; I promise it will be all right."

"It will never be all right" she denies. "Sidney's dead, because she was doing her job, reporting for the people of America. Now murdered, and Des is hurt badly" she keeps repeating.

"Kat, listen to me" Snake says roughly. "You have to pull yourself together. Becoming hysterical is not going to help matters at all. Where are you right now" he demands to know. "KAT, WHERE ARE YOU?" he yells.

"Oh, sorry Snake, I'm at a side of the Capitol Building, southwest I think, about a block from the crater."

"Kat, leave that area now. We're unsure if there's another explosive device, so get the hell out of there until the area's been cleared."

"But"

"NO BUTS! Get out of there NOW!"

"Okay, okay, I'm going" she mumbles, shock on her face.

"Kat, listen to me" Snake says. "Meet me at the coffee shop, make your way there right now, we'll talk. You aren't good for anything right now, you've had too much of a shock. Just meet me at Mikes."

"Okay, I'll be there in about ten minutes or so. Des is injured pretty badly. I'm not sure how far she can walk like this. Can you call someone to help her when we get there? The streets are a mess, jammed with people. It's going to take me longer than normal and with Des injured it may be awhile. I have to find a car for transport, but I'm on my way now."

"Good, I'll see you in a few and I'll make some calls."

"Des, we're here, are you awake" Kat demands when they arrive at the coffee shop, after a long thirty minutes passed. It takes time to hot wire a vehicle. "I have to get you inside. There's Snake, thank goodness he'll help. Snake, it was bad" Kat sobs as he holds her close, trying to warm her up after the shock of seeing a friend killed.

"I know, shhh, it's all right, it's all right" he murmurs, rubbing her back up and down in a soothing motion. "It'll be okay" he promises quietly as Mike stands back with a look of shock on his face and Des sits in the car injured and in pain. "Let's go inside and sit down, have a coffee." Snake says with a questioning look at Mike to get her a cup of her coffee. That snaps Mike out of his shock and has him moving to help. After getting Des out of the car without causing more damage, Snake helps her into the coffee shop.

Kat sits down and takes a deep breath, trying to gather her wits about her. "I'm sorry" she says to Des, Mike and Snake. "I don't know what happened to me there" she admits.

"I do" Snake says "you just witnessed a friend killed and a partner injured. It's normal to be upset. This has never happened to you before" he says soothingly.

"I suppose" she agrees "but I'm not supposed to get upset or hysterical" she adds in anger and denial. "I'm a cop. I'm supposed to be able to handle these things, and help the public and my partner, if need be."

"You will," Snake agrees "you're just still emotional from your past experiences, but that will pass." With a door chime, in walks one of Snake's unit members, the Medic Rand and he's carrying his supplies. He walks over and starts to help Des as Kat and Snake look on. "Okay, we have help, better than the ones out in the field right now. He'll help her, he's good" Snake says reassuringly.

"Now what's the news" Kat asks. "There must be other things happening out there. I just don't know if there was anything else big."

"There have been more explosions, about five minutes ago. The one in D.C. destroyed the sidewalk on the southwest side along with most of the foundation across the front and now the southwest side of the Capitol Building. People have been evacuated from the vicinity of the Capitol and were asked to go home or to get out of town until the Capitol Police have a chance to do a sweep for any more explosives and get anyone still in the building evacuated."

"Oh. . . My . . . God" Kat says as she sinks into the seat behind her in shock. "Snake, that's the area where Des and I went to get away from the falling debris. We could have both been vaporized if you hadn't told me to come here. We could be dead" she says, eyes wide in shock.

"It didn't happen" Snake reassures her "so let it go, you can't dwell on it or it will make you nuts. You're fine, it's okay."

"There's been another explosion" Mike yells from the back "it's on the news right now. It's the sidewalk on the Southeast side the Capitol building. It sounds like whoever's doing this is trying to destroy the whole Capitol building. There's only one side left that hasn't been touched by explosives and the media is now reporting that the same thing is happening in every state at every capitol building. There won't be a capitol building left when this is over."

"Shit" Snake exclaims "I have to go, this is big. I need to get to my unit and start investigating. We need to find out who the hell is doing this. I can't believe it's a left wing Christian group. Whoever this is has some military background, because they know too much about explosives, how to set a charge to damage a certain area. I'll try to keep in touch with my cell, but don't expect too much for awhile. It could be days or weeks before I can get in touch again. Sorry Kitten, but work calls."

"That's alright" Kat murmurs "I'll be fine. I have to get to work too."

"Des, how's the shoulder?"

"A little better Sir, I'll be fine."

"Kat, leave her here for now, I'll get her home or to a hospital if that's what needs to be done" Mike offers.

"Thanks Mike, I appreciate it. I'll owe you."

"No you won't, just go but stay safe. Try to keep in touch so I don't worry my head off and I'll take care of everything on this end."

"All right, thanks again Mike. I'll talk to you soon, Des. Call me if you need me, otherwise I'll be in the field. Snake, be careful please and stay safe out there."

"You got it Kitten, I'll be in touch."

"This is Jim Cochran of WELT News Channel 3, Washington D.C., live at the Capital building. I've just received information that the President will be holding a press conference within the next half hour, live from Camp David where she was spirited away after the first explosion. I'll be covering that as soon as it begins. Please stay tuned for up to the moment information. Let's recap. Earlier, we reported that there was an explosion in front of the Capitol building, where Sidney Norwood was doing a live update. The explosion left a twenty foot crater where the sidewalk was, killing an unknown number of pedestrians, and her complete camera crew. That explosion occurred at eight forty three p.m.

"Just twenty minutes later, another explosion occurred on the south west area of sidewalk near the Capitol, shattering more windows and weakening an already wobbly foundation. Debris flew outward with that explosion, creating mass panic while also killing a large number of pedestrians. It looks like a war zone near the Capitol building. Dust is still settling, while the police, FBI, and any available military are trying to help the general public to evacuate the area."

"Breaking news just in. We've just had a third explosion, this one occurring on the opposite side of the Capitol. Each explosion that's occurred at the D.C. Capitol building has also occurred nationwide at every capitol building in every state."

"It looks like whoever this is, is trying to destroy all of the capitol buildings. Maybe due to what they represent, since they're recognized as the center of our country, and of each state, more so than even the White House. These buildings are where the laws are created for this country. That may have something to do with it, but that's just conjecture on my part. I have heard nothing like that from any other source. Since the third explosion, there is only one side of the building that has not been affected by this. The structure is almost completely destroyed and very unstable. Every capitol building has been damaged in the same way. With each explosion, the same exact thing has happened all over the country, at the same exact moment. Whoever did this has synchronized the explosions."

"Please pay attention to this public announcement: Now that the sun has completely set and darkness is rapidly approaching, finding and helping everyone affected by this terrible bombing will be much more difficult. If you are able, please evacuate the area. This will better enable the safety forces in looking for and hopefully finding those injured by the blasts. The bomb squad has been called in along with the bomb sniffer dogs and the crime scene techs with the cadaver dogs. Everyone is arriving at the Capitol building area to help in any way that they can. Stay tuned for further information.

This is Jim Cochran of WELT News Channel 3, Washington D.C., live at the Capital building. The President is due here via satellite in the next two minutes to address the public regarding the explosions. Here she is now at the podium and she is live:

"Thank you everyone, for joining me tonight. This has been a confusing evening. First the good news about the vote on the chip, as I reported earlier, it passed, and now I want to reiterate the landslide that it passed by. You're decision came through loud and clear with the huge amount of votes that this chip received. I am very excited about this passing and now the American public can receive what they deserve and keep those out that are undeserving. Thank you for your support on this vote and of me, as your new President."

"Next, I must inform you that the explosions that have occurred near the capitol building were created by some as of yet unknown subject or subjects. I promise you that we will find out who created these disasters and they will be brought to justice. Until then, I have declared martial law. The military has taken over for the local police in every state, since every state's capitol building has been bombed. You must listen to what the military tells you to do. They will gain control of these problems and reinstate your normal laws. Once they are able to regain normalcy, they will be turning everything back over to the local police. The sooner that you, as part of the American public understand what must be done, and do it, the sooner things will get back to normal."

"It is with a heavy heart that I inform you of the death of one of Washington's' finest reporters, Sidney Norwood. She was reporting live from in front of the capitol building where the first explosion occurred. Her crew, along with herself and an unknown number of innocent bystanders, were killed in the first explosion. Another unknown number of innocent bystanders were killed in the second and third explosion. The military and the capitol police are at this moment doing a search of the area for any other explosive devices. Please, go home and give the military a chance to get some answers and secure the area from any further potential explosive devices."

"Please stay tuned. I believe that I will follow through with my previous plans for the morning.

Originally, I had planned to introduce you to the founder and creator of the implanted chips. He will still address you and explain to you the chip and all of its potential. This is a scheduled appearance for ten a.m., so please prepare for this information. The investigation into this attack will continue on until we find out who did this and apprehend them. Be prepared citizens, for once we know who did this and capture this/these individuals, you will again be asked to act as judge and jury. Thank you for joining me and I will be back as we gain information" President Martin adds as she finishes the broadcast.

"This is Jim Cochran of WELT News Channel 3, Washington D.C., live.

"Devon, I'm glad I caught you" Kat says as she rushes into Capitol Police headquarters. "I need to talk to you in your office if you can spare a couple of minutes."

"Sure, let's go. What's up" he asks as he closes his office door.

"I just left Snake. He had me meet him at Mike's after the explosion that killed Sidney. Des got hurt when a brick fell off the building after the first explosion, it looks like a broken shoulder. I admit that I kinda lost it but I thought we should talk."

"Fine, what about?" he says on a sigh.

"Martial Law. It's been enacted by the President?" Kat asks.

"Yes, but let's talk about something I don't know, alright? I'm a little busy at the moment."

"Have you heard anything about who's claiming responsibility?"

"We just received word that a left wing religious organization has claimed responsibility. They're protesting the chip implementation, claiming that not enough was made known about the chip and its actual uses. They believe that the President is withholding information that is detrimental to the public. They also believe that this will be more harmful than helpful to the American people."

"Wow, I hadn't heard that, I'm glad I got you before you left. Did they mention which group issued this?"

"No, they were just described as a left wing religious organization. My personal opinion is that this is one of the underground groups."

"What underground groups?" Kat asks with a confused look on her face.

"According to the information that I received from Eli, this is a group of people led by Reverend Johnson. They believe they're living in the end times, have actually built doomsday shelters in New Mexico, Colorado, Utah, Arizona, god knows where else. They believe they will survive doomsday and it will be their job to re-populate the earth. Along with average people, the brightest and youngest people are welcomed in this, the doctors, scientists, and engineers, anyone that knows how to rebuild the infrastructure. The average people are there to supply the man power to rebuild it."

"These places are like Taj Mahal's of the underground, with all the comforts modern society can conceive. They've been in existence since before the Y2K scares more than ten years ago. I didn't know places like that existed, and if these people believe that the chip is likened to the mark of the beast, then why did the Reverend get the chip? He found out the hard way that it couldn't be removed and when he found out by trying to remove his own chip the same night that he got it, he started moving his people. Being underground allows them to do and say things that others living normally would never do. The normal groups really have their hands tied due to the new way of the law that the President instituted. It would be way too dangerous for them to voice anything negative. The people would judge them and find them guilty, and you know what happens after that" Devon says.

"What's your decision, are you going in search of this group?" Kat asks.

"No, not while martial law's in effect. My job's on hold unless the military asks for help. Since that's not going to happen, all we can do is search through our own channels and get an idea of who did this. But first, I need to get a body and head count from the Capitol. Those people are my responsibility and I will not let them down. I need to know how many were in the Capitol during the first explosion, how many escaped and how many are still missing. We'll have to set up a command station, and find these poor people as soon as the bomb techs clear the area."

"Someone needs to be held accountable for this travesty. I have a hard time believing a religious group killed all of those innocent people, before coming out and complaining about the chip. It just seems to me to be totally backward. I thought religious groups put people first. I guess not though, at least this one didn't" he adds in disgust.

"Do they have an estimate of how many were killed in these two attacks?"

"I believe it's in the hundreds already but that's not an exact count and that's only the D.C. count. I'm sure it will grow once people realize whose missing and then report them. Since there were explosions in every state across the country at every capitol building, the death toll rises every minute. When it's all done, we'll no doubt be in the thousands maybe even tens of thousands. Not to mention how long it's going to take to find all the victims. This is big, bigger than a religious group, is my thinking."

"Have you talked to Eli and Mallory? How are they doing with all of this?"

"Yeah, Eli phoned about two hours ago and confirmed that in Los Angeles, martial law was also instituted which gives him time to look into this, the way I am. They lost quite a few people there, too. Mallory, she's been out in the middle of small town USA so wasn't as affected as we were or even as Eli was. They both plan on getting here, but they have to wait until they reopen the airports and start clearing flights. That's probably going to take a few more days. Until then, it's just you and me. What about your office?"

"My captain quit early this morning. He said he'd had enough and that he and his wife and kids were going west where there are less people, less stress. It totally came out of the blue, so I really haven't had time to process that, what with the explosions and such. My department is officially without a department head, but I'm sure it won't be for long.

They always have someone waiting to fill in or take the position.

"Deputy Chief Callander, I have some information regarding the bombs. We were able to obtain an intact bomb from the manhole behind the capitol building" informs his bomb tech after barging in.

"It was actually located in the manhole that leads underneath the sidewalk. Luckily, one of the bomb dogs sniffed it out. Once we were able to find it, we had the bomb robot brought out. We were able to direct it into the end of the manhole using one of its arms and telescope it far enough to be able to reach it. The tricky part was the motionlessness that it had to be done in. Any amount of sudden jarring could have detonated the bomb. Since we were unsure of exactly what was used, I think we all held our breath until we were able to remove the wire detonator. If that robot would have malfunctioned, we'd have been dust."

"It was actually a simple bomb consisting of a block of Semtex and TATP (Tri-acetone:Tri-peroxide) which was being used as the booster for the Semtex. They loaded the needed amount into a small prescription bottle with no label, added a wire detonator which they attached to the Semtex and then a cell phone, used to detonate. The explosive would have been large enough to take out the sidewalk and leave a crater. Unfortunately, this is such a simple bomb that anyone could have gotten the information on how to make it, simply by going to their favorite science pages on the internet."

"Since they used a throw away cell phone, it's not traceable. All anyone would have had to do is call the number. However, since we were able to retrieve the TATP undisturbed, we may be able to obtain fingerprints from the bottle that it was in. I doubt that they were expecting anyone to be able to retrieve an unexploded bomb. So we're hoping that whoever did this didn't figure that we'd be able to get our hands on a whole explosive device and left fingerprints all over the bottle. Once we retrieved it, removed the wire and then placed it safely in the Total Containment Vehicle (TCV), we moved outside of the city to the two acre plot that we maintain just for these purposes. We dismantled it so that we could preserve the TATP bottle, stored the Semtex separately and are now in the process of fingerprinting the bottle and the cell phone" the bomb tech says.

"Notify the Lieutenant and tell him to put the word out to the other states. Hopefully we can stop any more detonations. Put a rush on that." demands Deputy Chief Callander. "I also need your written report, please, as soon as it's available."

"Yes sir, I'll finish it sometime today. The Semtec that the bomb was made out of is an old Russian grade, not the same that we have in the United States. But it wouldn't be unusual for some third world country to obtain plenty of this. For the right price, anything's available. The TATP is available anywhere, especially at any beauty supply store. There's no way we can trace that since there are beauty supply stores everywhere."

"This looks like it's from a large terrorist cell of unknown origins. We're hoping for more answers that might pin point who may have done this. My guess is some middle east group, they like bombs and aren't afraid to use them everywhere. This was well planned out and an extremely large group since every state experienced some destruction, all at the same time. We'll be looking into all the security tapes that surround the capitol, looking for anyone suspicious that was working on or around the building in the past week. If we're unsuccessful, then we'll go back farther."

"So far we've received calls from twenty three states with successful completion of the same job that we did. Let's hope the rest of the states end up the same."

Chapter Two

"This is Jim Cochran of WELT News Channel 3, Washington D.C., waiting for the President to arrive at the podium at Camp David where she went after the first bombing occurred at the capitol building. This is her pre-scheduled meeting with the creator of the FIQH Chip, the CEO of Farhquest Industries. She's due here momentarily. Here she is:

"Thank you for joining me, Ladies and Gentlemen. I would like to introduce to you Mr. James Fahr, Owner and Chief Executive Officer of Farhquest Industries. He is the creator of the FIQH Chip that you saw implanted into my hand, the Vice President's and the Minister's. I'm happy to say that we have experienced no problems with this chip, there have been no side effects from the placement of the chip, and that I do not expect any problems to arise" reiterates President Martin as James Fahr walks forward to the podium, a tall, regal looking gentleman in a dark suit and crisp white shirt with a subdued red tie. With his classical features he could be a prince from another country.

"Thank you President Martin, and thank you American citizens, for allowing me to talk with you today, after all the terrible things that have been happening in this country" announces James Fahr. "This chip, the FIQH chip, has been worked on for more than ten years now. FIQH stands for "Fahrquest Industries Quality Healthcare" and each chip is marked with this name so that in the future, no one will ever be able to say they do not know what this chip is.

"We have worked hard at removing any potential problems by refining our product. It's working perfectly. We've checked with multiple types of scanners and have not found any problem. The information comes through smoothly and quickly after each scan. I am declaring all of these tests to be successful. I believe we can now start to mark our calendars and prepare to administer these chips to each and every citizen of the United States. I want to thank President Martin for her support in this endeavor and for allowing us to use her and her closest advisors as examples for demonstrating how well this product is working and will continue to work.

"Now as for dates of when these chips will be implanted. Of course, it will not be fast, however, production is to the point now that we may begin within the next few weeks. I expect that we will be ready very soon. I also want to remind everyone that these chips will have a new program installed on them, due to the reports from the general public of possible election fraud. There will now be no way, for anyone that is not the rightful person that was implanted, to vote."

"These chips are also not able to be removed without our knowledge. Once you're implanted, it will remain permanent. In order to keep these chips secure when in your body, we had to come up with a way of proving that the chip was yours. A special chemical was added that is absorbed into the skin with the first injection, marking the person with the chip, permanently. That chemical cannot be removed and will be easily seen. It's similar to a tattoo yet dissimilar by way of type of chemical. These are all ways for us to protect each and every one of you. We had your best interests in mind when we discussed what could be done to reassure you that no false knowledge could be transmitted, and that no one could remove your chip and use it as theirs.

"Remember, these chips will benefit you, this is your health information and it allows you to be treated at any medical facility. It also acknowledges you as an American Citizen, giving you free health care coverage, compliments of your country. I will be releasing information regarding these chips so that you may read up on what they are and what they will do. Check your local on-line news daily for this information. I want to thank you President Martin, for allowing me the honor of speaking to you and the American citizens."

"You're quite welcome Mr. Fahr. We appreciate you sharing your information with us. I'm sure the American people appreciate all that you and your company have done for us.

"I have just a couple of more items that I would like to discuss and then I will leave you" states President Martin after Mr. Fahr leaves the podium. "First, the area surrounding the Capitol building is restricted and the military are asking all citizens to stay home. Remember that we're under martial law which makes them the governing body. I would now like to introduce to you General Richard Bossley, the General of the Armies. This is a rank that has only been bestowed twice before in U.S. History. He's a five star general and has served this nation diligently for the past thirty years. The reason I gave him this rank is in the event that full martial law is invoked. He will be the man to run the country if I, in fact, cannot. Martial law has been declared to maintain order, add security and provide essential services for our people. The military will also help to locate any and all explosives that could still be hidden and not exploded at this time. They are also securing our government buildings. I want no more innocent people killed or injured by some fanatics that have eschewed the law because of their own inability to understand.

"We will find the people responsible for this terrorist act, and I promise that we will bring them in front of you, the U.S. authority. They will not be allowed to escape your judgment. As of now, all law enforcement will be handled by the army. We are asking the capitol police, FBI, local police and any other federal, state or local authorities to surrender their facilities to their local military so that this investigation continues on track with no interference.

"Now, the news regarding the chip. This chip will help to secure our borders by insuring the freedom of our nation and that only legal American citizens receive the health care rights that they deserve. Soon there will be no American citizen that will not have health care coverage. Everyone legally born into this country by legal American citizens will have this chip. You voted on this and it has become true. This is now law and is already being written into our laws so that everyone that is a true American citizen will be required to get the chip. After the chaos of the bombings has cleared up, we will make the decision on the dates that the chips will be made available to each of you. As you've seen, I received the chip on television, to prove that it is easy and painless, and I repeat that again, it is easy and pain free.

"Do not fear when you are notified that it's time for your chip implantation. Show up at the address that they give you and I promise within five minutes, it will be completed, and you will be happily on your way. If you get hurt or sick, every hospital will have the ability to read your chip and know how to treat you. The goal is to have every American citizen implanted before year's end.

"I am very excited about the direction that this new America is heading in. We're moving into the future and solving many problems as we go. I look forward to helping this country achieve everything it has ever dreamed of.

"We will not allow a few disgruntled people to end the new direction that we are going in. I will always be available to you, my public, for even the smallest of matters. I wish you a good night, stay home and stay safe. We will get those responsible for the destruction that has occurred in every state including our own D.C." President Martin finishes, turns from the podium and leaves amid loud applause.

"It looks like the people are very happy with our new President" comments Jim Cochran, WELT

Channel 3 News. "It will be interesting to see how all of these new things come to pass. I hope it will be as easy as she seems to thinks it will, but I have a bad feeling that today has changed the course of humanity. We'll just have to watch and see. This is Jim Cochran from WELT News Channel 3, Washington, D.C."

That's done, Jane thinks as she heads for her hidden office, where she can think and say whatever she wants. *The one room at Camp David, that no one is allowed to go in unless invited by me. Ahhh, life is good. Stage one down and only twenty more to go, before finally receiving all that is due me.* "Please send in Quinton and Jerry" she demands after calling her press secretary. "Thanks for coming" she says after Quinton shows up. "We're waiting on Jerry, he should be here soon" she informs Quinton. "Sit down, get comfortable and have a drink if you wish. We have a couple of things we need to talk about" she says quietly just as Jerry knocks and then walks in.

"Well, this has been a day" she admits wearily. "But it hasn't been all bad. We did get the vote we wanted, with a little help of course" she adds with a smirk. "It doesn't matter how, we got what we wanted and that's what matters. I think we need to contact our group and set up a day to transport them out of here quietly and send them to the Shah as an envoy. That would be the easiest and least questioned way. I shouldn't have to answer to anyone, but that day isn't here yet. I need to play the game a little longer" she says tiredly.

"Everything is going according to schedule, Jane.

Don't worry; you'll be in position when you're supposed to be. Until then, we need to control this country better than it's ever been controlled. Passing that law for the chip was the smartest thing ever done in the history of these United States. You're brilliant, I must say" Jerry assures her.

"I would have to agree with that, Jane, you are brilliant. You have achieved this much faster than any of us ever dreamed possible. There's no stopping you now" Quinton admits with a smile of delight. "So who are we sending as your envoy? I wouldn't mind going, but I probably

can't, since I'm the Vice President. It would be too obvious, I think."

"Yeah, it would be, Quinton, that's why you're not on the list for the envoy. I'm sending Ron Grayson, Jill St. George, Edward Sehgman and David Williamson. Those four people are the ones I placed into their positions more than a year ago. If only the public knew how long this has been going on, they'd be shocked" Jane admits with a laugh. "They're ready and eager to go. This has been a dream for a long time. My parents have sacrificed their lives for this to happen. This will happen because I will not let them have anything about their lives wasted. Not after all the sacrifices that they've made. We will be the world power, soon. Just a few more things that need to be done, but I'm on schedule, so that makes me happy.

"I believe all the bombing was completed today. That leaves one side of the capitol building in every state, intact. However, in a day or two, if the public doesn't crawl away to their homes and stay hidden, the last side may need to be sacrificed. I was hoping for today to be the last day, but Americans are a stubborn people. Every state has felt the power, maybe now everyone will believe and listen" Jane says firmly.

"This is Jim Cochran from WELT News Channel 3, Washington, D.C., with a breaking news update. The President of Iran is holding a news conference directed at the United States with a message for our President, Jane Martin. Here he is, live:

"I, President Murabbi Abdul-Majeed, the President of Iran, want to inform the people of the United States of America and President Jane Martin that we are, as a nation, appalled by all that has transpired in the U.S. during the past twenty-four hours. We are ready and able to assist you in your recovery from the damage that occurred during the bombings of your capitol buildings. What beautiful landmarks, giving the United States its dignity and freedom, to be taken away by some mad man's bombs, just because they disagreed with the votes of the citizens of America.

They will be caught, and dealt with justly. But in the mean time I am offering you our help to try to put things back to normal as quickly as possible. This act is being offered as a hand of friendship. It is time to put all the bad behind us and move into the same future that the United States of America is moving into. Please, do not hesitate to contact me, if there is anything that we can do, money, equipment, anything, we will be glad to do it. I, President Murabbi Abdul-Majeed thank you for your time and attention."

"That was President Majeed of Iran offering us help in the clean-up of our Capitol's. It will be up to our President to accept such an offer. This is Jim Cochran from WELT News Channel 3 in Washington."

"That was nice" Jane says to Quinton and Jerry, after watching the President of Iran's message on the flat screen in the corner of the office. "After that nice message from President Majeed, I'm moving forward with our plans. I'll let the group of four know about their approaching trip to Iran tomorrow. Tonight, I'm finished. I could use some sleep. It's been another hectic one and I'll be glad to put this behind me. It's time for the next step, starting tomorrow. Good night Gentlemen."

"Mike, what did you do with Des" Kat asks after finally reaching him after a sleepless night.

"I ended up taking her home, that's where she wanted to go. She promised to call her doctor today to have her shoulder checked and treated professionally. Not that the Medic didn't do a good job, I just think she should have it checked. It hasn't been x-rayed yet. I'm hoping that there's no damage except the break. How about you Kat" Mike asks quietly.

"I'm good, not sleeping, but that's not because of yesterday, it's become a chronic problem. Have you heard anything from Snake" she asks hesitatingly.

"Nope, not since he left yesterday, but he did say it could be awhile."

"Yeah, I know, but I was hoping" she admits wistfully.

"Kat, when are you going to tell him how you feel" Mike asks.

"I don't know Mike, honestly, I don't."

"Maybe you should think about it more" he advises. "Snake's a guy after all. They don't wait around forever, you know."

"I know, but I'm just not ready, not for a relationship at least. I promise I'll think about it more, but just tell him I inquired if he calls, please."

"You know I will, but the odds of him contacting me are much smaller than the odds of him calling you."

"I guess" she admits "but just in case. I think I'll head over to Des' house and see how she's doing. The streets in D.C. are almost totally deserted now, so hopefully normalcy will return quickly. Looks like the message from the President and the military presence did some good for a change" Kat says.

"Yeah, it looks like it, so all may be back to normal soon" Mike says.

Kat pulls up to Des's house with a screech of tires, jumps out and heads up the stairs to the front door. "Come in" Des yells after the pounding on the door stops. "Kat, I'm not deaf, it's my shoulder not my ear that's broke" she reminds her.

"Sorry, sick to me is sick, besides, I wanted to make sure you heard me" she admits with a grin. "So, what did the Doctor say?"

"The Doctor did X-ray my shoulder and it is broke, but the rotator cuff was also damaged by the brick, so he wants to do surgery to repair it. It looks like I'm going to be off work for awhile, Kat. I'm sorry" Des admits, discouraged.

"Hey, it's not your fault" Kat reassures her. "You had nothing to do with that brick hitting you, unless you bombed the building" she adds teasingly.

"There's no way, Lieutenant, I would never do something like that" she swears.

"I know, I know, I was just kidding" she adds with a laugh.

"Yeah, sorry Sir, I guess I haven't been up to laughing much lately" she admits.

"You will be soon" Kat reassures her as she heads to the door. "Let me know what's going on with your shoulder, Des. I'll talk to you later. Oh, and don't worry, I'll put your name and information in to human resources for workers comp insurance."

"Hey Mallory, when did you get in" Kat questions in excitement after she walks into FBI Headquarters.

"I got here about an hour ago. Why are all these military type people in here?"

"Haven't you heard the news?

"No, what news?"

"Martial law was declared in every state, everywhere."

"WHAT! No, I hadn't heard that. I was listening to CD's all the way here, instead of trying to get the local stations in on the radio. I didn't wait for the airports to be cleared. I decided to just drive back since it was only about a twelve hour drive and I figured, better driving here than waiting in some dinky airport for a ride. Besides, there's no telling when airspace will be allowed to reopen. Then when all the flights get caught up, who knows, it could be weeks."

"Yeah, that's the truth. I would rather be doing something productive than sitting and waiting for things to happen. There's nothing more boring than waiting.

"The streets look good" Mallory says after she's done greeting everyone.

"You should have seen them two days ago" Kat says. "It was crazy. Wait till you see the Capitol building. It's pretty much destroyed. The pictures on the television don't do it justice" Kat warns.

"That's where I'm heading next. I want to see just how much damage there is."

"Hey Devon, what are you doing here?" Kat says when she notices him getting off the elevator. "I'm here because the military has taken over my office and I heard Mal was coming in, so I came over here to see her."

A tall, military looking stranger walks up to the microphone at the front of the room and announces, "Ladies and Gentlemen, may I have your attention. On the screen behind me you will see the picture of the man that we have information on as being the mastermind behind the bombings. This is Lieutenant Jacob Callander, who, along with his squad, disappeared off the face of the earth a few weeks ago. They are an elite special-ops group and are considered a very worthy opponent. When they left their headquarters, they left them totally empty. I am very familiar with this man, since he was under my command for more than fifteen years."

"That's bullshit" Kat says loud enough to draw a quick glance from the gentleman at the microphone.

Devon quiets her and insists that they leave immediately. After getting out on the street, Kat turns on Devon informing him "you can't let them accuse him of that, that's crap. You know he didn't bomb anything. He's not responsible, he's was on their side. Let's go to Mike's and see if we can contact him."

Kat pushes through the door at Mikes and finds a group of military police handcuffing Mike and bringing him past her on the way to a military vehicle parked out front. "Hey, what do you think you're doing?" Kat demands.

"I think we better get out of here, that Lieutenant just pulled a picture out of his pocket and looked at you" Mallory says quietly to Devon. After moving quickly into the alley behind Mike's, Kat informs them "we need to go to my place; I have a way to reach Snake."

Kat picks her helmet up off her nightstand and puts it on. After it's in place, she pushes the button on the side that Snake had told her would contact him in an emergency. Just a couple beeps and Snakes voice comes through loud and clear. "Snake, they're accusing you of blowing up the Capitol and everyone's looking for you and they arrested Mike."

"Whoa, slow down Kat, calm down, and repeat what you just said, only slower this time."

"You're being accused of blowing up the Capitol and everyone's looking for you to arrest you, and they arrested Mike."

"I was afraid this was going to happen when I let you know that I was undercover. Right now, everyone that knows me is in eminent danger. See if you can get hold of my brothers and sister and go to the first place I ever took you to."

"I don't need to try to reach them since Mallory and Devon are standing right next to me right now."

"Good, then go to the first place I ever took you. I'll see you in an hour or so."

"All right, ladies and gentlemen" announces President Jane Martin to her handpicked envoy. "Airspace will be cleared very soon and your flight will be leaving. You'll be traveling on my personal transportation, but not Air Force One, that can only be used by me. However, I have other transportation that is being readied for you.

"Have your things gathered and ready, take off is tomorrow morning at zero eight hundred hours. The Shah is expecting you. I have a few things that I want you to take to him, so please do not leave tomorrow until you have them in hand. Go home now and prepare, this is a very important meeting that you are attending for me. I expect great results and answers that I have been waiting for all of my life. Things are now coming together for me, as I always knew they would, but it has been a long wait. Remember, you are not to speak of this trip to anyone outside of this room right now."

"You are four people specially chosen for this trip. No one else can know about this. Part of the reason each of you were chosen was because I knew I could depend on your silence. This is a special envoy chosen by me, just for this trip. Remember your loyalties and where they lay. I trust in you to do what is right and report back to me. I usually prefer to handle these things myself but because of the timing, it can't be done. I will attend the next meeting, however, so please inform the Shah of that information. Thank you, I'll be talking with each of you tomorrow morning, good night."

"This route is never ending" Kat complains after being on the road for almost an hour. "You sure you didn't take a wrong turn? Whoever Snake sent to meet us isn't going to hang around forever."

"Kat, stop your bitching, we're almost there. This is the end of the road for us, so to speak. Look, there's someone walking up ahead, towards the left side of this road, which is nothing more than a dirt path" he grumbles.

"Stop, what if he's on the wrong side? Maybe we should have our weapons ready, just in case."

"Fine" Devon agrees tiredly and pulls out his sig. "Better?" he asks Kat sarcastically.

"Yes, thanks" Kat says absentmindedly.

"That guy looks familiar to me, anyone else feel the same way?"

"No, I don't remember seeing him before" Mallory decides. "I'd have remembered him if I had" she says with a smile. "He's not bad looking, just the way I like them" she admits with a sigh.

"Wait, I remember, he's the medic."

"What? What are you talking about?" Mallory demands. "What medic?"

"The one that works with Snake. He came to Mikes and helped with Des' injury. Snake said he was a medic."

"Oh, I wasn't there, so I didn't meet him" Mallory remarks.

"Rand, is that you" Kat calls out from the safety of the car.

"Hey Kat, it took you long enough to get out here" he says with a serious look on his face. "Did you have some trouble?"

"No, we just had to borrow this vehicle and make sure no one was following us, so we took extra precautions which made us take a little longer than normal. But, here we are and we weren't followed, at least by anyone we could see."

"Great, follow me then, we're leaving this vehicle here. No time to hide it and where we're going, you can't drive. We have to move at a quick pace, though. I don't want to take any chances with being caught or observed. This is the only safe place left on this earth, everything else is known by too many people. You can never divulge this location or even the existence of this facility. It could mean the death of people too numerous to count. Their lives all depend on your ability to keep this a secret. Any questions, before we head out?"

Silence met his question and after looking at each one of the group and spending just a slight amount of extra time on Mallory, Rand starts walking. "It won't take long to get where we're going. This is through some rough terrain, so I hope you all wore your walking shoes" he says as he takes the lead. Thirty minutes later the group is starting to wonder where the hell they are. I'll never find my way out of here, Kat realizes. It seems like we've been traveling in circles. I hope Snake's there; I really need to see him.

"Ready everyone" asks Rand. "This is where we

change our direction" he says mysteriously with a small smile. "Stand to the right a little." After pressing a small spot on a tree, the ground starts to move, enough that you can see some rock steps leading down. "Let's go, we don't have time to stand around. We need to get this door closed again before someone see's it. Don't worry, there's air down there and there will be light, as soon as the door closes."

After everyone gets into the doorway and starts down the steps, Rand enters, closes the door and watches their expressions as the lights come on illuminating the stairway like an airport runway. At the bottom of the stairs is a floor covered with white tile, lighting the whole atmosphere. Everyone quickly looks at each other and no sound can be heard during the transition. Rand just starts laughing, "I wish I had a camera; that was awesome" he admits with a chuckle.

"So, are you ready to move" he asks when everyone just stands and stares in shock. When it finally sinks in, the questions start flying fast and furious. Holding up a hand to stave off the questions he reminds them where they are and what they're doing next. "Save the questions for Lieutenant Callander. He'll answer them all for you, but me, I want to get going. It's getting close to dinner time and I don't want to be late" he adds with an enigmatic smile."Just another half hour or so and your questions will be answered. Let's go."

After walking the same hall for a half hour, they enter a room guarded by two military personnel. Rand supplies a code and a retinal scan in order to open the door. Snake greets them with a salute and a smile when everyone crosses into the next room. Every square inch of the room is covered with electronics. There are people talking quietly everywhere or staring at screens. It's a huge war room, and everyone's busy. "How was your trip" Jacob asks as he glances at Devon and Mallory while reaching out for Kat. Once Kat is standing next to him, he moves into a relaxed stance.

"Snake, where are we and when was this place built?" Kat asks in shock.

"Let's see" he says thoughtfully while he runs his hand over his whiskers, rasping them. "About twenty five years ago I guess, maybe more. It was originally started in the fifties, but then the builder lost his income and had to find more, so it just sat for awhile. Then, a few years prior to Y2K, he continued on with this compound. There are more of these out west, but this is the only one this far to the east, so we took it over. It has everything we need. Food, air, water, places to hide safely. You can't ask for more" he adds seriously.

"Are there other people here" Kat asks.

"Oh, there are a lot of people here, but mostly they're military personnel. We try to send all the civilians out west. It's safer out there and it's easier to maintain military rules when there are only military present and their families of course. This is for the long haul. None of us are sure when or even if we'll ever be able to live outside of here. It all depends on what the future holds."

"What about our families" Devon asks.

"Oh, you mean Mom and Dad?"

"Yeah, what about them?"

"Not to worry Devon, Mom and Dad are already here. They've been here for a couple of weeks now and they actually seem to like it. Mom gets to cook as long and as much as she wants" he says and laughs at Rand's smile of bliss before continuing "and Dad, he's got as many military ears as he can handle. He tells stories all the time and has gained quite a reputation with the guys. Everyone loves them. They're perfectly happy and quite safe here. You'll be seeing them momentarily."

"Welcome to your new home. I won't be able to leave here since there's such a big price on my head. You won't be safe outside of here either, since you're known to keep company with me. I'm sorry, but I'm afraid you're lives have all just changed drastically. We'll talk about this all later, but first things first, let's eat. Mom doesn't like her food getting cold. We have the first shift. I figured you'd want to see them for yourselves."

Chapter Three

"Devon, is that you son" Joe Callander asks when he sees the group that just entered the dining room.

"Yep, it's me, Dad. I'm glad to see you both here safe and sound."

"Of course we're safe and sound. I doubt your brother Jacob would have it any other way. He was pretty insistent when he came to see us a few weeks ago. I guess you could say he wouldn't take no for an answer. What with everything that's happening, I'm sure glad he didn't. Ma, look who's here" he says on a laugh when Sandy comes through the door.

"Devon" she screams when she sees them "and Kat, Mallory, thank God you're all here. I've been so worried" she admits as she hugs everyone with relief.

"Why didn't you tell us Jacob, I would have made a special meal" she admits with a watery smile, tears gathering in her eyes.

"Mom, as far as I'm concerned, every meal you make is a special meal. Besides, I didn't want to give you false hope. You know how this group is, stubborn, totally stubborn, so I really wasn't sure if I could get them all here in the first place."

"Lunch is ready; shall we sit and eat while we talk?"

"Thanks Mom, we're starving, it's been a long time since dinner last night" Devon admits with a grin, relieved that they're all together and safe. All except Eli, he thinks.

"Jacob, we need to contact Eli, I'm worried about him. He hasn't been able to get out of L.A. since this all started. Too much going on out there and with airspace still restricted, he hasn't been able to get a flight."

"Yeah, I've been thinking about him and that situation. I have some plans just about ready. Let's eat first, then I'll tell you what I have planned. We eat here in groups, that way we're never without guards. So we're eating first today, we have a half hour, then the next wave will come through."

"Wow Mom, you alright with all that? That seems like a lot of work for one person."

"Devon, it's not just me, I have a bunch of kitchen helpers. I couldn't do this on my own. No,

I'm like the chef, with a kitchen full of people to help. Jacob makes sure I never have to do anything on my own. But, with all the help, I have a lot of fun. It keeps me busy and makes everyone happy. They all seem to like my food" she admits with a blush.

"Are you kidding Mom, I'd be lynched if I didn't take good care of you. These guys take their food very seriously."

"It's just a simple meal of fried chicken, mashed potatoes and gravy, green beans and some strawberry shortcake for dessert. It's no big deal."

"If you eat like this at every meal, it's no wonder everyone's in love with you" Kat admits with a smile. "I know I'm in love with you already." After everyone finishes they sit back with a groan thinking wow, stuffed, a nap would be good now.

"Let's move to the conference room, that way the

mess hall is ready for the next wave. We can talk there easier." Jacob suggests. After everyone gets settled into the conference room, Jacob reminds them of the reason why they're all here. "President Martin is not what she portrays. We're in the process of doing an in depth background on not only her, but also on her parents. There's just something that's not right there.

"Her parents are originally citizens of Iran. There's definitely a connection. Now with all that's happened, the President of Iran offering help, that just brings everything under suspicion. We haven't been able to connect her to him yet, not officially, but we have connected her parents to a Shah in Iran. I believe he's some kind of relative. It looks like maybe second cousins, but that would be her parents to him. She would then be a third cousin. That's enough of a connection to cause alarm. The way everything happened, putting her in the presidential position, and the speed that it was done in, is definitely not normal.

"My supposition is this has been a long term goal, and everything that happened to bring her this far was done on purpose. That would be including the deaths of all those congressmen and then the Director of Homeland Security and the President and Vice President. It looks like it was all set up to occur just the way that it did. No accidents, everything was preplanned. I know we briefly talked about this a few weeks ago, but really had no proof, just supposition. Now, we're obtaining some of the proof that we need. If everything shows up that I think will, we, as American citizens, are in mortal danger. This country no longer belongs to the American public, but to the

President, and she is not representing the country, but herself and whatever her goals may be.

"This whole problem was caused from terrorism from within. It's been a hostile takeover by a woman with an agenda. That agenda is to take this country and turn it into a dictatorship. She will be the final judge. The American people have no more freedoms. She's just done this under the pretext of making the American people feel like they are ultimately in charge. When there's absolute power, there's absolute corruption, like what's occurred in the past four months or so, there is no out.

"Unfortunately, most people are walking around thinking they're in charge, when in reality they are in charge of nothing. Not even their safety or their destiny's. That was given over and is being kept in reign by the President. The chips that are being readied to be implanted, they're more than health care chips. They contain a dye that shows who has taken the chip and they also contain a GPS unit along with all your health care information, all your affiliates, where you work, what your political agenda is, and your religious standings.

"They can also track who and what you voted for. These chips will create a country that is completely under the control of the highest power in the U.S. In the near future, they will control what you may buy, food, clothing, essentials. It will also track how much you spent and on what. The sad thing is, those without the chips will not be allowed to buy anything. You will be required to have the chip, to live. Newborns will be implanted on the day they are born. Everyone, by law, will be required to have the chip.

"We're in big trouble in this country. I'm officially in hiding. I can't do anything above ground without the military finding me and probably killing me. I'm now on the Presidents hit list. Even though I've done nothing to cause any of this to occur, I previously worked directly for the President, as I always have. Unfortunately, in order to maintain my capabilities, I had to move underground and not let the President know. Now the General of the Armies is trying to hunt me down. Unfortunately, I was trained by him, so he knows me and what I'm capable of. Fortunately I was expecting this, since I've kept the President and her office along with the new military regime under surveillance for the past few months.

"I had a bad feeling after observing what was going on, when we were losing Congressmen and women. Now the chip, no one truly understands exactly what this chip means to the country, to the people who choose to have it. She's made it sound like manna from heaven; hope for the masses, but in actuality it's the complete opposite. This is the FIQH chip and it literally means the true understanding of what is intended in Islam. Everything that has been done was intended. FIQH has been embedded on each and every chip.

"Now, the question is, what are you going to do? You're in as much danger as I am, since we're related and are known to visit each other and maybe even work together. Since I have a pretty hefty price on my head, you're no longer safe. They will try to get to me through you. I would prefer it if you just stayed underground with me and worked towards the same goal. I can't help you if you choose to go above ground again. I no longer have any power above ground. I know this is asking a lot, but for your own safety and the safety of all the people that came here trustingly, I ask that you take this under consideration.

"You're lives would not be worth much if they caught you above ground. Torture is a big price to pay, but pay it you would and since you've seen this place they would be able to find us. No one can withstand torture; it wears you down after a while. They'd get the information, sooner or later, and the outcome would be the same. This place would be overcome with the military and all here would be either put to death immediately or put in front of the American public, either way the outcome would be the same, death.

"Are you willing to chance all these people and go back above ground, or will you stay and help all of us try to put the U.S. back where it came from. Free. I know it's a lot to think about, but I'm asking that you seriously decide. If you leave, portions of this place will be moved and destroyed and you won't hear from me or anyone down here for a long time. Nor will you be able to find us. This is just a small part of the underground. That's all I'm going to say, but please, think about your decision. It could mean the difference between life and death, yours.

"I'll leave you now so that you can talk without pressure from me, or anyone else. You can find me in the war room. The guard outside the door will show you the way there, after you've made your decisions." Jacob leaves through the only door visible in the room.

"I'm stunned" Mallory says quietly. "I guess I was suspicious too, but I never thought that it was as bad as it is. I'm staying, that's for sure. I'll help fight this war, through underground means. No way would I ever put anyone down here in jeopardy. My decision's final. I'll make a new life down here. I don't need anything above ground. Devon, what are you going to do? Please don't go back; I can't stand the thought of never seeing you again. Kat, what about you? Please say you'll stay."

"I have to think about all of this, Mallory. I have friends above ground. What about them? How can I help them if I'm underground? Who's going to protect them? I can't make this decision quickly. I have to think long and hard before I decide. How can I help from down here? What can I do from here to help put the country back the way it was? What about Mike and his family. They're like family to me. All the family I have left."

"Hey, what about us" Mallory demands "we love you too. We're like family too."

"I know" Kat says on a big sigh. "I'm torn right now between the family above and this one below."

"I'm sorry Mallory" Devon says "but I don't feel like I can stay underground right now. There's too much responsibility for me above ground. I take my job seriously. It's not something I can just walk away from. Besides, all I have is Jacob's word for all this. He could be wrong or jumping to conclusions. I need to learn these things too. I can't just take his word for everything. Yeah, he's my brother, but truthfully he was gone most of our lives. He's really only been back for the past few months, and I'm supposed to take his word as truth for everything? These are

serious accusations and I need to trust my own instincts. I'll go back to my job and find the answers. If what I find is the same as Jacob's, then I'll somehow find you and come back. But I won't just follow him blindly. I can't."

"I trust Snake with my life, but I've always been responsible, and I also have responsibilities above ground. I have friends, co-workers and a job. They all depend on me to do what's right. It wouldn't be right for me to just walk away from everything that I know, from everything that I am. What about the future. The American citizens deserve people that will protect them, stand for them, and help them to stay safe. This is a whole country we're talking about. It affects them all, not just a chosen few. I know that Snake is going to do everything in his power to help us all, but in the mean time, I have to do everything in my power to protect and serve. Those are the vows that I took as a police officer. Nowhere in those vows did it say run and hide. I can't just not help it's not in my personality. "I'm going to go back home and take up my job right where I

left it. I have to. I'm sorry Mallory" Kat says quietly while Mallory starts to cry. "I promise I'll be careful and see you again someday, maybe even someday soon."

"Jacob, we've made our decisions. I'm staying" Mallory informs him after locating him in the war room. "There's nothing above ground that I need. From now on, this is where I'll be."

"I can't stay Snake. I have to go back. There are things that I have to do, people I have to protect. I can't just turn my back on everyone and everything. I promise to be careful though. I won't draw undue attention to me or to the ones I'm taking care of. Mike was being arrested when we came here. I need to find out why and how to help him. He's the big brother I never had. That's a responsibility that I can't leave. There's my partner too. She's injured and needs help. She can't protect herself right now, so she needs me. I also took an oath when I became a

cop, to protect and serve. There are a lot of Americans that are depending on all of us to protect them from everything, but especially the President. Unfortunately, they don't know about that yet. I can't in good conscience, leave them vulnerable."

"I'm afraid I feel the same way. I'll do my part, but it will be above ground. I have a job, people to protect and serve. I need to go back" Devon says firmly. "I will try to keep out of the limelight, but I won't run from my responsibilities, ever."

"I was afraid that you'd feel this way. I'll try to keep in touch with you, but I won't put these people underground in any kind of danger. You'll be in danger constantly, and I'll try to help when I can. However, my first duty is to this country. If we can save the country, then I won't have to worry about either of you. If the country continues on the way it has been, it won't be long before your jobs are nonexistent. The Military will assume your jobs and you will be left with nothing but running for your lives. I wish I could make you stay here, but I can't. It would be no different down here then it is up there, if I went that far. You won't be able to contact me once you return to your jobs. The underground will still be here, but not in this location. You will not have the capability to join us, not for awhile. I can't risk the safety of all these people. They depend on me to keep them safe."

"If this is your final decision, then so be it. I'm sorry you won't stay. I'll have Rand escort you to an area that you can leave through safely. Kat, the helmet will no longer work for reaching me. I can't take the chance that someone else won't take it and try to reach me. It will be for your own safety since you're going back, to not have the capability to reach me. That way, no one can accuse you since they will have nothing to accuse you with. Please, guard everything that you say, do not mention me at all, by any name. God be with you both."

"How much farther do you think it is?" Kat asks Devon.

"I don't know, but we've been walking for an hour with no sign of anyone. I can't believe these woods here are so dense."

"Shhh, I heard something" Kat says quietly. "It sounds like traffic, maybe over to the right."

"I see it" cries Devon with excitement. "It's the highway. Finally, we found civilization. Let's see if we can hitch a ride into D.C." he says.

"I'll talk to you later Kat. I'm heading into the office." Devon states after they arrive at the Capitol Police headquarters.

"Yeah, me too, I need to see what's been

happening in the past day, see what I've missed. I guess I could get that information from Des. Maybe I'll just head to her house first. Then I need to find out about Mike and what they've done with him. I'll call you later to update you."

"Thanks, Kat, I appreciate it."

"Hey lazy, how are you feeling" Kat asks after Des finally opens the door.

"I'm okay, a little painful yet, but okay. I'm scheduled for surgery tomorrow then hopefully I'll be on the mend."

"You will, it will finally be able to heal right. So, any news, work or other" Kat asks.

"No, I haven't heard from anyone, it's been kind of quiet since the explosions the other day. I don't think too many from our department have been working. It's all military right now. They've taken over our offices and jobs. So there really isn't much that we can do."

"No one's in the office, really? Have they hired someone to take over Captain Hill's job, yet?"

"Nope, not yet, they said there was no need since the military are doing all the police stuff right now. And since they've taken over the office's, there's nowhere for a new department head to go. I think they're waiting for the military to turn the control back to us and then they'll put someone in that position."

"Okay, I guess I'll take a ride there anyway, just to see." Kat says contemplatively. "What about the news on TV, anything new?"

"Haven't you been home Kat, how come you're

asking all these questions?"

"No, I was hanging with Snake for a couple of days. I haven't seen a TV since the day of the bombings. So what's new on the TV?"

"Then you don't know" Des says quietly.

"Know what?"

"They arrested Mike, the day of the bombings. He's going on trial in front of the American public, tomorrow."

"What! What for?" Kat yells.

"He's being charged with treason. They say he's the number two in charge of the bombings. That Jacob Callander is the number one person responsible and that Mike is the number two. They haven't been able to find Callander, but they grabbed Mike from his coffee shop and put him in jail."

"He was questioned in front of the public yesterday and goes on trial tomorrow. The voting takes place tomorrow night and into the next day. They want to execute him live on TV, just like they did to Addy."

"Oh My God" screams Kat. "They can't do this. He's not guilty of anything. He doesn't even know Jacob Callander. Shit, shit, shit! What am I gonna do" she cries, tears streaming down her face. "I can't reach Snake anymore. He can't help me with this. I gotta go. Maybe Devon can help" she says as she runs out the front door.

"Devon, can I come in" Kat asks after knocking loudly on his office door.

"Hold on one second" he says. He pulls open the door and places his finger against his lips to warn her that he's not alone in his office and to be careful what you say. "I need to talk to you" she says intensely but quietly.

"Can it wait" he asks just as quietly.

"No, it really can't" she insists. "Can we go somewhere private" she asks quickly.

"Sure, just give me a minute or two."

"Alright, let's go and get some lunch" Devon suggests when he leaves his office and finds Kat standing in the hall, just staring at the wall.

"Great," she says. Once they're on the street together, he starts questioning.

"What's going on Kat?"

"It's Mike. They arrested him and are trying him tomorrow on TV and then the public is voting on guilty or innocent. They want to execute him just like Addy. They say he committed treason, against this country."

"I heard about that when I got back to the office today. I doubt that there's anything that can be done to save him Kat, I'm sorry."

"No, that's not good enough. He's never done anything to justify this. The only thing he's ever done was befriend people, including Snake."

"Yeah, I know and that's why this is happening, I'm sure. They're going to use this to send a message to Snake and his underground group. He's the real trophy, not Mike. But they'll use him to justify a means to an end."

"Oh my god" she moans as she collapses onto a park bench. "I have to stop this. I can't let them do this to him. I'll have to do this alone. Snake warned me that I wouldn't be able to reach him now, at least for a long time."

"I know" Devon says quietly and with pity. "There really isn't anything that you can do. He's being guarded by the military and they won't listen to anyone except the President. She's never going to listen to either of us. We're part of the group she's trying to annihilate. She won't even do something if we tell her everything. She'll just do the same thing to each and everyone in the underground and to us, too. I'm sorry, but there really isn't anything either one of us can do about this. It's gone too far."

"My suggestion, go to his family and take them and deliver them to safety. It's what Mike would want. He'd want his family safe. Then you can let him know and it may give him peace. But that's really as much help as you can give him. You can't stop what's been set in motion."

"Yeah, your right, I can save his family for him. Damn it" Kat cries scrubbing the tears from her face. "Nothing I've done seems to help anyone."

"That's not true" Devon says in denial. "Remember, we're living in very rough times. Unfortunately, the American people can't see what's really under their noses. They can rightfully plead ignorance, because they are truly ignorant. This has become a bad joke, in the worst possible way.

"I'm sorry Kat, but I need to get back to work. I don't want to draw undue attention to either one of us. I'm sorry about Mike. He was a nice guy and doesn't deserve any of this. Go, find his family and take them to safety, somehow. I'm not even sure how to do that."

"Thanks Devon. I appreciate your talking with

me."

"This is Jim Cochran of WELT News Channel 3, Washington D.C. I am live here at the White House. President Martin is due here at any moment to address the American citizens. Here she is now:"

"Welcome, American public" President Martin says after arriving at the podium. "We have much that we need to discuss tonight. First, I want to thank you for your support of my office. I am here to help and we will put a stop to these fanatical groups that think it is right to bomb and kill innocent people, to destroy our government landmarks with no thought to anyone else. We cannot tolerate these individuals. We must stop them before they destroy more Americans, before they destroy all of our landmarks, those places that give us our sense of purpose, our freedom. It will, of course, be up to the American public, what happens to this individual. He has been found, and now you will hear what he has to say for himself. How he is the responsible person for the bombings a few days ago that occurred all over our beautiful United States. That he is the second in charge of this terrorist group. How they are a group of cowards that do the deed yet hide so they do not face the consequences, who are afraid to be brought before you to face your justice.

"Let's bring before you now Mr. Mike Vickors, the owner of the Capitol Coffee Shoppe. The second in command of the terrorist group that bombed all of our Capitol Buildings killing numerous citizens on the sidewalks and in the buildings. What do you have to say for yourself, Mr. Vickors?"

"Ms. President, I haven't done anything wrong. I was never a part of any group. The only thing I am guilty of is serving coffee to the citizens of Washington D. C. I have never done anything wrong. You arrested me without cause, without proof. This is not the America I have known and loved. This is a justice system that claims to be for the people but is in fact against each and every one of us. I was doing nothing more than serving coffee on the day you barged in to my coffee shop and arrested me without just cause. I want to make sure that the people are aware that if you can do this to me, than you can do this to anyone. Be careful, citizens, be warned. This could be you, standing here, defending your life."

"I'm sorry Mr. Vickors. I'm sorry that you cannot see how much this hurts me and every citizen out there that has to listen to this and to vote on your innocence or guilt. Do you think it's easy for our compassionate citizens to make these judgments? But they must take this very seriously, and they do. This is not something that you tune in to laughing and leave laughing. Most of these people cry when they vote. But they are strong and they will make the right decision. Their justice is true."

"Citizens, you have heard all that has been said today. Now it is time for you to make the decision. Is he guilty or innocent? Please vote; you have until tomorrow at noon to participate in this vote, so please, make your decision. I depend on your good judgment to come through. Thank you. I will see you again tomorrow night with the results of this vote." President Jane Martin says as she turns from the podium and leaves.

"You are going to die" Jane threatens Mike as she walks by. "You are going to die, in two days time, after the vote is finalized, if you don't tell me where to find Jacob Callander" she promises with a small mean smile playing around her lips and a blank look in her eyes. "If you do tell me, then maybe you can live" she says slowly. "It's your choice, live or die.

"I told you that I didn't know a Jacob Callander!"

"And I told you that you did. Life or death, your choice."

"Eli, its Kat. I need to talk to you. Is it safe?" she asks quietly.

"Not at the moment. Give me ten minutes and I'll make sure it's safe."

"Sure, call me at this number."

After waiting nearly a half hour, the phone finally rings. "Kat its Eli, what's up?"

"I have Mike Vickors family in hiding and I'm trying to get them to an underground group where they can be safe. There's a price on their heads because of Mike. I'm going to protect them for him, since I can't help him where he is."

"I heard about that Kat and I'm sorry. I wish I could do something myself for him. It's just not right what she's doing."

"I know, but I've exhausted all avenues and there's just nothing that I can do, or you either. But I can protect his family, so can you help me?"

"Actually, I can. I was just getting ready to join myself, so I have a pick up point. If you can get his family to me before tomorrow afternoon, then I'll take them with me."

"Awesome Eli, thanks! I'll have them to you by tomorrow morning, say around nine a.m.? Is that a good time for you?"

"Perfect" he says. "I'll be watching for you tomorrow morning."

"Here we are" Kat informs Mike's wife and two kids when they arrive at the specified building for transfer to Eli. "This is Eli Callander; he'll take very good care of you for Mike. It's what Mike wants. I was able to get a message to him briefly and he was very excited by this. I'm sorry that you weren't able to actually see him or talk to him, but it's the best that I could do. Just remember that he loves you all and looks forward to your reunion, in the future. Thanks Eli. I owe you for this one. Could you tell Snake for me that I miss him terribly? I have no way to contact him anymore, at least for now. I hope that will change in the future. Keep In touch with me if at all possible, please? Give my love to your parents and to Mallory. See ya."

Chapter Four

"Jacob, am I glad to see you" Eli says after finally reaching the underground command post. "It's quite a distance, isn't it" he admits in relief. "Now that I'm here, can we talk?"

"Sure, give me just a second and then we can go somewhere quiet."

"First, Kat wants me to tell you she misses you terribly. Then I wanted to let you know that Mike's family is underground safe and sound. Tonight's going to be a real bad evening for Kat and for his family. Tonight's the vote notification. Everyone will find out if he was voted guilty or innocent. We all know that there is no innocent, so we know the outcome. She's going to kill him. There's no choice. Kat's going to take this personal and she's a person to beware of. I really don't know what she's planning on doing, but it won't be good, not for anyone. There's just no way she'll be able to let this slide. She loves Mike like a brother and she'll go down with him, if she has to."

"Yeah, I know" Jacob says in fatigue. "I've been racking my brains over this and I haven't been able to come up with a save. I can't contact either of them, her nor Devon and everyone else is down here with me that I would have turned to in the past. So I'm out of pretty much all the options that I had in the past.

Do you have any thoughts on this Eli?"

"What about sending out some of your guys in disguises? Think you could pull that off?"

"I've thought of that. With the military looking so intensely for us, I'm not one hundred percent sure that we could pull it off. I guess we could try. I really don't want anything to happen to her. To Devon either for that matter, but I'd protect Kat first, she means a lot to me. "Alright, let's see what we can do, maybe another tracking device? I have one on her that even she'll never find, but I could always use more. I don't have any on Devon yet, but he needs at least one. I should be able to locate either one of them when I need to. I'll see if I can get everything ready for a forage tonight. Maybe I'll put on the disguise and head out. I'd really like to see Kat in person, too" he says quietly.

"You go and get ready. I'm going to try and reach Devon. He needs to be made aware of Kat and her probable moves in the next few hours. I'll see if I can find him."

"Devon" Eli says "where the hell are you? I've been trying to find you for hours now" he snaps angrily.

"What, I've been here the whole time. There's not much I can do at the office, so I decided to just sit at home until something comes up that needs my attention. I didn't hear the phone ring before this."

"Well, no, of course you didn't. I've been calling your cell phone, not your apartment phone. Since when don't you answer your cell?"

"Since it went dead and I had to charge it. It's

turned off right now, sorry."

"Fine, anyway, we have a problem. Mike's being sentenced tonight after the vote is announced. Everyone knows that he'll be found guilty and executed. You do know that Kat isn't going to take that well, so we need to set something up to protect her. There's really nothing we can do to help Mike, but we can protect Kat."

"Yeah, I've been thinking about her. She's had a rough few months and now this. Mike's family to her and she doesn't let go of family easily. Not that I can blame her. She's lost a great deal in her life. Besides, he didn't do anything wrong. These charges are a bunch of bull shit, you and I know that, but we can't help him now. Once he was arrested and charged, there was nothing we could do to stop the end from happening."

"Do you have any idea where Kat may be? We might be able to talk some sense into her before she does something stupid that puts her in danger" Eli says.

"Truthfully, no. I've tried calling her at home and there's been no answer. I've tried her cell, nothing there either."

"Shit, hang on, maybe that's her at the door right now. What do you want?" he yells at the officer at the door.

"I'm sorry Sir, but you'll have to come with us."

"Why, what for" he asks in anger, loud enough for Eli to hear him on the other end of the phone.

"We have proof that you've been in contact with your brother, the brother that's in charge of the underground group. You're under arrest Sir, for aiding and abetting a fugitive from the law. You're wanted downtown for questioning. I'm sure once you tell them what they want to know, they'll set you free."

"This is bull shit; I've had nothing to do with the underground. I'm Deputy Chief of the Capitol Police, this is some kind of a huge mistake" he argues as they spin him around and handcuff him, letting him know exactly where he's going.

Just before leaving the apartment, the officer in charge notices the phone lying on the table by the door.

"Who's on the other end of the phone, Mr. Callander?" demands Officer Jenkins.

"No one" Devon insists. "It's just sitting there, see for yourself" he offers sarcastically. "All you'll hear is a dial tone when you turn it on."

"Fine, I believe you. But you had better be telling us the truth, because we'll know if you aren't. We have that phone line under surveillance. We'll be able to tell you if there was anyone on the other end, who it was and their exact location."

Shit, shit, shit Devon thinks with a sinking heart. Please God, don't let them be able to find the underground. Protect all those innocent people down there. Please Eli, send help. I can't get out of this one on my own. The Military is so far under Jane's power that it's sickening. They've become brainless idiots, existing at her whim.

"Jacob we have a problem" Eli says into his radio. "Devon's just been arrested. We have to do something. Let me know how I can help, what I can do."

"Eli, its Jacob, calm down. Call me on this cell."

"What happened?"

"I was on the phone with Devon, talking about Kat and the problems that could happen when I heard a knock on his door. He laid the phone down but left it on so I could hear what was going on. A group of military police were at the door and when he opened it, they arrested him on charges of aiding and abetting a criminal group, the underground group. They also told him that his phone was tapped and they would know who was on the other end and where they were located.

"We're screwed, Jacob, they know it was me or someone from the underground and where we're located. What are we going to do?"

"Shit! Alright, damn it, get me Rand on the line, I'm heading back in. We have to move fast or we won't have the time we need to move."

"I think we have everyone, Sir."

"Thanks Rand, we'll get them with this. It will be the last thing they're expecting. Have you shut the east tunnel door? Once they enter through here, we'll close them off and it will blow, just like we planned. I'm heading west now. They should start entering in minutes. Keep an eye on the video; we don't want any of them to get out of there alive. Unfortunately, we have to do this. It doesn't make me happy, but I guess I was expecting it."

"Lieutenant; they're entering the east door now. There looks to be about twenty five in the group. They should all be inside in a matter of minutes.

Alright, they're in Sir."

"Shut the door now, both East and West." The doors slam with a loud bang. "Now, ignite and now, the button." A huge explosion can be heard, a lot of dust is flying through the tunnels. Enough force was used that there's nothing left of the one hundred feet of tunnel that just went up in smoke.

"Report" Jacob yells into his headset.

"Clear Lieutenant, the barrier held, there's not a speck of dust that made it through. All people are safe and accounted for, we'll start reassembling. Everything should be back to normal in a couple of hours."

"Excellent work Sergeant."

"Thank you Sir."

Meow….meow…..Kat swings around at the sound. A kitten? Where, she thinks with a little jump of excitement in her veins. Last time I heard a kitten, it was Snake! "What are you doing here" she cries in excitement when she finally recognizes him. "You don't look like yourself" she proclaims loudly before Snake has a chance to warn her to be quiet. "Oh, sorry" she whispers. "So, what are you doing here? I thought you said you couldn't chance coming out of the underground. What's wrong, something's wrong?" she says in a panic.

"Not really, I was just worried about you" he says quietly.

"There has to be something else. There's nothing to worry about for me, I'm fine" she insists. "Okay, its Devon" he admits to shut her up. "He's been arrested, aiding and abetting a criminal. They took him in to custody about two hours ago."

"What? Shit!" she exclaims in fear. "I can't get to Mike and now it's Devon too. Crap. Okay, how are we going to fix this one?" she asks him quietly.

"Let's go somewhere safe to talk, we can't talk here. I don't trust buildings, not even this one" he insists.

"So, how have you been, Kitten? I wish you'd reconsider joining us in the underground. I can't help you out here like I used to. We just had a military group infiltrate the east end of the underground tunnels. We had to move fast, before they got there, and then we sealed them in and blew it up. This is happening because of the outside contact we made. They traced it back to the underground, so we won't be able to use the disposable cell's that I obtained. We're going analog. There's plenty of equipment that we gathered, we just won't be able to use anything digital. The underground is going further under. Please reconsider.

"In the meantime, there's nothing that you or I can do for Mike. You know the vote will find him guilty. You also know what the outcome for that will be. Please, you must let it go."

"I know" Kat cries with tears streaming down her face. "If only I would have been more careful. He'd be safe. If only I hadn't befriended him, he'd be safe. This is my fault" she sobs.

"Shh, it's not your fault Kitten, none of this is your fault" he says as he holds her tight. "It's the world we're living in now. You didn't cause that, and neither did I. But we do have to learn how to live in it. It can't be done up here, unless you want to be a part of what the President has created.

"We are the true Americans; the underground. But it won't be forever, I promise you. Things are going to change for the better, soon I hope. Right now though, we need to figure out what to do about Devon. It's all going to depend on where they're holding him. If it's near the Capitol Police station, then we may be able to do something about that. It's going to be risky, but it's do-able."

"I need to contact Rand. Hopefully by now, he knows where Devon is. I'll head over to the bridge and try to contact him. You stay here and think about what I said. I have to go back underground as soon as possible. The longer I'm out, the more chance there is of them finding it and infiltrating it again."

"I refuse to let anything happen to those people, they're under my protection. We have to move" he says when he walks back to Kat. "I may be able to get him, but it has to be now. They're moving him in ten minutes and if I don't get him first, I won't be able to. This is the only shot I'm going to get. Are you in Kat? I don't want to leave you."

"Fine, I'm in, and I'll go underground with you too, after we get Devon. There's nothing much left for me up here. What about Des?" she asks. "Should I contact her, see if she wants to join us?"

"No. Des is definitely on the side of the government. We can't bring her she's too big of a liability. I'm sorry Kitten. You can't change what people are."

"Run" Snake yells when he spots the MP walking towards her. After getting a hold of him and knocking him out temporarily, he whistles for Kat to join him. "Now, I just need to get Devon" he says quietly as he busts open the door of the room in the basement of the Capitol Police Department. All the guards are unconscious" he informs Devon when he reaches him.

"Either you're going underground with me, or you're on your own. I can't rescue you again. The next time they arrest you, they'll keep your sorry ass. So decide now. I'm heading back under." Snake informs him angrily. "I've put enough people in danger for you, Devon. This is not a game that's being played. I warned you" he continues on in his tangent.

"Fine, fine" Devon says in anger. "It's not my fault that this is happening, you know."

"Yeah, I know, it's none of our faults. But it is what it is, so live with it." Snake starts walking quickly, in a hurry to put some distance between him and the Capitol Police station.

"We need to hurry. I can't take the chance of any of us being seen."

"Welcome home Devon" Eli says in relief. "Kat, you okay?" he asks.

"Yeah, I'm fine, just a little tired from the run. We had to hustle to get here without drawing any attention to us. But we made it, right Snake?"

"Yep, we made it without a tail" he admits as he picks her up and hugs her. "Let's go and see if there's any food left from dinner. I could use some, how about you two?"

"I've got the TV going, thank goodness for the old analog stations. Some of them are still broadcasting, enough that I can get the national news on. We can monitor the city and the president without worry of being found out. They don't know about this old stuff still being used." Rand informs them.

"Thanks Rand, good work."

"Now let's listen to what's new in the city.

"The Vote on Mike Vickors was announced last night. Tomorrow night is the night justice will prevail. The plan is executing him live on this channel, the same way they did Addy, some four months ago or so. I've been requested to notify you that if you have a weak stomach or are a small child, maybe you should stay away from the TV tomorrow night. This is not for the weak stomached. This is Jim Cochran of WELT News Channel 3, Washington D.C."

When the report is done, a pin could be heard dropping, everyone is glancing furtively at Kat, to see her reaction. Kat is appalled, her face has gone white and she's silently crying tears for her best friend. "I'm sorry" she says when she realizes that everyone's watching her with pity in their eyes.

"We have work to do, so the TV will be off. I'll have one of the MP's monitor it for useful information. This assassination will not be viewed by anyone in the underground. It's not right. No one's going to watch a friend die.

"Lieutenant, I have some news. I just received this information from News Channel 3 in D.C. It looks like there's rioting going on everywhere across the United States. The people are burning any buildings that are responsible for holding, making or distributing the chips. It looks like the citizens of the good ole U.S. of A. finally woke up. They're not happy with the chip issue, so they've decided to destroy them. The Military are having a hard time catching them."

"It looks like it's been well planned; a group goes out, burns a building and disappears. No one's admitting to seeing anything. You wouldn't think something like this would work, but it is" Rand exclaims in amazement.

"Can we get the TV on in here, I think everyone needs to see this" Jacob suggests. "This is the kind of stuff that I've been hoping for, the American citizens finally getting fed up. What people don't seem to realize is that they're a power to be reckoned with. I wouldn't want to be the troop that went up against them. When they're united, there's no easy way to stop them."

"Mom, Dad, hey everyone, check it out" Jacob yells in excitement when the picture comes in crystal clear, you can see everyone and everything. "Check out the guy with the face mask on, he's dousing the building with, it looks like an accelerant or maybe even gasoline. They're wearing Halloween costume masks. No one will ever be able to identify them. Good thinking guys. You see, all it took was uniting, they can go anywhere now, united they can stand. Oh, no, run buddy. Don't let them touch you."

"Shit, well, he was a little slow, and he ended up taking one for the team. I just hope that he didn't say anything or leave any clues. This is one fight that's worth it."

"I'm going to have to say, if the President wasn't pissed, she is now. This is blatant in your face war.

These people are not the ones that she thought would just sit down, shut up and do whatever she says. These are the Americans. It may have taken a while to wake them up, but I never had any doubt. These people know what fighting for the right and freedom is all about. They may have acted noncommittal, but inside, they were coming alive. After all, these are the type of people that came here over two hundred years ago and conquered this county. They're the ones with the power. They just needed to be reminded."

"This is Jim Cochran of WELT News Channel 3, Washington D.C. I've been standing here near the armory building watching people for the past hour. It's the strangest thing. Every person that I've seen out here is wearing heavy gloves and a Halloween mask. There has been no one seen today without those items. I also have not been able to interview anyone, no one will talk to the media."

"I have, however, received hundreds of notes. Not one of these notes admits to finding Mike Vickors guilty. The people are actually accusing the government of lying about the vote. No one says he was guilty, everyone that has handed me a note proclaims his innocence. Looks like the president may have a problem since the people don't believe that he was voted guilty. Now what will she do. She has to address this issue, especially since he's scheduled to be executed this evening. In approximately eight hours, he's scheduled to die in front of the American people because they supposedly found him guilty. Yet not one person has accused him, they have all actually requested his release."

"I'll be monitoring this situation closely. It's vital that this issue be addressed. The president will lose all of her support if this is in fact true. Since she's so new to the position of president and wasn't voted in by the citizens, she's in a very precarious position.

This is Jim Cochran of WELT News Channel 3, Washington D.C."

"The President is due any moment now. She has requested this news briefing in response to the outrage by the public on his guilty vote. We aren't sure what exactly she's planning on discussing, but we're hopeful it will answer the public. This is Jim Cochran of WELT News Channel 3, Washington D.C."

"Good afternoon everyone" greets President Jane Martin. "Thank you for tuning in to this meeting. I am greatly distressed that so many of my people are accusing me, the President of the United States, of voter fraud.

"I would just like to begin with, there is no way that an inaccurate vote occurred. It is possible that the only people that are contacting us are the ones that voted against the execution, not the ones that voted for it. If that is the case, than it is believable, unfortunately, that there are a great deal more people that have not contacted us, that did in actuality vote for the execution.

"I cannot, in all honesty, only believe those that were against it. I'm sorry that this has upset the American republic, but it is impossible to please everyone. I will have to say that the majority has voted for the execution and only a small minority has voted against. Since that is the case, the execution shall move forward as planned. I'm sure that this will upset some people, but like I said, it's impossible to please everyone. If this type of execution upsets you, than please do not turn on the television. You have been pre-warned; this is going to happen at its scheduled time. There really is nothing that you can do or say that will change the outcome of this.

"Just remember, I, Jane Martin, President of the United States, stands firm on the vote that occurred. I do not believe that it is wrong. I have seen the numbers for this vote, and the majority has won. Mike Vickors, accused of treason against this land will be executed at the prescheduled time. Again, thank you for your attention to this matter."

"Well, I didn't see that one coming, but if it's true, than the government has no other recourse than to do as she just said they will do. There are millions of Americans that voted. There were only thousands that dropped me a note to dispute it. If in fact the millions did vote for the execution, then they are justified in moving forward with this execution."

"Mike Vickors will be executed in less than eight hours from now. This is Jim Cochran of WELT News Channel 3, Washington D.C."

"I'm sorry Kat" Snake says after watching the news brief with her, his siblings and a few unit members. "I wasn't sure if the notes to the media would work, but it was worth a try. Unfortunately, nothing has changed. If nothing else, she's learning how to work the people. She will get even. The people actually tried to manipulate her and I'm sure she didn't like that at all." Kat just sits there staring at the screen that's scrolling the information about the execution time and place, a blank look on her face. Jacob requests everyone leave silently, so that he can talk with Kat.

"Kitten, it's alright. I'm sorry about the way this turned out, but in reality, I knew the notes just wouldn't work. Like she said, there are a lot more people out there that voted than just the ones with the notes. Even though we know she's lying, it's impossible to prove it. They're too good at hiding things and manipulating everyone."

"I know" Kat says quietly, despondently. "I knew that there was no hope, and yet I allowed myself a small amount of it. Now I'm paying for it."

"Come here" Snake says. "I wish I could do something to change what's going to happen, but there's nothing" he admits discouraged as he hugs Kat, rubbing her back up and down in a comforting motion. "They haven't even released where they're going to take him for this. I think that was for their security, so that they wouldn't be interrupted. Unfortunately, I don't have any spy's in their camp. It's been nearly impossible to find someone that can infiltrate her office, but I'm still working on it."

"I'm so sorry, Kitten. You've lost so much already and now this." he says quietly. "I promise that you'll never have to worry about me leaving you, if that helps."

She just wraps her arms around him and holds on tight.   "I'm

so tired" she admits with a sniffle."I couldn't stand it if anything happened to you Snake. I love you. I have for a long time" she mumbles.

"I love you too Kitten, I'll do anything for you, just to make you happy and keep you safe."

"Okay, I need to get to work. I've got lots to get done today. We're working on Jane's background. I'm looking for all her connections. Her parents, where they're from, who they're related to, anything. There has to be something there and when I find it, it will give me great happiness to throw it in her face while showing the world just who and what she is."

"Fine, I think I'll go spend some time with your Mom. She's so easy to be around. I'll see you later Snake."

"What kind of information have you been able to get so far" Jacob asks the unit. "I need more background on Jane Martin, as soon as possible."

"She was born and raised in Texas. She went to the public school out there and the community college for journalism. It really doesn't have anything negative, so far. She was a member in good standing of the Peoples Church. It actually looks like her parents helped found and build that church. Now the parents, that's another story. They're originally from Iran. They felt they were in mortal danger and left the country about thirty two years ago, after getting out of a Muslim extremist group. It was two years before Jane was born. After they arrived in Texas, they became citizens of this country, and gave up their citizenship to Iran. They haven't left the state of Texas in the thirty two years that they've lived there."

"Their background requires a much more in-depth look. There's something they're hiding, I think. I just need to find out what and prove it. It looks like they've come from a family with money. After checking their financials for the time they've been in this country, there's been money put into their account from a foreign source. Some of it's been quite a chunk. They live on a modest income, yet they live in an above average house. The money that was deposited always disappears with-in the week that it was deposited. It was always withdrawn as cash, and then the trail seems to end. It's going to take a little time, but I should be able to trace the cash."

"Excellent Dave, keep up the good work. I'll be in the kitchen, so page me if you need me" Jacob commands.

"Mom, where's Kat?" Jacob asks.

"I don't know, I haven't seen her today. Is there a problem?"

"No, she just told me she was headed this way about an hour ago, so I'm surprised you haven't seen her, is all. I guess I'll start looking for her. I don't want her to be alone when they have the execution tonight. She's going to take that pretty hard and I wanted to be with her for support."

"I'm so sorry about all this" Sandy says in pity. "The poor thing's been through so much, and now this."

"I know, but I'll find her. She'll never face anything alone again, not as long as I'm breathing. I'll talk to you later, Mom."

"Eli, have you seen Kat?" Jacob asks as he passes through the war room.

"No, not today, I've been in here all day, helping with the backgrounds on the Martins. She hasn't come through here while I've been here."

"If you see her, will you tell her I'm looking for

her please?"

"Sure, no problem."

Where the hell did she go he wonders as he does a quick search of all the dorm rooms off the hall? This is a big place and there's lots of hiding areas. Why would she hide, though? Maybe a coping mechanism, I suppose.

"Lieutenant, are you available, over" the radio on Jacob's shoulder crackles to life.

"Yeah, go" Jacob says.

"You need to come to alpha level, room 138, East wing."

"Problem?" Jacob asks as he heads toward that direction.

"I believe so, but I don't want to say over the radio, Sir."

"I'll be right there Sergeant."

"Copy Sir."

After finally getting to room 138 East wing, alpha level,

Jacob knocks quietly on the door.

"In here, Sir" he hears as he enters slowly, weapon drawn.

"I found her this way. I don't know what happened to

her, but she's unresponsive" Rand says quickly as Jacob drops to his knees next to Kat.

"I don't have any of my stuff with me, so I haven't been

able to check her vital signs. She's breathing but seems to be bleeding, judging by the pool of blood on the floor. I think we better get her to the infirmary as soon as we can."

"What the hell. I've been looking everywhere for her,

and now this. Just let me pick her up, I'll carry her it'll be faster. Any idea if there's a Doctor on staff here?"

"I think there is, I'm just not sure of his name and location. I'll do what I can to stabilize her, if you want to do a point check for him."

"Fine, I'll be right back" Jacob promises as he rushes out of the room.

"Kat, can you hear me" Rand says as he gently smacks her face.

"What . . . stop, leave me alone" she says as she tries to focus on his face. "What are you doing to me" she cries as she notices pain in her stomach. "Stop, leave me alone" she says just before she screams.

"Kat, Kat, you're okay, I'm not doing anything to you. Listen, relax, Snake's going to be here any minute. Just listen" he says urgently.

"Kitten, stop fighting me; look its Snake. You're okay, I won't let anything happen to you" he reminds her firmly. "What's wrong, who did this to you" he says in a loud and demanding voice, causing her to really look at him and quiet down.

"Snake" she gasps as she realizes who's holding her. "I'm okay" she says automatically. "I'm okay" she repeats.

"Do you have any pain, Kitten? Tell me what the problem is, you know you can tell me" he says worriedly.

"I'm okay" she keeps repeating.

"I found the Doctor and he's on his way here right now. He was in the West wing, Bravo level"

Jacob notifies Rand.

"Good, because this is beyond my abilities" Rand says.

"Dr. Carson, reporting as requested Sir."

"Thank goodness, Doctor. This is Kat; she's under my direct protection. She was found about a half an hour ago by Sergeant Rand. He's a medic but believes this to be outside of his knowledge base. He found her unresponsive, lying on the floor in a small pool of blood. We aren't sure why she's bleeding, so we located a doctor on staff, and you're it, it's your lucky day."

"Yes Sir, if you'll leave me, I'll do an exam and see if we can find the problem."

"Thank you Doctor Carson, I'll be right outside the door."

"I'm done Lieutenant, and have some news. She was hemorrhaging, it's looks like she was approximately four months along, and went into a miscarriage. She needs some blood, to replace what she lost."

"Unfortunately, there was nothing I could do for the fetus. It was a well developed boy, Sir. There's some damage, but it doesn't look like new damage, it looks like it was a few months old. I'm not sure what caused the hemorrhage, but if I hazard a guess, it was probably caused by the pre-existing damage. It's doubtful that she'll be able to carry a baby more than four months. I'm sorry, Sir. My recommendations would be a complete hysterectomy. There's no point in trying and going through this every time. It would be too hard on her mentally and physically.

Unfortunately, we don't have an OR available at this facility, that I'm aware of, at least."

"You can go in and talk to her, if you wish. I'm keeping her on bed rest until we can figure something else out."

"Thank you, Doctor. I'll see what I can figure out, but first I want to talk with her. Does she know anything about this, Doctor?"

"No Sir, she was unconscious while I did the exam. It looked like a panic attack and she just passed out. It could have been her blood pressure, but it wasn't that low" he finishes thoughtfully.

"Kitten, wake up. Everything's alright. You're going to be fine" Snake says as she wakes slowly.

"Hi" she says quietly. "What happened to me, how did I get here?"

"A doctor just finished examining you to find out what the problem was. You passed out before he did the exam, that's why you're confused. Do you remember anything about any of this?" he asks slowly and quietly.

"Not really. I remember getting a really bad stomach ache, I thought it was the flu or something I ate, but it wasn't, was it? The next thing I remember is seeing you when I woke up. It wasn't the flu, was it?"

"No Kitten, it wasn't the flu. The Doctor says you had a miscarriage. You were about four months along and then you started to hemorrhage. There was nothing he could do to save the baby, he was born dead."

"What" she gasps. "I was pregnant? That's impossible" she stammers in denial. "No way, that can't be true. I haven't had sex since I . . . was . . . raped. Oh . . . my . . . God . . . that monster, he did this. He did this, didn't he Snake" she sobs in anger and fear as she grabs hold of him.

"Shh, I'm sorry Kitten. I'm sorry. You'll be okay though. I'll always be here for you; you know that, don't you? It'll be okay, I promise" he repeats over and over until she stops shaking and sobbing and lays back in exhaustion.

"Is he ever going to stop haunting me and hurting me?"

"He will, I promise" Snake says to comfort her.

"I'm glad" she says suddenly. "Does that make me a terrible person, being glad that I lost that baby? I would never have been able to look at it, even though I know in my brain that it wasn't its fault. It was still from a monster. I'm glad. What day is it" she asks cautiously.

"It's still Wednesday, only it's after ten at night. You only lost a few hours. We found you pretty quick, but promise me next time you feel sick you won't head to a deserted area. You're lucky to be alive. You could have bled to death before anyone located you."

"After ten o'clock." She repeats slowly. "No, please" she whimpers and starts crying again.

Snake just looks at her in confusion until reality slowly dawns. Mike. He was executed at nine p.m. She knows that, that's why she's crying. "Kitten, I'm sorry. I'm so sorry."

"Mike" she moans out loud at the pain in her heart. "He's dead, isn't he" she asks Snake hopelessly.

"I'm afraid so, Kitten I'm sorry, so very sorry. Come in" Jacob says to the knock on the door.

"Sir, we've found everything we need to make an OR. I can do the procedure here without any outside help. We actually have an outfitted room complete with oxygen. I've done this procedure before, so you don't need to worry. I just need to find out what blood type she is and then we can get going."

"What procedure?" Kat asks suspiciously. "I'm not having any procedure" she says in denial. "I don't need any procedure Snake, do I? What's he talking about" she asks in fear and confusion.

"I didn't get the chance to say anything to her yet" Jacob states in anger.

"I'm sorry Sir. I just assumed that you had time." After glancing at Kat he decides to go ahead with the information. It's probably better coming from a doctor than a friend.

"Hi, I'm Doctor Carson. I took care of you a little while ago. You had a hemorrhagic miscarriage. I did the exam, but you still need a hysterectomy. There's just too much damage to try to repair it, the only option that you really have is to remove it all. Since you're so young, we really hate to do this, but whatever happened to you was pretty bad and left quite a bit of damage. We need to give you some blood and repair what the problem is, so that you never have to go through this again. I'm sorry, because you'll never be able to have children once this procedure is finished, and you're so young. But there isn't anything that can be done now. I'm sorry, Miss."

The complete silence of the room is the only

indication that everyone heard the prognosis. Kat just looks defeated while Snake holds her hand protectively, thinking, I wish I would have taken my time killing that bastard. That quick death was just too damn easy for him.

"How long will this procedure take" Kat asks quietly.

"Probably no more than an hour" Doctor Carson assures her. "The recovery will take a lot longer, but you'll recover just fine. We can take care of your every need, here. We're well equipped to handle this and even bigger emergencies. Whoever set up that OR had excellent knowledge and made sure everything was up to date. We're ready when you are" he assures her as he leaves the room.

Chapter Five

"I want to thank you for coming here early, before your flight. It's been a crazy few days, but I wanted to talk to you before you left to see the Shah. I realize that you were supposed to leave a few days ago. Well, today's the day." Jane Martin says to her envoy. "These are exciting times for me. I wish that I could join you, but unfortunately, the American public wouldn't take kindly to me going to Iran right at the moment. There's too much anger out there still. I don't want to chance the possibility of an uprising. I feel I need to be here, to maintain control of everyone, including the military" she adds with a smile.

"I haven't had the opportunity to see the Shah in the past five years. I've missed our visits, too. I do have a box here that I would like you to deliver for me though. He'll be surprised and pleased with what's inside. Since he's expecting you today, I won't keep you. Just remember who you represent and maintain your pride and dignity, in the same manner that I would. I know that he'll treat you very well, since you're going there on my behalf. No expense will be spared to make you feel welcome and at home. Go now, and have a safe trip" President Martin finishes.

"Welcome to Iran" the Shah says after the plane

lands safely and the envoy exits the cabin. "If you'll follow me, we'll head straight to my palace."

"Wow, that was quite a welcome" Jill says after she's seated in the limo. "A stretch limo and champagne, some cheese and grapes (cold too!), wow this is nice, really nice" she admits with a smile.

"Thank you all for coming" the Shah says at dinner that evening. "It's a pleasure to have you all come here. I am honored by your visit and I hope everything is to your liking. If you find displeasure in anything, please let me know. I want your visit here to be memorable."

"It can be nothing but memorable, Sir" replies Jill. "I've never seen anything as beautiful as this palace. My room, it's larger than the whole first floor of my house in Washington. And the decorations, they're amazing. Everything is perfect Sir. Thank you so much for allowing us the pleasure of this visit."

"You are more than welcome, my dear. We are, after all, comrades. We're working for the same purpose so naturally I want you to have the best. So tell me please, how is Jane" he asks everyone. "I haven't had the opportunity to see her in many years. It has been a disappointment to me, but she's doing what she was born for now. That brings me great pride and much hope for the future. All is going as planned" he reassures them smoothly.

"How do you know Jane?" Ron asks the Shah.

"Didn't she tell you the story? I'm sorry, I had assumed that you knew her story and that's why she picked you to come here. I will be happy to tell you the story, though. It's quite long but well worth the telling. This whole story begins more than thirty years ago. Right here in this palace, actually. I wasn't the Shah at the time, of course, but everyone knew that I would be in the future, it was my destiny."

"The old Shah, he was too flexible with the world. He didn't like rocking the boat and looked at the United States of America as a future friend of ours, an ally. We all know that that is not possible, at least as far as the people can see. Our religions are too different to allow us to become friends. We, as a nation, were going through some rough times back then. There was much fighting, bombs were going off constantly, there was war in the streets, by the insurgents. People were dying, being maimed, losing their lives and limbs."

"The country was in turmoil and the Shah, at the time, vowed to act as a constitutional monarch who would willingly defer to the power of the parliamentary government. Instead, he involved himself in government affairs that he shouldn't have, stopping strong prime ministers. He tried to revive the army by promising that it would remain under his control, royal control. Later on, there was an assassination attempt on him and he blamed the pro-soviet Tudeh Party, and then banned that party, expanding his own constitutional powers. He tried to establish himself as an ally of the West. He created a program known as the White Revolution.

"He even crowned himself as Emperor of Iran, back in sixty seven' which made the people of this land unhappy. The religious leaders of this country were afraid of losing their traditions and authority, so they criticized the Shah for a violation of the constitution, placing limits on the royal power.

"He even went so far as to replace our Islamic calendar with the imperial calendar. By the middle of the seventy's he reigned by continually repressing the socioeconomic changes that only benefitted the upper class, increasing the gap between the elite and the unhappy regular class people. That's where my grandfather comes in. He helped with the reform of our great country, by bringing back our Islamic principles, causing the Shah's government to collapse, allowing the Islamic Republic to take over."

"With all due respect Sir, why are you referred to as a Shah, since there hasn't been a Shah in Iran since nineteen seventy nine?" Jill asks.

"Hey, why are you being so rude, we're guests of the Shah's right now" Ron says in a low voice.

"Nonsense, it's okay my friend, I understand. Please let me explain why my friends refer to me as the Shah. Since the death of my grandfather, the Ayatollah, the founder of the Islamic Republic, this country has been run by weak minded men that are too afraid of the western world to stand up to them. They're so busy counting the money that they have left causing the true foundation of our religion to crumble like a foundation of sand. The believers of my grandfather feel that I should be the Emperor of Iran and Shah is a form of address for an Iranian Monarch, thus they refer to me by that name as a form of respect."

"But I digress; now let me get back to my story of Jane. Jane's parents were very good friends of my grandfather and when he died, they feared for their lives. So we sent them to the United States with the understanding that their first born child would be groomed as a great Islamic leader to not only rule Iran in the future, but to conquer the western world and spread the word of Allah across the globe. They settled in Texas because in order for this to work, we had to have a strong Christian front.

"Therefore we found a young Christian minister, funded his church and helped to create the largest non-denominational Evangelical Christian Church in the world."

"Jane has been a very good student of Islam and will serve our purpose well. The righteous Reverend Johnson, who owes everything to us, is now in a prominent position in your country and will do as we say because money is his God, as it is for the rest of the western world."

"Sir, I have a gift for you from Jane."

"Wonderful, I love gifts" he admits as he claps his hands in excitement. "Let's see what's in it" he says and with a gasp, he pulls out an old book. "Do you know what this is?" he cries in excitement. "It's my grandfathers Quran. This was given to the Muhsin's by my father on the birth of Abr'ar."

"Who are the Muhsin's Sir."

"Oh, forgive me, they're Jane's parents. Jane's Islamic name is Abr'ar. In reality, she is called Abr'ar Muhsin, and her parents are Da'wah and Tariq Muhsin, but as you can plainly see after hearing them, those names would not work in the western world. So we gave them new names, American names and created a whole new history for them. I'm afraid that they have had to live very boring and empty lives, all for the sake of Allah. Da'wah has worked in a retail store all of his American life. They have not left the state of Texas since their arrival thirty two years ago and unfortunately they were never able to return to the land that they truly love. They understood this was a possibility when they took the mission.

"They're good people and were willing to sacrifice their lives for the cause. They will be greatly rewarded by Allah for the sacrifices that they have made, for the spread of his kingdom."

"Now let's get down to business, the purpose that you are here for. I have many powerful and influential allies throughout the region. They have assured me that when the time comes, they will be more than willing to participate in our little peace conference. For this peace conference, even Jordan and Palestine have agreed to temporarily give up their fight in the West Bank to draw Israel into these talks. So on the outside it will appear that there is peace in the Middle East. Everyone knows that you can't believe everything that you see. Once we reach our ultimate goal, Allah will rule the world. We will finally have everything back that belongs to us."

"We'll schedule the Peace Conference for two months from today. In the meantime, we have much to do before this date. Now if you'll excuse me, I have other business I must attend to. I'm sure you're fatigued from your trip. This is Wal'i, he'll show you to your rooms and we'll get together again tomorrow for lunch. Rest well tonight, my friends."

"If you will come this way, lady and gentlemen, I will escort you back to your rooms."

"I don't suppose you could take us back the long way; I would love to see more of this beautiful palace."

"Certainly lady, I would be happy to escort you back and show you parts of the palace that I believe you would love to see."

"Amazing" she says after reaching her room in the palace. "I've never seen so many beautiful things being used for normal everyday life. This place is amazing. With its huge vaulted ceilings and the painted/glazed tiles that cover every square inch of the walls and ceilings. The thick hand tufted Turkish carpets, especially the tree of life carpet. I'm just amazed. It's so totally beautiful it's hard to comprehend. Thank you Wal'i, for the tour."

"You are welcome lady. I will be back in the morning to escort you to the dining hall. You have a luncheon engagement with the Shah. Goodnight."

Wow, I didn't think she'd ever be done looking at everything. I hope they could hear everything that was said in the dining room tonight. I thought that discussion was perfect. The information they received was really invaluable. Maybe I can manage to make it home now. I know I'm getting pretty sick of this country. I've had to be on guard at all times lately and then I'm never really sure if it's safe, Wal'i thinks, being the black-ops plant for the past six months.

"I got it all Sir. It's copied to a file so you'll be able to hear it at any time."

"Thanks Josh, notify me if there's any more that comes through. I'll be in my office." Well, well, Jacob thinks after he closes his office door. That was quite an educational dinner for them. Thanks for the information. Now let's see if I can reach Wal'i before anything happens. I think it's time for him to come home, his job's done for now. After listening to all the clicks representing the digital age, he finally comes to the end. Wal'i, its Snake. If you can hear me, I'm just passing on the information that it's time to hit the road. You're expected back in two days. Reservations are for the normal place. Should you have any problems, you know what to do." Okay, I need to gather the team and discuss what we were told. I knew that she had some background that was causing this. I just never expected it to be so far back and so twisted.

"Devon, Eli, Mallory, Rand, Mongoose there's a meeting in the delta west wing, ops center. Meet me there in a half hour."

"Hey, glad you all made it. I'm sorry, you haven't met Mongoose yet. This is Elsworth Langley the III, known as mongoose to all of us. Judging from his given name, I can't blame him for taking on the nickname" Jacob admits with a grin and a duck from the slap that Mongoose tried to deliver good-naturedly. "He's our sharpshooter, but he's also an expert on all weapons. He's actually earned his nickname Mongoose, so watch out for him. He's going to help protect this facility and all that are in it."

"Now, to the reason I called you all here. I just finished listening to a direct audio feed from the palatial palace in Iran. The Shah just greeted the Presidential envoy that arrived there earlier today and after the niceties were finished he gave them a pretty thorough history lesson on our very own President Jane Martin."

"It's actually more than we thought. She was born for this purpose and only this purpose, his words not mine. Her parents were sent over here thirty two years ago to have a child that would be born and raised to conquer the western world, while spreading the word of Allah and preparing for the future ruling of Iran. That pretty much explains why the Iran President keeps offering his help to her. He has to know what her reason is. He also must notice that it's moving forward in the way they obviously expected and planned for her to go. She's definitely more than anyone expected, at least she's more than I expected."

"Now that we know the reason and who, we can start looking into more of her parent's background and "The People's Church." That church is the focal point. It sounded like the Shah was responsible for finding Reverend Johnson when he was a young and promising Minister, and her parents took him under their wing and helped to build the church as it is now. They have unlimited funding and the goal of making it the largest non-denominational Evangelical Christian Church in the world. It looks to me like they've succeeded completely."

"This is going to be the fight for the life of the world as we know it. If she gains enough power, she won't stop here. She wants world domination; she wants to be the Dictator of the World. I hate to say this, but if things continue on as they have been, it won't take her long to gain that position" he admits in disgust.

"We're all responsible now, for finding a way to hinder her, if not stop her completely. It won't be easy, since she seems to have eyes and ears everywhere. We all have experience with someone that powerful. I don't believe she's done anything in the past that didn't promote her cause, even while proclaiming her kindness and how she's put the American citizens first."

"I can even now see what the importance of the chip is. It's not for healthcare reform. It's more an obedience form of torture for the people. She doesn't care about helping them, she wants to control them. With this chip, she can control them. At least the ones that take the chip. Now we need to find out anything else that we can, about this chip and the magnanimous gesture that she made to the public. We have our work cut out for us. Every day that we delay means more confusion and disruption for the people, and definitely more danger."

"In order for her to gain the power that she needs, she's got to punish those that refuse the chip. Without the chip, she can't find you. Each chip has a GPS unit in it that allows it to be found wherever it is. She's also underhanded enough that it must have other things that it can do to hurt the person wearing it, at her whim."

"Keep your eye on what she does, not what she says. Seldom does she do what she says. I think it's time for all of us to start working long shifts, gathering intel on the church, the minister, her parents, her past, the Shah and anyone else even remotely connected to her."

"There's a lot more to our Darling Jane than we expected."

"Let's work on this and meet back here once a day to share any information. We're running against the clock. We need information before she starts the chip implantations. I have a feeling the beginning is just days away. We can meet at five pm every day and then head out for dinner. That way we can also visit while we have the chance."

"Hey Kitten, how are you feeling" Snake asks when he gets to the recovery area. Kat's just lying in bed, staring straight ahead.

"I'm okay, I guess."

"Have you been up for a walk yet?"

"No, I've just been lying here. Too much effort to walk" she admits quietly.

"Come on, we're going for a walk. You'll never get better if you don't move. The goal is to get you back to normal. We need you, we've got some more information about Jane, and I want you to help where you can."

"Fine, I'll walk. Just help me up" she demands in a churlish tone of voice. "Shit shit shit" she says once she's out of bed, in a hunched over position. "That really hurts. I had no idea how much this was going to hurt."

"Yeah, the Doctor said the first time up would be tough, he did slice through all of your stomach muscles and it takes a while for that to be less painful and heal. He recommended that you just fold this blanket into a hard pillow and hold it over your stomach. He said it would feel like your guts are going to fall on the floor, and that this would help to support your incision and keep the pain under control."

"Stop, Snake, I'm tired already" Kat says after walking to her room door and back to the bed. "I didn't get very far, but I'm really exhausted now."

"It's only been about twelve hours since your surgery. You're bound to get tired easily; it takes a while to recoup. Besides, you lost a lot of blood and had to have a transfusion. Have you eaten anything yet?"

"No, but I'm not very hungry."

"I know, but you need to eat. Let's see if we can come up with say, some soup and crackers. That's nourishment and its light, so it shouldn't upset your stomach."

"Fine, if it will make you happy, I'll eat" she agrees tiredly. "So tell me the news. Have you heard anything, what about the country, how's it handling everything? Is there anymore rioting, burning of buildings, anything? I'm getting desperate to hear something. I was hoping for something positive though, but that's probably wishful thinking. It's just that it seems that the only thing I've heard lately is bad news, and most of it affected me, I'm sick of the bad.

"As a matter of fact, I talked with Kathy myself and she says they're fine. They know what happened, miss Mike and are hurting for it but they'll be okay, she's assured me. She sounded like she was taking it pretty good, and she knows that we tried everything within our power to change the outcome, but were unable to. She's appreciative of it, anyway

"Good, that's a relief. I'm going to miss him forever, but he's gone and I've accepted it. Now I'm planning on getting strong enough to get out of this room and help to make a difference. I will help with this problem."

"I've been thinking about Des. Do you think

she's in any danger? She had to have surgery on her shoulder and I haven't even contacted her to see how she's doing. Is there any way that I could call her?"

"I'm sorry Kitten, no phones here. They can trace them too easily. There's no outside contact from here. I'm sorry."

"That's alright, I understand" she says despondently.

"Knock, knock, anyone in there" Mallory says as she pushes open Kat's door.

"Hi Mal, how are you" Kat says in surprise and pleasure.

"I'm great, but how are you, you're the one that had the surgery and has to rest a lot. Me, I'm the same old, same old."

"It's good to see you. Can you stay awhile?"

"Sure, I can stay all night if you'd like. But wait, I brought a surprise, something that you need while you're stuck in that bed.

"Ta da" it's a color TV and a DVD player and look, I even found some movies, some old and some not so old. It's better than lying there and staring at the walls, not that they aren't lovely, but with no way to look outside, it's boring, at least for me. Since I think we're a lot alike, I thought you'd like some mindless entertainment."

"Mallory, you're awesome. Thank you so much. Isn't that nice of her Snake, she brought me something to do."

"Geez, if I'd have known the reaction you would have had if I'd have brought a TV, I would have gotten it first" he admits with a laugh and a look of thanks to his sister. "I should have known with that active mind of yours that you needed something to do, to help take your mind off of things. Mallory, you're brilliant. I was just going to go and wrangle up some soup and crackers for Kat. Have you eaten yet?"

"Not yet" she admits.

"Then it will be soup for three and we'll eat right here."

"Better make that four, cause I haven't eaten yet either" Devon says as he wanders into Kat's room. "Is this where the party is?" he asks with a grin.

"Hey, wait a minute, your having a party in here and didn't invite me?" complains Eli when he walks in.

"Looks like the gangs all here" Snake adds on a groan.

"What are we watching first" Eli asks after he shuffles through the pile of DVD's. "I say True Lies. That's an awesome movie. I love it when they question her but she doesn't know it's her husband and his friend that's doing the questioning" he adds on a laugh.

Mallory's just sitting in the chair by the bed with her head on her hand, wondering where all the quiet went, and how this many people fit into a room this small.

"Excuse me" the Doctor says when he walks by the room and backtracks. "She's supposed to be resting, not hosting a party. What are you all doing here?"

"We came to visit. She's one of us you know, and we take care of our own."

"That's nice, but you can't all stay. She needs to

rest."

"No, really Doctor, I want them here. Besides, if I get tired, I'll just sleep, even with them here. I feel better when everyone's here" she admits shyly. "I promise that I'll rest. It's just so much easier when you're around family, and this is my family."

"Okay, if you promise to behave and not overtire yourself, I'll let them stay. If I find you worse tomorrow, then this will never happen again."

"Deal" Kat says with a smile.

"Dinner is served" Sandy announces from the doorway. Behind her, Joe's pushing a small table loaded with a big pot of soup, some bowls, spoons and a couple of boxes of crackers. Behind him is Rand, pushing a small table with Soda in cans and bottled water, some grapes and apples to complete the meal. "I tried to keep it light and to make it something that would tempt you, Kat. I hope you like chicken noodle soup, it's homemade. You can't beat it for its healing properties, it is called nature's penicillin, you know."

"Mrs. Callander, you shouldn't have gone to so much trouble. Really, I appreciate it, but I don't want to cause anyone any trouble."

"Nonsense Kat, what are friends for, and this was no trouble, besides, I like to cook. There's just nothing more comforting than a kitchen when you have troubles, at least as far as I'm concerned."

"Thanks everyone" Snake whispers two hours later, after a soup dinner, some grapes and water and an hour of True Lies, Kat's deeply asleep. "She's resting very comfortably. Your visit made a world of difference. She's been hammered with a lot of bad things in the past few months. I hope she experiences only happy things now, at least for a while. I know your visit helped her to forget, so thanks."

Chapter Six

"Hey Mongoose, where you been hiding" Snake asks after nearly running him over in his haste to get to the conference room.

"I was looking for you, Lieutenant. When you have time, I wanted to show you something. It's in the north wing, Delta level."

"How about if I meet you there in, say a half hour. Right now I'm needed in the conference room, east wing, alpha level."

"Great, I'll meet you there."

"What's the problem" Jacob asks after he reaches the conference room.

"We're getting some chatter, Sir. I thought you'd want to hear what's going on, for yourself."

"Alright, let me see what's going on" he says after he grabs a chair so he can see the computer screen a little easier. "That's Wal'i, damn it . . . aww man . . . damn it, he was a good guy. Those bastards, they didn't need to do that. Those blood loving fucking bastards. I am going to pay them back for this" Snake swears after watching his best operative killed by a group of Iranians.

"They think that was funny, look at those bastards laughing and joking. I warn them now; there is no where they can hide from my justice. I'll serve them justice, as soon as I can get over there; they are not going to walk away from that unscathed. They'll be met with the same justice that they just gave to Wal'i. He was supposed to be on his way home, something must have happened to tip them off. Sergeant, you find out how they heard about him. I want that information today."

"Yes Sir, I'll find out."

"Down here Sir" Mongoose yells when he see's Jacob enter the wing. "That's the last time that doorway will be available. I left it open for you to be able to get in here. From now on there's only one way in and that's this door. I'll put signs up on all the other levels, to let everyone know."

"What are you doing in here" Jacob asks as he scans the area to see why he wants all the other doors blocked.

"Well, since we can't go outside easily, yet everyone needs to stay practiced with their weapons, I set up this area for target shooting. We need to be kept sharp, since it's the way we'll probably have to stay alive. I wouldn't want someone hurt or killed because they were out of practice."

"This is a great idea Mongoose. Thanks for thinking of it. I've been a little busy lately, but I should have thought of this, it's a safety issue. You have no idea how much I need to shoot at something today" he admits as he moves to the front of the area and stares down the hall to the picture of the President that's being used as a target.

"Nice target" he adds dryly "I won't have any trouble aiming at that face."

"That's what I thought, Sir" Mongoose admits with a smirk. "I doubt anyone will have trouble hitting that target. I know we'd all be happy, given the chance, to shoot at the real thing. I've also set up an area to use your knife in, and a room off this end is set up with weights and a treadmill for work outs. We need to stay in top form if we're going to stay fit enough for a fight. Besides, we need something to take our aggressions out on besides each other. So, I consider this the gym of our underground."

"Good deal. We'll need to make out a schedule to keep people moving in and out so that everyone has a chance to use this. But first, let's have a little practice" Jacob says with a light in his eyes and a smile on his face. After aiming his weapon at President Martins face, he fires six rounds in rapid succession, then wanders down the hall to see how well he did. "I've still got it" he says to Mongoose. "She's got no forehead left. I hope you have lot's more of these" Jacob adds with a smile. "I think this will probably be the most used target in the world. I wonder how she'd like it if she saw this" he murmurs with a wicked smile. "Maybe I should send it to her, by a circuitous route, of course. It would give me great pleasure just knowing that she saw it."

"I'll take care of that for you Sir. It would be my pleasure" he admits as Jacob slaps him on the back in appreciation.

"I'm leaving you in charge of this area. It's up to you who can come here and when. Everything about this place is yours" Jacob states. "Now, I gotta get back. I haven't checked on Kat yet today, she's probably wondering if everything's all right."

"I'll be glad to help with that too, Sir. When she's well enough, I'll bring her up here, she can start on the treadmill at an easy pace, to build herself back up. Then we'll throw in some weights and then weapons training and practice. She'll be good as new in no time, Lieutenant."

"Thanks Mongoose, I appreciate it."

"You might want to include a ring to work out in. Kat does like her kickboxing and I know she appreciates it when she can take her aggression out on someone else. She actually tried to get me, one time when we sparred. She just doesn't realize how small she is" Jacob admits with a shake of his head and a grin. "Thanks Mongoose, this made the day just a little bit better."

"Any word on how they found him out" Snake asks when he gets back to the conference room.

"It was a delegate, Sir. One of them knew him from before, and recognized him."

"Which one" Snake demands.

"It was Ron Grayson, Sir. He's the only one that had any knowledge of Wal'i. He was introduced to him in the states, as a sergeant of the U.S. Marines but because he's been undercover and changed his looks dramatically, we never expected anyone to actually recognize him. Obviously we were wrong. Ron Grayson must have recognized him and passed on the word."

"Damn it" Snake yells. "Why weren't we informed of this sooner? We could have prevented this. Son of a bitch!"

"I'm sorry Sir; we only found out because we went pretty far back and were looking for it, we would have never known otherwise."

"Well Mr. Ron Grayson, you will pay for this. No way am I sitting back and letting you get away with this" Snake warns.

"Sir, there's some news coming through right now, level one. It's says that an American delegate, part of the Presidents special envoy sent to Iran to help schedule the upcoming peace conference, has been found dead. This happened sometime early this morning. It looks like he was murdered in his own bed, since that's where he was found. This happened mere hours after a staff member of the Shah's was killed in a brutal manner, by an Iranian group of extremists."

"Sir, who do we know over there that could have gotten into the Palace and killed Grayson, without being found out? Do we have special-ops over there still? I know we did at one time, but with everything that's been going on in the States I just assumed that everyone was called home."

"We still exist outside of their knowledge base, and we didn't go back for new orders. We are legend, and it's very possible that they are legend too." Snake says thoughtfully. "This is good news. Now find out who was in charge of that unit, I want to talk to them. If this is true it makes our lives a whole lot better. It means we aren't the only ones. It also means that we can depend on some help when and if we need it."

"I'm headed over to the recovery area to check on Kat. Contact me if you can get anyone on the line or on the computer."

"Hey Kat, how are you feeling today?"
"Much better actually, it seems as every day

passes, I feel more hopeful and not nearly as exhausted. I'm getting better. Pretty soon I'll be up to work again. It won't be too soon as far as I'm concerned."

"There's no rush, you know. I want you back to a hundred percent before I'll even consider letting you work again" Snake informs her.

"I know, but it won't be that long now. I'm about ready to start walking, at least a lot more than I have been."

"Good, then I'll send someone over to talk to you about it. His name's Mongoose, maybe you can set up a tentative schedule. We'll get you back to normal, fast" he promises with a grin.

"Mongoose, that's his name? You people use the weirdest nicknames" Kat says in disbelief. "His real name is Elsworth Langley. How would you like to carry that kind of baggage around with you? Mongoose is a good nickname, and it's pretty descriptive of what he actually is, fast and good. He's the sniper of our unit, and a weapons specialist. But he's also set up an entire exercise area and shooting range that he's now in charge of. You'll like him, Kat, I promise."

Just then Snakes pager goes off and he turns away to glance at it to see who wants him. "Look Kat, I'm working on something, so I gotta go. You can reach me by pager anytime. We aren't using anything digital anymore, so no cell phones unless it's on the old analog ones that we used years ago. At least no one realizes their use, so we have plenty. I'll see about getting one for you, today. I'll also notify Mongoose that you're ready to talk to him about the next step in your recovery."

"Thanks Snake" Kat yells after him, he left in such a hurry she thinks with a grin, always running.

"Sir, we have Domino on the line, he's the Lieutenant of the special-ops unit in Iran."

"Thanks, I'll take this in my office. Jeremy, is that you?" Snake asks tentatively after he reaches his office.

"Jacob, that you" he hears on the other end of the phone.

"My God man, I thought you were state side. I didn't know you took over that group. How long ago?" he asks in surprise.

"Been here about two years now, but I'm getting pretty sick of it, although from everything that I've heard about what's been going on in the states, I think I'll stay here. The lesser of two evils, I suppose you could say" he adds quietly.

"You're right, it's definitely the lesser of two evils, although I think it's headed your way, so beware."

"What can I do for you Lieutenant?"

"I think you already did it and I wanted to thank you."

"For what?"

"Wal'i"

"Enough said, Lieutenant. That was our pleasure, Wal'i was one of the good guys and he certainly didn't deserve what they did to him. It made my blood boil, Jacob. I realize that you're not supposed to let your emotions rule, but they did, and there are no regrets on this end. We would do it again, if we had to."

"Well I thank you for it. And I'm also pretty excited to know that there's another group out there like this one. We've gone underground, just prior to the president gaining any knowledge about us, so that made it easier."

"This world has become a dangerous place to live in. The group I'm with is not taking the chip. We don't want anyone with knowledge of us, our whereabouts and exactly who is here. We're legion."

"This stretches from D.C. all the way to Texas, and down south. We're using some of the old underground, but have enlarged it and modernized it. We don't have to leave here for anything, but we can, although it has to be done carefully. We certainly don't want anyone to know of our existence."

"Lieutenant, this brings tears of gladness to my eyes" admits Jeremy. "It's a relief to know that there's another like us in the states. We thought we were totally alone here and I know the unit was disappointed with that. Our resources aren't as large as yours obviously, but we do have some. Now we can back each other up. That's makes my job a hell of a lot easier. I go by the name of Domino here, we try not to use our real names, that way no one can hurt any family out there."

"Understood Lieutenant. I'm Snake, same reason."

"Great minds and all that" Domino says. "I'll keep in contact Sir, and definitely let you know when anything major occurs."

"Thanks Lieutenant, the same here, out."

"I can't believe this" Jane Martin shouts to her Vice President. "They were hand chosen by me for this matter. Damn it, no one should have been able to get to them, they haven't even talked with the President yet. Who the hell is responsible for this disaster? I want names, do you understand, Quinton. I want whoever did this. They will not get away with this. He was picked by me. No one should have known anything about him other than what his position was in the House. That's public record. The rest was inside information. We have a fucking leak somewhere. I want that information before the sun sets today." Jane demands, voice rising with anger.

"Calm down, President Martin, calm down. We don't want anyone finding this secret room of yours, but if you insist on screaming, you're going to have the General in here. Then what? Use your brains, Jane. Calm down, we can get more accomplished quietly than with that roaring temper of yours." After taking in a couple of deep breaths and holding them, Jane calms enough that she's able to talk in a normal tone. "I'm sorry Quinton. I didn't mean to scream like I did. I'm just so angry that it exploded out of my mouth. I have to hide this side of me so often that when I can let go, it takes over. Sorry"

"Alright, first things first, his family needs to be informed. Then we need to talk with the other three envoys and see if they heard or noticed anything. Then I need to talk with the Shah. He's got to be as angry as I am, if not more so since this happened in his own palace. What an insult that was" she murmurs thoughtfully. "Maybe we're looking at the wrong reason. Maybe there's more to this than being my envoy. Maybe this had to do with something else that went on over there. Call the General and see if he has any knowledge of what could have caused this. If so, maybe we can piece together exactly what's going on, on his turf. If not, then we need to figure out how to find whoever did this. They will not get away with this. I cannot and will not tolerate this."

"Yes Madame President, right away" Quinton murmurs and then leaves the room.

"President Martin of the United States to speak with the Shah, please" she requests after reaching the Shah's palace on her hidden phone. There's no way anyone can trace this, she thinks as she waits for the Shah to come to the phone.

"Lieutenant, there's a call being made to the Shah. It's the President."

"She didn't wait very long for that" Snake says with a wicked smile. "Let's listen to what she has to say. No doubt she's pretty unhappy right at the moment. I'm sure she heard about her envoy by now, she's got to be spitting tacks" he laughs.

"Uncle Rahib, its Jane. What happened to Roy, Uncle? I thought your palace would be a safe place, how could anyone enter that huge place without your guards knowing?"

"Jane, it's good to speak with you. I don't know how they got in, but I will. We are questioning everyone that may have been around at the time. Trust me, Jane, if there's anyone that saw or knows anything, I will find it out. I will have answers by the end of today, I promise you."

"So how does it feel to be the President? Is it as

awesome as you once said it would be? Have your dreams come true, my dear?" the Shaw asks with a smile in hi voice.

"It's a lot of work and a lot of secrets, but I think I'm getting the hang of it. The people seem to love me at least. They're doing exactly what I ask them to do, so they either love me or they fear me. Either way is fine with me." She adds with a happy giggle. "We will conquer the world, Uncle. You'll see, it's going to happen just as we planned."

"I believe you Jane. I believe it will happen. You have my support, you know. I just can't show it yet. Some thing's need to remain cloudy for a while and you have much to do before you can be brought over here for your true goal. Be careful Jane, we don't want anyone finding out about your ways to communicate. It would be a dangerous thing for anyone to find out about this and about our relationship. Of course I told your envoy, some, but not all of it. But as far as I know, they are the only ones that know your story. I doubt the American citizens would like this information too much. By the way, your envoy should be arriving at any moment. They left during the night, so that we could track anyone that could have been following them. I thought it best that they get into American territory as soon as possible, after the murder of Ron. Let me know what you learn after questioning them. I'll keep looking on my end, too."

"Thank you Uncle. I'll be in touch. Please let me know when you find the answers to this dilemma."

"That was enlightening" Snake says. "I had no idea that she was actually related. I don't think she is.

I wonder if that's a courtesy title between the two of them, because I really don't think that the blood is connected here. Let's do some digging and see" he orders his group.

"This is Jim Cochran of WELT News Channel 3, Washington D.C., live in our downtown studio. We have some breaking news. We've just received news of a rather loud explosion being heard near Capitol Hill. We have Jennifer Sanderson live near the Capitol with news on what the explosion was. Jennifer, can you hear me?"

"Yes, I can, Jim. There's been a large explosion at the Capitol Building. It looks like it's located near the rear of the building. The last portion of the sidewalk that was left from the previous explosions has gone up in smoke. The area was cordoned off, allowing the explosion to affect the building only. The strange part is that the area was cleared of bombs, previously. They had sent in the bomb sniffing dogs, then the bomb robot which was able to gain possession of the complete bomb, which they were able to dismantle and identify. Somehow, another bomb was either still there or someone gained access to the cordoned off area and planted a new bomb. The military will probably use any surveillance cameras working nearby to try to identify any person that they were able to tape, who may have been in the area possibly planting the new explosive device."

"Hold on" says Jim of WELT News Channel 3, Washington D.C. "I'm receiving more breaking news. There have been reports from multiple cities across the country of explosions occurring at the capitol buildings in their cities. This sounds like what happened a few weeks ago when these bombs first went off. It's almost like Déjà vu or like we've gone back in time and this is just now happening for the first time. Unfortunately, this is the second time and thankfully the military is maintaining control of the cities. They've been on duty since the President issued martial law following the first explosions. No one knows why the first bombs went off and certainly, they

don't know why, now. Why did these bombs go off again? This time, the buildings are gone, there's nothing left of the capitol building that has stood in Washington D.C. for the past two hundred plus years. From the reports that I'm hearing, all the cities with a capitol building have experienced the same explosion. The damage sounds to be the same. There's nothing left but rubble where these majestic buildings once stood."

"Wow, someone's pissed again. This sure is looking presidential. I know there'll never be a way to actually prove that our president is causing these explosions, but I think she's pissed because of the death of one of her envoy, and this is her message to those that know anything about that, probably a warning of some sort" Jacob murmurs. With a wicket grin, he looks to his unit. "Well, looks like she don't like us none, this was an attempt at a warning. She ballsy, I'll give her that much. What she doesn't seem to realize is, we aren't scared of her. We need to up the ante, let's start creating chaos everywhere. The least we can do is help her to show her true colors to the world. This has been a pretty good day so far" Jacob admits with a laugh.

"I think she greeted her envoy and will be meeting up with them pretty soon. If we listen in, maybe we can get a heads up on who the snitch is in that little group."

"Thank you for taking the time to talk with me so soon after your arrival. Unfortunately, this is an urgent matter and I want it taken care of immediately. What do you think, David, Jill, Ed? Do you have any clue who might have given information away? It looks like we have a leak somewhere. Think back and let me know who you spoke with prior to your departure. There has to be someone that talked with one of you and let this out or planned it. Either way the information was leaked, causing the death of Rob. It can't be that hard to figure out, there are only three of you left. Let's start talking, list who you saw and spoke with just before your departure."

"President Martin, I spoke with no one before we left. There really wasn't time to talk to anyone. You informed us on what you wanted us to do, then told us to pack and meet at the airport. I didn't have time for chatting, not with anyone" denies Ed Sehgman.

"That's true, Ed, I did give you pretty abrupt orders and really didn't leave you any time to talk with anyone. That was part of the whole plan. I didn't want the information getting out about what you were getting ready to do. Unfortunately, someone had to have let the information out, so one of you talked to someone, now who was it?" Jane says in an angry tone. "No one is leaving until I have some names. I know it was one of you, which one" she demands loudly.

"President Martin, it was probably me. I had time to talk with my house service. I had to leave some orders for the time I was going to be gone. I never dreamt that just talking to the housekeeper would cause all of these problems. I promise you that I'll personally bring her here to talk with you and as soon as I'm free to go."

"That won't be necessary, Jill. I'll dispatch a military person to go to your house and bring in the housekeeper right now. We can question her together."

"What about you David? Did you speak with anyone prior to departure? It's possible that it wasn't the housekeeper, but someone else. You're not off the hook so easily, I want names."

"I did actually have a brief talk with a couple of friends. I didn't tell them exactly what I was doing, but gave them generalities. They shouldn't have been able to figure out exactly what was going on, but I suppose it's possible. I talked with Pete Townsend and Rachel Madison. Both are close friends of mine and truthfully, I can't see either one of them breaching our confidences. They've been friends of mine for more than half my life. They've never told tales outside of school before."

"Thank you for that David. I also want to remind all of you that this is not acceptable. The next time your president gives you orders, you need to follow them word for word. If I tell you not to talk to anyone that means ANYONE, do I make myself clear" she yells in her rage and embarrassment. "Now that those things are handled and we have some time, tell me what you thought of the Shah and the President. What was your first impression of them?"

"The Shah was very forthcoming and seemed affectionate toward you, President Martin. He told us a little bit about your past and your parents and a little about Iran's past and the upheaval that occurred that caused all of this to be put into motion." Jill says quietly with a smile.

"It was actually pretty impressive. Your parents deserve much credit for sacrificing everything that they had to sacrifice. It's amazing that they're so focused on the right and wrong of things and how they embraced the west and helped to build a church that they can't even worship in. You and your parents are very special people" Jill admits in awe.

"Thank you Jill, that was a very nice thing to say. I agree; my parents are perfect, they have given everything for these things to succeed. Allah will smile on them when it is time, they will be blessed."

"I agree" David says. "You've given your whole life, childhood and adulthood and have stayed so focused with your goal. You're very impressive, President Martin. We, speaking for this great country, have been truly gifted with your abilities."

"This is Jim Cochran of WELT News Channel 3, Washington D.C. The President's news conference is about ready to start. Let's go to the White House to hear what she's got to say. Jennifer Sanderson is live at the White House. Good evening Jennifer."

"Good evening, Jim. The President is due at the

podium in just about a minute. She plans on discussing the chip and when the public will start to receive it and how. Here she is" Jennifer fades out, and President Martin comes into view.

"Good evening Ladies and Gentlemen of the United States. I am distressed about some things that have been happening to the United States of America. The newest explosion at the Capitol Buildings across the states has me extremely angry. How dare someone take out their frustrations and misplaced anger on our history? Those buildings held a lot of American dreams in them. It's where our laws were written and voted on. It's where our great country was represented in each state. I, as your President, will not tolerate the further destruction of anything American. We are looking for those responsible and I have every faith in our military, that they will find those that created this uproar and they will be brought before you, the judges of the new American justice system."

"Also, I recently sent my own handpicked personal envoy to Iran to meet with the President there and give our thanks for offering to help us in our darkest times. We were able to handle our problems within our own country, but are appreciative of his offer. Unfortunately, someone was not happy that I had sent delegates over there and they killed an envoy. This has made me extremely angry. How dare someone just kill another person for no good reason? Attending to the President of Iran was not a good reason. Those people went there in peace, attempting nothing stronger then thanks. They were not there to cause any trouble, were greeted by the Shah himself and housed in his palace."

"Just prior to meeting with the President, someone was able to gain access to the Palace and murdered one of my personal envoys. I will not tolerate that, nor anymore stupid moves by the outlaws. I have been informed that the person responsible is Jacob Callander. Again we hear that name. We will now be looking for him thoroughly. I have no doubt that we'll find him and when we do he'll pay for what he's done."

"I would like to let you know that if you have seen him or have any knowledge of him, there is a reward. You will receive a million dollars if you find him and we are able to get him and bring him before you for justice. You will find a link to a special page on the web site that will allow you to sign in, and explain everything that you know. If we can apprehend him, you will get paid. That's a pretty easy way to make some easy cash, compliments of the White House."

"And now we finally move on to something good. I am happy to be here today to talk with you about the chip. We discussed earlier the vote and how much the chip passed by you, the America public. I know that there has been some confusion, some upheaval after the chip vote. Let me assure you that those people that created the problems, they were not the majority. The majority voted and said yes, we want the health care, we want the safety and we want to be a part of the new vision for this country that we live in. Because of that, we are moving forward."

"The chip implantation, as you have requested, will begin at the beginning of next week. We have spent many months, weeks, days and hours preparing for this huge undertaking. The chips will begin to be implanted beginning next week. We have decided to use the high schools of every community in your area. If you have children, then you know where you will report to. If you do not have children, but the neighbor does, then you will hear from them where to go. If you're still unsure where to report to, then please don't hesitate to go on-line and look it up. It's posted on the web site. You must call to set up a time to have your chip implanted."

"Please go on-line and set this up, once you know which high school you need to report to. The first visit is free. All you have to do is set up the appointment. If by chance you miss your appointment, then you will still need to make a new one, unfortunately, we cannot as a nation, cover the cost of a missed appointment. Therefore, you will be responsible for any charges incurred due to the first appointment being either missed or canceled. If your appointment is during work hours, your employer is legally mandated to allow you time to go and get your chip and then go back to work."

"We've tried to think of everything. If by chance you are in the hospital or ill at the time of your chip implantation, do not worry. We will be in every hospital, to enable you to receive your chip. The chips are so fast and easy that it won't matter if you're ill, they will not cause you further distress."

"Remember that you must be a real citizen of the United States to receive this chip. But I have great news for all those who are in the United States but are either from Mexico or Canada. These chips will soon be coming to your country."

"I have been in close contact with the President of Mexico and the Prime Minister of Canada. They have both enthusiastically decided to implant the chips just like the United States. We are in the process of forming what is called the Continental Triad."

"All people on this continent will have the chip implanted. That way, everyone will be able to get Health Care. Those with the Mexican chip, Mexico will pay for and those with the Canadian, Canada will pay for. All will have the health care that has become such a big issue in this millennia."

"I'm pleased to announce that the chip idea is spreading rapidly across the world and I'm sure that many other countries will want to follow suit. We are producing these chips at such a rapid pace that we may be able to help all the countries that wish to participate in a short amount of time. These are exciting times. New progress is being made as we rework the chip's information. Soon, you won't have to worry about anything, because the chip will help you in all matters."

Chapter Seven

"Kat, don't you think you're overdoing it" Mongoose asks after watching her run five miles on the treadmill and then look for a sparring partner. "Jacob told me to work you, but he didn't take into consideration your one track mindedness. You keep going at this rate and you'll be past normal. Can't you give yourself a break?"

"NO, I need to be in top form, now. The only way I know of to get that way is to work myself. I'm fine, I'm not overdoing it. If I were, I wouldn't be able to finish what I start."

"So what about weapons training; how's your aim?" Mongoose asks with a smirk.

"My aim is just fine, but I'll practice since I can't seem to find a sparring partner."

"Great, let's start with your police issue then we'll move up to bigger and better. Maybe I'll turn you into a sniper. We can always use more of those."

"Awesome, I'm in" she says enthusiastically.

"See that target? Let's see what you can do."

After loading her weapon and putting on the ear protectors, she stands on the line and fires six rapid shots at the target.

"Bring it back, let's see how you did" he says. "Not bad, you killed her, all six shots to the head; not an easy feat. You're pretty good, Kat. Where'd you learn to shoot like that?"

"My Dad, he was a hunter; small and large game. He used to take me hunting with him. It was one of the few times where we could spend time together, just the two of us. Those were good days" she admits quietly with a smile.

"He did a good job with you, then. You have great aim. Now, how'd you like to shoot like a sniper?"

"I'd love it. I'm a quick learner, so show me how."

"Remember, when you're taking the long shot, you have to adjust for wind speed and even temperature. They're all contributing factors on where the bullet will hit. Now, once you can feel the wind, think about how fast the bullet will go from this particular weapon, and how much it will lose as it travels, then how much it will probably drop. Now adjust your sites accordingly."

"Okay, let's see what you did" he says as they both take off walking towards the tree that the target was on. "You have to keep your eyes and ears open out here. If the Lieutenant finds out that we went outside for practice, he'd probably skin my ass. So let's do this quietly and get back inside."

"Wow, Kat. First time and you got a kill shot. I'd have to say you're a natural. Is there anything that you can't do?" Mongoose asks teasingly.

"I'm sure there is, I just haven't found it yet." She admits sheepishly. "Don't tell Snake about this, I want to practice more. I want to be the best sniper you've ever seen, and then I'll tell him and surprise him."

"That sounds good to me. I doubt it's going to take you long at all to be the best sniper ever. The record is one and a half miles I believe, but I'll investigate that more and let you know."

"Maybe I can find a sparring partner now. Someone else must have showed up to work out by now."

"Sure, we can check" he says after they make it back inside without being found out. "Hey, Devon and Rand are here now, anyone ready to spar" she yells when she sees them.

"I'll go" responds Rand. "I've never sparred with you so let's see what you've got."

"Rand, you okay" Kat asks with a laugh when she helps him up after the first round. "You were holding back on me, weren't you" she teases.

"Yeah, I was a little but you pack quiet a punch" he admits good-naturedly. "I won't make that mistake again" he promises as they square off again in the ring. After dodging as many blows as receiving, Kat still manages to get one under his guard and knocks him down again.

"Sorry Rand, you okay" she asks with a smirk.

"I'm fine Kat" he says disgruntled. "You're better than I was expecting" he admits.

"Sorry, I know I am. No one expects it cause I'm a girl, and not a very big one. They look at me and see weak. I'm not weak. Actually, I'm a fifth degree black belt in tae kwon do. No one expects that either" she laughs good-naturedly.

"Have you sparred with Jacob yet" he asks with a laugh.

"Yeah" she admits with a blush. "He won, but I wasn't at my best for that" she admits. "I was too distracted."

"What's so funny" Jacob asks when he enters the training room and finds Kat, Mongoose, Rand and Devon laughing.

"We just watched Kat whoop Rand in the ring. It was great" Devon explains around chuckles. "Rand stepped into the ring thinking he was sparring with a girl. Well he was, technically, but Kat's not just a girl. After watching that, it makes everyone want to either spar with her or leave before getting talked into sparring with her and losing."

"Yeah, I know she's good. She gave me a run for my money when I sparred with her. I wasn't sure who was going to take that one. Finally, she gave up" he adds with a laugh. "We'll have to try that again when I have time and you're up to it."

"I can understand the time issue, but up to it, really Snake. I'm up to it now. Well, maybe not right at this second, I'm a little tired right now, but the next time for sure" she advises him smartly.

"Okay, I'll plan on the next time then. Just let me know when" he adds with a smile completely expecting to win that easy round.

"Now, Mongoose, I want to talk to you, privately, please."

"Sure, I made an office out of one of the rooms off the gym."

"Good, let's go there" Jacob says with a look.

"You were found out, Mongoose. You've got NO business going outside of this facility. There's too much danger of someone finding out about us. Not only are you not allowed to go outside, you're definitely NOT ALLOWED to take KAT! Are you freakin nuts? You didn't expect me to hear about this, did you?" Jacob yells. "Do you know what would happen to her if she were captured? Do you not understand how much they want me? One million dollars worth, that's' how much. They also can figure out if Kat's around, then so am I. Her partner with Metro One D.C. is still out there, and she's totally on their side."

"Lieutenant, I'm sorry. I had no idea that it would be a problem for anyone when we went outside. She's practicing to be a sniper, and wants to surprise you with her skill. But in order to practice, we have to go outside. There's nowhere underground that's long enough to shoot at. It's too contained. What if I promise not to let anything happen to her; not let anyone see this location. We can get lost deeper in the woods, and if we're doing the sniper thing than we can kill anyone that appears to be a threat."

"I'll have to investigate this more before I decide. There are a lot of people that I'm responsible for. We've already lost a whole bunker. We can't afford to lose this one too, and too many people could die if we aren't careful. Let's work on what's available out there, and see if we can tighten up the perimeter security."

"Yes Sir. I'll look into the outside security right away. When that's done, we can spend some time outside. I think everyone needs to go outside and see blue sky. It'll help make their circumstances easier to cope with."

"Alright, Mongoose, do it and let me know. In the meantime, I promise not to say anything to Kat about what's she's doing."

"Thank you Sir, I appreciate it."

"Lieutenant, we have some information coming through. I think you may need to hear this, Sir." Jacob's informed through his radio.

"I'll be right there. I'm leaving the gym right now."

"Yes Sir."

"What's going on" he asks as he strides into the war room.

"We've picked up some chatter. It doesn't sound good. Someone's complaining about the military presence. They're accusing them of committing atrocities on the general public. It sounds like the military's decided they're above the law and are doing anything they want."

"There's a woman crying, I can hear her, saying how they're taking all the females out of their houses, accusing them of being traitors and then passing them around among themselves, forcing them to do all manner of sick things. They don't seem to care about the ages of their victims, either. I've just heard of an eight year old being gang raped. She didn't survive that, Sir" the Sergeant claims in a shaken voice. "We have to do something. How can we let this happen to our people? This is wrong, we have to do something."

"I agree Sergeant, we have to do something. Put out the call, I want every able trained person to meet me at the exit, tell them to bring their weapons. We can't let the people fall this way and we can't allow those people to do that to anyone. We're going out, Sergeant; we'll get as many as we can."

"People, listen up. Some of the military's gone corrupt. They're treating America wrong by hurting those they're supposed to protect. It's become a corrupt world and you're now assigned the job of protecting the citizens, those that made us hide, now need our help. They don't realize what's happening to them, now that they're under the thumb of the military who answers to the President only."

"We're going out in short spurts. Each of you has an hour to make as much confusion out of this situation as possible. Let's take their minds off the public and bring it to us. We can deal with them on more of an equal footing; the public doesn't stand a chance. Anyone with sharpshooter experience is front line. Try not to let them see you just let them see what you can do. Take them out, as you will."

"This is war now, rules of engagement have changed. Remember to protect the innocent. I want everyone to sign out and time out, and then give us a general direction that you're headed in. That way we can keep a tab on everyone. If anyone is gone much longer than their scheduled time, then we'll be notified and may be able to do a search. I want you working in pairs. Take care of each other. We use radios only and on our band, no digital communications, since they can be intercepted too easily. Good luck out there. Remember, we're defending the citizens from their own military."

"MY God" Kat says to Mongoose. "How can this be happening? It's only been a couple of months since we went underground, and look what the world's become. The only people seen are the ones that the Military has taken out of their houses. Those poor people, no, hold on you bastard, you're not going to hurt that child." Kat brings her weapon up, sites, and pulls the trigger. The person dressed in military garb goes down dead, middle of forehead.

"Nice shooting" Mongoose says to Kat as he brings his weapon up and shoots the other military person. "Two down and thousands to go, but at least we're helping someone. Keep moving, stay in the woods as long as possible. That way we can get more before being found out. Remember, we only have an hour to get these monsters."

"This is what people become when their leader is corrupt. I believe we're experiencing the Absolute Power equals Absolute Corruption rule, first hand."

"Time" Mongoose commands discouraged. "We didn't get as far as I'd hoped. Hopefully, we'll be back out in an hour or two to start again."

"Yeah, okay" Kat agrees. "We have to come back out. This is horrible."

"Where's Snake" Kat asks after returning to the bunker by way of the long way. *Wouldn't want to lead anyone to our door* she thinks after wiping the sweat from her face and eyes.

"He's still out" the young officer says after checking her name off on the returned list.

"What, what time did he go out" Kat demands to know, angry and about to take it out on the kid. "He's been gone almost an hour, Ms. He should be returning momentarily."

"Okay, fine" she says, determined not to worry.

After all, if anyone can take care of themselves, it's Snake.

"There he is Ms. I told you he'd be back soon."

"Thanks, Officer. I appreciate your help" she says as she advances on Snake with long strides, looking for any injuries or damage.

"Kitten, glad you made it back okay. What's the good word" he asks as he gives her a big hug.

"Mongoose and I need to go back out, Snake. It's bad out there. We need to continue on with the decoy work. We may be able to stop some of the worst crimes that are being committed. At least we'll take their minds off of what they were doing and switch them over to us."

" Let's see what the word coming through the radio is, first. We fought long enough to grab the attention of the leaders. Let's see what they're going to do about it" Snake replies.

"This is Jim Cochran of WELT News Channel 3, Washington D.C., with a special announcement from the White House. The General of the Armies is about to make a statement concerning the problems that have been occurring in the area today. He's ready now, here's General Bossley:"

"Thank you for giving me a few moments of your time. We've been experiencing some difficulties relating to the safety of our citizens today."

"The underground group that's being run by Lieutenant Jacob Callander has gone crazy. We're being fired upon in the very streets that we're trying to protect. I've heard the rumors that our Military had gone rogue, but that's not the case. The one's you need to look out for are the very ones that you have mistakenly proclaimed as your saviors from us, your true protection."

"My people are not responsible for doing any of the vile things that you've accused them of. They would never do anything to create a poor light to be shown on our Military nor on our President. They're professionals and are only doing what they've been ordered to do, they will not harm you. You must help to keep our streets safe by listening to what they tell you to do. Do not side with the underground, they're not on your side."

"We, your Military, are the ones that are protecting you and keeping you safe from those in the underground movement. Thank you for your time" and as he turns to leave, questions come flying in from the media and with flashbulbs going off every second causing utter chaos, but no further answers are forth coming.

"This is Jim Cochran of WELT News Channel 3, Washington D.C., "Wow, that was brief and to the point. I have to agree with the General. The Military are the ones responsible for the protection of the citizens, that's why martial law was enacted, so that you would be protected by the President's very own troops.

"They would never do what the public has been accusing them of doing. It's hard to believe that the people actually believed what they heard, panicked and contacted the underground, who just made matters so much worse. We have definitely fallen on hard times in the U.S. This is Jim Cochran of WELT News Channel 3, Washington D.C."

"I can't freakin believe that the General actually stood in front of the millions of viewers today and lied. How does he think the public's going to react to that? They're not stupid, and it's them that have been affected, not the military. Except maybe by not getting away with everything they're trying to get away with. By being picked off one at a time, trying to stop the chaos and being made to stop hurting the very people they're supposed to be protecting. Will the levels of corruption never end? Is there no hope for this world any longer?" Kat adds through anger and heartbreak.

"I know, Kat. It's not going to improve, at least not in the near future. Just because the General wants the public to turn to the military, it's not going to happen, at least not to those that have experienced the military at its worst."

"We have a job that still needs to be done, and we'll be doing it. I believe it's time to get back out there and take out a few more of those, the ones that are using their jobs to perform the vilest of acts. I can't in all decency not help those poor people, and stop the terrible injustices that are happening to our people, our children. Prepare yourselves, we begin again. No one will be left out there preying on our youth, our babies."

"Rules of engagement still stand. One hour, pairs and return for check in. Be careful out there, watch your backs. I do not trust this military, they're a corrupt bunch of cowards preying on the innocent."

Chapter Eight

"I asked you here to inform you of a decision that I made earlier today, while we were above ground trying to protect the public. We've got a whole group of people out west in those undergrounds.

"I'm planning on heading out there. I know that we have experienced people out there and they just need to be rallied and guided on how to help the American people during these trying times. I'm sure similar if not the same things are happening out there that are occurring here. They need to be shown that they too can help our country by helping to protect the American citizens.

"I trust the people here to know what needs to be done and continue doing it. I'm going to leave Rand and Mongoose in charge at this end while I go west and help them to gather forces to begin to protect the people. Once I've completed that, I'll be back. I prefer to stay at this end, close to the Capitol.

"It feels like things are going to start escalating in the near future. The military don't realize the extent that they've been slowed down, thanks to our expert marksmen here. We'll continue to slow them down, by taking them out when needed. Just think of it as weeding. Hopefully we're making a difference. It's just hard to see to what extent right now.

"My plans are to return here within the next three weeks. I should be able to get quite a bit accomplished in that period of time. I'm reachable, in an emergency. I just won't be able to get here as fast as normal. Anyone have any questions? Good, then I'll be leaving."

"Hey man, how the hell are you" Snake says to his old biker buddy, Cougar, after he reaches Montealth, about ten miles south of Sturgis. "It's been what, ten years?"

"No way man, it can't have been ten years, maybe five, but ten, that can't be right" Cougar says in denial.

"Yeah, I'm pretty sure it's been ten, but whatever, it's good to see you alive and well." Snake says with a slap on Cougar's back.

"What's happening with you" Snake asks as he sits as if settled in for the night. "I'll have a draft" he yells to the waitress. "Nice place" he says as the waitress turns back to get his beer.

"It's not bad, I'm here most nights. There's just nothing going on in this one horse town" complains Cougar. "I don't know why I stay, except, it's free so why not? So how's the bike business going? Are ya still creating those custom bikes and selling them for that ridiculous amount?"

"You bet" Snake replies with a laugh "hey, if they're willing to pay that much, why shouldn't I charge that much? The beers on me" he tells the waitress when she brings his drink. "Get my buddy here another one, would ya, doll? Thanks."

"So, what's the news, have you heard from any of our biker group lately?

"Naw, they don't stop in. No idea where any of

them disappeared to. They just took off one day and that was it. You're the first one I've seen in years" Cougar admits.

"Wow, I would have thought they'd at least dropped in. I wonder what happened to all of em. I know what happened to Bad Ass, he met his maker oh, about six months ago I guess. They found him in a burned out house in D.C. but it wasn't the fire that killed him. He was stabbed to death first. Not surprised, he had it coming to him. He was a son of a bitch. I never did like that guy anyway, so I say good riddance" Snake adds. "Been to the biker rally this year? I haven't had time to get there in so long that it's hard to remember how much fun it always was." Snake says reflectively.

"It ain't nothin like it used to be. This year, there was hardly anyone there. I think everyone's a little nervous about travel, what with everything that's going on in this country now. It's just become a really boring world to live in. It's not like the old days when we rode free and did what we wanted, when we wanted. I sure miss those days. It's just too bad you can't go back.

"Yeah, I miss those days too; there was a lot more freedom back then. We didn't have to worry about nothin, especially a business" Snake admits in a grumble. "So, there's nothin going on in this one horse town, hmmm."

"Not really, nothing that interests me, as long as those military idiots leave me alone, then it's all good" cougar adds.

"What military idiots, I ain't seen no military around here" Snake admits in a questioning tone.

"Oh, we got a bunch of military idiots that think they own the place running around here, nosin in on everyone's business. They leave me alone, they don't want any of this, I tell you" Cougar says with a fist waving.

"Hey, I don't blame them none, I've had some of that myself and it ain't no fun" Snake admits with a rueful grin "don't want no more of that either" he admits with a teasing smile.

"That's right" Cougar says, puffed up with pride.

"So where are these military? I didn't see any when I got here today, they hiding from you?"

"Naw, they don't hide, they mostly search the areas out by the caves. Don't have no idea what they're looking for, but if it keeps them out of town and away from me, they can do what they want. Ain't no skin offin my nose."

"Caves, what caves. Now you got caves around here? I never heard of no caves out here by Sturgis" Snake says slowly.

"Oh, we got tons of caves. Lotta people buying them up for a lot of money, the rich bastards. They don't know what to do with all their money, so why not buy a cave? They're scared of the end of the world. They're buying up all the caves after they been fixed up. Don't want to live above ground like normal people, no, they'd rather be hermits. Stay away from the above ground people. We might contaminate them, or something. Hell, I don't know. All I know is, they want to live in those underground caves. Go figure." Cougar says in disgust.

"Caves, awesome, I want to see some, can you tell me how to get there? Snake asks excitedly.

"Why you want to see those places, they're just holes in the ground, that's all. Nothin to really look at, but if you want I'll show you where they are. Maybe you can get a tour, you make enough money to buy one, so they'd probably let you see some."

After a twenty minute road trip, by bike of course, Cougar points out some rocky areas, supposedly containing entry areas to the caves. "This is as far as I'm goin, I don't want to see no stupid caves. I like life above ground, not like I'm buried early. No Sir, I don't like them under the ground things."

"Hey, thanks Cougar" Snake says. "I'll be back in a few hours or so, but I'll meet you at the bar. You don't need to hang around just cause of me. Here's a fifty, go buy yourself lunch and a few drinks. I'll meet up with you later."

"Hey, thanks Snake. See ya" Cougar yells as he turns his bike around and roars out of the area.

The road is pretty nonexistent out here, Snake decides as he travels slowly toward the rock outcroppings. This place reminds me of Afghanistan with the rocky outcroppings, caves, temperatures and all. After getting as close as fifty feet to the nearest rock formation, a whistle is heard near his face. I'm being shot at, he realizes, son of a bitch! Okay, you want to play that way, I'm in, he decides.

"Stop where you are. You're trespassing on private property. Just turn around and leave and nothing will happen to you. If you continue on in this area, we will use force to stop you." Snake moves forward slightly and raises his hands in surrender and waits to see what's going to happen next. A lone figure starts walking towards him with a gun pointed at his chest.

"I don't want any trouble out here, Mister. But I'm not afraid of having any either. State your business and I'll let you know if you're in the right or wrong spot."

"I want to talk to someone about purchasing an underground facility."

"Your name, Sir"

"My name is Andrew Callwood, I'm from Vegas."

"Well Mr. Callwood, you're in the right spot then. Come on this way and I'll show you the entrance."

"Thanks Mr.?"

"Just call me Mike, Mr. Callwood."

"Okay, Mike. Thanks."

"Here it is, Mr. Callwood. If you come here alone, you'll be stopped every time. We have to take care of the people living underground. "I'm part of the security force that searches these areas for friendlies and not so friendlies." Mike reaches out and touches a small mark on one of the rock surfaces. Out comes a lookalike rock, blocking a large steel looking door. Once the door's exposed, a small area towards the left side is dirt free. Mike touches that area with his index finger, print side toward door panel. After checking his fingerprint, the door soundlessly moves down into the ground. Ahead is a stairway down into a dark, cavern like area. After both of them move in, the door raises and locks and the lights come on, similar to an airway runway.

"Wow" Snake says, impressed. The seamlessness of all the actions was impressive.

"We have to take all these precautions, Sir. There are a lot of people out there looking for us and we can't afford to have them find us, at least not right now. I'll introduce you to the leader here, his name's David Hall." Mike knocks on the third door down the corridor and after hearing come in, he opens the door and gestures for Snake to go first. "Mr. Hall, this is Andrew Callwood. He was wandering around outside and has asked to see the underground, says he's interested in purchasing one."

"Welcome Mr. Callwood. Please, come in and have a seat. I'll answer whatever questions that you have."

"Thanks Mike, see ya later" David says.

"What can I tell you Mr. Callwood?" David asks after they both take a seat at the small desk, one of the only few pieces of furniture in the small office.

"First, my name is not Andrew Callwood. That was just something that I made up so that I could meet you and see the underground. Now wait, there will be no need for that gun, Sir. I come here in peace, not to harm."

"What's your name, Mister, your real one this time" David demands in a firm voice, gun still at the ready.

"Fine, my name is Jacob Callander but I'm also known as Snake and I've come from the east bunker, the one in D.C."

"Lieutenant Callander? You're Lieutenant Jacob Callander, ex Special-Ops unit leader." "Wow"

David says as he drops his weapon and re-holsters it. "This is an honor Sir. What can I do for you; really, we never expected to get a visit from you. Thanks for coming Sir."

"First, all we want is to make sure that everything here is going smoothly. There are a lot of innocent people out there that are having major difficulties with the military. We set up a special sniper group back east, to take out the ones in the military that have become corrupted. There are some that are hurting the very people that they have sworn to protect. We can't have that kind of behavior, not even among the military, so we're disposing of those that are guilty of doing the crimes.

"Not all military are corrupt, but the ones that are, are giving the whole a bad name. Since all this is occurring in D.C. and we know people are the same everywhere. I figured that you were probably having similar problems out here. I've come to help you set up sniper groups to stop the crime waves. The last things we want are the people being afraid of leaving their homes. No one should have to live that way."

"Thank you Sir. You're an answer to a prayer. We are having those kinds of problems, but I wasn't sure about sending people out of here to commit crimes themselves. I understand the need, but couldn't figure out how to transform them, yet keep their consciences clear."

"I can and will help you in that area. I just need you to get a hold of as many weapons trained people as possible. A tour of these facilities would be appreciated also."

"Glad to, Sir."

"I want to thank you for your attention and for showing up here for this impromptu meeting. It took me four days to arrive here since travel has become so burdensome. I had to take the long way out so I didn't bring the military right to your door, but I want to say thanks for gathering here today."

"My name's Lieutenant Jacob Callander. I'm from the east end underground. I've been running that part of the underground since we were forced to move there a few months ago.

"Truthfully, none of us ever thought that things would get as bad as they have, and certainly not as quickly. We've had to resort to leaving the underground in short spurts in order to help protect the citizens in the cities. Unfortunately, we've experienced an increase in military abuse and I'm saddened to report the corruption that's been occurring.

"Some of the Military have started to harm the citizens that they're supposed to be protecting. My group, which mostly consists of sharp shooters, has had to resort to leaving the safety of the underground to help stop the corruption that's been occurring. All manner of evil things are being committed against the public, murder and rape of all ages of children and adults. We can't in good conscience allow that to continue.

"You've probably heard about what's been happening in the Capitol. Unfortunately, I expect that it's already begun here, also. Unlike what you've probably heard, my people are all doing this voluntarily. I will force no one to participate in this, but I do want you to be aware of what's going on, on the outside.

"I want to thank David Hall, former Captain of the Metro D.C Police for his welcome when I arrived. This place is set up really nicely, whoever created it thought of everything. Mr. Hall, can you tell me why you're here?" Jacob asks.

"My wife and I moved out here just prior to the vote on the chip. We didn't like what we saw was happening with the new President and came out here to get away from so many people. But since the bombings that have occurred in every state and with the military occupation since the martial law was declared, we decided that even going west, we were sill in danger. So then we sought out the underground. It's probably been the best thing that we've ever done. Here we feel safe and our children seem happy, we don't have to worry as much as we did. The people here are like family; we all watch out for and take care of each other."

"That's excellent, Captain. Since you're in charge here I assume, I want to hear what your input is on what's been happening, and what you think you can do about it from this end."

"I'm hoping to make this place impenetrable, for the protection of all who have chosen to go underground to live. I certainly don't want to leave anyone out. Realistically, I know that there's never going to be enough room for everyone. But if there's any way that we can help those above ground, then I think we should. Since we're lucky enough to be able to stay down here, then morally I believe we must help those less fortunate."

"It does look like there are those that are corrupt in the military. Unfortunately, in any large group, there will always be the good and the bad. I'm not saying that all of the military are corrupt, but enough that they are giving the military a bad name. We're living in terrible times Lieutenant and I'm sure that I can find a number of sharp shooters at this end, since we have quite a few underground people that are ex-military. I'm sure they'll be happy to help in the sniper roles when the time comes and the people need them.

"We can't let the martial law sway us from helping the helpless. There are so many people that they can prey upon that it worries me."

"I agree, Captain, we have to stop them from committing any more atrocities. We can't allow them to hurt and kill the citizens of the U.S. without repercussions. Thank you for allowing me this time. Talk to the Captain here, he's going to start scheduling sniper fire to remind the military that they are not allowed to do whatever they want. They, too, have someone to answer to regarding the citizens of the U.S. and their treatment of them. Thank you for your time." Lt. Jacob Callander finishes in dismissal.

"We've saved some small rooms for anyone that's new here to use, until more permanent places can be prepared. I'd be happy to show you one, if you're interested."

"That would be appreciated Captain. I've been up for the past few days. Travel isn't as easy as it used to be, especially for the underground and it's only going to get more difficult as time passes."

"I plan on staying for maybe two weeks and help

in setting up the groups of weapons trained individuals. If you have any military or ex-military, I'd like to talk with them first. They'd make excellent trainers."

Chapter Nine

"Mongoose, you ready? It's time for us to go out and create a little confusion." Kat says with a look of determination.

"You bet" he adds as he grabs his weapon and some extra loads.

"Think you've got enough fire power?" she asks dryly.

"Hey, pot calling the kettle black?" he points out with a smirk.

"Yep, I know" she admits with a puckish grin "I'm ready."

"We only have a few minutes left of our time, but at least we stopped a few things from happening. It looks like the Military's starting to act a little skittish, don't you agree?"

"Oh yeah, they aren't too comfortable. It's hard to do much when you have to look over your shoulder all the time, but hey, we're just doing our job and rather well too."

"Hold on" Kat says quietly. "I just heard a moan or something. It sounded like it was up ahead and to the right."

"You bitch; you aren't going to get away with that. You drew blood when you hit me in the mouth. Now you gotta pay" says the soldier in a hard voice as he grabs the twelve year old girl and throws her to the ground, making her scream. She starts to whimper in fear as he jerks his pants open and prepares to rape her, kneeling in front of her and grabbing at her shorts.

Unfortunately for him, he was so busy talking to his victim and threatening her that he didn't hear Kat come up behind him. She places the tip of her gun against the back of his head and then clicks it in warning, demonstrating a load being put in the chamber, making the soldier go real still. He gets a strange look on his face when he's told to slowly turn around, by a woman no less. He just doesn't realize what woman's gained the upper hand, but Kat's ready for him. With the gun ready to go off and a knife in her other hand, he doesn't stand a chance. He tries to stand, and Kat moves in close, suggestively. "What's the matter, little man, a real woman too much for you" she says in a smoky flirtatious voice, close to his ear. After seducing him with her deep voice, she slides the knife in her hand between the two of them and with a swift downward movement, slices off his penis. The knife's so sharp that he didn't feel a thing and it happened so fast that he just watched everything then screamed.

"Are you in the habit of raping young girls, Corporal? She can't be more than eleven or twelve. What were you planning on doing to her, soldier? Aren't you the ones that are supposed to be PROTECTING the citizens" Kat yells in his face. "Nothing, Sir, I wasn't going to do anything, I swear" he says and then he passes out cold.

"Are you okay?" she asks the young girl, lying on the ground near the soldier.

"I'm okay" she says with tears streaming down

her face, in a state of shock.

"Did he touch you" Kat demands to know.

"No, he never touched me in that way. He hit me and knocked me down, but I fought him and hit him in the mouth, I made it bleed. That's when I saw you come over here, into the alley. You saw everything after that."

"Good, then I want you to get up, brush yourself off, be thankful that there are people out here that do want to help and then go home. Shut the doors and windows, cover them and stay inside. It's not going to get better out here and you could be caught in the middle of some really bad stuff. So go home, and forget you ever saw me. That way I can help more people."

"Soldier, get up and get out of here. This is your only chance" Kat says with a kick.

"Remind me to never get on your bad side" Mongoose says to Kat, dryly.

"Sorry about that, but there are some things I can't handle, and that's one of them. He had it coming. He'll live, but now he'll always remember what he was planning on doing and now can't."

"Let's head back; we've gone over our hour by a few minutes. Someone will probably be getting ready to come out here and do a search for us and I'd like to get back before that happens" Mongoose says quietly.

"Alright, I've had enough" President Jane Martin says in anger to the General of the Armies, Richard Bossley. "My military are being hurt and killed by this damn underground. We've got to find them and put an end to this. They can't continue on with the things that have been happening. Too many of our fine young men are being seriously injured or killed by this group of renegades. We have to find these people and stop them.

"The citizens are starting to trust the underground and not listen to our leaders and that puts us in a precarious position. It will be hard to regain control of our country if we can't gain control of the underground. Something has to be done, and soon." she yells in warning.

"President Martin, I understand, but you don't know who these people really are. Sure, the leader of the group is Jacob Callander and he's really good. I know, I trained and worked with him myself. However, he's obviously trained many more to fight the same way, and with that many as capable as he is, it's going to be hard if not impossible. You saw what he did with the first wave that found him. He trapped them and destroyed them like it was nothing. We haven't even been able to glimpse the opening for their underground. They're cautious; they have the perimeter guarded heavily. We can't get close enough to see anything. All we have is an approximate area, nothing exact. He's good, President Martin and he's your biggest threat at the moment."

"So, what you're saying is he's better than our whole military, better than the thousands that you have available at your finger tips. That's a very sad state of affairs, General Bossley. If only I would have known that he was better than you then I could have looked him up and made him General of the Armies. At least I would have had the best, which is what I was supposed to have right now, by giving you that title" she replies in anger and frustration.

"I'm sorry President Martin. I'm sending out more troops to see if we can locate their hideout. If we can slip someone past their security, then maybe we can get the upper hand" he promises quietly. *I've got to get that bastard. Callander, you're giving me a bad name, you bastard. I promise to make life hell for you and turn you into a huge example for others, he thinks to himself.*

"I want all marksmen in this building within the next hour. They're going to be getting some new orders" General Bossley informs his Lieutenant after he leaves the President sitting in the Oval Office and get's back to his own office.

"Yes Sir, right away Sir."

"This is going to stop, I will not tolerate anymore of this bullshit. If he wants a war, he shall

have a war. More than he can handle, the bastard" the General murmurs to himself. *I must have trained him too well, instilled the wrong loyalties, evidently. Well, I can fix that. If you take away something important, he'll come to the rescue.* "I want intel up here also" the General snaps at his Lieutenant. "We'll find out who he's close to, and it will be my pleasure to create chaos in his life" he decides with a grimace like smile. *He won't like this much, but then I haven't liked what he's been doing to my military, how he's been making us look. It's time.*

"Thank you for being here in such a timely manner" the General addresses his marksmen. *There must be over a hundred people here he thinks, perfect. The more guns pointed at Callander, the better chance of getting him.*

"From this moment forward, you are under my direct command. You have one and only one order to follow. Get Jacob Callander. He's the person in charge of the underground. He's also been wreaking havoc with my military personnel and I'm done playing by his rules. Now, we go to mine."

"I do not want him killed. You people are the best, therefore I expect the best. I want him alive. I don't care if he's wounded but I don't want him dead. He's got a lot to answer for, and information that we need; locations of all the undergrounds, who's working where and when. We're going to put a stop to the insurrection that he's started, so your work begins today."

"I brought intel up here for a reason. They're going to let you know where he probably is and who he's going to protect with his life. That person will be a valuable asset to us. It'll help to bring him out into the sunlight where you'll be waiting. Any questions?" he asks and when silence meets his question, he orders "Sergeant, please let these people know whatever information you have on him."

"Jacob Callander has two brothers and a sister. They're actually quadruplets. His brother Eli is with the FBI out of Los Angeles. However, he dropped out of site a few days after the bombings occurred at the capitol buildings. We believe he's joined Jacob underground. His other brother, Devon Callander, is the Deputy Chief of the Capitol Police Department. He was last seen near his apartment, close to the Capitol Building. Since we've been under martial law, he has not been seen. We believe that he too has joined his brother Jacob underground."

"His sister Mallory is with the FBI out of D.C., in charge of the serial killer group. She was out of town during the bombings, somewhere in the Midwest, but drove back here shortly after the bombings occurred. She also has dropped out of site. We also believe that she joined her brother Jacob, underground.

"His parents live just outside of D.C. proper and have not been seen in the weeks since the bombings, so we believe that he took his parents with him when he moved underground."

"Jacob Callander is a long time Special-Ops leader and has been extremely successful in the past. He's known as Snake by quite a few people, especially underground although his men call him by his rank, in a gesture of respect."

"He's a very dangerous individual with multiple specialties. He's an expert with weapons and at hand to hand combat. He's also an explosives expert, among many other things and he has no problem sliding through areas like a ghost. I've never met anyone that admits to seeing him. He's silent and deadly."

"He's believed to have gone underground in answer to something that occurred right after the President took office. He has a "friend" that he protects and he treats, similar to a younger sister. They've been friends for more than fifteen years. She would be an excellent catch, so be on the lookout, her name is Lieutenant Kathleen Thomas, previously with the Metro One D.C. Police Department."

"I received word from an inside source just before I left my office that Lieutenant Jacob Callander is not around here at the moment. It looks

like he left for the west coast a few days ago. Rumor
has it that there's a huge underground out there that
he wanted to visit. We believe that he's going to try to
set up that underground the same way this one is set
up, which means that there will be military shootings
happening soon."

"They're not shooting at all the military but at the
ones that have been accused by the public of rape,
murder, injustice. Even though we police ourselves it
doesn't mean that we always catch everyone that
commits a crime."

"The snipers, however, shoot to kill and don't
ask questions. If a military person is accused of
something by an American citizen, then the snipers
go out, search for that person and kill him when
found. It's their code and there isn't any leniency, at
least not as of right now."

"Thank you, Rick, that's good information"
praises the General. "I'll contact the west coast
military commander and let him know of the
possibility of catching Jacob Callander out west. He
can step up his search and start looking for him in
particular. Let's hope we get this man since he's
become a thorn in the side of the government. The
President wants him and she shall have him. Now go
out there and stay out of trouble. If I find out that
what the people are saying is true, I myself will find
the individual that's been accused and kill him
myself."

"I want to thank you Captain Hall, for the
opportunity that you gave me to help set up a sniper
group. The ones that are committing the crimes need

to be taken out, but I know that your group won't take out just anyone. They'll stick to what they've been told and will take action only for the protection of the people. We won't need to worry that everyone is the target. I know they'll use their brains and stay with the proposed target. That takes a load off."

"We live in tough times and if we can trust, then we are lucky. Now I need to get back to the east end, there's so much happening all the time that it's hard to get away. But I promise, I'll be in touch, and if you ever need anything, I'll get it for you if at all possible. Just use this number and I'll be paged. I'll get back to you as soon as I'm able to. Oh, and thanks for the hospitality, it's appreciated."

"Thank you Sir, for taking the time to help us out on this end, and if ever the need arises, we'll be there to back you."

Damn it's hot out here, Snake thinks as he walks quite a ways to get to his bike. I shoulda parked closer he decides after feeling like a sitting duck. Damn it, someone's got me in their sites he realizes as the hairs on the back of his neck stand up. Not one to discount his gut instincts since they've kept him alive many times in his life, I need cover, he decides. Now where the hell am I going to find cover out here in the middle of nowhere? If I can make it to that small stand of trees, maybe I can hold them off, at least for a little while.

After a bullet goes whizzing by thanks to a sharp move on his part, he just makes it to the trees when a bullet tears into his calf. Not letting that hard sharp burn bring him to his knees he continues forward until he finds a sheltered area. Son of a bitch he decides as he grabs his knife, tears his pant leg and field dresses his injury. I hate it when they hit me, he grumbles. It really pisses me off. Damn it, I should have been faster, more on guard. I better call base and let them know that I have a problem.

"This is Snake, get me Mongoose" he orders the Sergeant that answers his page.

"Lieutenant, what's up man, you lost again?"

"Listen, I'm stuck out here near the west underground, in a stand of trees. I've got a freakin sniper taking pot shots at me and he's already hit me once in the lower leg. I'm going to need an extraction, so send out a sniper and a ride, as soon as you can. I'll send you my coordinates. Snake, out."

"Rand, report to the office, Rand, the office" Mongoose says over the intercom. "I just got a call from Snake. He's stuck out west, above ground in a stand of trees. Here's his coordinates. He's got a sniper on his tail and he was bit once in the lower leg already. He wants an extraction and requested a sniper. I'm going to send Kat and you. Kat, because she's the best sniper I've seen in a long time, you because you're a spotter and a medic. He's going to need something for his leg, and she's going to need a spotter if she can't get real close."

"We have anyone on the military side of things that are on our side?"

"Yeah, I got a buddy or two out there" Rand admits.

"Think you can get transport for the both of you out there."

"Probably, let me get a hold of him and see if he can help" Rand says as he turns away to make the connection. "When, excellent" Rand declares and hangs up. "He's got the availability of a Black Hawk, he's a pilot and he said that no one would think anything of him taking a chopper out, it's what he does. He's going to wait for us in this old beat up airport on the edge of the Virginia and D.C. border. It's been closed down for years, so no one would ever think anything about that."

"Good, now all you need to do is find Kat and let her know. When are you leaving?"

"He said he could meet us in two hours, at the airfield, so as soon as I find Kat, we'll head out. It may take that long to get there from here." Rand says.

"Keep me informed on your status."

"Will do, see ya."

"Kat, you up for a field trip" Rand asks after he finds her in the kitchen, helping Jacob's Mom with lunch.

"Always, where we going?" she asks with a grin in response to his question.

"Let's head out and I'll let you know" he says with a quick look at Sandra and a no shake of his head telling her it's not public information.

"I gotta go, Mrs. Callander, but I'll see you later" Kat says with a quick hug and cheek kiss.

"What's up, Rand. We don't usually keep secrets around

here, so this must have something to do with Snake. What is it?"

"He's still out west, was actually trying to get to his bike to head back when he got cornered by a sniper. He called and requested an extraction and you're the shooter Mongoose picked. He says you're the best, and I'm a good spotter so he wants me to go too."

"I've arranged for a helicopter through a buddy of mine, he's meeting us in an hour and forty five now, since it took me fifteen minutes to find you. So grab your gear and move your rear, make sure you get lots of ammo and meet me at the west end exit. We're going to have to hustle to get there on time. I need to get my stuff too, so I'll see you in ten minutes."

"What's up with the first aid kit? Was he injured, and if he was, why didn't you tell me" she asks quietly.

"He was grazed in the calf of his leg, but he's fine. I want to be prepared in case any of us have problems. Better to have the stuff you need than not."

"True, I guess. But I'm sure he was more than grazed, you're just telling me that so I don't panic" she accuses.

"Not true, but you can't panic anyway. We have a mission and you're the one that has to do it, so let's move. Jacob's depending on us to get him out of there."

"Ten more minutes" Luke, the pilot of the black hawk

informs them after hours of flying "then we'll be in site of the area that the Lieutenant's in."

"Kat, you tell me where you want to be and I'll make sure you get to that area. Keep on the lookout for the sniper and for the Lieutenant."

"Will do Luke, thanks."

"I think I see him" Kat says in excitement. "Look at the stand of trees, see to the left. He's standing out so that we can see him."

"Hey, shit, look out" Luke says as a bullet hits the bottom rung on the chopper. "We can't land here and we can't take any gunfire to this baby, I just waxed her. Hold on, I'm going down on the other side of that ridge. Let's hope that the sniper's on this side, or that there aren't two of them, one on each side" Luke says grimly.

"Shit, look to the north. I see some company headed this way. They must have heard the gun fire, or they've been contacted by the sniper. I'm counting close to a hundred troops. This may make the extraction a little more difficult. How far would you say the sniper is from the Lieutenant?"

"Oh, let's see, about five hundred yards give or take. That should be an easy target for me, five hundred yards is nothing."

"We're taking more fire; we need to get down fast" Luke mutters while trying to keep the helicopter upright and not let her be hit by any more bullets.

"I'm going to try to bring her down over there, Lieutenant. Hold on, this could get hairy" Luke warns as he throttles down "I need away from those snipers. Okay, we're down, let's go" says Rand after a harrowing couple of minutes of trying to land as he grabs his bag and shoves Kat's at her when she finishes loading her rifle.

"I can't see yet, too much dust blowing around. Where was Jacob, just before we landed?"

"He's was to the west of us, so he's probably to the right of where we are now."

"Okay, the sniper was to the north east of Snake, so we're good. Let's go hunting" she adds in grim amusement.

"I think I've got him" Rand says after a half hour of searching and then lowering the binoculars. "He's trying to make that rock outcropping protect him. He's about a mile, maybe slightly more, away from here. That's a tough shot, Kat, but I've heard of longer shots. Just take your time youngster, you can do it."

"Let's hope. I'm good, but this is a lot of pressure. Let's see if all my practice pays off. Tell me where Rand, set me up. Be my eyes."

"To the left, one click Kat, the winds are coming out of the north at about five and a half miles an hour. Almost there, and I think that's it, give it a try Kat. On two" Rand says. "One and two" and on two Kat fires while Rand's watching through the binoculars and see's the sniper go down. "Yes" he yells "you got him Kat, excellent!" he says as he jumps up and slaps her on the back.

"Hold on" Kat says. "I want to make sure there are no others out here. The troops that we spotted from the air must be getting close. We're going to have to move, or we're going to have more fire fights. Alright, let's go and get Snake and see how bad he's hurt."

"Snake" Kat cries in jubilance when she finally lays eyes on him. He's just sitting with his back against a tree, waiting for them to show up.

"Hey Kitten, it took you long enough" he says teasingly with a smile.

"I saved your ass, buddy" she adds with a smirk, teasing him back.

"I'm not so sure of that. I think he probably dropped over dead from waiting so long."

"Stop it, both of you. Let me see that leg, Lieutenant."

"It's fine, just a little scratch" Jacob insists.

"It looks like the bullets still in there Sir. It's not a graze. You wanted to keep the bullet, did you?"

"Naw; it just annoyed me more by staying, that's all."

"I'm going to have to remove it. It's going to hurt a little" Rand warns.

"Just do it" Jacob says "so we can get out of here. I've had enough of the one hundred degree temperatures. It's time to go home."

As Rand prepares the injury for bullet removal, Snake stares straight ahead, ignoring everyone else. As he reaches into the injury to grab the bullet with some forceps, Snakes breath hisses in through his teeth until the bullet is successfully removed, then he breathes out slowly. When the wound is finally dressed, he gets up as if nothing happened and states "let's go check out that sniper. I want to see just how good you were" he says to Kat teasingly. Kat replies back in a much quieter tone; face white, tears in her eyes that she refuses to let fall.

"He's over to the right, and north. Out by that rock outcropping. It's about a quarter mile from here, maybe a little more" she says. "Should you be walking that far Snake? Why don't you give yourself a break and we'll just get in the helicopter and head back now?"

"Why, you did get him right? Don't you want to see for yourself? Come on Kitten, lighten up, let's go see, it could give you bragging rights if it was that difficult."

"Okay, fine, whatever" she says in annoyance "Let's go look, but we need to hurry, there're more troops headed this way."

After walking for slightly more than a quarter mile, they come across the sniper lying on his side with the gun almost at his finger tips. He was barely disturbed when he was shot. "Hey, look at his scope" Rand says. "You shot him through his scope, straight into his brain. I've never seen anyone make a shot like that one. Good shot Kat" he praises as he grabs her and gives her a big hug.

"Kitten, that was an incredible shot" Snake says after he stares at the sniper and registers everything that must have happened. "I've never even heard of a shot like that one. It was just slightly over a mile and you killed him through the scope, amazing. I suppose I better let everyone know never to under estimate you. You've gotten pretty dangerous Kitten!"

"Thanks" Kat says with a bright red face "but I was shooting for his crotch" she replies with a smirk. "Can we go now? I think it's time to go home."

"Shit, that hurt's" Kat says as she grabs her right shoulder. "Run, we need to get out of here; I just got nicked by a bullet. I told you I didn't need to see my shot. Now the damn troops are close enough to do some damage" she complains as she runs away from the area with Rand and Snake behind aiming and shooting, trying to keep her covered.

"Rand, can you contact Luke, he needs to get started, before they catch up. They'll pin us down and we'll never get out of here. Damn it, I only brought so much ammunition. I'll never have enough to keep a hundred troops at bay. We've gotta get out of here."

"We will" Snake says reassuringly as he runs behind her, keeping her covered.

"We're almost there" Rand says breathlessly. "Damn, it's hot out here, almost too hot to run. Only thing keeping me going are those damn bullets. They'll catch up if I'm not careful." "Ahhh, shit, they caught up" Rand says as he staggers after getting one in the back of the right arm. "Damn it, I hate getting shot."

"Get in, get in" Snake yells as he grabs hold of Kat and throws her in to the helicopter, which is starting to take off. "Rand, jump" he yells as he grabs him by the arm to help him on. "Go, Go" he yells at the pilot. "It looks like we might make it, they're shooting at us. As long as all they have are guns, we're okay, but if they have a freakin rocket launcher, we're in big trouble."

"Go, shit, I spoke too soon, they have a launcher. Keep her steady, I'm going to try to take it out if I can hit it from this height."

"It looks like they're getting ready" Rand says after watching through the binoculars. "Maybe if you both use the long range rifles, you can hit the shooter. You're going to have to be fast though; he's lifting the launcher and getting ready to sight it. Fire now, hurry, we're out of time. Kat, you got him. Good shooting. That made them all scramble, awesome."

"Shit, there's another one, a different shooter, same kind of weapon. Aw, shit, there's no time, he's sighted, we have to jump, get out, hurry, before he launches. Here, grab this and jump, go go go" as they all jump the helicopter explodes in the air leaving four free falling people with emergency shoot bags in their hands, pulling the wires and hoping they'll be able to hold on and land a little easier than without one, while trying not to get hit by any shrapnel from the black hawk.

"Everyone alright" Snake yells after he lands. Not a gentle landing this time, he thinks.

"I'm okay" Rand says as he tries to sit up after half landing on a cacti. No answer from Kat, she's lying on her stomach in a very still position. No sign of the pilot, shit.

"Here, grab my hand" Snake tells Rand. "Start looking for the pilot, I'll check on Kat."

"Kitten, you alright" Snake asks gruffly, worry in his voice when she fails to answer. After checking her for any bleeding, he calls Rand over so they can turn her and check for injuries. "Looks like a pretty nasty bump to her head, let me check her over. Could you look for Lucas, I didn't see him close by. He must have fallen further out. We have to hurry; we have to get out of here before those troops get here. I'm sure they watched where we fell and are changing direction as we speak. We don't have a lot of time and now no transport. We may have to try to get into one of the caves until this blows over" Rand says worriedly.

"There's a cave about hundred yards from here. I can see it with no binoculars, so it's pretty close. Let's try to head in that direction. If she's knocked out cold, I'll carry her. Just give me a second to try to find Luke.

"Let's go" Snake says. "Luke's headed in that direction. He's pretty beat up, but says he'll make it. We're all lucky to be alive right now. Let's head out"

Snake says as he picks up Kat and carries her gently to the cave.

"Sir, what happened?" Mike asks when he spots the bedraggled group making their way to the cave entrance. "I got caught by a sniper after I left here earlier and had to call for an extraction."

"This is my group from out east. Anyway, we got caught by a squad of about a hundred. Unfortunately they had a couple of rocket launchers. They blew our bird out of the sky, but luckily, we were able to get clear before it exploded in the air. We're injured a little and could use some help here. Let us in please and inform the Captain of our arrival."

"Yes Sir, right away. Come on in, you're all set. Just head into the room on the left, there's a couch in there you can put her on. I'll find the medics and have 'em head this way.

Chapter Ten

"Captain, sorry to inconvenience you, but I had to seek shelter in one of your caves. We got caught by the military, and after they blew up our helicopter, we lost transportation. I'll have to contact the home base and see what we can arrange. Until then, we need a medic to check out some injuries. Looks like Lucas and Kat here are the worst.

"Kat? Shit, Kat . . . wake up Lieutenant, can you hear me" demands Captain Hall after seeing his Lieutenant lying on the couch quietly. She slowly moves her head, but winces as she does so that Snake grabs her head and holds it still, until she's examined and found to not have a neck injury, she's not moving at all, he decides.

"Captain, Captain Hall, what are you doing here? Where am I" she says in a panic, not recognizing the room she's in, but once she see's Snake, she relaxes.

"You're in the underground out west. Lieutenant Callander carried you in. I guess you passed out or something, but the Medics are on the way, so you'll be fine."

"Snake, what happened? Why are we here?"

"We were in a fire fight in the helicopter, remember? We had to jump before the rocket hit it and blew it out of the sky."

"I remember a little. Was anyone else hurt?"

"Yeah, you and the pilot, he had a hard landing.

Looks like a slight injury, but he needs to be checked over, anyway. Here come the Medic's. Captain, if I could talk to you while they're doing their thing."

"Sure Lieutenant, let's move over here to the door."

"What can I do for you?"

"I need to contact my east end group and arrange for transportation."

"I have transportation available here, if you're interested."

"Really, that would help out a lot, thanks. We're going to need to move as soon as they're checked over and treated. I have to get back east as soon as possible." Jacob insists.

"Not a problem Lieutenant Callander, I'll arrange for it. It'll only be an SUV, but it will get you where you need to go. Why the urgency, Sir?"

"The only people that new where I was were the ones I spoke to here, my old biker buddy that I spoke with just before coming here, and the east end underground. Somewhere in that group, I've got a leak. I need to get back and start setting up some different scenarios to draw him in. It's too costly and not good for your health to have a leak, so I'm going hunting."

"I'll take care of this end, whoever the leak is I will find him, I promise" Captain Hall assures him grimly.

"Good, but don't kill him, I want more in-depth information. If he can leak this than he can leak other things, so once we catch him I'll interrogate him."

"As you wish, Sir."

"Looks like the Medics might be done, let's go

find out the news." Jacob says as he starts over to where Kat's sitting on the couch.

"She'll be fine Sir, she has a mild concussion. She'll be tired for a while but she can sleep, only someone will need to wake her every two hours to make sure that she's okay. Just wake her and ask her questions that she should know the answers to. If she reaches a point that she can't remember, you need to get her to a Doctor, fast."

"Thank you PFC Taylor, appreciate the help. What about my pilot, how's he doing?"

"He has a dislocated shoulder and some minor cuts and bruises, but he'll be fine. He'll need to wear the shoulder sling for the next two weeks, long enough for his shoulder to learn to stay where it belongs, but other than that, he'll be fine and he's able to travel."

"Excellent PFC Taylor, thank you."

"Looks like we can take you up on your transportation, Captain Hall. When will it be available?" Jacob asks.

"Whenever you're ready, but you can stay as long as you like, I'm sure we can find rooms for everyone."

"Thank you for that, Captain, but we need to hit the road ASAP. Too much going on right now, but maybe when it gets a little quieter, we can come back for a visit."

"Any time Sir, you're welcome here any time."

"Kat, do you think you can travel soon?" Jacob asks. "We need to hit the road. We've got a long trip ahead of us, some of it in occupied territory, so we'll need to be ghosts."

"I'm ready whenever, Snake. Is Lucas ready, was he hurt bad?"

"No, just a shoulder issue, he'll be fine."

"What about Rand, is he okay?"

"Yep, the only injuries were you and Lucas, and you're both going to be fine. You've both been cleared to travel."

"Then let's go, I'm ready." Kat assures him.

"I'll show you the way to the parking area. We've had to create an area that's pretty much undercover since we need to keep our transports safe. It won't take long to get there, just follow me."

"Thank you Captain Hall, we appreciate all the help. It will be returned if and when you need any help. Please contact me at the east end underground at this number, and I'll make sure help is dispatched as quickly as possible."

"Remember, this underground is not alone. There are also other Special-Ops located in different areas of the world that are there for our back-up. Things may get crazy for a while, but persistence pays off, so we'll do what needs to be done.

I'll send you some intel about our President, it will make for some interesting reading and is actually an eye opener, but I won't send it through the normal ways. We've got some trouble within, so I'll dispatch it here as soon as someone's going in this direction or when we can stop our leaks."

"Now, the last thing we're going to need besides gas stations that are friendly is more ammo. I'm not sure what we're going to come up against. We'll be traveling the same roads as everyone else is, so hopefully we can get a good idea on how the average

Americans and small town America is doing at this time. It may be the best thing that's happened to us, traveling the same way everyone else has to. We'll get a bird's eye view."

"We've arranged for an envelope of cash, you'll find it in the glove box and also, the ammo you requested, under the floor board in the spare tire compartment in the back of the SUV. Is there anything else, Lieutenant?"

"I think that about does it, thanks Captain Hall. I'll contact you once we reach our underground. I think we'll enjoy going home this way, out in the sunshine, leisurely. Thanks again, Captain Hall. I'll talk to you soon."

"When can we stop for some food" Rand complains after traveling for five hours nonstop.

"Soon, if we can find a place close to an exit, then we'll get off and get some dinner. But if it looks like it'll be difficult to get back on, or if there seems to be a heavy military presence than we'll keep going. I want to have a little peace when I'm eating, and not look constantly over my shoulder."

"Deal Lieutenant, thanks."

"Let's get off here" Snake says when he recognizes the name of the town. "I've been here before. I hope they left it the way it was. It was a nice little town, very country. It was just a normal small town with kids playing at the play grounds and parents sitting, and talking together as they watched them. Turn right up there at the light. It'll take us right into the down town area."

"I thought you said this was a nice small town,

with people and stuff. It looks deserted to me. When was the last time you were here Snake? Could it have become deserted that fast" Kat asks confusingly. "None of the stores even seem open and the restaurant looks like it hasn't been open in a long while."

"Damn it! They've destroyed this little town. Either all the people left for fear or they're all hiding out somewhere they think will be safe. This used to be a perfect little town, alive with laughter and kids, adults and music, damn it!" Snake growls.

"I'm sorry Snake. I'm really sorry" Kat says in sympathy, feeling his pain.

"Let's get back on the highway. We'll go somewhere else. Somewhere has to be the same. Not everyone could have hid or left" he says sadly. "Get off at the next exit and we'll check that one out." After getting off at the next exit they find the same thing "damn it, nothing's the same as it was."

"Stop in Kansas City, there's got to be someone around that town. That city's way too big to have everyone hide in it. Besides, the last polls I saw had most of the major cities happy with the president and what's been happening. I think they're supposed to start the chip implantation this week. From what I heard, it's being done in the high schools of each town, so there's has to be something going on."

"There're a lot of people wandering around, everything looks almost normal. There just doesn't seem to be a lot of laughter or smiling going on, everyone seems pretty intense, but at least there's food available. Let's find an off the beaten track place and see about refueling our bodies, then we can take on the gas tank for the car. Hopefully we can take care of everything at the same exit."

"Try to act subdued like everyone else. And try NOT to look military. Just act yourselves" Snake says as they enter the Italian restaurant.

"Can I help you" the hostess asks somberly.

"Yeah, we'd like a table for four, in the back if you have it."

"Right this way, Sir" she says as she leads them to the back room in the restaurant.

"Can I get you something to drink while you look over the menu?"

"Please, I think we'd all like the house wine" he says as he glances at each one and gets a yes nod.

"I'll be right back with that, Sir. The specials today are the spaghetti and meatballs and we also have stuffed manicotti. I'll be right back with your wine and to take your orders."

"So what do you think?" Snake asks quietly. "On the outside, it looks like everyone's trying to act as normal as possible. But the feeling I'm picking up on is suppressed fear, subdued, but anxious."

"Yeah, that's the feeling that I'm getting too" says Rand.

"I don't know, it seems pretty normal to me" Lucas says "but I've been out in the public with the military during the martial law institution. This is what we find everywhere; the people are quiet and scared. They want business, but they don't want to draw attention to themselves. I think they're just really afraid of the military."

"Yeah, that's my take also. They shouldn't have anything to be afraid of with the military occupation.

I'm sure the underground news is happy to report on all manner of atrocities. Which actually seems to make the public fear the military even more, even though most of the military are just trying to help everyone" Jacob says quietly.

"Now wait just a minute, the military aren't trying to help. They've gone out to scare people and intimidate them, which breeds fear. They also want the people to bow down to them. I'm sorry that you're all military but you know what they say, one bad apple . . . Well, that can't be truer." Kat says hotly. "Just because you're military, it does NOT give you the right to treat people poorly. You've been trained wrong if you believe that's the only way to help the country. It's not, what about the people. Shouldn't they come first? In this world, the reality is that the people have lost all of their freedoms. They can't just go outside doing nothing. If they do, they get harassed by the very people that are supposed to be protecting them. The people of this country, they've become the bad guys. Now all people fear arrest and judgment by their neighbors. They all know how that would turn out."

"No, when the President did what she did, she created a country of fear. It'll be a long time before people will feel free and happy again, if ever. We may never see that happen, at least not in our lifetimes. This President has created a disaster, under the guise of help. Now if the people decide they've had enough and start an uprising, she may have more to deal with than she could ever have envisioned."

"Let's head east, it's time to get back to our underground, see if anything new has happened in the past few days. We should have enough gas to get us there now" Snake decides.

"This won't be easy since we're surrounded" Snake growls after he sees the crush of military personnel that are surrounding the entrance area to the underground. "Word's gotten out on our entrances, now we'll need to figure out a new way to gain access."

"Damn it, we've got an underground leak, that's the only way they would have known where to gain entry. I will figure out this leak and whoever it is, they're going to be real sorry they ever messed with me" Snake says angrily. "From now on, no one talks to anyone about this place without writing down what they said and to who they said it. We're going to set a trap and catch that son of a bitch."

"We'll have to go to the other entrance and hope that it's not surrounded, too. It's going to take us the whole day to get back. This was the closest way in, damn it."

"Look out Lieutenant" Rand yells as he takes out a sniper who's trying to catch Jacob. "Got him, go, go . . . we'll make it, I think he was the last one around" Jacob says as they run the last hundred yards to the underground entrance.

"That was hard" Jacob says as he finally shuts the entranceway to the rear of the underground. "Okay, our first priority, new exits and entrances. Let's hope someone down here thought of that and started it."

"Lieutenant, it's good to have you back, Sir" Mongoose says when he catches sight of Jacob.

"It's good to be back."

"Where's the rest of the group?"

"I had to sneak them in at all different locations. It looks like someone gave away some of our details to the wrong group of people. We've definitely got a snitch in here somewhere and I promise you, we're going to find him and then, no guarantee's. It's taken me the better part of the day to get everyone back underground safely. I want a report Sergeant; let's head to my office so we can get started."

"We started having these problems a few days after you left Sir. It's taken every ounce of manpower to keep the military from getting in. We've had to set up guards. I've sent snipers out to help get rid of some of the problems, but there doesn't seem to be an end to how many troops they're using. For everyone that we take out, they replace it with two more. I'm really glad you made it back, Sir. I'm at my wits end on how this information's getting out and how they're replacing people with double the amount. I will gladly hand over everything to you. I could use a break, maybe a nap. I haven't slept for more than an hour at a time in the three weeks you've been gone."

"Take off Sergeant. I'll take over. Thanks for all the hard work that you did" Jacob tells Mongoose as he's leaving. "I'm going to call a meeting and see if we can find the leak. Rand, put the word out, meeting in the dining room in two hours. We can take care of a few problems at one time."

"Hey Mom" Jacob says when he gets to the dining room ahead of the others.

"Jacob, thank God you're back. It's been crazy around here for the past few weeks. Everyone's been putting in double time just to keep ahead of the problems."

"Where's Dad? Is he gonna be able to be here for the meeting?"

"I'm sure he will; he's probably out in the rec room telling his stories, as usual. That seems to be what he does most of the time. He's got a lot of ears and loves his stories. Everyone seems to like hearing them too, so he's happy."

"Any idea of what kind of stories he's been telling?"

"No, I never have time to sit and listen, besides, I've probably heard them all anyway" she admits rolling her eyes and smiling.

"Jacob, glad to have you back man" Devon says as he wanders in hoping for a quick snack before the meeting. "Hi Mom, you got any of those cookies left from yesterday?"

"Sure, let me get some and some coffee. We have a little time before lunch, so a snack might be good" she agrees with a smile.

"Mallory, how are things?" Jacob asks when she walks in and over to him for a hug.

"Great, Jacob, really great" she says smiling. "I'm so happy you're back and no worse for the wear."

"Eli, it's good to see you!" Jacob calls out when he sees him enter. "Let's start taking some seats. I've called a couple of meetings this morning, so we need to get started as soon as possible. Rand, Kat, Mongoose, Lucas, thanks for coming" Jacob says as he catches a glimpse of them entering the dining area.

"Looks like everyone might be here" Jacob says

as he walks to the front of the room. "We have some rather large issues right now. Dad, come on in, we're just getting ready to get started. Okay, like I was saying, we have some problems. There's a leak here somewhere. Someone's giving information to someone outside of this facility. This has got to stop. I'm not sure who's responsible yet, but believe me, I will find out. Once we take care of this problem, then we can move on with the protection of the citizens again."

"Remember people, there are those on the outside that need our help. We can't help when we have to fight the military. So, first thing we must get done are the new entry and exit areas for this underground. Whoever's leaking the information has notified them of where our entryway was and where our exit areas are. It took the group I was with the better part of the day, trying to get back underground. The entryway was totally covered by the military, waiting for anyone to show up so that they could gain access along with whoever was entering."

"There's no way that anyone should be handing out this type of information. Even if you think it safe or the person you're telling is close to you, if they don't actually live here then they can and will pass the information on, they may even be ignorant of the danger of sharing this information."

"I want everyone that lives in this facility to be constantly on guard as to what they're saying and to whom. Who leaves this facility frequently and who stays away? That's no longer going to be acceptable. You come here from now on and you stay here. I'm sorry if this causes you trouble, but my first priority is the safety of all of those that have taken the underground as their homes."

"Now, we have to repair the damage that was done with the intel leaks and start changing things up. New entryways must be created along with new exits. We can't afford to have anyone knowingly or accidently sharing this information. It's going to take us weeks to get things back to the security level that it was before I left. Everyone's going to have to do their part to help get this facility back in order. Pick people to make groups and then schedule the groups to start working on the new exits. I chose exits first because they're more important than the entrance ways. If we have to evacuate, then we need to be able to leave fast. I'll be meeting with everyone here at one time or another within the next week. Until then, we have a lot of work to do."

"Devon, what's the word. Have you heard anything about where the troops are coming from? How they're getting advance notice, how fast they're replacing the ones we take out? I need as much information as possible. Why don't you take charge of that, get me that information as soon as possible. Head over to my command center and see what kind of information you can come up with. I'm going to show everyone else where to start working. We need emergency evacuation routes for the safety of the underground. Today is as good a day as any to get started with this."

"I'm on it Jacob. I'll get back to you as soon as possible."

"Thanks Devon, appreciate the help."

"I thought you had this under control" President Martin yells at General Richard Bossley. "They weren't supposed to be able to get back in, isn't that why I keep sending you so many troops, to stop anyone from entering the underground? Apparently, you're not capable of handling this issue. Should I get you another helper?" she adds sarcastically. "Just how many is it going to take to stop this from growing any further?"

"The last thing I need is more underground people. I'm already having a bit of a problem dealing with them. Stupid, narrow minded, indecisive people. I had no idea this was going to be so freakin difficult. And now this, you're telling me my biggest threat, Jacob Callander, managed to get back to his precious underground, with no problem? He's now in the one place that I have not been able to infiltrate, and you couldn't stop him."

"What would you like me to do Jane? I have no more power than you've given me. If you want me to apprehend this individual, then I'll need complete control."

"Hell no Richard, you'll never have complete control. You work for me, remember? I'm the one in control, the one holding all the power. As it should be and has been meant to be for my whole life. I will help you, as I have been, but you will never have complete control. Remember who you answer to, Richard, remember. I can make you or break you; I have no need to share my power. I'm quite capable of controlling and handling everything. You were given this duty and have been totally unsuccessful with it and I'm extremely disappointed" Jane finishes in disgust. As she paces back and forth, thinking, General Richard Bossley just stares at her with a blank look on his face thinking, *Bitch,* why did I ever decide to help her out.

She sure doesn't show what she thinks. I should have read her better, maybe then I wouldn't be in this position, at her mercy. Damn it, this is not going the way I envisioned it. She's really not capable of wielding as much power as she has, he thinks with a smirk. She's nothing really, just a plain Jane, delusional.

"Earth to Richard, are you in there General Bossley?"

"Oh, sorry President Martin, I was thinking, sorry. What was it you were saying?"

"I'm sending you another two hundred troops. That's my max. From now on, you'll have to give me something to get anything more. I'm giving you a deadline now since you've had enough time and wasted it. As of now you have two weeks to bring this underground to my door. I will not wait any longer. If you're unsuccessful, then I will assign someone else this problem, but if you're successful then you needn't worry, you're position will stay secure with me and my office. I'll see to it, I promise. And now, I have a country to inform about the starting of the chip implantation. Tomorrow's the big day and I'm so excited. Things will finally be moving forward. Finally."

Chapter Eleven

"Good Evening ladies and gentlemen, this is Jim Cochran from WELT News Channel 3, Washington, D.C. live from the White House. President Martin is scheduled to give a news briefing within the next few minutes. She's promised to announce the start of the chip implantation, where to get it and who's going first. This is a big night for the American public, the thing that everyone's been waiting anxiously for. Here she is, President Jane Martin."

"Good evening everyone. I am so very happy to be here tonight for the big news. I know how you're all awaiting the information I'm about to tell you."

"The chip implantation is scheduled to begin tomorrow. In your own towns, the high schools are going to be used. This has taken a lot of planning and work. The United States is a huge country with a lot of people and we've had to prepare and train enough people to be able to do these things. The production of the chips was a huge project, but I'm told that all is in place. Each person that lives in these United States will be called on their home phones and cell phones notifying them of the time that they are scheduled to be at the school to receive the implant."

"We've made a few adjustments to the actual chips, all for the benefit of you, the American citizens. I have a wonderful surprise for you. The chip will now take the place of your check books and debit cards. You're payroll's will be directly deposited into your bank account, minus the tax moneys. We have adjusted the taxes so that you will only have to pay them once, and everyone will be treated equally. For each paycheck a percentage will be taken out prior to deposit."

"You will never again have to file taxes, nor carry around the cumbersome check books or wallets with the debit cards. That in itself is an added bonus. But wait" she adds with a grin "you don't need to carry around anymore plastic. We've gone to the paperless society. Everything you need or want can and will be purchased with a swipe of your chip."

"We will track for you the amount used and the amount left. We're cutting down on people being robbed by another for their money, check books or credit cards. All you will need now is the chip and since the chip is mandatory, then everyone will have one. We have tried to simplify things for you and everything looks promising. This will save you money. You will now be able to leave work and stop at the store if you need to without going all the way home for your check book or credit cards."

"Anyone that has lots of cash at home is going to be informed that in the near future, it will no longer work. You will never have to see cash again; that filthy, smelly stuff that has been in everyone's pockets, on the floors, in the dirt and who knows where else. The germ infested papers that have come from the old will now become extinct."

"If you have a lot of cash on hand, you need to take it to your bank and they will deposit it into your account. It will be safer there than anywhere else and you can still save money this way. This saves money not only on printing costs, but also does away with the germs that have been passed around for years and it will also stop all counterfeiting. It saves your government money; we can do away with a whole department and use those people in other areas. It's time to move into the future, and I am so very happy that I have been given the honor and am the President that is helping this along."

"Now onto some different information: we're still having problems with the people that have decided they do not like their new country and have run to the underground. They are becoming increasingly more resistant to anything new for this country."

"I'm asking for your help. Since you're the Americans that love this county and only want what's best for it, I'm asking you for help with this underground problem. I've decided that if the American public works towards discovering who's in the underground, what their plans are and comes up with a way to stop them from creating so many problems, then you should be paid for those services. After all, it's a job and if you do the work then you should receive fair trade. So with those lines of thinking, I've decided that whoever helps the Government capture and detain anyone living in the underground will receive one thousand dollars per person that you find."

"You'll be helping your country by delivering its enemies to your government. You will then act as judge and jury and decide how you want these people treated. I believe it's the only fair thing to do. After all, they were your brothers, sisters, neighbors and friends that have run to the underground. You can make a difference, you'll see."

"To find out more on this subject, please visit my website. There you will find the link that will give you all the information you need to begin the job of finding the underground. I think I've covered everything that I needed to. Thank you again for listening to me. If anything comes up that pertains to the American people, I'll be in touch. Good night."

"Well, that was interesting. It's a good thing when the President guarantee's work for money. I'm sure all the American citizens will be diligently looking for the underground. A thousand dollars is not a bad sum for notifying the government when an underground person is found. I'm sure there will be a lot of names on the list soon. This is Jim Cochran from WELT News Channel 3, Washington, D.C. Good night."

"Well, we need to get this word out to everyone that has come to the underground for safety. No one will be safe anymore, once they leave the protective cover of the underground" Snake admits in dismay. "We should have expected this, and I suppose I did, just not this fast. She sure doesn't like to let things go. I think an underground news paper should be in the making. I wonder if Dad would mind getting that going, it's a good way to let everyone know what's going on here and out there."

"Hey mom, have you seen Dad anywhere recently?" Snake asks after he walks into the kitchen and finds his Mom in the middle of lunch preparations.

"No, Jacob, I haven't seen him since breakfast this morning. That's not unusual for him though, he disappears every day after breakfast, and I have no idea what he's doing or where he goes, sorry."

"That's alright, I'm sure I'll find him. What are you making, it smells wonderful in here."

"I thought I'd make some old fashioned chili. It sounded good to me and I think most people like it, so that's what we're having for lunch today. That and some fresh homemade bread" she adds with a smile.

"Awesome, I can't wait for lunch now" he admits with a grin and a little hug, happy to be able to see her every day.

"Hey Mongoose, have you seen my dad today?"

"Yeah, he just left here about a half an hour ago. Said he had some guys that were meeting in a room on the alpha level for some talking. He likes his stories and so do the older guys that have nothing better to do than to sit around, listen and kiblitz. They're a pretty big group now, I think twenty or so. You should be able to find them pretty easy, they aren't real quiet."

"Thanks, I'll head over there now."

On the way over, he notices empty halls and some loud laughter coming from one of the larger conference rooms in the alpha wing. After standing outside for a few minutes, just listening to his dad and the story he's telling, he just shakes his head and walks in on quite a few people sitting around the conference room table, talking and laughing.

"Hey Dad, what's going on" he asks with a grin. "Now you know you can't be telling anything that puts me in a bad light, right" he says innocently.

"Ha, Jacob, there are no stories about you that put you in a good light. You gave us a run for our money you did, when you were growing up" Joe declares with a straight face but a smile in his eyes. "Did you need something Jacob?" Joe asks when he realizes that his son looked him up for something, certainly not old stories.

"As a matter of fact, yes I do. I need someone to take charge of writing a short paper for the underground. There are a lot of people down here that I need to communicate with and I thought a paper would be a good way of doing that. I thought if you all worked toward that end, you could tell your stories and keep people informed at the same time. With all the news broadcasts going on, I felt it would be the easiest way to keep people informed on what's going on above ground and underground. Especially with the things that affect them, like the Presidents broadcast a hour ago."

"That sounds like a great idea Jacob. I'll get started on that right away. I'm sure my friends here will help and we'll get this going in a matter of days. It won't take long at all."

"Good" Jacob says. "I appreciate it, since the announcement today affects everyone that lives here and out west in that underground. I'll see about getting the news sent to them also. Maybe through either a radio, or an email. I'll have to look into both of those before I decide. It has to be something that doesn't put anyone in harm's way. No aboveground transport anymore. It's not safe for anyone living in the underground to go above ground. There's a price tag on every underground person's head now, and we can't take any chances with anyone getting caught."

"Let me know what you decide, Jacob. We'll start writing things down and get the information from the broadcast today."

"Thanks Dad, I'll see you later."

"Hey Mongoose, how's it going?"

"Good Lieutenant, real good."

"Where's Kat?" Jacob asks him suspiciously since Mongoose and Kat have become joined at the hip after she started to train as a sniper.

"Right behind you, Sir" he says with a smirk. Jacob slowly turns around and almost bumps into her, she's standing so close.

"Kitten, learning how to sneak up on people" he asks with a grin.

"Yep, I got ya, didn't I" she asks with a smile.

"You did" he says and grabs her in a hug.

"What's up Snake" she asks in concern, feeling the tension in him.

"Nothing really, just wondering what you're doing, that's all."

"Me, just practicing. Did you come for the sparring match?" she asks with a challenge in her tone.

"Sure, why not, I'm up for it. How about you? Head all better after your concussion?"

"I'm fine and raring to go."

"Then let's do it."

After nearly ten straight minutes of trying to get the upper hand on Snake, Kat's feels like a wet noodle. Fatigue is starting to set in and no victory is in sight yet.

"You tired Kitten? Snake asks with a tease, barely sweating.

"Not yet" she says breathlessly.

"I think it's time to end this" he says as he grabs her and sets her down gently on the mat, and holds her there till she stops wiggling. "Sorry Kitten. Remember what I said about size. Well, I'm a lot bigger than you and there's not much else but equal strength that can stop brute force. To win a match like this, you have to be sneaky and underhanded, in other words, cheat. There's no way you can win unless you try cheating, but it was fun" he admits with a smirk.

"Let me up Snake, no need to gloat."

"I'm not gloating, just enjoying the moment, since I don't get to hold you often enough for my liking."

"Snake, shhh" Kat says quickly with a blush. After glancing around and discovering that they're alone, she relaxes a little more, but becomes a little nervous with his intense stare.

"Here Kitten, grab my hand, I'll help you up."

"Thanks Snake" she says as he pulls her to her feet and then into his arms, for a long hug.

"What's gotten into you, you're awfully touchy today. Something happen?"

"Nope, everything's good right now. I just felt the need to hold you. Thanks Kitten, for being here for me to hold. You know how I feel about you, don't you?"

"Yeah, I do and I feel the same, but I just can't, not right now."

"I know and I'm not asking for anything, just time to spend with you, nothing else right now. I know you have some things to work through, but I can wait. I don't see any problem with spending alone time with you though. Just the two of us holding each other, nothing else; a little peace and quiet, maybe some music, maybe some talking like we used to do."

"Sure Snake, I'd like that. I actually miss our talks at Mike's. We can figure out something, somewhere here that we can spend some time together."

"Thanks, how about you meet me in my room say an hour after dinner?"

"I can do that" she agrees nervously.

"You know, you have nothing to fear from me" he says as he touches her on the face gently.

"I know, I'm just being the nervous nelly sort lately, but I'm working on that."

"Good, then I'll see you at dinner and then later."

"Yep, I promise."

"Hey Rand, have you seen Mallory today?" Jacob asks after having searched for the last half hour to no avail.

"Umm, yes Sir. She's just down that hall in the sitting room."

"Sitting room" he asks with an eyebrow raised in question.

"Well, it's like a sitting room, you know, with the couch and chairs and a coffee table and TV, you know."

"Oh, right, sitting room" Jacob says with a small smile as he moves towards that area. After knocking on the door and hearing a come in, he enters the "sitting room."

"Mallory, I've been looking for you for the past hour. Since when did you start spending daytime hours in a "sitting room?""

"Uh well, I was just cleaning, yeah, this room needed cleaning and I thought, well I'm not busy, so I can clean it." she admits innocently.

"Would the room cleanliness have anything to do with the fact that Rand happens to be just down the hall" he asks smoothly.

"Well, if you must know"

"No, stop, I don't need to know. Just be careful, you're an adult, you don't need my permission for anything personal. By the way, Rand's a great guy" he says as he turns and leaves the "sitting room."

"Rand, did you say something to tip off Jacob about us" she asks him as he enters the same door that Jacob just left through.

"Nope, I didn't say anything, but I guess he considered us guilty anyway. Of what, I'm not sure, but it must not have bothered him cause he didn't say anything negative to me. Did he say anything negative to you?"

"Nope, he said he didn't want to know, that I'm an adult, etc. so I guess it's okay with him. Oh, yeah, he said you're a great guy" she adds with sparkling eyes and a grin.

"Oh, he did, did he? Well, come here and let me show you what a great guy I am" he says seriously with a smoldering look of promise.

"Can I get everyone's attention please? I have a couple of things to say to everyone tonight" Jacobs says. "Tomorrow is C Day. Chip day. Tomorrow begins the day that everyone that accepts the chip becomes the property of the President of the United States. I don't expect that everything will be going smoothly tomorrow. There are a lot of people that really don't want to accept the chip, but are being forced to."

"I expect violence to erupt in the streets again with the military trying to maintain control. I believe a lot of people will be either hurt or killed tomorrow and that we'll be needed to help as many of the citizens as we can. We may have to start shipping them west, to our underground if they have the room. Room will be an issue, so we'll try to get everyone to just go back into their houses, lock the doors and windows and pretend no one's home."

"Granted, that won't last more than a couple of days, but that's better than none. In those couple of days, we may be able to come up with another way to protect the people. Any time we get will be well used to try to figure out a way to stop the violence that will be occurring. It's the best that we can do for the American public. I wish there were more; unfortunately our numbers aren't nearly big enough to stop what's going to happen."

"After the chips are completed, probably months from now, then we'll have to look into how we're going to survive since you'll need the chip to purchase things, like food. We need to think about what we can do here, in the underground, to add to our food rations. How can we feed ourselves without getting the chip implanted? If anyone can figure that out, I would appreciate the help."

"Let's make it an early night since all hell's

about to break loose tomorrow. We'll need to be at our best, since we are wanted so heavily by the President. Let's meet up in the practice room at zero five hundred tomorrow."

"What are we going to do Snake" Kat asks as she joins him in his room on the night before Hell breaks loose.

"Kitten, don't worry, we'll be able to do this. You just have to be extra careful, do not get captured. It would make me feel a lot better if you'd consider staying underground tomorrow, but I won't even ask because I already know what your answer would be, the same as mine actually, so I understand."

"Thanks" Kat says with a small smile and a tender heart.

"I just want you to know, Snake. I love you."

"I know you do, Kitten, and I feel the same about you."

"Thanks, that means everything to me, if only you knew" she says with a murmur.

"I think I do. Let's talk about something else now, enough with the maudlin thoughts" he says as he guides her to lie down next to him and cuddle. "We may not get the chance to do this again very soon. If tomorrow goes like I'm expecting it too, there will be no relaxation time for awhile. Just promise me that you'll be careful so that when the time comes, we can be here, just like this, again."

"I promise."

"Mongoose, where's Kat? She came out here with you hours ago I know, but this is the first chance

I've had to get over this way."

"Last time I saw her, she was guarding the rear of the exit for the underground. She's a hell of a sniper, man. I never thought she'd be as good as she is." Mongoose says prideful of her accomplishments.

"Yeah, she the best, but where is she" Jacob demands. "You're supposed to be her back up. Why aren't you watching her?"

"She's fine, Sir. I just came over here to check on things on this side. I've been with her all day. I'll show you where she is, just follow me. Look out Lieutenant, behind you" Mongoose yells, Jacob spins around, weapon ready, and fires off a round just before a Corporal takes his shot.

"Thanks Mongoose, now let's get to Kat. I'm not comfortable with her having no back up. We're going to talk about this when we get a chance. From now on, you do not leave her alone for any length of time, understand me?"

"Yes Sir, I'm sorry Sir. I wouldn't have left her if I thought for one second that she couldn't handle whatever came her way."

"I understand that, but I know that things happen to her. You just need to follow my orders."

"Kat, where are you" Mongoose yells when he finds the area empty that he left her in.

"Look out, Mongoose, down" yells Jacob as he fires his weapon at the armed guard. "Damn it, I knew there was something wrong" Jacob growls when he can't find Kat. "I told you never to leave her" he swears at Mongoose.

"She's here somewhere sir, she was just here a couple of minutes ago, I swear."

"There she is, sir" he says in relief when he spots Kat about two hundred yards away, faced in the opposite direction, staring intently at something on the ground in front of her.

Jacob throws his hand in the air and makes the quiet motion for Mongoose to shut up. "Something's on the ground in front of her. It's not like her to not turn at the sound of voices." Both men start the walk towards her, spreading out to cover her more easily. After the long two hundred yard travel, they finally reach her and see what she's staring so intently at. On the ground in front of her, is a skinned out body, just the body no skin.

"Snake, do you think this is one of the bodies that we never found that goes with the skin that we did find? It smells like it could be. Shit, that was six months ago or so" Kat adds in disgust.

"We can't stand here all day Kitten. There are too many Military searching for us. Come on, let's go" he says insistently as he grabs her arm and turns her toward the entranceway of the underground and comes up with a group of military on the hunt for none other than themselves.

"Shit, take cover" Jacob yells as he hits one of the Corporals. Kat takes aim and takes out two while Mongoose runs forward and takes out one with a kick. Soon all hell breaks loose. Jacob knows that they can't be taken in; it would absolutely be the death of them all. What a coup that would be for this little group of military. Soon the ground is littered with bodies, some dead, others unconscious. "Let's get the hell out of here" Jacob yells after they finish off the last. "We need to get underground right away.

We can't be caught" he says as they run towards safety.

Chapter Twelve

"We're going up" Jacob says to his group of family members and the group of Special Forces. "The longer we hide in the underground, the more damage is happening above. It's time. We can't hide any longer, not if we expect to change things. I believe it's time to go above ground and get into the groups up there that seem to be wreaking havoc with the underground. Once we've infiltrated, then we may be able to change the course of things."

"I'm not saying to go above as you are, but disguise yourselves. Since the Callander's all have similar looks it will be harder for us to change. I do know that we can't change the fact that my face is known and hunted. The same applies for anyone that looks like me. Unfortunately, we all look enough alike to be recognized. So we change our looks. Go older or younger, blonder or red, add glasses, anything that will make you harder to recognize."

"Kat, you're the only other one that's recognizable, so you too will have to alter your appearance."

"We've stockpiled quite a few disguises you ought to be able to find something appropriate. Meet back here in a few hours and we'll check them out and see if they're good enough."

"While you're at it, make sure that each of you has a GPS device hidden on your person. Non-detectible is best. Keep it small and simple. Something that no-one would bother to look at. I want to be sure that we can track each person that leaves this facility to infiltrate the above ground groups. Meet back here at one o'clock, then we'll head out."

"I'm ready, Snake. I promise to be careful, but you have to promise too."

"I promise, Kitten."

"Wow, you don't look at all like yourself, I barely recognized you, Snake. You shaved your beautiful hair and added a goatee; did you have to have a goatee? It definitely throws the focus off your face and onto your chin. And with the glasses, who could have known. You're wearing contacts too, aren't you?" she asks in surprise. "Your eyes are the most beautiful shade of blue usually, but now they just look like mud brown. I hate it" she says sadly.

"It's still me Kitten. I'm the same person, whether mud brown eyes or a goatee and a shaved head, same person. I'm not looking like the same person, though. So do I pass muster?"

"Absolutely! There's no way anyone will recognize you now."

"That's a good thing; this disguise is the only thing that will protect me while I'm above ground. It better be good."

"Mal, is that really you" Kat asks in surprise. "You look awesome as a blonde. I would have never thought that it would make you look so different. Wow is all I can say. Nice hair cut, too. You had a lot done in a short amount of time."

"Devon, you look weird. You look like a father figure. A little heavier, some lines and creases on your face, a lot of gray in your black hair. So much that it just looks like an older person's hair. Even your eyes look different. Contacts too, right?" Kat says as she circles around him.

"Eli, you look like a country boy, baseball hat and all, your hairs longer, and a different color. It's brown, light brown. It looks good on you like that. I like the length too, not real long but longer than a military cut is. Everyone looks so different. How are we all going to remember who's who?"

"Kat, you're beautiful. I love the red hair and the short, curly cut. You definitely don't look like you did. And your skin color, how'd you do that. You're so much darker than you were; you look like a mixed race. I would never have recognized you in that disguise." Mallory says admiringly.

"Yeah, I'd have to say out of all of us, you look the most different. You won't be easy to recognize, but I'd still stay away from your ex-partner. She'd recognize you instantly by your voice." Devon says warningly.

"Really?" Kat says in a lower, smoky voice.

"That's good" Devon admits "but voices are the hardest thing to change. You have to constantly be aware of where you are and what you're saying."

"I agree Kitten" Snake says "your voice will give you away, why take the chance. I'd rather you be safe than sorry."

"Alright, I promise to stay away from Des. She'll never hear from me. I'll go near to just check her out and make sure she's fine, but then I'll take off. She'll not see me or hear me."

"Alright then, it looks like we're all set. Make sure you have enough weapons concealed on your person. Mal and Kat, you're going to get a room together, right? You're job is to infiltrate the General of the Armies closest workers. It's up to you how you're going to do that, but you shouldn't have a big problem with it. Stay in touch, but do it subtly. I don't want anyone to get suspicious."

"Make sure you have plenty of cash before you leave. There are NO credit cards and no credit accounts. Everything that you need will have to be paid for with cash. If anyone asks why you're using so much cash, just remind them that you have to get rid of the cash pretty soon, so you've decided to spend it. That makes less you have to trade in to the bank. I'm sure that will make perfectly good sense to most people above ground."

"Remember, you'll need places to stay, you can't go back to your previous apartments, they're being constantly watched. You may want to beware of old friends too since they won't know you in your new disguises, they'll be like strangers to you."

"We've managed to obtain transportation for each group that's headed up. Take care of these vehicles; they're the only ones that you'll be getting. If you don't want to walk everywhere, then take care of them. Take lots of gas money, you never know. You should be able to store quite a few items in them until you can manage to get an apartment or whatever. I would like everyone to check in at least once a week to let us all know how it's going."

"If we don't hear from you within that seven day period, then we'll hunt you down. Also, in the event of an emergency, you can contact me, Rand or Mongoose. We'll be able to drop everything to get to you as fast as possible. I think that's it. Go out there and create as much chaos as possible without getting caught. We need intel too, so keep your eyes and ears open. Stay safe people."

"Okay Mallory, we're getting close. The General of the Armies has taken over the Capitol Police building and all of the offices. They're also on the top floor of the Hoover Building. We just need to find a place to stay, cheap, unload this car and start looking into ways to infiltrate their offices. I think we should stick with the Capitol Police building since that's where the General is when he isn't at the President's side, which rumor has it, isn't very often. I don't think they like each other much" Kat adds with a smirk.

"I know of a place, it's pretty small, but since we're only sleeping there, it should suffice. It's cheap, it has a bedroom and it's completely furnished, just what we're looking for. It's only about three blocks from the Capitol Police building so we can walk most of the time, weather permitting" Mallory promises.

"Excellent" Kat says enthusiastically.

"This isn't bad" Kat says as she wanders around the small apartment. "It has everything you need for an apartment. I think we can handle this since it's for work, it's not like we'll be entertaining anyone. I'm hoping this is for the short term, not the long haul."

"Let's head over to the General's offices. We can see how things work over there, what kind of jobs they have and if they might have any openings."

"I'm going to look and see if they need

translators" Mallory says. "I'm fluent in three languages, one of them being Farsi, so I'm hoping that they need someone like me" she adds with a smile.

"I think we need to let them know that we're friends from a different state. Let's see, how about Montana? That way, the chip hasn't been given to us yet, but we're on the list in our hometown and are scheduled to receive it in about six weeks. That hopefully takes care of that problem, the last thing that we need is to be forced to take the chip."

"I wonder if they can set us up with legit backgrounds for these characters. I won't work if someone does an in-depth background and finds nothing for either of us in Montana. Maybe we should contact Snake and see what he wants us to do."

"Yeah, I think that's probably what we need to do."

"You contact him" Mallory says with a grin.

"Alright, I'd be happy to" Kat agrees with a grin.

"Snake, come in" she says into her radio.

"Go" he says without identifying himself. "We need backgrounds set up for both of us from somewhere in Montana. We're planning on hitting the General's office as soon as we have something set up. Today we're just looking around, doing a recon. As soon as the backgrounds are ready, we can try to get on his staff."

"Twenty four hours, out."

"Boy, that was brief and to the point, he must have concerns of someone else being able to intercept our radio contact. Maybe we should get real serious here. I feel like I'm having fun at his expense."

"Naw, he's just real serious sometimes and right now they're pretty dangerous times so he's real serious."

"We don't want to draw undue attention to ourselves by being something that draws eyes. We stay happy, sad and neutral, whatever it takes we do. That's the only way we can help. Our goal, get this done so we can rejoin our guys."

"Rand, Mallory? You've fallen hard, haven't you?"

"Yeah, I never thought I'd see the day that all my thoughts would be on a guy, but I can't seem to help it. Yep, I got it bad" she admits with a shrug and a smile.

"I don't know how he does it, but it never fails to amaze me. Every time I think about Snake, he leaves a message. Something personal, so I know it's him. This time it's a message about our backgrounds. Here's yours and here's mine. They got me down as a computer expert. That's gonna be difficult, darn it, I hate working on computers" Kat says in dismay.

"Wait" Mallory adds with a smirk. "This is your background, that one's mine. I'm a computer expert with translator experience, so he kept it close to reality for me. I suppose that makes it easier to blend. What's he having you do?"

"He's given me a military background, so it looks like I'll be the General's intelligence expert with a weapons specialty backup. That shouldn't be a problem, at least I hope not, since it's pretty much what I am anyway. I say we get a good night's sleep and then head into the General's headquarters bright and early tomorrow."

"Good Morning, My name's Cathy Brightman and I'm reporting for the General's staff. I've been assigned here as the intelligence expert."

"It's the room to the back, Miss. Just knock, he's expecting you."

"Thank you."

"Hi, I'm Tessa Ronales and I've been asked to come in today to speak with the General. He's been looking for a computer expert with translator ability. I have a zero eight hundred appointment with him."

"If you'll have a seat, I'll let him know that you're here, Miss."

"Thank you." Mallory scans the waiting area looking for anyone that might know her as she

takes a seat to wait for her appointment.

"Come in" the General yells at the knock on his door. Cathy smiles as she opens the door expecting him to be looking in her direction, but he's on the phone in a somewhat heated discussion. He turns to see who's coming in and motions her with one finger to wait a minute.

"Hi, my names Cathy Brightman and I was assigned to your office as the intelligence officer" she informs the General when he finishes his call.

"Welcome, it's been a little hectic today since the phones don't like to stop ringing for any length of time. If you could help out with that, it would be appreciated" he says distractedly as the phone starts to ring again.

"General Bossley's office, how can I help you?"

"Please hold."

"There's a man on the phone that wants to register a complaint against the military. What would you like me to tell him, Sir?"

"Just grab a tablet and take down the information. There must be something going on out there today since that's not the first complaint call I've had."

"Yes Sir."

"Could you give me your name, address and phone number sir" she says as she gets back on the line with the caller. "I'll be happy to take down the information and make sure that this get's into the right hands."

"Phew, that was quite a complaint" Cathy murmurs to the General.

"Yeah, they all seem to be. Do we have a full moon tonight or something? I haven't had this many phone calls since the chip was first brought up and the public informed. Not even when the President instituted martial law."

"It sounds like most of the complaints are similar if not the same. Has anything changed in the past twenty four hours to cause this problem, Sir?"

"The groups of military have changed. We rotate troops monthly in order to maintain the security level that I prefer. If we leave groups on too long, problems start occurring. I suppose it's some form of burn out. So we've been changing the guard, so to speak, on a monthly basis. The new group started yesterday. The phones were fine yesterday, but when I got in this morning, this is what I faced."

"It's possible that it's temporary, Sir, until the public get used to this group."

"I don't want the public to get used to this group. That's where problems first start. Everyone gets used to the same ones and then they stop listening to them. When we replace them, it reminds everyone that these people are doing a job, that they're not out there to be friends."

"Yes Sir."

"I'm sorry, I didn't get your name when you first got here, my mind was a little busy."

"That's alright, Sir. My name's Cathy Brightman. I was assigned here to be your intelligence expert."

"Thank goodness they finally sent someone. I've been calling for weeks to get that position filled."

"Here I am Sir, happy to be here and take charge of the position."

"Hopefully the phones will give me a break soon and we can get down to the real reason you're here. I'd like to spend an hour with you to catch you up on the problems we seem to be facing. By this afternoon they'll quiet down enough so that we can talk. In the mean time, please continue answering the phones and taking the information given, we can get down to what to do about them when we have a chance to think."

"I understand President Martin. Yes, as soon as I can get to that, it will be done. Thank you, yes Madam" the General says as he hangs up slowly.

"Alright Cathy, let's talk. I'm having some issues with our troops. We no sooner get a new group out there and we have the same problems that the prior group was having."

"I hate to think this way about our troops, but

there has to be an information leak somewhere. It's now your job to figure out what in the hell is going on. I don't have the time to take care of all the problems that the public are having. I can't believe that in every one of our groups, we have people committing the same crimes. This has been going on for way too long now, so it's now become an issue for our intelligence officer. That's you. I had to jump through hoops to get you assigned to this office. You now answer to me and only to me about anything that's happening with our military."

"This office must get control of the situation. There are a lot more things that will be starting in the near future by the Presidents directive and with the chaos that occurring in the streets, it will be a much more difficult thing to do. Do you think you're up to this job? Think carefully before you answer. It's imperative that you really believe what you say. It won't be easy, but it can be done."

"Yes Sir. I have no doubt that I'm more than capable of handling these problems. I will, however, need a staff to help out with this, since I'm only one person and can't be everywhere at once. Probably a staff of four or five would be sufficient."

"Done. I expect quick results, so please keep me informed of what's happening. I'll have your staff together by day's end."

"Thank you Sir."

"I'm Cathy Brightman, the intelligence officer for General Bossley's office. We're going to be working very closely and with some speed. There are a lot of things that need to be done, problems that need to be solved, but investigated first. Welcome to the team, Jason Mannering, Roth Montgomery, Susan Lehigh and Pat Reynolds. I've looked over your information and credentials and I must say it's all pretty impressive. I think we're going to work well together and solve some of the larger issues that the General's been handling. Since you're all experienced in the area of questioning, I'm going to set you free to visit the people on this list. Today I answered the phones for the past six hours. In that time, I took fifty-seven complaints regarding our military troops that seem to be wreaking havoc with the general public. Do I believe all of these people? No, but I'm sure as with anything else there is some truth in the matter. Your job is to sort the truth from the lies. I'm looking for a possible core group that may be spreading rumors just to create chaos with the public. I want to know where the complaints are really originating from."

"I want each of you to take a page from this tablet and follow up with the people and the complaints on each one. Once you're finished, you can head home for the day and meet me back here tomorrow at zero seven hundred. Hopefully, you'll have plenty to report. And just so you know that I'm not sitting here waiting and twiddling my thumbs, I'll be taking a page also and visiting those people before I finish for the day.

"Good luck and if you experience any problems, please contact me on my cell phone."

Chapter Thirteen

"Rand, you could have let me know what job you were going to be doing. When I saw you seated in my office with the name Roth Montgomery, you could have floored me. I had a hard time not giving myself away and treating you as a stranger. Next time you decide to surprise me, please do it when it's not in a public place or anywhere near the General. That's all I need, him questioning my every move with suspicion."

"Sorry Kat, I mean Cathy, I didn't mean to shock you. You can blame Snake. He didn't give me my packet until barely an hour before I was to meet in your office. It wasn't enough time to give you fair warning. He probably didn't want to tell you in advance. I'll take it up with him at the next available time for the two of us to meet."

"What did you get from your interviews?"

"Oh, you won't believe it. It's just like you thought. The Military are being set up by a group. Every time a new group is deployed, someone starts to go to the neighborhoods and complain about bad treatment from them. They tell the same stories, mostly because they already have them on paper. It's a lot easier to just change names than to think up something even worse that the troops are doing to the people."

"Someone wants the troops to look bad and so far they're doing a good job. They start the rumors, the

General is called by one of the good neighbors and complained to and then they move on to the next neighborhood. By sending someone different each time, the people aren't seeing the same complainers, but different ones. If they change the issues just by even a word, then they change the problem and a whole new one takes over. Not all of the complaints are trumped up, but the majority of them are. The problem is, there are real issues and the ones that do commit the crimes can't be allowed to get away with it. It's going to come down to he said she said."

"Yeah, that's what I was afraid of, that's where I'll take over the investigations."

"What a day" Kat says to Mallory as she closes the door to their shared apartment. The room's small, a tiny window that barely let's in the light let alone the air, not that the air is refreshing since it's in the high 80's with 100% humidity.

"We should have gotten an apartment at least with air. I'm going to suffocate in this place" Mallory complains.

"Yeah I know, but at least it's safe and not bugged. Who'd have thought to bug this place? I checked it anyway, when I got home, I just don't trust anyone" Mallory replies during a yawn.

"Yeah, me either."

"So, what happened to you today" Kat asks as she re-enters the living room with shorts and an old T-Shirt on. "I'm having a drink, want one" she asks as she wanders into the kitchenette part of the living room.

"Please" Mallory replies, not moving from her

comfortable position.

"I started working on the computers today. It looks like I'll be able to access the information on the chip. It could prove invaluable, at least I hope. As soon as I break the code, and find someone else's password, a computer that's untraceable, I should be good to go. I figured I'd put the order in when we check in tonight."

"Awesome."

"I was put in charge of finding the Callander's, all their family and friends, anyone that had anything to do directly with them. The General's on the war path" Kat reflects with a smirk.

"He has grandiose plans and fortunately for him, he has me" she adds with a laugh. "I bet he's going to be real happy, real soon. I've been ordered to go out and find anyone, maybe even the ex-detective of Metro D.C. Police that hangs around with Jacob. His words not mine."

"Oh, that's priceless" Mallory says with a laugh. "If only he knew, wouldn't his life be grand."

"Actually, it wouldn't be worth a cent, it isn't worth much right now."

"Rand showed up today" Kat says quietly, watching Mallory for her reaction.

"What!" Mal says as she sits up quickly on the couch.

"Rand showed up today" Kat repeats somberly.

"Why, what happened, is he okay" she asks quickly.

"Of course he is. He showed up as part of my new team, a Mr. Roth Montgomery. He's going to be investigating and looking for anyone in connection to

Jacob Callander. Snake sure knows how to plant people" she admits with a grin.

"Where's he living? Mallory asks quickly.

"I can't tell you, at least not yet. We can't jeopardize the positions that we're in. But" she holds her hand up in the stop position as she see's Mallory open her mouth to argue. "But, it's only for a couple of days. After that, then it should be okay, I promise."

"Fine" Mal agrees with a big sigh. "I guess the mission must come first, since it affects so many people. You can bet that I'll be working overtime to get to the chip information. There's got to be some way to wreak havoc in the actual chip program without anyone noticing right away."

"We better eat soon, so that we can join Snake and whoever else shows up, in the video conference. That way when we're done, we can get to bed. Tomorrow looks to be a long day and I don't want to screw up by falling asleep."

"Good morning Cathy" Roth calls out when she walks in and heads to the General's office. "Same to you Mr. Montgomery, I see you're punctual, a good sign."

"Always, Cathy" he adds with a smile.

"I have to talk with General Bossley, but I'll be back momentarily."

After knocking and being told to enter, Cathy enters slowly and quietly, observing and gathering emotions that seem to be flying around the office.

"Yes, Madame, I agree" he says and motions with his hand for Cathy to take a seat.

"Fine, I'll handle it, I promise" he says, rolling

his eyes. "Yes, Goodbye, Madame President."

"Alright, that was the President, as you no doubt figured out by yourself. There are just some days that I'd rather not start the day talking to her. Anyway, how was your first day? Please tell me you've got some good information to share."

"Absolutely, I did get somewhere, just not as far as I would have liked. The Callander family is rather large and I've been given some names that are connected. Those are the people that I'm putting on the list today for my group to start looking for. I'm hoping that by day's end we'll have a definitive place to find one or more of them, and I'll have set up times to go there. I'll have to detain them, but I wanted to make sure that it was fine with you before I actually started."

"You have my permission to do anything you think is best for the cause. If I don't give the President something soon, she's going to start taking matters into her own hands and if that happens, who knows what's next. I'd rather get the job done this way then have her send who knows who out there and muddle through things. Her ways aren't necessarily the right way, if you know what I mean. She's just not used to letting someone else do the work, take charge. She thinks she needs to be doing everything."

"I understand Sir. I've worked with people like that too" she says in commiseration.

"I knew you'd understand" he says in gratitude. "So what did you find?"

"First thing; Jacob Callander is an ex-special ops leader. He ran the states side unit with a steel glove. His people, considering how strong his leadership is, are very protective of him. But I can break them" she admits with pride. "There's no one that I can't break. I've found multiple groups of his that live above ground. Unfortunately, Jacob and his siblings and parents are no longer above ground. They've all taken shelter below. But that won't be a problem. He's loyal, tough, but loyal. If he finds out that some of his groups have been found, detained and are being interrogated, he'll show up. I'm sure he'll even show up in person. He's arrogant enough to believe he can do that and get away with it."

"Excellent, Cathy, you've really gained ground. You got a lot farther than I expected. Good work."

"Thank you Sir. Now I need to go and get this started. Time's wasting."

"Not just yet, please. I have some thing's I need to discuss with you. The President is furious. She wants Callander and she wants him now. We talked for quite a while about this, this morning, and have come up with something that just may work. I know you just started yesterday, but do you think you have anyone that can take over for you for a few days? I have something bigger that I want you to handle personally."

"I believe I can hand off what I was going to work on today, to one of my new team members. His name's Roth Montgomery. He seems to be quite capable, at least from talking with him yesterday, that was the impression I got."

"Good then we'll work on Callander together today. I thought for sure that when I arrested that weasel Mike, that it would draw him out. Obviously, he's not that loyal. He saved his own skin that time by staying away and quiet" the General admits chagrined. "Now the President thinks I'm incompetent, but I'm going to show her that I'm better than she'll ever be."

"Yes Sir" Cathy agrees with a smile on the outside and anger so hard that she's afraid he'll see it before she has a chance to exact revenge.

"I want you to try and find Callander, use whatever it takes to set up a trap for him and draw him out. Bring in anyone that even remotely worked with or knew Jacob Callander. We'll put them on trial in front of the American public. We'll execute them the same way we did Mike."

"But just because they know him doesn't make them guilty of anything" Cathy declares emphatically.

"Sure they are, they're collateral damage. We can't have anyone out there that sided with Callander. They were aiding and abetting. The American people would love to execute them, just on principle. The end justifies the means you know" he reminds her confidently.

"As a matter of fact, he was pretty close to an ex-detective from Metro D.C. police by the name of Kathleen Thomas. If we could get our hands on her, we'd have him, hands down" he adds with a grin of anticipation.

"Maybe you could start with her partner, whom I believe is still in the area. If we bring her in and question her, I'm sure if she knows anything, anything at all, we can get it from her, by fair means or foul. You know what they say, all's fair. Well this is war and in war you do what you must."

"I promise to have to you by week's end, Jacob

Callander. If you'll give me that much time, I know I can find him. Look at how the President would treat you then. You could be the hero for a change, in her eyes. I'm sure she'll reward you hugely for that information and for the chance to put Jacob Callander on TV in front of the American People."

"Done" he agrees in gratitude, visualizing how the President would react to his news of the capture of Jacob Callander and the end of the underground.

"Roth, I need to talk with you, my office now" Cathy informs him brusquely.

"Yes Sir."

"I had plans on locating some of the people in Jacob Callander's cells today. Unfortunately, some thing's have come up and I need to hand this off to someone I can trust. You're it. I hope that I'm not making a mistake."

"Just start visiting the addresses that I have listed here and see if you can find anyone, if so bring them in for questioning. I now have a deadline. I promised the General that by the end of this week, I'll have located and found Jacob Callander and that he will be brought in for the President and the General to question. He'll then go before the American public on trial for treason, crimes against the American government. Do you feel capable of handling this duty?"

"Yes Sir. It will be my privilege to assist you in this matter."

"Thank you Roth, I appreciate it! That takes a load off. If you need me I've listed my cell phone on this sheet, just give it a call. I can meet you anywhere you need me to."

"Thank you Sir."

"Mallory, are you ready?" Kat asks after they both arrive at Mike's coffee shop. Empty and dusty from non-use, Kat wanders around the small building noticing how empty it feels, and has difficulty just being in the building. My best friend, she thinks in tears. I should have saved you, Mike. I'm so sorry, I miss you so much. If only we could go back, I'd do anything to help you, to save you she thinks.

"You okay Kat?" Mallory asks as she gently touches Kat on the shoulder.

"Yeah, I'm okay" she admits sadly. "I didn't realize how difficult this was going to be. Maybe I should have gone to a different location. I can still see Mike's laughing face behind the counter; his joking as he mixed up the coffee's that he was so well known for. Mal, I'm never going to see his face or hear his voice again. He was my best friend, like a brother to me, the brother I never had. We've been close since I moved here at fifteen, to start college. I guess he kinda took me under his wing. My parents had just died and I must have looked like I needed someone. He took that place so easily. Damn it, the man wouldn't hurt a flea. What they did to him" she says in anguish.

"Shhh Kat, you can't think like that, not today. Today we're going to get a little even for Mike. I know it won't bring him back but maybe justice can be served. Maybe it will help you to move on, give you some closure" she promises softly.

"You're right, this is for you Mike. I couldn't stop what they did to you, but I can do this.

"I'm gonna call him now, Mal. Let's set this in motion.

"General, its Cathy, I've been snooping around to find some leads on where Callander might be. I've looked all over this city and then remembered what you said about Callander's buddy Mike. So knowing how close they were and how loyal Callander is, I thought why not check out the coffee shop that Mike owned. I didn't find Callander himself, but I did find some things that you might find interesting. I'm at the coffee shop right now, if you want to see them for yourself."

"Cathy, this better be good, I'm too busy to be chasing ghosts" he chastises.

"I promise you that you won't be disappointed, however, there's a leak in your office somewhere, so I don't feel this is something I want to discuss on the phone or in front of anyone else until we find the leak."

"Fine, but if this doesn't pan out you may be the next collateral damage of this war. I'll be there in a half an hour" he says and hangs up with a bang.

"What a fucking bastard. He's so full of himself, Mal. I'm proud to be serving our country this way" Kat admits with feeling.

"You ready Mal. The General's due here momentarily. Sit in this chair over here and I'll tie you up lightly. You can get out of it anytime you want, it won't be a secure tie."

"I'm ready" she says as she sits quietly and lets Kat tie her hands to the chair.

Kat stands back looking around to make sure that there's nothing left out. It all looks believable. "I think I hear a car."

"He's here" she says quietly after looking out through the curtains. "General Bossley, glad you could make it" she says derisively after he enters. He glances at her sharply and only see's an innocent face, so believes he heard wrong. Then his gaze swings quickly back to Mallory and he frowns.

"Do I know you" he asks suspiciously. "You look familiar."

"Right, you probably think you know everyone" she says in sarcasm. "Well let me tell you, you'll never get Callander. He's the one prize that you'll never lay your hands on." She promises.

"General Bossley, let me introduce you to Michelle Treyhurn, she's Mikes cousin. I thought you'd like to talk with her yourself to hear what she has to say about Callander."

"I would, I would indeed" he assures her as he rubs his hands together in anticipation while staring at Michelle. "So my dear, you know Jacob Callander, do you" he asks quietly as he walks towards her. "What can you tell me about him?" he demands.

"I'm not going to tell you anything, nothing, especially after what you did to my cousin. Bastard" she spits at him.

"Oh, I think you will" he promises in a deadly voice as he raises his hand to make his first slap.

Kat moves into position just behind him and before he can get in the first slap, she hits him on the shoulder, demanding his attention.

"What" he yells as he spins around "I was just getting ready.....uhh, what the hell" he says when he feels a burning pain in his stomach, enough of a pain to take his breath away. "What the hell…" he says again as he sways on his feet.

After informing him "this is for Mike, you bastard" Kat places both hands on the knife handle that's sticking out of the Generals stomach and pulls up and over quickly. He drops to the ground when she releases him, but she leaves the knife in place while he lays there groaning.

"General, I'd like to inform you that you just messed with the wrong bitch. Remember that friend of Jacob Callander's, the one from Metro Police? Well, that would be me and my face is one of the last face's you'll ever see. Don't close your eyes" she warns him and moves the knife a little to wake him back up, hearing him scream in pain.

"You killed my best friend; he was like my brother, like my father, the one person that meant the most to me aside from Snake. He was my confidant, he took care of me, we were family. My name's Kathleen Ann Thomas. I'm also known as Kat and the woman you were planning on hitting, her names really Mallory Callander, she's the sister to Jacob Callander. Oh yeah, one more surprise" she says as Jacob walks in from the back room, disguise in place "meet Jacob Callander. I thought it only fair that you had the opportunity to meet the one and only."

"Pleased to meet you, General" Jacob says with a sneer.

"Guess you didn't need my help, Kat" he adds teasingly with a grin. "Looks like you got this under control."

"Yeah, I didn't remove the knife yet cause I didn't want him to bleed out too quick. He had some people to meet first" she admits with a smirk. "Besides, I want him to suffer a little, especially after what he did to my best friend, Mike. A quick death's too easy for the likes of him" she says as she kicks the knife again, just to hear him scream.

"I agree" he says compassionately. "Mal, you okay?" Jacob asks.

"I'm fine" she admits, watching the drama unfold. "Kat didn't even tie me up completely. That stupid idiot, he was just getting ready to hit me when Kat stepped in and tapped him on the shoulder to get his attention. After that it was fast, so fast I didn't realize what she'd done until she moved sideways so that I could see. I have to say, don't mess with Kat, she's a dangerous woman."

"Don't I know it" Jacob agrees with a smile. "It's time for me to go before someone tries to collect that million promised by the President. Take care of yourself Kitten. I'd be really pissed if anything ever happened to you, so make sure you take care of yourself. Remember what I told you months ago, what your helmet reminds you of" he adds and leaves.

"Kat, you okay?" Mallory asks after they get ready to leave the scene, checking for anything that could lead the police or the Military to their doorsteps. "You were sure cold acting when you took out the General. I'm worried about you, you're not the cold hearted person that you're pretending to be."

"I'm fine Mal, really. I had to do what I did, I promised Mike's soul that I'd give him justice and that's just what I did. Since I can't kill the whole United States, I can take out its commanding officers. That gives me some justice at least. I just hope it's enough."

"Let's do dinner, remember that little Italian place we all used to go to, let's go there" Kat says wistfully as they leave Mikes for the last time.

"Morning Mal, I have to run. Everything needs to look normal today, since the General isn't coming in, ever again, but no one else knows that yet. We have a couple of day's reprieve I think; unless someone happens upon his body, then all hells gonna break loose. I'll see you there, later."

"Yeah, I'll see you Kat. I've got a long day ahead of me. I'm going to figure out the code to hack into the chip program. I think it's time for a little confusion in that area" Mallory adds with a smile of anticipation.

"Hey, have fun Mal" Kat grins and waves.

"Roth, my office" Cathy says as she strides into her office with suppressed anger. "That bitch. The stupid bitch! President Martin, you will pay for your part in everything that's happened in this country. One way or another you will pay." Cathy promises in a mutter.

"What's up, Sir" Roth asks as he quietly takes a seat, aware of the anger emanating off of Cathy.

"I am so pissed" she says quietly to Roth after she regains more control of her emotions. "I was just informed by the President of my new job. She wants me to find out where the General is, as if I'm responsible for him every minute of every day. I don't know or care where he is. He's not my responsibility. How dare she order me to babysit him."

"But" he starts to say when Cathy warns him

with a hand up and a negative shake of her head, then a sign meaning bugged office.

"I want you to start making calls and see if you can find him. I have a whole lot more on my schedule than hunting down the General."

"Yes Sir, I'd be happy to" Roth replies quietly.

"Thank you Roth. I've only been here a couple of days, but you've already become indispensible to me. I appreciate your willingness to do whatever it takes to get the job done" she adds with a grin and a roll of her eyes.

"Your welcome Sir" he replies with a similar grin, two cohorts doing what they want when they want.

"Call me if you get any information. I'll be sure to let the President know as soon as I hear anything."

"Yes Sir" he replies as he leaves the office.

"I demand to know where he is" President Martin yells into the receiver "I don't care who you have to put on this, put everyone in that office on it, I want him found" she yells before slamming the phone down.

"Wow" Cathy says to herself as she hangs up the phone slowly. "She's quite angry." With a smile she turns back to Roth and just shrugs. "I can't help it, I love pissing her off" she admits quietly with a laugh. "It gives me something to look forward to everyday that I'm here" she says to him. "Did you need something else Roth?"

Roth just shakes his head slowly back and forth while enjoying the same feelings as Cathy. "I'm sorry Sir that she's got such a bad temper and continues to take it out on you. That's just not right,

Sir." Roth says seriously but smiling huge because no one can see him.

"You would think that after three days of the general missing, she'd use a little common sense and figure out that he might be dead. But no, she thinks he's off playing games on her for some reason. I wonder what their relationship was really like. I don't think the General liked her much, but a job's a job. Anyway, it's a moot point, since he doesn't seem to be coming back anytime soon. He could have at least called."

"Call the troops and let's start a search for him. Go building to building. Start at his house and then hit the west end and do say a hundred blocks in all directions. It may take a week, but at least we're looking. Let me know how that turns out or when you hear anything, whatever comes first."

The phone ringing jars Kat out of the fugue she's been in for the last couple of minutes. Remembering Mike, remembering the first time she met Snake. How he looked and acted. That carefree time of her life compared with now. "This is Cathy, what can I do for you" she asks after she grabs the phone up impatiently.

"Cathy, its Roth. We've found the General. His body was discovered about five minutes ago by my team. It looks like he's been dead a couple of days, smells like it too. I called for the Coroner; he's on his way now. I'll be back in the office within the hour to fill out the reports and give you cause and time of death."

"Thanks Roth, for the notification. I think I'll wait on the official reason and time before I notify the

President. She's going to want those answers too, so I might as well wait. I'll be watching for you to get back here" she says before hanging up, smiling in anticipation, now it's begun.

I can't wait to see how the President's going to handle this. Too bad I can't get face to face with her since she'd probably recognize me, even with this disguise. I spent too much time with her when all those House of Representatives were killed, one by one, well before she became President. Things have sure changed in the past six months. Who would have thought, she thinks with a small shake of her head.

"Cathy, can I come in?" questions Roth after the knock on her door.

"Please" she replies. "What's the word, Roth?"

"The Coroner identified General Richard Bossley as the deceased, death approximately three days ago. Cause of death, a stab wound to the abdomen that was moved in the Japanese style of Hari Kari, which is normally a suicide, but in Bossley's case, it was murder. There was no sign of a weapon, nor any fingerprints. It looks like whoever did this was a pro, since there was no sign of anyone else having been there in a long while."

"That's the official, so now I contact the President."

"This is Cathy Brightman, I need to speak with the President."

"President Martin, I've just received word that General Richard Bossley has been located. His body was found at Mike Vickors old place, Capitol Coffee Shop, lying on the floor. It looked like he lived for a short time after he was stabbed, but whoever stabbed him took the knife. There was no sign of anyone else in that place, just a lot of dust lying around, but no footprints, no finger prints, nothing, just the body of General Bossley. I'm sorry President Martin, your General is gone."

"Son of a bitch" she yells "who the hell could have pulled that one off? It had to be Callander. He's the only one capable of committing this kind of atrocity and leaving no trail. I know he's the one that did this; he did this just to get to me, that son of a bitch. Wait till I get my hands on him" she says and after a short pause "I will get my hands on him, soon" she swears before she slams the phone down.

"Well, that went well" Cathy says to Roth, then shares a huge smile with him "justice has begun" she predicts.

"This is Cathy" she says automatically as she answers the phone. "President Martin here, I'm just calling to notify you that I've chosen a replacement for Bossley. I'm holding a news briefing at eighteen hundred hours today to notify the public of what happened to Bossley, who did it and who the replacement for him will be. I can't leave my military out there enforcing justice without a leader."

"Well, that was fast" she says to Roth as she looks at her watch. "It looks to me like she had a replacement already waiting for the news. She's already contacted the media and is set to hold a news briefing at eighteen hundred today. That's only four and a half hours from now. In less than five hours she finds out about Bossley, throws a huge tantrum, schedules a news briefing and picks the new General. No one is that good or that fast" Cathy says to Roth in shock. "Of course, she didn't bother to notify me of who the new General will be. I guess I'll find out just like everyone else does, tonight at eighteen hundred."

Chapter Fourteen

"This is Jim Cochran of WELT News Channel 3, Washington D.C. We're waiting for the President. She's scheduled to appear here at six p.m. with a special news bulletin. We have no idea really, what this briefing's all about. It's been kept very quiet, no one seems to know what this could possibly be about. Here she is now:

"Thank you American Citizens. I requested this news briefing to impart some tragic but very important information to you. General Richard Bossley, the General of the Armies has been found murdered." Gasps can be heard all over the briefing room from reporters and Congressmen, Senators and White House staff.

"I realize that this comes as quite a shock to you, a much unexpected occurrence. He disappeared three days ago and regardless of how many people I put out there to find him, he wasn't located until earlier today, and he was dead. The Coroner says that he died about three days ago but his body wasn't found until earlier today."

"This is obviously Jacob Callander's fault. He's the one that murdered General Bossley. General Bossley was apparently getting too close to finding Jacob Callander and therefore had to. I have no doubt as to who murdered him. Jacob Callander is the only one with the resources to enable him to commit this atrocity."

"I will miss General Bossley. He was a good man and ran a good organization with strong convictions, he'll be missed. I must take into consideration the safety of our American public and it is to that end that I am naming a new General tonight. As President, I can't let the American citizens down by not doing my job. My job is the protection of this country and all of its citizens. I can't leave the military operational without a leader."

"I want to introduce to you, your new General of the Armies, Admiral Teri Auliya; the previous Admiral of the Middle East Naval Fleet. He comes to this position with thirty years of experience, was tried and tested during Desert Storm where he earned the Silver Star for saving the life of four other team members. Here he is now. You may ask him a couple of questions if you must, but please keep it brief, very brief, since he has much to do." General Teri Auliya walks onto the stage area, tall, dark, thin and regal in bearing.

"Thank you" General Auliya says as he moves into position at the podium. "I want to thank President Martin for the honor that she has bestowed on me by choosing me as the new General of the Armies. I am honored by this decision. I promise to hold this position with the utmost respect for the Military, the citizens of this great country and the President of the United States. I will never do anything to cause the President to regret her decision of naming me the General of the Armies."

"I have a few questions, Sir. I'm Jim Cochran of WELT News Channel 3, Washington D.C. Can you tell us where you were born, what did your childhood consist of, when did you join the Navy and what makes you capable of doing this job?"

"I was born in the United States, as were my parents. I was raised on a tobacco plantation in Georgia, went to school also in Georgia and continued on with my career in the Navy. I have many silver stars but they don't mean as much to me as the people they represent, the soldiers that I helped off of battlefields. Those are the things that mean something to me" he admits quietly, in his deep smooth voice.

"I am prepared to do what must be done to help the President with the smooth running of this country. You will never need to fear the military, not while I am in charge. The military are your friends and I want every American citizen to always remember that."

"Do not run and hide from them, they're only trying to help, they will not hurt you. If one Military person harms one citizen, they will be punished by me personally. I will not tolerate the abuse of the citizens of these United States. I want this country to be back to the way it was when I was growing up. The biggest fear being is it going to rain today. Thank You" he says and turns to walk over to the President who takes his arm and walks off the stage area with him arm in arm.

Once out of site of and headed to her private rooms, Teri whispers "Hello Jane dear, how is your father Da'wah and your mother Tariq? I hope they are doing well" he inquires with a smile. "They're great Teriq, I will tell them that you asked after them. It will please them to know that you have not forgotten."

"I do want to apologize to you though, on how long it took me to get you into this position. No matter how hard I made it on Richard, he refused to resign. He actually thought I needed him, can you believe it? I will need to thank Jacob Callander before I cut his head off, for taking care of the General for me. It's appreciated" she admits with a soft laugh.

"Tell me Jane, why didn't you put me into this position in the first place? Why did I need to wait so long and be second choice?"

"Teriq, you were never second choice, with me you are always first. But I had to show the American citizens that they could trust me, and I did that by hiring people that they would be comfortable with. I am replacing them as I can, you were always meant for this position, you know that. Now that we have the trust of the citizens, you can take over and do what you must."

"You see, everything is falling into place the way it was planned" Jane murmurs.

"Well, that was definitely a shock. I don't believe anyone in my office even knew that the General was missing, Jim Cochran says. "They have certainly been able to keep their own council lately. It's a sad thing that we heard about the deceased General Richard Bossley. He seemed like a nice enough guy; no one seemed to have any problems with him, so it's a shock to find out that he was missing and then murdered and by Jacob Callander no less. That was quite a feat. We are living in difficult times; let's hope that only good comes from what happened. This is Jim Cochran of WELT News Channel 3,

Washington D.C., Goodnight."

"Kat, I'm headed into work early today" Mallory informs her. "Today's the day."

"The day for what" Kat asks.

"Today's the day that I make a change for the better on the computer side of this chip issue. I'm headed for Fahr Industries data base and the program for their chip. I want to know more about this chip and how it works. I think I can make a difference for the world if I can get into the program. Who knows what it says and does but all that can be changed once I see what they've done and study it. Then once I'm sure of the program and how to change it subtly, I will."

"How long do you think it'll take to get into it?"

"Depends on how many security layers there are as to how long it'll take. I can't just jump into it, I have to go slow. I sure don't want to tip off any of their programmers. That would be certain death, since what I'm about to do is illegal and I can't afford to be caught doing it."

"Hey, good luck Mallory. Stay safe, work quick and I'll see you tonight. I get to meet the new General and see how well we'll get along."

"Good luck to you today, too!"

"General Auliya, my name is Cathy Brightman. I'm the Intelligence Officer for your office. I worked previously with General Bossley. It's an honor to meet you Sir."

"It's good to meet you Ms. Brightman. We have much to do. This office has been without a head for too long. I'll look things over here, investigate a few things and then plan a meeting where we can talk and catch up on everything that's been happening. I'll get in touch with you in a few days, if that's all right.

"A few days, Sir? That seems like a long time to wait before we can start working on the problems that we have out there with the public."

"It's not so long Ms. Brightman. I really must take the time to catch up on all the issues but I promise to call you in as soon as I have all the information that I need. You're dismissed."

Well, Cathy thinks as she leaves the Generals office. Now what the hell am I supposed to do. What's up with that guy? I have all the answers the idiot needs. Who the hell does he think he is?

Oh well, let him get them from some other source. It's probably the male/female thing. He probably doesn't like working with females. I wonder how he likes working for a female President? That's got to rub him wrong.

Since I have some personal time, I think I'll try to reach Snake and have a visit with him, I really miss him.

"Hey Kitten" Snake says as he wanders into the Italian restaurant that they all frequent when they're able.

"Hi" she replies softly. "Want to have some lunch? We can order it to go and take it back to my apartment, that way we're not in the public eye very long."

"Sounds good to me" he answers with a grin.

"Here we are" she says as they park and walk to a small apartment door on the third floor. "It's not much, but we only sleep here and shower so we didn't need much. It's close and cheap, two requirements."

"It's fine" he says as he follows her inside. After finishing the meatball subs that they got at the restaurant, they sit down to talk and relax.

"That new General, he dismissed me today, said he'd call me after he has time to look over the information on what's been happening lately. The idiot, I'm the one with the information. Go figure" she says in disgust.

"He's probably looking into your background, that's what I'd do. He's not going to discuss anything with you without knowing everything about you. He's not stupid" Snake replies quietly. "So, what time does Mallory work till?" he asks with a grin.

"Oh, she said she'd be late today, she starting to hack in to the Fahr Industries chip site and see what kind of information is available and what she can do to mess with the program."

"Late, huh" he repeats with a devilish grin. "That sounds real good to me" he says huskily as he moves closer to Kat. "I've missed you Kitten. How about a cuddle" he asks as he grabs her hands and pulls her closer.

"I'd like that" she admits shyly, a light blush on her cheeks and a slight tremor to her hands.

"Kitten, you have no idea how long I've wanted to do this. At least fifty times every day for the past two months. I want you Kitten" he murmurs in her neck as he holds her gently, rubbing her back in an erotic fashion. "I love everything about you, your thoughts, your moods, your happiness, your sadness, you."

"I know, and I love you too, Snake, but I'm

scared. I can't. Not yet, maybe never."

"I know, and you don't have to. Just holding you is enough for me. I don't need anything more, not right now at least. I promise to tell you when, but not right now."

"Thank you Snake" she says around the lump in her throat and the tears that are threatening to blind her. "You have no idea how much that means to me, how much you mean to me" she says as she holds him even tighter, afraid to let go, to never touch him again, to have him never touch her again.

"Let's just cuddle. Maybe take a nap?"

"That sounds wonderful to me. Maybe I can sleep for a little while. I still find it pretty illusive. Maybe someday, I'll be able to be normal again."

"You will be, I promise. It just hasn't been long enough yet. Your mind is still healing. Come on, up you go. If we're going to take a nap, it might as well be on the bed."

"There, how's that" he asks after lying down and pulling her down next to him. "Comfy?"

"Yeah, this is nice. Thanks, Snake" she murmurs as she closes her eyes and tries to sleep. He lies there quietly, pretending to sleep and notices that she never relaxes, just lays in that stiff position, pretending to sleep.

"I think I know what the problem might be" he says quietly and feels her jerk at the sound. "You need noise, something that makes your mind work, giving it a rest, not thinking just listening. Have you tried noise therapy?"

"No, I've never even heard of that" she says with a grin. "You just made that up, didn't you?" she says teasingly.

"No, really, there's a treatment called noise therapy. When you have things that bother you, your mind can't shut down, so you give it a peaceful kind of noise, tricking it into thinking that it has to stay busy. Then, all of a sudden, you fall asleep. Let's try it at least, it might work for you."

"I'm willing to try just about anything to sleep. I'm tired all the time and afraid that I'll be too tired to stay two steps ahead of the General."

"There, the TV. It's boring enough that it will probably put you right out."

"It is boring, so okay, let's try it." Ten minutes later she starts the deep even breathing that indicates sleep. The first real sleep in a long time he realizes with sadness and anger. I wish I would have taken my time killing that bastard. He deserves to suffer for what he did to her, damn it. If only I could go back.

"Kat, it's me, shhh, everything's all right, I just wanted to let you know that I have to leave. It's about eight pm and I have a shift I need to cover for the underground. I didn't want you waking up to find me gone and panicking."

"Isssoookkkay" she says sleepily. "Thanks . . . bye . . ." she murmurs as she goes back to sleep.

"Bye Kitten, I love you" he says quietly and with a gentle kiss, he leaves the room, Kat sleeping soundly.

Wow, Mallory thinks, after gaining access to the Fahr Industries FIQH Chip. I bet the people of this country have no idea just what the chip is capable of. The GPS portion, they can find anyone at any time for any reason. Then they've included a program for de-programming certain chips.

Of course on that list is the President, Vice President, the Reverend, the people in the President's special group. They don't want anyone to be able to find them, but the same courtesy isn't given to the U.S. citizens. They want total control of the people. You'll also need this chip to do anything; buy groceries, get health care, pay taxes, get paid by your employer. It doesn't look like they forgot anything.

Shit, it says here you can commit genocide. Damn it, she can kill anyone she wants, when she wants, for any reason she wants, and make it look like it was from natural causes. I need to call a conference with the group. We need to fix this before they can actually use it.

There's got to be some way to secretly stop some of these capabilities yet leave it looking like it's still there and running.

"Kat, are you here" Mallory yells when she gets back to their apartment. "I've got some important information. You're not going to believe what I just learned" she says when Kat comes wandering out of the bedroom area, hair tousled, yawing big.

"Hey, were you sleeping? I'm sorry to wake you; I know how little sleep you actually get" Mallory says chagrined.

"That's alright" Kat says while yawning. "I got some sleep" she says in shock.

"Yeah, you did, finally" Mallory agrees with a grin.

"So what's all the noise about" Kat asks sleepily.

"I just left the office. I know it's late but I got

involved with the chip program and when I finally got in, I was shocked with what I learned. They can trace anyone with the chip, but that's not the worst of it."

"The things it's capable of, it's brilliant really and if I were a ruler I'd want all my subjects to have this chip. I could kill anyone I wanted, just by going into the chips programming, putting in the number on the chip of the person I want to kill and then pushing a button. I could do that with as many chips as I wanted at one time. I can kill by gender, religion, race or even age, and it would look like death by natural causes. I can also stop people from eating if they don't take the chip. They won't be allowed to purchase food without the chip. No health care without the chip, no paydays for anyone without the chip. She's even funding this whole project plus the country on these chips by charging fifty-five percent on earned income for taxes. It's actually so diabolic it's frightening."

"Holy shit" Kat murmurs in shock "How are we going to make a difference with this? This is huge and she wants the whole world to be on the chip? She's moving towards world domination. We need a meeting. This is too much for just us to handle. We need to talk and make some plans. I'll try to contact Snake and see if he can set up a time and place to meet safely."

"Snake, it's me, Kat. Mallory's uncovered some interesting things programmed into the chips that are being placed in the hands of the American public. We need to talk about these things, fast. The programs are unbelievable. Call me back when you get this message and let me know where to meet. Better make sure that Eli and Devon are included, this is big."

"Head to the underground, it sounds like whatever we need to discuss, it needs to be in confidence. I don't want to take the chance of anyone overhearing this. Tomorrow morning at zero seven hundred at the west side market entrance, out."

"That was Snake" she informs Mallory after she gets off the radio. "He wants to meet tomorrow at zero-seven hundred at the west side market entrance. He sure was brusque, I hope everything's okay with him" Kat mumbles in guilt, afraid she awakened the beast and then ignored it, leaving him feeling unappreciated and frustrated.

"Good, then I'm going to head to bed. I've had a long and stressful day and I just need a break. Night Kat."

"Night Mal."

"So what do you want from me" Mallory yells at Devon. "I didn't create the damned chips.

I just found out all this yesterday, and scheduled this meet right away. Don't you think that I'm worried about this too?"

"Sorry Mal. I didn't mean that the way it sounded. I know you're worried about this, how couldn't you be. It's just such a shocker. I let my emotions get in the way, I'm sorry."

"Alright, now that we've all calmed down a little, I want to share some information with everyone. These are some things that I heard, first hand, from the President's very lips. Let's see if we put our heads together, what we can figure out" Kat says.

"I was listening in on the President while she was

in her secret office that only a very few know about, mostly her closest allies. Dad, this is especially important for you to know, since you have the biggest following here in the underground and can reach so many people."

"The President was on the phone with the Shah, the family friend of hers, at least we thought he was just a close friend but she addresses him as Uncle which puts a much closer relationship between them. From what she said and he concurred, she was born for this work. Her parents were not only close friends but had a blood tie to the old Shah. They also belonged to the Savak, Iran's Security and Intelligence organization that existed prior to the Islamic republic being created, which came after the first Shah was overthrown."

"During that time in Iran, Khomeini was just coming into power. They were extremely loyal and very good at what they did, just two soldiers that had given their country and their religion everything they had. They weren't married but were partners, not even boyfriend and girlfriend.   Anyway, to get to the point, they were wanted people at that time and the only thing that they could do to further the Shah's goals were to leave the country under the guise of fear for their lives which is what a large number of people that were loyal to the Shah were doing. In actuality I'm sure that wasn't the issue.

"Picture a war torn country, bombs going off constantly, people dying everywhere. Nothing was the same. It took years before the country was calm enough for the people to venture out into the streets again."

"Fortunately, Jane's parents were related to the future Shah who was able to totally fund their lives while working towards a common goal. That goal was the birth of the next total ruler of Iran."

"They were told to settle in the states, pick a town that was unknown, find someone that wanted to start his own church, to become a minister and help him to build the largest church in the United States. To have a child, raise him or her as an American citizen, outwardly as an American Christian with strong ties to the church they were building while in reality they were raising her in the Muslim way. Now we have the adult version, Jane Martin, who in reality is one hundred percent Muslim. She's good at proclaiming who she is but really isn't."

"Every once in a while she'll slip and you can see her true colors. Her goal, as far as I know, is to become dictator of the United States with everyone powerless except her. She's done a good job informing the people of her strengths yet she prefers to show herself as innocent and wronged."

"The people really believe that they have control over everything when they have control over nothing. The voting thing that's being done on-line is a fake. She decides who lives and who dies. There's a voting mechanism in place should anyone want an audit, but she has the ability to change the outcome to suit her wants and needs."

"So what we're now facing is a President that is under Muslim religious control, who wants to be completely in charge of the states. So far, that's happened and with an ease that makes me sick. It didn't take her long at all, once she removed all obstacles that were in her way. She now holds the highest office in this country."

"This is a dangerous woman. She's very vindictive and extremely determined. It's as if she has a due date for things that only she knows about. My suggestion is to keep her in sight at all times. It wouldn't be a good idea if she had the opportunity to do something massive. She could destroy not only this country but others as well in her quest to control everything."

"The truth is not a pleasant thing. The United States is now in a fight for its very survival, the people are afraid of what's happening yet they're afraid to get involved, also. We have a lot of work to do if we plan on protecting these shores and keeping them from being totally destroyed." "Okay, I think that covers most of it, now you know why I wanted to talk to you all. We need to get back to where we were" Kat says.

"The chips, Mal, what can you do without getting caught?" Jacob asks.

"Well, I can disable the chips but I can't do them all. That would be too noticeable, there's no way I could get away with that. I may be able to change some of the programs just enough to stop the orders or to cause the order to change enough that no one would get hurt. That's my main issue, the ability the President has to kill at whim. I can de-program chips in the event that anyone of the people underground would be safe. Their chips would be useless, but then the food issue would become a problem. It's damned if I do and damned if I don't. You tell me what you think would be the right thing to do. I'm in a quandary right now."

"Mal, you're not responsible for any of this. You're capable of helping, but you're limited too. You can't think like it's your fault. All we can do is take it a day at a time and fight for what's right. None of it will be easy, but we'll all share the burden" Eli says.

"Thanks Eli, for understanding" Mallory says with tears in her eyes. "I didn't realize how hard this was going to be, and I know it's only going to get worse" she adds with a sniffle.

"Okay, so let's make a list. Then we can decide which ones are most important and what can be done to change the outcome" Jacob decides. "List the positives and the negatives. The negatives: killing at whim, unable to purchase food, no paydays, tracking each person. The positives, if you can call them that, health care, taxes pre-paid. Looks like the negatives far outweigh the positives. Unfortunately, we'll have to let some of the negatives stay. If we change too much we'll be found out and then we'll do no one any good.

"So Mal, what do you think. Can you change the program enough that no one will die from the chip?"

"Yep, I can do that, but I think it would be better if we left some of the people on that part of the chip. The President may be able to kill on a whim and if she tries, then is unsuccessful it'll be found out that the chips have been changed. I'd rather not have that found out too fast, because they can change it back and make it a lot more difficult for me to gain access."

"True, true, but who gets to stay on that list.

How are you going to decide who go's and who stays?"

"I was thinking of the Presidents staff. Since she works so closely with them, she could get angry with them and decide she's tired of them and kill them. If she's unable to do that, then she'll blow a fuse. I'd rather she was successful in the beginning. That way, she might not catch on when the general populace stays alive. It's not like she's going to be inside their homes when she pushes the button or calls for it to be done, so there's a time lag there that might be able to help us."

"Good Thinking Mal. I suppose, if you leave anyone, it would be most appropriate for those closest to her. They chose sides, so really there's nothing we can do to help them, not that they'd believe anything negative about her. I think that's the way to go." Jacob answers in agreement.

"Yeah, I have to agree. If we want to save the majority, then some will have be left as sacrifices" Kat murmurs in agreement.

"Does anyone have a problem with this decision" Jacob asks as he looks at each and every one before making the final decision. "Mom, Dad?"

"No, we're good with this."

"Devon?

"I'm good with it."

"Eli?"

"Yeah, we don't have a choice, so yeah."

"Rand?"

"Good with it."

"Mongoose?"

"Good."

"Lucas?"

"Good, sad but good."

"Anyone here have a problem with this decision?"

"Alright, it's a go, Mal. Do what you must and keep the Presidents group on the chip and active. Hopefully we've gained some time with this decision. How long do you think, to get the job done?"

"It'll probably be a week, maybe longer, but minimum I'd say a week."

"Good, let's get to it."

"Good luck out there Mal, try not to get caught." Jacob says as everyone gets up and starts to leave, ready to start another day.

Chapter Fifteen

"Why don't we use our Military to help with the chip placement? It may help the people accept the military faster and learn the need for them. We can create some things that would scare the citizens and allow the military to come out on the side of the protector, showing us in a good light. It's easier if we take the public this way, it lessons suspiciousness. We can finally be reported in a positive way. That way, the citizens will follow us willingly. It just makes more sense."

"So what do you say Jane? I could have the Military help bring the chips to each and every house in this country. It would be an easier transition for most."

"I'm not sure" she says thoughtfully. "I want the people to fear me, they need to realize who's in charge now and that when they don't listen they will see what I can do to them."

"I understand that Jane, but sometimes you have to start out with patience. That's all I'm suggesting, not change but patience."

"Fine, it's temporary though. I want to have ALL the power over these people. That will bring me great delight and I don't want to wait too long. I'm impatient. Do you know how long I've been waiting, Teriq, can't you understand the importance this has for me?"

"Yes, Jane, I can and do understand. Just a little longer, that's all. Soon it will all be rightfully yours."

"Okay then Teriq, let's get the military moving. The sooner the chips are all in place, the sooner I'll have complete control. Thank you for coming up with this idea. It will speed things up. It's time" she adds with a smile.

"I'll plan a news conference for this evening, early. I'll let the people know about the decision and the change in the chip implanting. They'll be happy that you're going to be bringing the whole chip process right to their own homes. They no longer will have to worry about how to get to the schools and what time, can I get off work, etc. This is going to work beautifully, I believe."

"I'll let them know that at the beginning of next week, this will be instituted. Soon the whole country will be done."

"Then maybe I can move further in the planning issues with Canada and Mexico. We'll get the Continental Triad going stronger. I feel the chip is going to travel quickly around the world. Soon everyone will have the chip, in every country. I can stop any and all that want to create problems, those that refuse to bend to my will. That's true power. These are exciting times" she adds with a gleeful laugh, anticipating how close she is to having it all.

"I need to talk with Jerry, because I've heard some rumors that I don't like the sounds of. I can't believe everything I hear though, besides, he's been like a father to me since I was born. I can't believe he'd do anything to hurt me or my destiny. He's actually helped me thus far. I'll talk to you later

Teriq. I need to get this done, put any problems to rest with Jerry."

"Jerry, can you meet with me in my non-public office" Jane asks after he answers her call.

"Sure Jane, anytime. You know that I drop whatever I'm doing when you need me."

"Yeah, I know, thanks Jerry. Meet me in twenty minutes, thanks."

"Come on in Jerry, have a seat. What can I get you to drink" Jane asks.

"Just a soft drink, thanks Jane. I've got other meetings today and can't go to them with alcohol on my breath. I'll save that for later."

"Jerry, I've heard some rumors that have me confused" she admits when she hands him his drink. "I wanted to check them out with you before I got upset or angry. They're not pretty rumors and I'm hoping they're totally unfounded."

"What is it Jane, what's got you upset?"

"Well, I've heard that you've sent quite a few of your followers underground in Texas. I hope that's not the case; there was no need to send anyone underground. I happen to have a friend that's infiltrated the underground and is keeping me informed of what's going on down there and up here. I'm so disappointed in that, Jerry. How could you do what he says you've done? Why send anyone underground? You know those people are making my life miserable, so why add to the list? Please tell me that you didn't send anyone there." Jane says in anger and disappointment.

"Jane, I would never do anything to give you pain. I have sent no one underground. Yes, some of my congregation has gone underground, but none of them were on my orders. How could you even think that I would be responsible for any of that? Haven't I supported you for your whole life, given you everything I had to give, just to make sure that you arrived at your destiny? I'm one of your biggest supporters, how could you think otherwise" Jerry asks in denial.

"I know Jerry and I'm sorry for believing what I heard. I knew that you wouldn't betray me. I had a moment of weakness, I'm sorry. I believe you. I know that you want me to succeed" Jane says near tears. "You've been my friend my whole life and you knew where I was heading, what my parents had sacrificed their whole lives for, so you knew. I am so sorry. Can you ever forgive me for doubting you?"

"Jane, Jane, no harm done, please don't cry. Your life has never been the easy one and you yourself have sacrificed also. Its fine, we're fine. I'm not mad, just a little disappointed, but not angry."

"Thanks Jerry, for understanding. I won't bother you anymore with the trivial, stupid questions. From now on, I'll believe only what I already know. Who's on my side and who isn't. I'll use my own judgment, I'll also make sure that my underground plant learns a lesson from me, he will never again bring me false information."

"I have another appointment in a few minutes so I'll have to get going Jane. But anytime you feel doubtful about me, please call me. There's no need for you to worry about us. We'll always have that special relationship" he says as he kisses her on the cheek and leaves the room.

"Good Evening ladies and gentlemen, this is Jim Cochran from WELT News Channel 3, Washington, D.C. live from the White House. We're here for the live broadcast of the Reverend Jerry Johnson, Minister of 'The Peoples Church' near Lorado, Texas. Here he is, live:"

"Thank you, ladies and gentlemen of this beautiful country, the United States of America. I'm talking with you tonight to dispel some of the rumors that are flying like wildfire throughout the country. I hope that you feel that you can trust me, because this can in fact be life or death. This is my plea, a plea for unity and peace, unfortunately, this has not been happening throughout this country."

"We have been overcome by evil in its most base form, the form of the President. All true believers of God need to be aware that this country has become a farce. You need to stand as the Christians that you are and take back this country; our freedom to worship is being destroyed. There is evil happening all around you; it is against God our Heavenly Father and against our Lord Jesus Christ that these things are happening. Believe NOT what you hear from the Pres
. . .

"You're off the air Jerry" Jane says as she advances on him slowly. "How DARE you talk to MY people that way" she yells. "They are MY people and will follow me. You are the sick, evil soul that has been hanging around my neck my whole life.

Well, no more, you are finished Jerry. Bring him to my personal office please, General Auliya. I have some things to discuss with him privately."

"Damn it Jerry. You betrayed me in front of the whole country. How could you" she demands as she watches him. "You will no longer be welcome anywhere, Jerry. Your church is forfeit; it no longer belongs to you. My parents built that church, they befriended you, they helped you and this is how you repay them? You better run Jerry. Your life is worth nothing any longer. Run". . . she watches him run down the hall towards the main stairs realizing there's no one that's trustworthy anymore. It's a lonely life that I must lead now, she decides as she picks up the phone and dials. "Teriq, I need to see you in my personal office, now."

"Yes Madame President, I'm on my way."

"Come in Teriq" Jane says at the knock. "I have a problem that you must help me with" she informs him. "It's Jerry, my Minister from Texas. He's betrayed me; he's sent many of his flock into the underground to get away from the future. They didn't want to take the chip and so he gave them amnesty by sending them underground."

"I can't have anyone that freely betrays me on my staff. However, I don't want this to become public knowledge, so I'm asking you to handle the problem quietly. He can't live in the world that I'm creating; he'll only become a problem. Problems I want handled the best way possible and as soon as they come to the front. I leave how up to you, you're the professional and that's why you have the position that you have. I expect this problem handled today, I don't want to worry about this any longer."

"Yes Madame President. Your orders will always be followed by me and by your military. It will be done today."

"Thank You Teriq. I'm scheduled to go live for a news briefing. I must repair some of the damage that Jerry just caused. I'll do what I must to fix this problem. Then, we'll announce the new plan for the chips. How the military, under your direction of course, will be going house to house to help the people to obtain their chips. With your direction, this process will be completed much earlier than anticipated. That's a bonus for us, since it will allow us to move quicker to make sure that every citizen is covered with insurance."

"I thought that you could give a demonstration of some of the capabilities of the new chip programs. I believe it will impress the public. They'll feel safer after seeing the chip in action. I thought you could set that up for me, since it's your game that we'll be playing."

"I'm honored, Madame President, that you trust me enough to allow me to do this thing for you."

"Of course I trust you Teriq, did I not appoint you to this position, because of trust? I will trust you until you do something that causes me to lose that trust. But I really don't believe that will happen, at least not right now."

"And now, moving on: I also have another issue. I've been informed of a secret meeting that's been planned. The Senate, Congress and the House of Representatives are going to be holding a meeting at

'The People's Church' in Texas. How they thought they could get away with that I have no idea."

"My parents helped build that church, there's nothing done there that they don't know about, so of course they notified me. I was shocked. I just spoke with Jerry and he didn't even mention this. I know he's the one behind it. I also know that he had a meeting when he left me, with the Speaker of the House. They seem to be working together and against me at the same time."

"I've taken as much as I'm going to take with traitors. They all will pay for what they're planning. So, I have an idea that will fix the problem and bring a smile to your face at the same time."

"You know that we're scheduled for a test of that new radar system, the one called the DB six-nine-six. I thought that since we have to turn off our old reliable radar to try this new one, we may just experience a national security issue."

"Someone could bomb the church and destroy everyone in it. It would be such a shock and such a waste, but in reality, we don't need those Senators, Congressmen or House of Representatives any longer. They actually fill empty seats, seats without any power. I've already stripped them of most of their power, so taking the rest will pose no problem for me. I already have all the power; they just don't want to admit it."

"Anyway, I propose calling the Shaw and he can in turn contact President Majeed. I'm sure President Majeed would have no problem launching a nuclear warhead at the church, and I also plan on accepting his offer of troops. Yes, it will be the first time since the revolutionary war that foreign troops have set foot on our soil and I believe it's only right that it be by my command. We're going to need a lot more man power to control the problems that Jerry caused."

"The bombing can be blamed on someone else, after all that wouldn't be a problem. We'll just pick someone believable to blame it on. The people of this country will believe me if I say it's so" she adds with a deep sigh of satisfaction "or they know what could happen to them. Fear is a powerful tool."

"Do you have the date that the meeting is planned for, President Martin? I can start the process if I have an exact date to go with."

"I do, but I will handle this situation, I just wanted to see how you would react to it. Some of those people are friends of yours, are they not" she asks coolly, knowledge bright in her eyes.

"Yes President Martin, I have friends that are Senators. You will not see me notifying them of course, since my loyalty is all yours" Teriq replies his gut twisting in fear.

"Yes, Teriq, I believe you" Jane says quietly. "Trust me, no harm will come to you, you have been only extremely loyal to me" she adds as she leaves the room.

"Good Evening ladies and gentlemen, this is Jim Cochran from WELT News Channel 3, Washington, D.C. live from the White House. President Martin is scheduled to appear here in a matter of moments. She's says she has a surprise for the public. I can't wait to hear what she says" he adds with a smile. "Here she is now:"

'Thank you, ladies and gentlemen of the United States of America. I have some exciting news to give you this evening. General Teriq Auliya, the General of the Armies, has promised a demonstration for you so that you may feel comfortable with the chip and its many capabilities. General, welcome, please go ahead with your surprise" she says with a girlish giggle.

"I've decided to demonstrate for you what would happen to a robber if they tried to rob anyone, a store, a bank or even yourselves. The chip will make your life so much safer that anyone would want to have it, just for this reason. I have set up something on video that I want to show you. Now watch closely and you'll see just how safe you will be."

Live camera shot, a person robbing another person on the sidewalk in front of the White House. After almost getting what he wants by hitting the victim a couple of times all of a sudden he drops to the sidewalk, jerking and a military person walks over to him, turns him face down on the sidewalk and handcuffs him, then pulls him up to his feet. The robber just stands there as if in a daze, not even trying to run.

"As you could see in that short video, the robber was getting away with a little bit of violence before all of a sudden falling to the ground and jerking around. That was because a person in our military that was monitoring the video of that area noticed the robber, quickly did a scan of him to get a reading on his chip. Once the reading was in, he pressed a button that acted as if the robber was hit by a stun gun, causing him to fall onto the sidewalk, never leaving the scene of the crime. It was all caught on tape and he was apprehended mere minutes after he started the robbery. No one was seriously injured and now the public will be the judge of what will happen to him."

"Awesome" claps Jane with childish delight and a laugh. "This takes so much worry away from me, since I do worry about our citizens. I feel that we have become friends in the few short months that we've worked together. It was wonderful to catch that robber within that very short time frame, before he was able to injure the person he was trying to rob and before he finished his crime. Plus he's on tape, so there's no mistaking who did what. That was wonderful, General Auliya, wonderful" she repeats with a smile. He thanks her formally, a twinkle in his eye for the praise.

"And now on a more serious note, the final information that I share with you tonight is that I am declaring total martial law. We have had so many things happen in such a short period of time, so much unrest that I believe the only way to gain safety and get peace for the citizens of this country is to command the General of the Armies to institute total martial law. This makes the General responsible for the country. He will be in charge of everyone and everything. The first thing that he's done since this declaration is to institute a curfew. You must now be in your homes no later than twenty-hundred hours. That's eight pm for those that don't know military time" she adds with a smirk.

"We need a meet" Eli notifies Jacob. "We've got a problem and it's going to affect everyone in this country and abroad. We need to talk about it. I've just received information from one of my sources."

"How about tonight at say twenty-one hundred, same place?"

"Yep, same place, see you then.   I'll notify everyone else."

"Thanks for coming so quickly. This is urgent, that's why you didn't get much notification.   Eli called the meeting based on some intel from one of his sources. Eli, go ahead" Jacob says.

"I was informed earlier today of a planned bombing of 'The Peoples Church' in Texas. I just don't have the exact date. It's going to happen within the next week, so we have seven days, but I'm not sure on which day they're planning it. I'm also not sure what type of bomb they're using; it could be any number of bombs, coming from God knows where. I did find out though, that the Congress, the Senate, and the House are planning a meeting at this same church. The date is within the next week, but there too I have no exact date and time. Some things are discussed and others are being kept totally dark. I'm working on my source to get me an exact date for that meeting."

"In order to pull this off, she's disarming our phased-array radar system temporarily, to try out the newly developed DB six-nine-six. This radar is so far advanced that it can seamlessly track numerous targets at one time, the biggest advantage being its ability to cover a large area with this single system. If this were the only reason why she was disarming our normal system, then I'd be just as excited as everyone else is, but it's not."

"She has an agenda that includes a much more underhanded reason. I think I've got that covered though. I've sent a team to West Virginia, there's an abandoned mine with the national radar (phased array) still in place. I think they can get this back on line, I'm just hoping that it's in time. If so, we can at least track the bomb. It's a given that once we see the blip, there's nothing we can do. So in reality, we'll be able to see it coming, but it'll be too late to save anyone. I'm not sure that it's worth all the effort, but, they're on the way."

"This meeting with all the political leaders is definitely not being broadcast for the Presidents ears. My guess, they're not happy with her leadership. She's taken everything away from them; she's left them pretty much without jobs."

"So what you're saying is they're going to bomb the church but no idea of when, or even who?" Devon asks derisively.

"Yeah, sorry, but at least I heard of the bombing. I guess now we start bugging more sites and try to get the information that way, hopefully before anything happens. Geez Devon, you have a bad attitude, bro. Lighten up a little, why don't ya? I don't see you contributing much except attitude lately, so back off."

"Sorry Eli, it's been a bad couple of weeks for me."

"It's been a bad couple of weeks for everyone. Maybe you need to keep that in perspective."

"Fine."

"Kid's, kid's, enough; we're all under a lot of stress so let's just cool the attitudes" Jacob says with authority. "We're having enough problems; we certainly don't need the bad attitudes to go with them."

"Now, we know there's a bombing in the works, we just need to focus on the when. We already know the where, so we can start listening for key words and try to nail down the when. We'll never know the why, at least not for a while. Let's get back out there and do our jobs. Stay safe everyone and as soon as anyone hears anything related to this, radio in please."

"Kitten, can I see you for a couple of minutes, privately?"

"Sure Snake, what's up" she asks after moving down the hall to a room never used. "Looks like a storage room, maybe we should clean it out and make use of it" she murmurs when he turns around and locks the door behind them.

As her heart starts to race, visions of what happened start flying through her brain causing her to gasp for air.

"Kitten, it's me, no need to panic. I'll never hurt you" he says quietly in anguish. "Shh, you don't need to be afraid, I just want to talk to you, that's all" he says as he starts to rub her back in a soothing motion, dispersing the fear and reminding her who she's talking to.

"I'm sorry, Snake. I'll get better, I promise. It was the locking of the door, it brought back sharp memories, memories I thought were gone."

"They'll go away, I promise. I just need to replace them with good memories, which I'm working on" he adds with a grin and a hug.

"When I saw you last, you were sleeping, and I wanted to know how well you slept, that's all. I also happen to know how you feel about your privacy, so I didn't want to ask in front of everyone."

"Thanks Snake" she says with a big hug and a smile, eyes a little clearer. "I slept great" she exclaims. "It was the first great sleep I've had since I stopped wearing my helmet to bed" she adds with a blush, realizing he didn't know that she slept in the helmet.

"You used to sleep in the helmet?" he asks in surprise.

"Yeah, it was the only way I could get any sleep. It kept the nightmares at bay. I forgot you didn't know" she admits with chagrin. "I don't suppose you'd forget I said that if I asked you too?"

"No way, Kitten. You know me better than that. I will never forget you said that. It makes me feel good to know that you trust me enough to sleep well when you hear my voice or feel my body near yours" he admits with a strong hug, a feeling of closeness enveloping both him and her, a feeling of peace.

"How about I come to your place every night to help you sleep" he asks seriously. "I really don't mind, you know."

"I know, but I live with Mal right now and I don't want her to know" Kat admits, chagrined, the thought of Snake sleeping next to her, almost more than she can bear. The wanting, the comfort, the happiness she always feels when she's around him. The safety in his arms warring in her mind with the knowledge of how close she is to accepting. "How about you staying in my apartment at night, and meeting Mal in yours in the morning. The only thing she'll know is that you're not sleeping at the apartment. She may even believe that it's because of the nightmares."

"Really, I didn't know that you had an apartment, where is it"

"It in the same building as yours. I wanted to be close in case of emergency, so I rented one on the top floor."

"Wow, that's awesome" she admits thoughtfully. After a few quiet introspective moments she decides. "I'll stay at your apartment, starting tonight. Thanks Snake. What would I ever do without you? I love you, you know."

"I know, Kitten, I love you too, I just wish you knew how much." he murmurs quietly. "Soon, you'll know how much, soon" he promises to himself.

Breaking News... Breaking News . . . "This is Jim Cochran of WELT News Channel 3, Washington D.C. Thank you for joining us. There have been some reports of a large explosion occurring in Texas. We are unsure right now of where this took place and what happened. We're waiting right now for a sister station to go live and update us with this information. Hold on, I hear Lester Van Goff from WELK News Channel 7, Dallas, Texas. "Lester, can you tell us what happened, where the explosion occurred?" asks Jim.

"Yes, sorry, I can barely hear you. It's a catastrophe, to be sure" Lester says to Jim, loudly, emotions building from the shock. "We've just been informed that the largest non-denominational church in the country, known as 'The People's Church' has been completely destroyed by a bomb, can you believe it? Do you know what kind of bomb it would take to destroy something that large? This is unbelievable. From all sources close to this explosion, there's NOTHING left of the church. No sign that it ever existed. This was a huge church and to have no sign of it points to a pretty large explosion. There are bomb squads on the way to the site with the military, trying to figure out just what caused this destruction, the devastation. Hopefully we'll know soon how many fatalities have occurred."

"Since it's the middle of the week, we know that the people that attend this church, the members, were not in the church at this time. The church has a small staff that works weekdays, but the majority of the congregation is only there on Sundays."

"More Breaking news is coming in, hold on. The areas surrounding the church are showing signs of radiation! 'Oh my God' this could have been a weapon of mass destruction. If that's the case, it's very possible that this bomb came from terrorists possibly located within this country or by another country. We may have been struck by a different country. That would mean war; it would mean that we're at war" Lester remarks quickly in a voice full of shock.

"As everyone is aware, the United States has been threatened quiet frequently in the recent past by nuclear weapon threats from multiple countries around the world. Since the site is showing signs of radiation, there will be no interviews close to the area of the explosion. The area is now closed to the media and to the public until exact cause is known and all threats of imminent danger have been handled. They have evacuated an area five miles in radius and they aren't even sure if that's large enough. I don't think I'd be any closer than ten miles, but that's my own opinion."

"Watch now, we've got some video feed coming in from our news chopper, they're hovering close enough to the sight so that we can see some of the damage. Wow, look at that, there's a huge crater where the bomb hit. No sign of any church. Watch the monitor now; we're going to show you side by side pictures, one with the church, the other now, after the bomb went off. Shit, look at that, the one on the left, it was a huge church, the one on the right, there's absolutely nothing left, nothing but a huge hole where the church was standing and lots of wood that from this distance looks like match sticks. Hey, Mike, doesn't radiation go up too. Aren't you exposing yourself to large amounts of radiation, should you be that close to ground zero?"

"No, we shouldn't but decided we needed the pictures; we were only close enough to the radiation for just a couple of minutes. Hopefully that won't cause any problems. We're heading away now, but will stay in the area for awhile in case of more film being needed."

"Breaking News" This is Jim Cochran of WELT News Channel 3, Washington D.C. We've just been notified that there is an area in the bombed site that is releasing large amounts of radiation. Since so much radiation is lingering, they have now issued another evacuation area. Due to the wind that's blowing southwest to northeast, they are evacuating an area five miles southwest of the site to 20 miles northeast.

They're asking people to get in their vehicles and leave the area; this area is considered a plume area and moves according to wind speed and direction. The further away you get, the safer you'll be."

. "Go in the opposite direction. Do not tarry, grab what you need for an emergency and get out of the area as quickly and as orderly as possible. Take your pets with you; they will not survive being left in the area. Anyone that was out of the area at the time of the explosion will NOT be allowed to go home for anything. If you had pets, they will not be able to be saved unless you have a neighbor that can grab them as they leave. Unfortunately, your cell phones will not work at this time. There's too much disturbance in the air, too much dust and too many people trying to call out. The lines are jammed. This is an emergency of mass proportions. The World Trade Center was terrible, it destroyed much, but this, this is far worse, and we still don't have any idea who did this to us. Are we under attack, is another bomb pointed in our direction, ready to be launched?"

"Here's Doctor Whilker, WELK News Channel 3, Washington D.C. our on staff Doctor with some extremely important information. Please stay tuned:"

"If you feel unusually ill and were in the area that is now evacuated, you may need to report to an emergency room. If you touched anything that was near the site of the explosion, you may need to be seen at the ER. If you feel you may be contaminated with radiation, then listen to this. Find a shower outside of the evacuated area; wash your body and hair with a gentle soap in slightly warm water. Wash gently; do not scrape your skin off trying to remove the radiation, that won't fix the problem. The goal is to wash it OFF, not into the skin. If you're unsure if you need medical attention, go to the nearest health care facility that is outside of the evacuated area. This is Dr. Bill Whilker of WELT News Channel 3, Washington D.C."

Chapter Sixteen

"Madame President, there's been an explosion of mass proportions at "The Peoples Church" in Texas" remarks Teriq to Jane, who's video conferencing with the President of Mexico. "From all reports, there's nothing left of that area. I've issued a Homeland Security Red Alert. I'm citing belief that there could be more bombs aimed at the United States."

"President Whuarez, I must go, this is national security, but I promise to contact you when I know more about what just happened" Jane says before she ends the video connection.

"What else, Teriq?"

"The military in Texas have also detected radiation surrounding the explosion, leaving the area uninhabitable. However, they've cleared an area five miles out surrounding the church that they believe is clear of the radioactive danger. They're saying the majority of the danger is found within close proximity of the crater that was left by the explosion. There have been no reports as of yet, about who was in the church at the time of the explosion. As far as I can discern, no one has come forward about the secret meeting of the Senate, House and Congress. Fear of reprisal is probably keeping that information quiet. I'm sure it will break sometime today. Once that information is out, all hell's going to break loose. I've started calling in more troops for Texas and of course, here in D.C. "

"Thank you Teriq, for the information" Jane says with a smile, eyes shining. "I love it when things come together" she murmurs in satisfaction.

After Teriq leaves, she grabs her private phone. "I want to speak with the Shah. Thank You" she says just prior to being put on hold.

"Jane, my dear, how can I help you?" he asks with his deep, smooth voice.

"I want to thank you, Uncle. Everything has gone as expected. The United States must learn her lessons hard, as usual. The explosion was perfect, it destroyed what we needed destroyed, stupid Americans. They actually thought they could meet like that and get away with it. Stupid people" she adds with a laugh. "Please pass on the word of the success; I want to share this with those that are closest to me, Uncle. I'm going to call my parents next, just to check in with them but pass the thanks on, please Uncle."

"Of course I will Jane, of course."

"Notify the media that I plan on giving the Country a briefing. They need to be informed where this attack came from. Schedule it immediately. The sooner the word is out, the faster I look good to my citizens."

"Right away Madame President" Teriq promises. "They'll be here for a live briefing within the next half hour."

"Thanks Teriq."

Why isn't mom answering her phone, surely they're home. Where else could they be? It isn't a church day so they wouldn't have been there, so where else could they be. I wish they would have accepted the cell phones as a gesture of good will from me, but of course, they had to make that difficult. I'll have to keep calling until I can get a hold of them. News conference now, I'll try them again later.

"This is Jim Cochran of WELT News Channel 3, Washington D.C. with a live briefing from President Jane Martin at the White House. Here she is:"

"Thank you for pulling this meeting together so quickly. It's appreciated, Jim. Ladies and gentlemen of our great United States, I'm here to inform you of an attack that has occurred on our beloved soil, in the great state of Texas."

"I can't begin to explain to you how I feel about this. My own home state, within miles of my parents home, whom I haven't been able to reach as of yet" she exclaims with tears in her eyes.

"Before I called for this briefing, I did some investigating as to who could possibly have done something this horrendous, and have received information that I want to impart to each and every one of you. The country responsible for sending this weapon of mass destruction is China."

"As the President of these United States, I am declaring war on the country of China. They are the ones that are responsible for dispatching the nuclear warhead that destroyed my church, the church that my parents spent their life helping to build. This is a personal insult against me, your President. I will not tolerate anyone threatening or sending any type of bomb at our beautiful country."

"We will use every ounce of our power to stop them from continuing with the destruction that they've started. We have weapons aimed right now at their country. The United States has the power to take care of its own. Sending that bomb was the wrong thing for them to do, they need to beware now of the wrath of these United States and it citizens. I bring with me today to talk with you, the General of the Armies, the person in charge of bringing our strength together and stopping China from committing any further acts of war. Here to speak with you is General Auliya."

"Thank you President Martin. I appreciate the time that you're allowing me to have to inform our citizens of what has happened and what they will be seeing done in the very near future."

"We cannot and will not sit back and allow anyone, not even a country such as China, to bomb our soil, to destroy our churches, to kill our people, to threaten anymore of the people of the United States."

"Directly after this happened, bomber jets were dispatched in retaliation of the bomb that destroyed the Presidents home town church, Jerald Johnson's church, the minister that has befriended and helped our own beloved President to obtain the seat that she now has. Don't be afraid in the future when you hear of China being bombed. It is with great sadness that this must be done, but unfortunately for them, the United States will not sit back and allow this to happen. President Martin has declared war, war against the far east, war on China and Korea."

"As of right at this very moment, China has

received four of our numerous nuclear warheads. There's damage being reported all over their country, millions are thought to be dead or will be after the radiation sickness sets in."

"Their largest city (people per capita) is Shanghai which has received two of the four bombs as a direct hit. Bejing has received one and Chongquin the other. As the day progresses, more nuclear warheads are to be dispatched to a few of the other larger municipalities. China has been unable to fight back since our retaliatory attack on them. You need not fear any longer that they will bomb us again; they are so busy right now protecting themselves that they have no time to bomb us. We're watching right now and waiting and have our anti-missile aircraft at the ready. We have also sent our Navy to station just outside of Korea. We're invading Korea to use that land mass to help further our cause in china. No one will be able to sneak a bomb through our defenses again. In order to defeat the dragon, you must cut off its head" General Auliya says.

"This is Jim Cochran of WELT News Channel 3, Washington D.C. with live coverage of the bombings. We've received reports from the American Embassy in China. They've informed us of a secret meeting that was occurring in China with the President of North Korea. North Korea initiated a meeting of the Nuclear Non-Proliferation Treaty, meetings of that type are normally held partly at the "Great Wall of the People" meeting place in Beijing which has been destroyed. If that's where they were at this time during this secret meeting, they're gone. There's nothing left of that meeting place."

"People are running through the streets, crying out names of missing loved ones, and scrambling desperately through the streets which are covered in a thick dust that's most probably radioactive; along with the dust from the buildings that were destroyed, millions of wood pieces, broken glass and concrete that's scattered over the area. After looking closely at the scattered debris, you can see thousands of bodies lying in the ruins and the dust. This definitely looks like a war zone and it's only just begun. This is Jim Cochran of WELT News Channel 3, Washington D.C. with live coverage of the ongoing chaos in China."

"We need a meeting, now! Drop everything that you're doing and meet me where the last meeting was" Eli informs each of his siblings after they answer.

"Sorry about the abruptness of this meeting, but as I'm sure you're aware, the explosion that rocked Texas killed more than just the weekday staff. I've been informed that the political meeting that was planned was taking place at the time of the bombing. We no longer have any Senators, Congressmen or House of Representatives."

"They were all in the meeting at the time of the bombing. I've also been informed that the bomb came from Iran, not China, that's being reported. It was a special nuclear warhead, the one that we were suspicious of for quite a while. Our suspicions were well founded since it was real and was successful. Underground word has it that it was ordered up by our very own military who, of course, are under the very tiny delicate thumb of our President."

"This has become war now. It's them against us. We may be small but we're gaining size as we speak. There are many that are loyal to us, probably more than are loyal to her, but we have to move much more cautiously. We certainly don't want to tip our hand too soon." Eli says.

"Mal, what have you learned from the chip program? Can we make a difference? We're going to have to be able to de-program them if we want to continue living above ground and infiltrating her groups. The only way that we can repair this problem is by infiltrating her people with ours and learning things before they occur. We may be able to stop the majority of the damage that's been occurring" Jacob says.

"I think that I can fix this problem, Jacob. The problems that I'm finding are whoever's behind this, they're quick. As soon as I change something, they notice and put it back. Somehow, I need to be a ghost in that program. If I just had some idea of what type of program they're using to follow me, then I might be able to rewrite it and change their capabilities. I'm getting closer at least. Soon, the underground will have de-programming capabilities including turning on and off the GPS signals. And the food portion, I'm just going to leave that one in, since we all need food for survival. I'm also re-writing some of the program so that everyone will have special capabilities of turning everything back on. It's really just a safety feature. If one of the underground gets caught and they check the chip, finding it changed, they'll send their own programmers back in to change it. If they change the firewalls, I'll have to start over. We don't have that kind of time.

"I may be able to do this and use a loop program. There are some out there that are so new they can't have the fix for them this fast" Mallory assures everyone. "Those are my plans for today. I need that program to speed things up on my end. We're running out of time with this whole scenario. If I can't get this, the citizens don't stand a chance. If I can speak freely, just for a couple more seconds" Mallory asks the group tentatively.

"Sure Mal, what's up?" Jacob asks.

"I hate to think this way, but I'm afraid we have a leak. Not in this group, but in the larger one, the one with Mom and Dad in it. I hate to think like this, like I said, but every time we tell Dad something, something that only a few of us know, it gets carried to Jane."

"Hey now, you can't say that Dad's the leak, Mal, that's just bullshit and you know it" Devon replies loudly in anger.

"Wait, wait, I knew you were going to take it bad, but honestly Devon, I'm NOT accusing Dad, I'm just saying Dad tells stories, he loves to tell stories. Where do you think he's getting the new stories? Not above ground. Everyone that's listened to him loves his stories. All I'm saying is that he's intermixing facts about now with his stories to freshen them up. He's not doing anything anyone else wouldn't do under the circumstances; I'm saying that some one that listens to his stories is reporting back to Jane, I'm saying we have a leak in the underground."

"You could be right Mal. I've had the feeling for

the past couple of weeks that we've got a leak. I just didn't take enough time to look into it, even though I should have. Now that you mention it, I have heard some of Dad's stories recently and he is adding some modern day into his old stories. Everyone loves them, but I think you just might be right about this. There's only one way to fix this and fortunately it's an easy fix. We just give Dad a tidbit of incorrect information and see how fast it gets to Jane. Then we watch who leaves the underground frequently and who doesn't."

All of a sudden, Jacob's radio crackles to life. "Callander, go."

"It's Mongoose Sir. We have a problem. I've just been contacted by the west underground. They're being slammed with people demanding entrance to the safe areas. The problem is Sir, there's not near enough room. It sounds like anyone living in Texas, Arizona, Utah, the 'Bible belt states' Sir, wants in. I put Captain Hall on hold until I could find you.

"Put him through."

"Captain Hall here, Lieutenant Callander are you there?"

"Yes, I am, what can I do for you?"

"I'm afraid we're going to need some help. I don't have enough manpower to keep the trouble down. I hate saying no to those poor people out there, but I have nowhere near enough room for everyone. What do you recommend, Lieutenant?" asks Captain Hall.

"I can dispatch some of our guys from here, but it will take them a substantial amount of time to get there."

"Let me look into where else we might be able to

send them, luckily there are multiple undergrounds out west. I'll contact them and see where we can send the majority of them, just do the best you can without getting violent. Those poor people are scared, they're just scared. Try to get them to listen to you. If you can restore calmness, then you will have done a great service to them today. I'll get back to you within the hour on how we're going to help, Callander out."

"You heard, what are your opinions? They need help but we can't get there that fast. I know that our militaries going to be pretty swamped for awhile with the bombings, so we might be able to find a pilot and a helicopter to transport some of us out there, but then we're leaving this area open. I think finding alternative housing for them is the best thing to do."

"I know that we have many underground areas in Nevada, they actually dot the desert in numerous locations. We can send them to Area fifty-one, that place has more security than the White House. I have thousands of Military personnel that have abdicated their positions to join our underground. The President has done many things that are wrong; those military that were fighting for our country will no longer be on her side. But Area fifty-one has plenty of room and is a safe harbor in this violent storm. I don't think they're even aware of each other but they surely have room available. They can't be full already."

"I'll see if I know any of the commanders of that area and give them a heads up."

"I agree" says Eli. "We can get some GPS longs and lat's and give them to Captain Hall and have him hand them out. If he gives the public somewhere with directions, they should be happy to head out. I doubt he'll have more problems once he takes care of that. The shelters should be up and running and willing to take people in, that's the whole point behind them to begin with. Once that forward motion is working, it will pick up momentum and word will spread. The people will be happy to have this idea and will probably jump at the chance to get into one of those underground shelters."

"Is everyone else in agreement?" After everyone agrees, "fine, I'll call him back and let him know. Eli, can you get me the directions? I'll send them out there to Hall. I have a feeling that it wouldn't be a good idea for any one of us to leave here right now. I think she's going to be expecting us to drop our guard and then she'll send in the troops. I don't want to take that kind of chance."

"This is Jim Cochran of WELT News Channel 3, Washington D.C. with an update from the President's Office. Here's President Martin:

"Thank you ladies and gentlemen of the United States, for your attention; I've obtained more information regarding this bombing. This is information that will hurt me to tell"

"I've just learned that the bomb that was used in Texas to destroy my church has not only taken out a very dear building but has also wiped out our whole Legislative Branch of Government. Every Senator, Congressman and House of Representative elected official is gone. I've learned that there was a meeting being held at the very church that was destroyed and the whole Legislative Branch was in attendance, a secret meeting similar to the ones held by the patriots of the Pre-Revolutionary war, for example, Adams, Hamilton and Jefferson. They're now all dead."

"It seems that this country is not only at war with the far east, China to be precise, but also that there is discontent within. Obviously, the meeting that was taking place was being held against me, since I wasn't informed about it at all. I can only believe that they didn't want me informed of what they were doing, so they kept me out of the loop. Certainly, if they would have been doing something positive for our United States then they wouldn't have taken the time to attend this secretive meeting and been in the very spot that was bombed. It's seems to be a pretty strange coincidence."

"I find it hard to believe that no one knew about this meeting. How can a group of more than four hundred people plan this meeting without anyone else hearing about it? I've never known a group that large to be able to pull something like this off."

"Be advised, if you are one of the ones that are against your very own President, then you are in danger. I will not tolerate people that are against my position. I can't accept that. The curfew that was instituted a couple of days ago is still in effect. If you are found outside of your home after eight pm, then you'll be arrested and brought up on charges of treason. I can only assume that if you're outside after curfew, then you're doing things against this country and against me and you'll be treated as such. If you know anyone that missed this news briefing, be a good neighbor and let them know the new law. You could very easily save their life. That's all, thank you and goodnight" she says haughtily as she turns and leaves the podium.

"Wow, I feel threatened" says Jim Cochran of WELT News Channel 3, Washington D.C. "That was a very scary thing that she just said to the public. It's a sad day when your very own President feels so let down and disappointed. It's hard to believe anyone could be against her."

"She's never done anything to deserve this. The only thing she's capable of is helping the United States, not hurting it. She's worked hard since she had to assume office, to do everything she could to help this country and its people. And now the people are treating her this way, it's shameless, a huge disappointment in the country."

"I have breaking news coming in from Nevada, a Reverend Michaels is live from somewhere near the Hoover Damn. Here he is"

"Ladies and Gentlemen of the United States, I'm just a simple soul that was asked to deliver an important message from the congregation of 'The People's Church,' the church that was destroyed earlier today by a nuclear war head. I'm standing here surrounded by thousands of people that are dislocated because of the nuclear fallout."

"They need places to live, places to go to stay safe. Although they're standing out here in the sun with a temperature of approximately one hundred and twenty degree's, they refuse to lose hope. They have demanded me to give the President of our Country a message. They want her to know that they are aware of what she has done."

"They all agree that the bombing that occurred in Texas in her church, her family minister's church was done on an order from forces from within."

"They say that this was NOT done by a foreign country, but it was a calculated move by the evil leader of this country. My church and country were destroyed by the President's order. The leaders in this country are evil and are destroying our freedom to worship who we want, how we want. If you follow what I am saying, then get out there and fight. It's the only way that we will ever be able to take our country back."

"If we all fight, then we'll become a force to be reckoned with, united we can stand but divided we will fall."

Chapter Seventeen

"Ahhhhh" Jane screams when she hears what's being broadcast over the television stations. "Shut them down, stop them, they can't get away with this" she yells at the General. "I can't believe the station allowed that to be broadcast."

"Get me their CEO's, I want to talk with them now" she demands, her blood pressure rocketing. "They're going to pay for what they just did. Isn't my job hard enough without rallying the people against me? Who the hell gave them that information? I want whoever told them, I want them dead" she screams in a temper at the General.

"President Martin, please quiet down. We don't need anyone hearing what you're saying right now, it would just reinforce what you've been accused of. Please Madame President, don't give them anything to back them up with. Your whole demeanor should be "I'm so disappointed in this country, how could anyone think me evil. I just don't understand how this all happened, yada yada yada. Never give them what they accuse you of. If you behave the way you normally would, then they would have nothing to fight with. If you give them what you've just been doing, then what they accused you of is all too real and close to home for everyone. They just might start believing instead of taking your side. Understand Jane? For your own benefit, you must portray yourself as the meek and mild tempered friend of the country, as you have been in the past. I understand all about getting angry, but at this time, there's no room for that. Save that for later when you have everything to your satisfaction. Keep the goal in site, Jane. I speak as not only the General but also your friend."

"Thank you Teriq, for grounding me. I have such a terrible temper that sometimes it's impossible to control" she admits in dismay. Tears running down her cheeks, she shakes her head slowly thank you "I did forget for a moment where I am and who I am. I'll try not to let that out anymore. I can't afford having everyone out there against me."

"I'm still going to discuss this with the CEO's of those stations. This cannot be allowed to happen again, it's a disgrace to the country and to me."

"President Martin, I originally came in here to inform you that the planes carrying the requested military back-up from Iran will be arriving shortly. Do you want to greet them?"

"That's not necessary. You're our military leader; you greet them and then send them where you want them. I'm sure you would know that better than I would."

"Actually, I was informed just moments before coming in here of a mass abandonment of our military. It sounds as if the troops have decided to leave your service. Large majorities have left their commands and are headed west. I'm still working on where they're going, but I do know for sure that it's not in your service. It looks like it's for the people of the country, not the President. I've also heard that some are taking over Area fifty-one. They've already started moving into the area and are killing any that disagree with them or pose a threat. Once they establish a safe zone, we'll have trouble getting them out of there."

"Not really, General. We can always take them out with a nuclear war head. That would clean up the area nicely" she adds with a smirk and a strange glow in her eyes.

"We can't bomb every town in every state in this country, President Martin. That would leave you with nothing and no-one to rule. Your whole goal has been as ruler of this country, changing it into the country of your dreams. Those dreams never included this country without people, what good is a country without any people?"

"You're right Teriq. I must be cautious. I can't let the people see or believe that they aren't important to me. Thank you for bringing me back to reality. We need to form a new command to include the troops that were sent over here from the President of Iran. Let's make this a Presidential decision, a Presidential military group that answers only to me, and you, of course Teriq. We can send these troops out to do the necessary things to keep this country safe from the underground military. Let's keep it as a secret group, I don't want the underground to have a clue. We can keep surprise on our side that way."

"Their first job will be to hunt out the underground forces and destroy them. Every one of them" she says in determination. "I'll not share my position with anyone, least of all them. Get them started within the week, please."

"Yes Madame President."

"Lieutenant, we've just received notification that the Islamic Republic of Iran, ground forces, have landed and are being dispersed throughout the city. General Auliya is commanding their officers, but in reality, once they landed they took over. This is a bad sign Sir. What do you want me to tell our guys?"

"Tell them to stay in the shadows and watch what the ground forces are planning. I don't want them to take action until we see what's going to happen."

"Yes Sir."

"Shit, what the hell am I supposed to do with our guys. If the ground forces become aggressive, then we'll have to send out our troops. I don't want to send them out unless I absolutely have to. They're way out numbered. Damn it, she should NEVER have opened our borders to those bastards. Once they get a foothold, they'll take over, they won't care who the President is. Then what's she going to do, after everything that she's done in the past seven almost eight months, no one's going to work for her, she's got no one that's loyal to her anymore" Jacob yells in anger.

"This country's been well guarded for the past two hundred plus years, when we defeated England and took these shores as American shores; we promised everyone and ourselves that no other country shall ever fight on these shores. If we must fight, then it's to their shores we go. We would allow no other military occupation, knowing what would happen if we did. What a freakin stupid bitch she is. I bet she's not going to like what's going to happen.

Actually, I can guarantee you she's not going to like what's about to happen."

"Lieutenant, I just listened in on Jane and the General in her private office. She's making a Presidential group of soldiers known as Muhsin (which happens to be her last name in Arabic) and sending them out with the sole purpose of finding and destroying the undergrounds. They will report only to her and to the General, but to her foremost."

"Now we know what to do with our troops. They'll have to guard the undergrounds and stop her group at all costs. Notify them that I'm going to have a meeting with them to give them their orders. I'll start here and move west, but first I'll notify the officers in charge of the west undergrounds. I'd prefer that I can get them all to give their troops this information. I really don't have time to head west myself."

"Kat, Mallory, you need to get back to your jobs above ground and see how much information you can get from everyone. Just try listening in, having lunch or whatever it takes. Mal, could you finish with the chip stuff. I believe the Presidents going to re-focus on that since that's really going to be her way of keeping track of people and either controlling them or getting rid of them. She'll probably do the chips on all the troops, including the Iranians. It would be the safest thing to do and the easiest way of controlling them."

"I'm going to work out of here and get the troops ready but we're looking at a lengthy process. I'll be available if needed, just radio in" Jacob says.

"Mal lets head out. I want to check a couple of

things, including Des" Kat says. "I'm wondering if Des's fiancé, Patrick, is the leak. He could be underground and above ground and if that's the case, I bet he's listening to Joe's stories and then carrying that info to Des, who happens to be completely brainwashed on how great the President is. If you could plant a bug somewhere in her apartment, we might be able to fix one problem at least. We'll just have to make sure Patrick isn't able to get underground any longer. I'd do it, but I can't go near her. We were partners for close to five years. There's no way she wouldn't recognize me."

"Sure, I can do it. I'll try it today, before I head into the office to work on the chip. There's got to be a way to fix the chip so that it blocks where people are and lies and shows that it's working normally so that people can get food once she institutes the food rule. We don't have much longer before the chips are far enough along to start using them for everything."

"Shit, looks like we're being pulled over. Were you speeding" Mallory asks anxiously.

"Nope, I have no idea why they're pulling me over. Be ready to fight because this doesn't
look good."

"Please step out of the car" the soldier demands after pulling up behind her vehicle, getting out of the car and pulling his weapon out.

"What's the matter, Sir? I wasn't speeding, I know I wasn't so why did you stop me" Kat asks quietly.

"Just get out of the car, Miss. There won't be any trouble if you obey my orders."

"Yes Sir" she says as she gets out slowly, hands in front of her. This soldier can't be older than eighteen if he's that old, Kat thinks.

"Turn around" he demands. Kat complies slowly making no fast moves then feels the cuffs being attached to her wrists. "You're under arrest for possession of cocaine."

"What! There are no drugs in this vehicle or on my person, Sir. You've made a mistake."

"No, I didn't make a mistake. See this" he says as he waves a small bag with a white powdery substance in it. "It was on your seat when you got out of the car. I got a tip that you were transporting drugs and it was right on, this just proves it."

"That wasn't on my seat, you just planted it; you never even looked on my seat."

"I guess it's your word against mine, right. Guess who's gonna be right" he adds mockingly.

"It looks like it will be us, right Soldier" Mallory says, surprising him. "Drop your weapon" she orders having gotten outside of the vehicle without being noticed. "Don't try anything stupid or you'll be dead. Just drop your weapon and everything will be fine."

"I can't do that Miss" he says as he spins around, points his weapon and fires. Kat slams into the back of him to knock him off balance causing his shot to go wide; however Mallory's shot is clean. One bullet and he's gone.

"Kat, are you alright" she yells as she hurries around the back of the car.

"Yeah, I'm okay. Can you get his keys and get these damn cuffs off of me please" Kat questions in anger. "I can't believe this whole thing" she says in anger. "Do you think he really got a tip or just thought that one up on his own" she asks Mallory outraged.

"I don't know" Mallory admits in concern. "If he got a tip, where did it come from and if he did it on his own, then why?"

'Who the hell knows, I hate it when kids get guns. He couldn't have been old enough to get in the service" Kat says in denial. "When you treat kids like they're soldiers and give them a weapon, who knows what they'll do. Shit, let's go before anyone else comes through here. We'll have a hard time explaining this."

"Where do you want me to drop you" Kat asks after they get into D.C. proper.

"Just drop me near Des' apartment and I'll see if I can get a bug in there without getting caught. I'm hoping she's not home right now."

"Okay, then I'll see you later at home."

"Cathy, I need to see you in my office" General Auliya announces when he notices Cathy walking towards her office.

"Yes Sir, what can I do for you" she says as she closes the door. A large office with bright windows, the air on so it's a comfortable temperature.

"Have a seat please" he says as she glances around and finds an empty formal leather chair in front of the large mahogany desk. After taking her seat and crossing her legs she looks up at him calmly and questions "is there a problem Sir?"

"Just a few things that I want you to be aware of,

that's happened today and will most likely continue for days to come."

"Yes Sir" she replies questioningly with raised eyebrows.

"We have initiated the bombing of China due to the nuclear strike that the United States experienced in Texas. That bomb created a huge amount of fallout and killed many of our citizens. It also contaminated a large area that needed to be evacuated. I need you to use your intelligence capabilities and find out if there's any chatter about another weapons strike. I prefer to be prepared this time and not lose so many people. We must protect the public from any more bombs."

"Yes Sir, I'll get right on the chatter and I'll do some investigating myself. I'll have some news for you within the hour."

"Another thing, be careful if you leave this office. We have ground troops from Iran out there that are taking over the jobs that our own troops were doing prior to the bombing in Texas. Once the bombing occurred, I had to pull our troops and send the majority of them to China, to control the country.

"Tens of thousands of people have died in the first four strikes against China, since they took place in their most crowded cities. It looks as if the President of Korea was in China at the time of the attacks and if that's the case, there's no way he survived that attack. We're deploying our troops to Korea right now and will be using it as the staging area for this war. We will not be defeated either in China or in Korea and have planned a minimum of five more strikes.

"There will be many more casualties over there but hopefully the numbers here will stay the same as they are right at the moment. Now, I have a card here that you need to carry with you whenever you leave this office. The Iranian soldiers will honor this card if they stop you, if not, I can't guarantee anything."

"Thank you Sir. I'll start the information digging and will have something to report to you within the hour" Kat assures him as she leaves his office.

"Kat, its Mal" she hears on her radio. "I have a problem."

"This is Kat, go" she says quietly as she walks the deserted hall outside of her office.

"I managed to get the bug into Des' apartment, but now I have one of those Iranian soldiers following me. What do you want me to do?"

"Head into the office and I'll meet you at the door."

"Copy, I'll be there in about seven minutes."

"Copy."

"Can I help you Soldier?" Kat asks when she sees him behind Mal. "No, I want to talk to this person, not to you" he says rudely.

"To bad" Kat says when she notices the weapon that he's holding. "This card should say it all" she says when she takes it out of her pocket and shows it to him.

"Sorry, Miss. I didn't realize you were part of the Generals' own staff. I'll be going now, but I recommend that this lady carry her own so that she isn't stopped by any more of the troops."

"You bet that I'll make sure she carries her own" Kat says sarcastically. "Your job isn't to harass the innocent people of this city, is it? Last I heard, your job was to keep the peace, and this sure isn't how you do it" she says dismissively as they both turn and leave.

"We're going to need to start working for the underground group while we're above ground. I can't just let those ass holes do what they want. Someone's got to make them back off. I'll contact Snake later and inform him of what's happening above ground."

"From now on, we stay together when we leave this building. You go work on the chip and I'll go get some intel for the General. Call me when you're close to being done for the day and I'll wrap up too so we can leave together, we're safer together than apart right now."

"I think I got it" Mallory says when they leave at the end of a long day. "It was a little difficult at first but once I broke the code, it was a lot easier. I actually just signed myself up as one of the programmers. There was a programmer that left last week, suddenly, and she hasn't been signed on since, so I thought I'd just borrow her password and sign on name. As long as no one looks too closely, I won't have any trouble. It even looks like it's coming from her IP address, so if they do figure it out; it will look like it came from her desk. They'll have no one else to go after then" Mal admits with a laugh. "Today was a good day for this" she admits. "Unfortunately, it hasn't been a good day for very many other people."

"Any word from Jacob" Mal asks.

"No, I've been too busy to be able to take the

time to contact him. I'll do that tonight from home. I didn't feel comfortable enough at work today. I felt like I was being watched closely, but I never saw who was doing the watching. It was creepy."

"Watch out Kat" Mal yells when she catches site of a soldier taking his gun out in the shadows near their building.

"I've got him" Kat says as she hits him with a upper cut to the chin, a kick boxing move. "What were you thinking" she demands from him after she gets him in a cuff hold.

"I wasn't thinking, I saw and I wanted so I did" he mutters angrily.

"Look, this isn't Iran, and in this country you treat people with respect. You never freakin touch or take just because you wanted. You want to die? That's what happens in this country to people who see and want and take action. Go the hell back where you came from, we don't need your kind here. You can bet the General will be notified of this behavior, asshole" she says after she shoves him away with disgust. "Just take a seat right there on the ground until someone gets here to take you in to custody."

"Kat, is that you" she hears after a police car rolls up and the officer gets out from behind the drivers wheel. Shit, shit shit Kat thinks after she recognizes the voice. With a quick look at Mal, she slowly turns around and faces her ex-partner.

"Wow" Des says when she looks Kat over. "You've changed your hair and your skin color, wow, you barely look the same. I almost didn't recognize you Lieutenant. Why all the drastic changes" she asks suspiciously.

"I needed a change, Des, no specific reason."

"I'd say you went through quite a change Sir. It seems like quite a lot for just needing a change. It reminds me more of when you went undercover; you used to change a lot for that. Is that what you're doing" she asks as she slowly unsnaps her weapon harness. "Working undercover? If I remember correctly, you were against the President, weren't you" Des says quietly as she draws her weapon and reaches for her radio. "Hold Detective, don't move, now drop your weapon" Kat yells as Mallory draws her weapon and stands ready to shoot.

"Now lay your weapon on the ground in front of you, Detective" Kat yells quickly, trying to keep Des off balance with her voice. As soon as Des drops her weapon, Kat reaches down and picks it up and puts the lock back on. "Now, stand at ease Detective."

"I don't understand, Lieutenant, why did you make me drop my weapon?"

"We seem to be of different viewpoints, Detective. I don't work for the police department any longer. There's been no need with the Military assuming control over all the offices. Why is it that you're still on duty, Detective? Who do you really work for" Kat asks in contempt.

"I work for the police department Sir. The police department is now and always has been loyal to the President. That hasn't changed at all. I've heard what's been going on in the underground, Lieutenant" Des admits in disgust. "You used to be loyal. What happened to you to change you so much? You used to be a good cop, now you seem to be a renegade" she adds in disappointment, striking Kat in the heart with the arrow of her judgment.

"Des, I can't explain to you the whys. You'll just have to judge me the way that you think is best. Just remember, I'm Kat, I haven't changed anymore than you have. Life tends to change us and life has certainly become different then it was a few months ago."

"I'm sorry you feel the way you do, but my conscience is clear. I can and do live with my choices. Can you say the same" Kat demands gruffly. "Take off the rose colored glasses; maybe you'll have a better vision of the truth than you do now. Now, I'm sorry but I have things I need to do. Have a good rest of your life, Des. I wish you only the best." Kat says with dignity and sadness then turns and leaves with Mallory, home bound.

"I'm sorry Kat. She really has no clue as to what's going on. She's blindly following the President, even with everything that's been going on. Some people refuse to really look at the problem. She's obviously been a follower all her life. That makes for a good cop, someone that doesn't ask questions, but follows orders. You're a leader, not a follower, it's what your personality is."

"I know. I just wish she'd listen to me. Something bad is going to happen to her with her following issues."

"We picked up a tail again. The car that's about four car lengths behind us, he's been on us since we left Des."

"Of course he has, let's see if we can lose him. I'm a little tired of fighting my way home every night. It's getting a little annoying."

Chapter Eighteen

"President Martin, the switch board has been lit up with calls for you. Of all the calls that I've taken in the past few minutes, they all seem to be coming from other countries. Not just other countries but the heads of the other countries. I've taken messages from Belgium, Austria, Denmark, Italy and Greece just to name a few. Everyone claims to have an urgent need to talk with you. How do you want me to handle these calls?"

"Start sending them in to me one at a time. For those that have already left messages, I'll start calling them back when I get through with the in-coming calls. Just let them know that I promise to contact them as soon as I'm available."

"This is President Martin, what can I do for you President Greavak?"

"I'm calling to discuss the Chip implementation and how we could see for ourselves the exact workings of this so called chip. We may be interested as a country in trying this out. It sounds like something that would work well for us here in the Czech Republic."

"I would love to show you how this works. I'll start setting up a time and date schedule that will allow me to demonstrate this to you and many others at the same time, since it seems as if at least half the countries of this world are interested. It would be my honor, Sir, to bring you all together and show you what we're talking about. I promise to get back to you within say two weeks, to show this to everyone. Does that sound okay? I'm a little busy right at the moment with China and some other issues that have surfaced recently. I don't see my schedule clearing up until next week at the earliest. But as soon as it does, I'll set it up."

"Thank you Madame President, I appreciate the gesture of goodwill and look forward to witnessing the chip."

"Martha, could you come in here please?" Jane says to her secretary, who comes strolling in, with her hair tucked up into an old person's bun, her dowdy black skirt and white blouse, flat black shoes and small plain glasses. Definitely no movie star here, Jane thinks with a smirk. "Pick a day a month from now and start scheduling all those countries that are calling for a chip demonstration."

"Plan it for Brussels at the European Union headquarters, some time mid week and make sure you keep my schedule clear for the day before and the day after. We'll need James Fahr scheduled to go with me also, so you probably should call him and give him warning. Just tell him that I said that I'd be pretty upset if he couldn't make it, so suggest to him that he do whatever it takes to be there. Now, put through any calls not pertaining to the chip. Any heads of countries that have concerns about anything besides the chip. You will handle the chip from now on until I go and do the demonstration."

"Yes President Martin" she replies quietly as she leaves the Presidential office.

"President Raphael Montegra of the European Union is on the line, President Martin."

"Thank you Martha, put him through please."

"This is President Martin, President Montegra, what can I do for you" she asks in her calmest voice, a smile in place.

"President Martin, thank you for taking my call. I have so much I want to applaud you for. You have handled these trying times in the United States extremely well considering you took office out of necessity. I commend you on how well you're handling everything that's been thrown your way. It's your type of leadership that we at the European Union are looking for. We have a chair open for you and it will remain open until the day that you choose to join us."

"Thank you President Montegra. It's been difficult but I believe that the United States is finally moving into the future with some guidance and determination. This will allow this country to become great again. With the correct leadership, all these things are being made possible. I'm proud to admit that I've been a catalyst, enabling the states to finally move into this great future that they've had the potential of for years. Once we're able to take care of China and stop the bombings we will again be on track.

"It's an unfortunate thing that they chose to attack us. I cannot and will not tolerate another country taking initiative and attacking this country. While I'm in charge, these states will be safe. This is MY country and is under my protection. I will use any and all of our strength to protect what is mine. I want to thank you for the offer of the chair at the European Union, and I feel that in the near future we will be joining the greatest Union the world has ever seen."

"Thank you for your positive remarks. I'm afraid that at this moment the people of the United States are confused from hearing negative things; a problem in which I'm trying to change. With my leadership, they will have excellent health care from our heath care reform and of course the chip. They will not have to support those that choose to enter this country by illegal means. They will only be required to support their own country as is right. They can vote and judge things that never before have they been allowed to do. They get to decide who was right and who was wrong."

"Because of the party reform, they don't have to worry about being on the wrong side during elections. There is only one side. The American Union, which takes the place of the Democratic and Republican sides, which is all that they have ever known. I see a bright future for these United States and I'm glad that you too have noticed the direction that we're heading in. Thank you, President Montegra, your kind words are greatly appreciated especially during these trying times."

That was really nice, Jane thinks as she dials her parent's number for the tenth time today. Where are my parents? I can't keep calling and getting no answer. I need to send someone out west to look for them.

"Martha, get me the General please."

"President Martin, this is General Auliya, what

can I do for you" he asks politely.

"Teriq, I still haven't been able to reach my parents. I want you to send a detail of our special forces out west to their home town, find them and bring them to me. I haven't heard from them since the bomb destroyed my church. I need to know that they're all right."

"I'll dispatch a group right away. Don't worry Jane, we'll find your parents. I'm sure it's a phone problem, nothing more" he says to reassure her, hearing the panic in her voice.

"Thank you Teriq" she says with a big sigh of relief. "It's so good to have someone that cares about me and my family on my side. It's not so hard and lonely that way" she admits shamefully. "Before you go, Teriq, what's the word on China? How's our bombing going?"

"It's going according to plan. We have successfully destroyed sixty percent of China and the last body count we had, over twenty-two million people had perished. China wants to talk, so I thought I'd let you know that. I was getting ready to call you when you called me."

"The new president of China wants to talk with you. I think he's hoping to stop any more destruction. He was in the mountains when the bombing started so wasn't affected at first. Now however, it's a different story. I believe he was the next in line to the Presidency; the original President was killed in the first wave of bombs. The country's unstable now; most of the leaders were killed. This is the new regime that I've been in contact with and they want to do whatever it is that you want, to stop anymore destruction. They're afraid that if we continue bombing them, the world will lose the Chinese race."

"What do you think Teriq? Have we destroyed all that's needed, is there anything left that can point the finger at us?"

"I don't believe there would be any way to prove that we caused the bombing in Texas. That secret's safe with us now, Jane."

"Thank you Teriq, that's what I wanted to know. Take this as orders from me. We'll stop the bombing, but if there's any type of retaliatory war we will finish destroying them."

"As you wish, President Martin."

"Son of a bitch" yells Jacob when he listens to this recording. "We knew she was bad but this, this is beyond bad. Who or should I say what the hell is she? How could she bomb her own church? She had to know that the entire legislative branch was meeting there. I'm sure that's why she bombed them. She won't tolerate anyone threatening her position and they did threaten her. They were tired of her orders and they knew she wasn't treating the citizens of this country fairly. The laws that she's instituted are wrong; they're corrupt and the chip, that's a whole different story but you can bet that it's definitely wrong. Mal said the chips were capable of being programmed remotely and that she could kill anyone she wanted at the push of a button. I'm sorry but I believe we're looking at the face of evil in its purest form."

"How's it going out west with her parents? I know that Captain Hall's group took them from their home and have stashed them underground, just in case we might need some leverage. That was a brilliant idea, Devon."

"Were there any witnesses to their abduction? Should I send more people out that way? It sounds like they're dispatching their new soldiers, the group that works directly for her. If they're any good, which I'm sure they are, they'll pose a challenge. I wish I could be out there but I can't leave right now, there's too much going on here."

"I think Captain Hall's got it handled, but I'll get in touch with him to give him a heads up and I'll ask him if he needs help. I'll let you know as soon as I get word."

"Good deal, thanks Devon."

"Has anyone heard from Kat or Mal in the past twenty four hours? It seems like a long time since they've checked in. We have the Iranian soldiers out there and that's a threat to any woman. Not necessarily for rape, sure, that's always going to be an issue, but mostly because they aren't submissive. It's so hard to believe that there are still people out there in this modern world that expect women to be submissive. They sure won't find that quality in either Kat or Mal" Devon adds with a laugh.

"Actually, they didn't check in yesterday but I assumed that you'd talked with them. If not, maybe we better start looking for them" Eli recommends worriedly.

"Yeah, we better start looking. I never heard from either one yesterday. Damn it, I hope they're all right."

"Mal are your okay" Kat asks in a whisper. "I think they're gone for now. Those bastards, they aren't taking either of us in for anything. We need to figure out how to get out of this. I'm sorry I got us in it" Kat says in disgust.

"You couldn't know that they'd be so close. I didn't know, either. I could have been the one that caused this just as easily" Mal says quietly.

"We'll get out of here soon, I promise" Kat whispers as she peers into the blackness of the room they've been hiding in for the past eighteen hours, black and airless. Talk about suffocating darkness. I guess this is it.

"I had to take out those bastards. They were going to kill that whole family all because they were women without a man in the house. I didn't see them until I'd already pulled the trigger."

"Shhh, I heard something, they're coming back" Mal says quietly but urgently.

"I told you there was no one in here" a black clad soldier remarks harshly. "You're wasting our time; you keep bringing us back to the same places when there's obviously nothing here." "But I could have sworn I heard something, Sir" replies a young man in the same black garb. "This is your last chance, the next time you lead us all on a wild goose chase will be your last time. I'm out of patience with you. Let's head out now. You better pray to Allah that you find those two before the President hears that we lost them."

"I think they all left" Mal whispers to Kat and then jumps back when the door that's separating them from the main room is thrown open, a black figure standing there looking at them with night vision goggles on.

"I knew you were here, I just couldn't figure out where" says a young Iranian soldier. "My commander will be pleased with me now" he says threateningly. "Out, get out of this room" he says waving an automatic weapon at them to exit the room. The sound of a weapon being thrown precedes their exit by a second, the young soldier dropping to the ground almost silently.

"Kitten, are you all right?" Snake asks when he quietly walks over to her.

"Yeah, we're fine, it's about time you got here, though" she teases with a grin.

"First I had to find you. Only after we all realized that neither of you had checked in for a day and a half. We need to come up with a better way. I'll think on that problem while we head back to the bunker."

"We can't go to the bunker with you Snake; we have things we need to finish up here" Kat replies in denial.

"How long will it take to finish up whatever it is that you're working on" he demands. "It's getting too dangerous for you to remain above ground for very much longer."

"I'm almost finished with the chip, I just have maybe a couple of days left" Mal admits. "I'm sorry, but I've had to change layers of security to get to the point that I'm at now. I have to finish this or we won't be any better off than we were."

"How much longer Mal" Devon asks when he over hears his sister.

"If I could have a full ten hours, I might be able to finish it" she admits slowly. "We've been under some intense scrutiny at the office lately. I think there are quite a few people that are suspicious of us; it's taken me longer because of that. I've had to work fast but briefly so that no one notices my work. When we go home at night, we have to go together, alone is just too dangerous. Then we've been spending the after dark hours, trying to help the people. Those damn soldiers from Iran are definitely causing problems by attacking people for no reason. Just wait until they start choosing their victims because of religion. I can admit though, I sure have been thankful for Kat's sniper abilities."

"It's been a little crazy in the bunker, too. That's why it took so long to realize that we hadn't heard from either of you. I've been working with our underground forces to prepare them for the war that's about to start. Jane wants the underground in the worst way, so she's declared us outlaws; which we technically are" Jacob admits with a smirk.

"As soon as they institute the chip for food rule, we're going to have problems. We have the underground sources, but with the way that the underground's growing, we can't keep up with the demand for food. We'll have to come up here for supplies. Sure, we've got some underground people living up here with chips, but not enough to justify the amount of food they'll need to purchase. With the chips tracking capabilities, everyone will be watched."

"Yeah, I know, that's the part of the chip I've been working on. It's for the one's that live above ground but belong to the underground. I'm trying to make the chip capable of being used without registering the use on some of them" Mallory reminds them.

"Since we found you and you seem to be alright, we need to hit the road. We have to get back to base, finish preparing for the takeover and contact the west underground. If you two can get back to your apartment, we'll take off" Jacob says.

"We're fine" Kat assures them.

"Oh, here's a bag with some items in it for you. I prefer to know where you are at all times, that way if something happens we won't need to search for you again. I hate wasting time if I don't need to. These are some personal GPS units and a couple of receiving/sending chips. If you can think of anything else that might be helpful, just let me know and I'll see what I can do."

"Thanks Jacob" Mallory murmurs with a tearful smile and a hug. "Thanks for not forgetting about us."

"Of course I didn't forget about you, you're my sister" he adds with a hug back. "This will all be over soon and then we can get on with our lives again. Hopefully be normal again. It can't go on like this forever. We won't let it" he promises with determination as he grabs Kat and hugs her tightly.

"Keep in contact with us please and put on your GPS units. Find somewhere to hide them that won't be easy to find. They're small enough that they won't be picked up by the normal security check point equipment and they should blend in easily. Take care of each other" he adds as they walk out the door into darkness.

"Alright, let's see if we can get out of here without anyone seeing us" Kat says when they're alone again. "Hopefully we won't come across anymore of the troops. I'm tired and don't want to have to deal with them."

Chapter Nineteen

"Martha, get me the General" Jane demands after touching the intercom button.

"Yes Madame President, right away."

"President Martin, General Auliya's on the line for you."

"Thank you Martha. General, what have you heard from my parents. Have you found them yet?"

"The troops searched the area surrounding the spot that your church was in and found nothing. They should be arriving at their home any moment. As soon as I receive word on what they find, I'll contact you Jane, you have my word."

"Thank you Teriq, at least you understand why I'm so upset."

"President Martin, I have the President of Iran on the line for you."

"Put him through, Martha."

"President Majeed, what can I do for you?"

"President Martin, it is good to speak with you" he says in his stilted formal English. "I was wondering if you were experiencing any problems with the troops that I sent to your aid."

"Actually, I was going to contact you. So far, they have not done anything that any other army would not have done, but I would like to offer them something that will place them into the future with the United States. I would like to offer them the newly created chip, similar to the one that we are using on the citizens of this country, yet different because these were made for your country. This will advance them ahead of your country's date for the chip but it will also allow us to make sure that they are functioning correctly. It will not harm them, but will allow us time to make any adjustments to them that we observe they need to function perfect. I would not want to place poor quality chips into your citizens, so with your permission I would like to test them on these troops. Do you have any problem with this, President Majeed?"

"No problem at all, President Martin. I am honored that my country will be the next to receive these invaluable chips."

"I have another call President Majeed. Is there anything else I can do for you" Jane asks hurriedly.

"No that was all, thank you for your time President Martin."

"President Martin, I have General Auliya on the line, he said it was urgent."

"Put him through Martha, thank you."

"Jane, its Teriq, I have some bad news. I'm sorry to report this to you but after a careful search of your parent's home I must come to the conclusion that they were at the church at the time of the bombing. I'm so sorry Jane. There is no way that they could have survived that as no one else did."

"No, Teriq, please tell me that's not true. They can't be gone, they're my parents, they wouldn't have been at the church at that time, please tell me that it's not true" she cries, devastation on her face.

"I'm so very sorry Jane, so very sorry."

"No, I will not believe that they're gone. They have to be alive; they must witness what was sacrificed for, how everything they worked so hard for is coming true. They must see this; it's what they lived for."

"I know Jane. There's no evidence that they have been here since the explosion. There is no sign of them having returned here from wherever they were. The only place they ever went was to that church, they worked there preparing the way for you. I'm sorry, their house was deserted; no sign of life since the explosion."

"That doesn't mean that they are dead. Maybe they just went out of town or something; it doesn't mean they were at the church. I will never believe that they are gone until I can see their bodies for myself. As far as I'm concerned they live, just somewhere else."

"If that is what you want to believe then by all means do so, you are the President of the United States" General Auliya remarks, saddened by the events that led up to this information.

"That's right, I am" she adds in wonder and with determination. "Thank you Teriq, for reminding me. Now, I have much to do today but please continue on with the investigation into my parent's disappearance."

"Absolutely Jane, it is my honor to help you in any way."

"Before we hang up, tell me your preparations for surprising the underground. I've had about all I'm going to take with them and their skirmishes, the unfounded attack on my soldiers. I'm ready to begin the cleansing of the underground. Tell me you're ready."

"I am close Jane. I await a few more troops in the west areas. They should arrive within the next few days. After that we can begin the cleansing. The special bombs that you had made were brilliant. Look alike smoke bombs with Ricin instead smoke. I think they'll work perfectly. Not only will people run, but they won't survive. You are brilliant President Martin, brilliant."

"Thank you General Auliya, thank you" she's says with a spark in her eyes and a big smile on her face. "I believe before we move ahead with this attack that I need to talk with the American public. I want to let them know what's been happening to the citizens of the U.S. and also what terrible things the underground has been responsible for. They will be informed before this begins so that I am not cast in a negative light to them. They will all follow me; I'm the one protecting them from their own. I'll schedule a media release for tomorrow evening. That way the soldiers that haven't arrived out west yet will have had time to do so. We can plan on the attack beginning out west the day after the media release. I'm just thankful that the underground doesn't have the capability to watch the media releases" she adds with a chuckle. "What they don't know can hurt them" she adds in delight.

"I will await your orders President Martin. This will begin on your order" he says as he hangs up shaking his head and grinning like a fool. She is way too much fun to work with he thinks as he prepares to head out and check on his troops.

Chapter Twenty

"Last night went well" Kat murmurs to Mal as they join the group at the door waiting to get through security so they can start their day.

"Yeah" Mal replies quietly "but I'm tired today. I need to get more rest at night; working on these programs is taking everything I've got. I'm almost there now, so maybe by the end of the week, we can finish up. I'd really like to see Rand soon, I miss that guy" she admits wistfully.

"I understand" Kat says ruefully "I kinda miss Snake, too" she admits.

"I'll talk to you later. From what I've heard through the grapevine, the President's giving a media release tonight and I don't want to miss that."

"Yeah, me either" Mallory says with apprehension. "You never know what she's going to throw at you next, so let's meet up here at six tonight and we can head home together."

"Deal" Kat says as she leaves the security area and gets lost in the crowd headed for the elevators.

"This is Jim Cochran of WELT News Channel 3, Washington D.C. with an update from the President's Office. President Martin is about to speak to the American public live. Here she is:"

"Thank you ladies and gentlemen of America, I have some important information that I wanted to give you personally. I would never want one of my citizens to ever be able to say that I have not taken every care in making sure that the American people have all the information they need to make sound judgment calls."

"It is with great difficulty that I inform you of the terrible things that our brothers and sisters of this country are doing, the ones that decided to go underground so they would not be a part of everything that has been happening. They have gone a step further away this past week, they are now attacking the military, the very ones that are out there trying to help our citizens."

"We've had hundreds of troops perish at the hands of those from the underground, all because they do not want the help. I can't allow this to continue any longer. These troops are under our protection, they should be able to do their jobs without fear of death looming over them."

"I'm sorry to inform you of these terrible things, but I need your help. How should we protect the ones that are trying to protect us? You, the American public have the authority to make this decision. I will put this on the web site for your vote. Please, take the time to go there and tell me how you want to move forward with this matter."

"As soon as I know your decision, I will begin it. Thank you for your time this evening and I look forward to seeing your decision. I will be back tomorrow night with the decision, so until then, good night" she says quietly, with a gentle smile before she turns and walks slowly down the hall.

"Teriq it's me, Jane. I just finished the announcement to the public and wanted to let you know that tomorrow night after I inform the people of their decision, you may begin the cleansing of the underground."

"Excellent Jane, I've got my troops close to being in place, we'll be ready by tomorrow night. It'll start as a wave with the first round beginning in the west; Nevada to be precise. I also left troops here so that we can hit both ends of the underground at the same time. Some of the troops will be waiting near the underground entrances for escapees; they'll be taken out then and there. This should work beautifully, Jane."

"Thanks Teriq. I appreciate your loyalty to me and to this country. Once we take care of those underground trouble makers things should start moving smoothly and I can move ahead with my plans, the plans to move this country into my future for them. It's nice to watch things take shape the way they were planned. Now, I have another question, any word about my parents yet? I know that I just spoke with you yesterday about this but time seems to be dragging while my parents are missing."

"No, I'm sorry Jane. We still have had no word but I promise that as soon as I hear anything, anything at all, I'll contact you. They too are on my mind constantly."

"We need to contact them NOW" Kat says in a panic. "Who knows what she's got up her sleeve, but you know it isn't nice. She's planning something. I just hope that the underground's already aware of what."

"I tried to call Jacob earlier but I got no answer so they're probably already working on a solution to whatever problem she's planning for them" Mal admits worriedly.

"Let's use our sending chips and see if we can get a response from them" Kat decides. "Let me do it from the bedroom, but we need to check for anything planted here first, or we could walk somewhere and do it from the outside. That way we won't have to worry about someone intercepting it."

"Yeah, I like that idea better, but we're still going to have to check our apartment out, I hate people listening in on my every word. I just can't relax that way and I really need to relax."

"Alright then, let's change and get ready to go outside. We might as well take care of some of the troops while we're at it."

"Snake, come in, please come in" Kat demands. "I'm not getting any return reply, and I've been trying to get a reply for the past three hours. They either can't hear me or they're so busy that they can't reply."

"I hope it's because they're busy. Do you think we should head over that way" Mal asks quietly.

"No, we don't dare head over to the underground; I don't want to be responsible for the troops following us and finding the actual entrance" Kat replies.

"I guess were done then. We've tried multiple times to reach them and nothing. I'm sure they'll contact us as soon as they can. Let's go home. I need some sleep. I'm hoping to finish up the chip by this weekend. Maybe then we can go home" Mal says hopefully.

"Get general Auliya on the line for me please, Martha."

"Right away, President Martin." After a short wait, Martha buzzes with "The General is on line two President Martin."

"Thank you Martha."

" Teriq, thank you for getting back to me so fast, I have the information that you requested. The vote is in and the people want you to put a stop to the underground. They believe that the underground is not conforming to the new laws. They want them gone for the good of all."

"Yes President Martin, I will begin the underground cleansing."

"Thank you Teriq, please keep me informed of your progress."

"Absolutely President Martin, you'll be the first to hear how things are going."

"President Martin, the phone lines have lit up" Martha says. The media are on three lines and some private callers on the others. What do you want me to do?"

"Send me one of the Media and I'll talk to them. We'll go from there. Just tell them that I'll be with them each as soon as possible."

"This is President Martin, how can I help you?"

"President Martin, this is Jim Cochran, WELT News Channel 3, Washington. I've just received word from a co-anchorman in Nevada. There are bombings occurring in the dessert with portions of the ground disappearing. Is this what's happening to the underground? Are we responsible for this latest problem? Is this what the vote last evening accomplished? I don't believe that this is what the public had in mind when they voted about the underground. The people would never have voted if they knew that you were going to kill everyone in the underground."

"Jim, Jim, hold on a second. I would never ask anyone to kill people. As far as I'm concerned they were stupid people, not reason enough to commit what you're accusing me of. I have not heard about any bombing, but I promise you that I'll get the General on the line and see what the hell's happening out west. I promise to get back to you as soon as I know what's what."

"Thank you President Martin, I appreciate it. I'll be waiting for your call."

"General Auliya, I'm getting complaints. I thought you were going to handle this quietly, not with the big explosions that are occurring."

"President Martin, we can't do as you've asked without making some noise. There will always be some way to tell but we were hoping that since it's out in the middle of nowhere, we would have more time before the public was made aware of what's happening. By that time we would have had a plausible explanation for what they heard."

"Damn it Teriq, how am I supposed to clean this up. I'll have to have a media release for the public and now I won't be able to wait. You give me something to take to them" Jane demands angrily.

"Fine, just inform the public that it was the military that was being fired upon, not the other way around. We fired back of course, but had not planned on this happening. We were just going to start grabbing the people of the underground as they left for food or whatever. We had not planned on hurting anyone."

"Excellent Teriq, I'll pass that word on. Now, finish this without so much attention if you will. I don't want to spend so much time explaining to the public. I want them willing to follow me, not fight me and if they think that I was responsible for this it will damage my reputation. I can't afford that. Too many things are resting on this cleansing."

"Martha, get me Jim Cochran, WELT News Channel 3, Washington on the line. I need to pass some information to him."

"Yes President Martin, right away."

"Jim Cochran here President Martin, how can I help you?

"I got the information you asked for Jim and I wanted to be sure that you were the second to receive it. The General has assured me that we did not start the problem. They were fired upon by the underground. What you heard about was retaliatory; the troops were just trying to protect themselves. They went out to escort the underground public and were attacked. They didn't bomb the underground on purpose."

"That's a relief President Martin. I'll be sure to pass that information on to the public. Are you scheduling a media release in the near future? If so, I'll try to hold off so that you'll be the informer for the public. The people love you enough that they will gladly wait for your word."

"I have scheduled a time today for a media release. It's scheduled for five p.m. I was trying to wait until most people are home from work before I gave the information. That way, I can cover more area."

"Excellent President Martin, thank you and I'll wait for the release since it's now near three-thirty anyway."

"Good evening ladies and gentlemen. I'm here this evening to inform you of what has been happening to the underground in Nevada. Earlier today there was a bombing. It was not planned but it was a reaction of the troops after being attacked. They were attacked by the underground shortly after zero-eight hundred this morning. They had arrived at the entrance to the underground and were in preparation of arresting those that exited the underground for one reason or another. Before they had the opportunity to begin to detain those that exited the facility the underground attacked them. There were many injuries and a few fatalities among our troops. Due to the way they were attacked, the troops fought back and in so doing they ended up destroying quite a large area of the underground. I don't have a list yet of the number of causalities there were, but I'm sure that it was heavy. As soon as I get that report, I'll be sure to pass the information on to you. I'm disappointed that you immediately thought that I would command something like that. I thought our relationship was more open then that" she remarks with a quivering voice and tears in her eyes.

"You know that you come first with me; that each and every one of you is important to me, including those that went underground. I didn't want them hurt, but detained so that I could hear for myself why they chose the underground over living in this beautiful land. Surely I have done nothing to warrant this type of anger. I promise you, the great citizen's of this country, that I do nothing without informing you first and usually asking you by vote. Don't you think it's time that you stood up for me? Stood up for what is right. Have I not done everything to help you, to make your life easier? Why are you treating me this way?" she quivers quietly in hurt.

"Oh my god" Kat exclaims in disgust. "She'll have the people believing everything she says. This is going to make our life unbelievably difficult. You can't fight an innocent, like she's portraying" she adds angrily.

"Talk about not fighting fair" Mal says turning away from the TV. "Now what are we going to do" she demands of Kat. "We still haven't heard anything from Jacob or Devon, really from no one in the underground. What the heck is happening that wouldn't allow them to contact us" she says fearfully, all manner of things running through her head.

"I'm sure they're just busy, maybe with the west end underground. There's been a lot of bad things happening out in Nevada, so who knows. You know

Snake takes his position seriously. Especially when someone needs help and from what Jane just said, they need a lot of help."

"I'm almost finished with the chip, so maybe this weekend we could go and see what the problems been?" Mal asks hopefully.

"Yep, that's the plan. We promised to get the chip done and then we could go home so let's work on that."

"There's going to be another media briefing this afternoon" Kat tells Mallory. "We need to hear what's going on, so let's meet for a late lunch and we can find somewhere to listen to what the news is" Kat says excitedly.

"Sounds good to me; if everything stays on schedule for me, I should be done around that time. Maybe we can take off and go home, finally" Mal says hopefully.

"Let's make that the plan then. It's only a couple of hours, so get finished Mal and we can go home to our guys."

"Yippee" Mal adds quietly but with eyes glowing.

"You need to get the hell out of here, right now" Jacob yells at the underground people still wandering around. "I told you people what they used in the west. We can't take a chance that they're not going to attempt the same thing here, so get out. Use the side entrances. I doubt they even know about them."

"But Jacob, we don't want to leave. This is our home now, son."

"Dad, this will only be home for the dead soon,

do you want to be a part of that? Home is no place if you're dead."

"Fine, your Mother and I will leave, right now."

"Thanks Dad; thanks. You have no idea how that makes me feel. Be safe out there, and I promise to find you as soon as possible. I'll find somewhere that we can all stay safely but until then try to get lost in the crowds. You'll be safer in a crowd then alone. Try to make yourselves look a little different too, anything that will help you survive this attack. It's all only temporary."

"Lieutenant Callander, we're being attacked at our doors. Anyone that leaves through the front or back of the underground is either being shot at or grabbed and arrested. What do you want me to do" Rand asks.

"Shit, I knew we didn't have much time but I sure didn't expect them to be that fast. Gather any snipers that are left and let's see if we can make it a little safer for us. Maybe we can get the majority of people out if we give them some sniper fire."

"Has anyone heard anything from the west? How many died in that explosion? Has anyone been able to contact Captain Hall?"

"No sir, there hasn't been any answer to any of our calls. No radio response either" affirms Rand.

"That's what I was afraid of" Jacob admits discouraged.

"I've got a call coming through right now, Sir. Yes, I understand, that is not good news Sir" Rand remarks before hanging up, "thank you, be safe out there soldier."

"Now what" Jacob growls.

"I was just informed that the bombs that were used on the underground out west were more than smoke bombs, Sir. They were chemical bombs."

"Shit" Jacob yells in anger. "What the hell did they have in them?"

"They were loaded with Ricin. Anyone that was underground at the time of the explosions is dead. They never stood a chance" Rand exclaims in anger. "We now know just how far this President will go to win. This is valuable information. Pass it on to anyone still underground. They need to look more closely at leaving as soon as possible. I don't want any deaths on our hands because I didn't force people to leave."

"Hold on" Jacob mutters as he answers his radio.

"Sir, we're taking heavy fire, as soon as we show ourselves we're being shot at. What do you want me to do?"

"On our way" he says as he barks out orders to follow him and bring your guns. "We have work to do." While running down the tunnel he starts explaining what the call was about. "Anyone exiting the underground is being shot at as soon as they show their face. We need to get rid of some of those snipers, it's the only way we can help these people now. When we get to the exit, I want everyone here to shoot their way out so that we can start picking the troops off. Make sure someone down here is informed about what's happening, about the bombs from out west and what everyone needs to do to keep safe. We can't leave anyone down here, they'll just die from the Ricin and that's not a pretty way to go. No exceptions!"

"Yes Sir" replies a young guardsman that joined them on their run.

"I'll stay Sir, and make sure that everyone's out."

"Thanks Soldier, I appreciate your help. On three" Jacob says "one, two and Go . . . GO . . . blinding light meets him and heat that makes it hard to breath as he barrels out the exit, firing as he goes. After a heavy firefight lasting about twenty minutes Jacob notices the quiet. *Maybe we won this round*, he thinks just as he hears a scream and a gurgle. "Now what" he growls between his teeth, anger forcing him quickly to the area he heard the scream in.

"You bastard" he yells when he rounds the corner and finds a soldier raping a child. After reaching the soldier and yanking him off of a boy of about eight, he throws the soldier to the ground, aims his weapon, waits for the soldier to start begging then shoots him in the groin. After the soldier stops screaming, he leaves him with a message. "Looks like you won't be raping anyone again, ever. You should feel lucky, at least I didn't kill you, even though it probably would have been doing the world a favor if I had" he adds in total disgust and then joins his Sergeant and the eight year old to see how he's holding up.

"How is he Sergeant?

"He'll be okay, but it's going to take a while to overcome this, if ever" Rand mutters in pity while trying to calm the child.

"This is what happens when you invite other countries soldier's in. Corruption and evil, they don't care, they don't live here" he grounds out, loathing for the world heavy on his shoulders, pity in his eyes.

"Let's head back to the underground entrance and see if everyone's gotten out" he suggests as he heads off towards the east, the injured soldier crawling away looking for safety.

"What's going on here" he asks when they reach the east end exit for the underground and he finds hundreds of people milling around. "We think everyone got out safely but we haven't been able to locate everyone. Some of the underground went out the other exits, I'm sure" Rand says.

"Who's missing?" Jacob demands.

"Well Sir, I haven't seen your parents yet. I did see Eli a few minutes ago and Devon came out when I did. They were packing a few things up when we came out. Neither one of us thought anything of it. They were getting ready to exit though when we left. I'm sure they came out a different exit and that's why we haven't seen them yet."

"Damn it" Jacob yells at Rand. "I gave you an order, Sergeant. I told you to get my parents out."

"Yes Sir, I know Sir, but like I said, they promised they were coming."

" I'm sure they did, I just don't know where they came out at. Devon's searching for them at the south side exit and Eli took off for the North exit. I've asked everyone here if anyone's seen them and no one has admitted to it."

"Get a hold of Devon and see if he's had any luck" Jacob orders worriedly, thinking where the hell could they have gone?

"Devon, come in" Rand says into his radio.

"Lieutenant Calendar wants to know if you've had any luck locating your parents. Yes, I got it, thanks Devon."

"I just spoke with Devon sir, no sign of them yet. He's questioned everyone out there and no one has seen them."

"More bad news Sir. The Iranian troops have managed to bomb the north end of the underground. Looks like the same type of bomb that was used out west. There's still no sign of your parents either."

"How many people are estimated at being in the underground when the bombs were tossed in?"

"We are unsure at this time, Lieutenant. I sent a couple of troops on the hunt for some Bio/Chem suits with respirators. Once we get them, we can send a couple of our guys into the underground and do a head count, maybe even identification for family members that made it out. It'll be a long shot, but at least we can see firsthand and who knows, your parents could show up at any time."

"Thanks Rand, I appreciate it. I'm sure they made it out, it's the only acceptable alternative" Jacob murmurs, a sick feeling in his gut.

"Snake" Kat yells when she catches sight of him. "I've been looking everywhere for you. Do you know how scattered everything is. It took me five hours to find you" she says as she grabs and hugs him in relief.

"Yeah, you have definitely not been an easy one to find" Mal agrees.

"We had to fight our way here, those damn Iranian troops, and sifting through everyone wandering around took forever. I didn't realize there were so many people in the underground. It had to have been thousands and that was just at this exit. If I would have had to go to the other exits, I'm sure it would have taken me days" Kat informs him.

"I'll take that as good news," Snake murmurs to Kat.

"Good news, why" asks Kat outraged. "I wander for hours and you say that's good news?"

"Yeah, it's good news. My parents are missing, so I'm going to believe it's because there're so many people wandering around that we just haven't found them yet."

"Oh no" Mallory cries at the news. "They got out right? They left the underground, right?"

"We can't be sure" Jacob replies "but since it took you two so long to find me I hope that's why we haven't found them yet."

"I'm sure that's why" Kat says reassuringly. "It has to be why."

"Actually it doesn't, but I prefer to think that way. Let's start the search here and we'll ask everyone. Don't leave anyone out. We'll find them. Devon's at the south end exit looking and Eli's at the north exit which is the exit that was bombed just a few minutes ago with the same type of bomb used out west, Ricin."

"Oh no" Mallory moans in anguish. "Please tell me they got out before the bomb. Please tell me" she sobs as Jacob grabs her and holds on until she gains control of her emotions.

"We're working on some bio suits with respirators so that a couple of the troops can go in to search for any possible survivors, but with Ricin, that's not usually probable."

"Eli, what about Eli? You said he was at the exit that was just bombed. Is he alright?" Mal demands of

Jacob.

"I believe so, but let me have Rand contact him."

"Sergeant, contact Eli please, at the west end exit. He was nearby when they bombed that area."

"I'm on it Lieutenant. Eli, come in, Eli come in" Rand keeps repeating.

Chapter Twenty-One

"Jane, it's started, the first bombing was successful and as of right now there is no count yet on how many deaths have occurred here in this underground. The ones that got out are wandering around the area no longer able to go to the underground. There are thousands of people displaced. Now they'll either have to go home or sleep on the streets. If they stay on the streets, we'll arrest them, so my guess is, they'll go home. Once home, they'll have to receive the chip and once that happens, they're all yours" General Auliya informs the President.

"Excellent Teriq, thank you. This is just what I needed to hear right now. It helps me to forget that my parents are still missing."

"I'm sorry Jane. I haven't forgotten that your parents are missing. Maybe now we'll be able to find them for you."

"Thanks Teriq, I appreciate your dedication to me and mine. If anyone can find them I'm sure it's you" Jane says quietly with confidence and hope, a rare smile lighting her face.

"I know that you've been busy Teriq, but how is the chip implantation coming. Have you heard from anyone about this?"

"Actually I have, Jane. It looks like we're close to twenty-two percent completed which is a lot higher than we had originally anticipated. It's coming together well, you should have no worries on that front."

"Excellent Teriq, thank you, I knew I could depend on you. Maybe it's time to prepare for the Middle East conference. There are a few countries that are opposed to the chip that I must recruit. We must have everyone on board for this Chip, without that I will not be successful and that is not an option. I must succeed. I want to be able to show my parents, when we do find them, that I have done everything that they planned and sacrificed for. There is no room for disappoint for them. I just wish I knew where they were."

"Soon Jane, soon we'll find them and when we do I will personally bring them to you" the General promises fervently.

"Thank you Teriq. Now I'll schedule a media release for this evening to inform the public of exactly what's happened. I promised to keep them informed and I am determined to keep my promise in this instance."

"Good evening, I'm Jim Cochran with WELT News Channel 3, Washington. The President has requested this news conference so that she can inform her people of what's been taking place this afternoon in the area around the underground. She wanted to inform you herself of exactly what has transpired. Here she is now"

"Thank you, ladies and gentlemen of these great United States. An exciting thing has occurred today in our beautiful city. We have managed to force the people living in the underground, the ones that have caused untold trouble to us, to leave their safe haven and come above ground to live with the rest of us. We managed to accomplish that before we used weapons that would force their hands. I'm happy to say that approximately seventy-five percent of the people that were living underground are now above ground, mostly back in the homes that they ran away from. I believe once they realize what is truly happening they will be grateful for their lives and for the chance to live as the rest of you have chosen."

"Unfortunately, these are trying times and in order to enable our military in the help of our citizens, sometimes bad things happen. Today, we had to use a measure that I had hoped never to have to use. Unfortunately, those that were left in the underground chose to side against this country, which is an act of treason and because of that we had to use a few bombs that destroyed the underground and a few of those that had refused to leave. This was an unfortunate thing. I, in no way, have ever wanted to harm anyone. But because of the danger that they posed for the rest of us, this had to be done."

"I do not at this time, have the exact number of those that didn't survive, but I promise you that when I do, you will be notified."

"Now on to more light hearted things. I have just completed the schedule for the world's first Peace in the Middle East conference that is to be held one month from today. On the fourth Thursday of next month I shall be attending a conference that will hopefully change the course of the world. I do this with gladness in my heart and a smile of anticipation, for once we can achieve peace the world will be held together with love instead of hate. We can all benefit. …..Ahhhhhhhh……"

"This is Jim Cochran, WELT News Channel 3 Washington. It appears that the President just came under fire. I heard something, a slight popping noise and then the President screamed and I saw her start to fall before we were cut off from the live video feed. As soon as they can re-connect us to the video we'll have the information for you. Who in their right mind would shoot the President? This is unbelievable" Jim explains loudly with shock in his voice and on his face.

"I think the video feed is ready now, let's go back to the White House and the live media release that was occurring from the President. It's General Auliya standing at the podium not the President. Let's see what he has to say about what just happened there."

"Ladies and gentleman of the United States, I'm sorry to report this but the President of the United States has been shot. She's alive at this time and has been taken to the nearest medical facility for treatment. I'm going to find out exactly how serious this is and as soon as I do, you'll be notified. It looked like it was a sniper shot from a very long distance, possibly someone from the underground that's not happy with what occurred earlier. I will apprehend whoever did this and they will pay, I promise you" he finishes and rushes out of range of the podium, swarmed by dozens of military personnel.

"That was brief" Jim informs his audience. "A little unusual considering what just happened but at least he took the time to tell us something. Who could have done something like this? She's got to be the most popular President that this country has had, at least in a long time. As far as I know, she had no enemy's. Everyone loved her or at the very least, respected her. She took this office at the darkest of times and has managed to make this country a better place for all of its citizens. There's no way anyone would want to hurt her. It has to have been some psycho; no one in their right mind would have done this. This is Jim Cochran, WELT News Channel 3, Washington, live outside of the White House. Please stay tuned for the most up to date information."

"Lieutenant, did you hear the news?" Lucas asks when he finds Jacob.

"What news, Sergeant?"

"Someone shot the President."

"What! When?"

"A few minutes ago, she was in the middle of briefing the American public regarding the underground, in the middle of a sentence actually when she screamed and fell to the ground. The media's reporting that she was shot, but alive and undergoing treatment at a local hospital."

"Who the hell shot her?" Jacob demands frustrated.

"They didn't give a name but I have a feeling that the underground is going to be blamed for this one, even if we didn't do it. We probably should disperse the people milling about. If the Military gets an order to arrest or detain anyone from the underground, we don't stand a chance."

"You got that right, Sergeant. See if you can get all those with a radio to start hustling the crowd; make them go home before they're arrested. They'll never get out if they catch them. Unfortunately there are only so many of us to protect them, not nearly enough."

"Yes Sir, I'm on it."

"Kitten, where are you" Snake says out loud while walking quickly through the crowd in search of Kat, Mallory or either of his brothers.

"Kitten, over here" he says when he finally catches a glimpse of her.

"What's up Snake" she says in answer to his order.

"Have you heard the news" he asks her when she gets close enough to hear him.

"What news" she asks.

"The President was shot" he says while looking at her and immediately notices a brief guilty look that crosses her features. So quick it was hard to register.

"Come with me" he orders brusquely.

"Where are we going Snake?"

"Just over here for a little privacy. Now, I'm going to ask you again" he says when they reach a relatively private area near the woods. "Did you hear the news, the President was shot?"

"Only when you told me a minute ago, that was the first time I'd heard that" she admits with a shrug.

"Kitten, tell me truth. You knew that she'd been shot, so how did you know."

"I told you Snake, when you told me a few minutes ago, that's the first that I'd heard that."

"Damn it Kitten" Snake yells in frustration. "Do

NOT lie to me, ever."

"What? I'm not lying to you, I told you…"

"Yeah, you told me that I told you about the President being shot, first. However, your face told a different story. Now, spit it out, how did you know that she'd been shot?"

"I did it" she mumbles guiltily, but almost silently.

"What? What did you just say?"

"I said, I did it" she admits quietly but proudly.

"Damn it, I thought that's what you said. We have to get out of here. Does anyone else know this?"

"Just a couple of people. I couldn't help it" she cries defensively when she sees the look of anger cross his face "they saw me do it."

"Who's they" he demands angrily.

"Just Mal and Eli, and maybe an under-grounder or two, I'm not sure. I had the shot and knew that I could make it so I took it."

"Kitten, she'll never stop looking for the person that shot her, whether they did or not, someone will pay for this."

"I know, I know" she admits tearfully. "I had to take it, it could have saved this country, but I missed my target. Damn it, I missed the kill shot."

"Yeah, you just injured her and created a very angry and vindictive President. If she ever finds out the name of the person that shot her, she will hunt that person to the ends of the earth."

"We're going to have to leave this group, head west, maybe northwest just to get out of her sights. It's going to be a lot more difficult handling all the problems when I'm not even near the area. I guess it's time to hand off. Let's see if we can find Devon and Eli, Mallory too. They're going to have to assume control of the militia around here. You and I are heading west."

"Devon, come in" Jacob mutters into his radio, angrily.

"I'm here Jacob, what is it?"

"We need a meet. Head to the coffee shop and let Mal and Eli know too, so they can join us. We're about ten minutes out, so we'll meet you there."

"Sure Jacob, no problem. We'll meet you there in a few."

"Head out Kitten, you caused the problem, now we all pay."

"That's not fair, Snake. I did what I thought would help the world. I tried to get rid of the President."

"Well you didn't succeed so now we need to go to plan B."

"Fine" she grumbles in anger and hurt "whatever."

"I see the gangs all here" Jacob says after Eli joins them at Mikes Coffee House. "We have just a slight issue. Kitten here decided to try to take the problems of the world into her own hands and get rid of the Chief of Staff. Unfortunately, Jane Martin lives, injured but alive. You all know what her reactions going to be when she starts looking for the person that shot her. She will not stop until she kills whoever dared to shoot her. There's a problem with that since our own Kitten shot her and I don't particularly want anything to happen to her, not that she doesn't deserve it."

"Hey wait a minute Jacob. Don't say things like that, she was just trying to help" Devon says hotly.

"I understand that, but she didn't help. It should have been brought before all of us before she tried something so hair brained. Now we need to take the precautions we must, in order to protect her. The only thing that I see that may protect her is by taking her west, way west. Not to the underground but out in the wilderness. Somewhere that has a low population. There won't be any military out in nowhere land, so we may be able to hide there until most of the heat is off of her. I'll try to do my share of work long distance, but I sure won't be able to do everything that I've been doing recently. That's the reason you're all here. I'm passing the reins to you. You can divide the duties up anyway that you want, but I can't do everything that I've been doing, so you need to take over."

"Sure Jacob, we can do that. It's the least that we can do to help you both out. We wouldn't be here if you hadn't taken us under your wing when you did." Eli says emphatically.

"You still need to search for Mom and Dad, but I'm sure you'll find them. And you'll need to take care of each other. Other than that, you'll just have to take everything one day at a time" Jacob says. "Any questions? If not, we're going to hit the road now, there's no time to stay and talk. I know that the President's alive which means that she's already giving orders to find us. I know she'll pick one of the five of us, because she can. It will be really easy to blame it on one of us, she's been doing that since the beginning anyway."

"Shhhhh, did you hear that" Kat asks quickly, quietly and intensely. "Someone's coming" she says quickly as she reaches for her weapon and rushes to a window.

"Crap, it's the General's troops" she says as she takes aim.

"Stop Kitten, do not shoot, because if you do, even if you kill him, we'll never get out of here alive. There are too many troops with him."

"Fine, but they're not taking me without a fight. I'd rather be dead then submit to her and then be beheaded in front of the world on national television. They're moving past us, they don't have a clue about this place or what it means to us" she adds in relief.

"Alright Kitten, let's get ready. We need to get out of here before they change their minds."

"Go on you two; we'll cover you if we need to" Devon offers as they take positions in all the windows.

"Thanks Devon, I'll owe you one" Jacob says in relief and thanks.

"Just go, before they change their minds" Devon says.

"Kat, move" Snake says as he rushes out the door. Just as he passes the window that Devon's looking out a shot is heard making him drop to the ground, a thud sound following his landing.

"Devon, Oh nooooooo Devon" he hears Mal scream from inside the store. After a heated skirmish with the military Jacob runs back to the store.

"What happened" he yells when he see's Mal and Eli huddled down by Devon who's laying in an awkward looking position, eyes wide open, face slack, gone.

"What the hell happened" Jacob yells as he drops to his knees, grabs Devon by the shoulders and lays him down, about to begin CPR.

"Wait" Kat says quietly but heard loudly in the silence. "Wait" she says as she lays her hands on Snakes shoulders.

"He's gone" she murmurs. "I'm so sorry, but you can't bring him back, he's gone" and she gently reaches out and closes Devon's eyes, tears blurring her vision.

"No, he can't be gone" Eli says brokenly.

"How could this have happened" Jacob murmurs, choked up, listening to Mallory sob in Kat's arms.

"He's our brother, he can't be gone, I can't believe this, he's....someone do something" Mallory screams, her hysteria building.

"Shhh Mallory, I'm sorry but there's nothing that we can do, he's gone. This is my fault" Kat admits, tears streaming down her cheeks. "If I would have never shot the President this wouldn't have happened. God, I'm so sorry, so sorry" she keeps repeating.

"It's not your fault" Snake informs Kat. "This has been building up for months. It was just a matter of time before they came after us. The odds of one of us getting taken out were growing substantially by the day. One of us was bound to take a bullet sooner or later. It's just such a shock, that's all. Now we need to do something to protect his body until we can bury it. That's gonna be tough since the military are everywhere. We might have to take his body with us for a few hours until we can find a place that's military free and appropriate for a burial."

"Hey, I was at a farm that borders Virginia, an old guy owned it and kept it real nice. He had lots of acres and I'm sure we could bury him there. We stopped in there when we were looking for witnesses to the plane explosion. He hadn't seen anything but was willing to help in any way that he could. I just remember him because his house was quaint and well kept. His out buildings were the same, he took good of care of things. I'm sure he wouldn't mind. It's only about an hour and a half from here."

"That sounds good" Jacob says thoughtfully then glances at his siblings to see what their opinion is.

"Sounds okay to me" Eli says slowly, still in shock from the death of his brother. "It will work for now and later on, if we feel the need we can move him and do a proper funeral service for him."

"Good, then we need to get to a mortuary, get a casket and a hearse. Then we can move to this farm, bury him and head further west. We have to get out of this area before the military come looking here again."

"Alright, I'll go to the Craven Bros' Funeral Home since it's the closest and see what I can find" Kat offers out of deference to the Callander Quads, providing them with a little privacy time to be with their brother.

"Thank you Kitten" Snake murmurs with gratitude. "Be safe out there."

"I borrowed the hearse and found a pretty nice casket in the store area. I borrowed that too but I did it with the owner's permission. They even helped me to load it up and offered to help. I told them thanks for the offer but no. I didn't want them being seen with us. It would make their lives way too difficult. Since we're heading west, we won't be around to protect them. I didn't want them to have to worry about their safety. Life's too difficult right now; no-one needs any extra help in the danger areas."

"Good thinking Kitten, thanks."

"Well Eli, you ready to do this deed?"

"Yeah, I'm ready" he admits with a quiver in his voice and a straightening of his spine.

After positioning Devon inside of the casket then sliding it back into the hearse, they prepare to close the cover and hearing Mallory's breathing becoming harsh and loud Jacob grabs her and olds on tight until the anxiety attack starts to subside, tears running down her cheeks, his eyes watery but determined.

"Thanks Jacob" she says with a sniff. "I'm okay, I'll be alright."

"I know but it's just real hard. It'd be easier if Mom and Dad were here with us. But you two will find them; I have no doubt. When you do, please tell them where we are and about Devon. That's going to be a tough moment and I'm sorry that I can't be there when you have to tell them, but you can promise them that we'll have a proper funeral service as soon as we can and remind them that he died a hero's death."

Chapter Twenty-Two

"I'm fine Teriq, please; just get me out of here, these people hover too much."

"Jane, you were shot and you happen to be the President of the United States, that's a big deal. The last time the United States had a President that was shot was back in the eighties, President Regan I believe."

"I understand that Teriq, but I can't get anything accomplished here in the hospital. These are trying times for everyone and I can use this atrocity to bring the American public closer to me. Besides, I want Jacob Callander. I know he's the one behind me getting shot. If he didn't shoot the gun himself, he gave the orders to do it, so just get me out of here! I want that bastard. I need to go after him before he gets too big of a head start on me."

"Jane, that's why you have me remember? I've already given word to get him. I have a couple of units that are responsible to me, and they're on his trail now. I should hear soon on whether or not they have him."

"That's awesome Teriq. I never should have doubted you, it's just that I've had a little time to think while waiting to get out of here and I'm pretty used to taking care of myself, so I automatically began the thinking process of how to get the person responsible for shooting me. I personally want to make him suffer for what he's done."

"I want him to suffer, too. He crossed the line when he shot you. He has to pay for it, one way or another. In the mean time, the Doctor's have to release you before you can leave here. As soon as they do, I promise, you're out of here."

"Thanks Teriq, I knew I could depend on you. I've got so much going on right now, I can't find my parents and I really need them now more than ever, the chip implantation is nearing the half way mark, the public is accepting this more easily than I expected. I also have to get in touch with the Shaw. I'm sure he's heard about the shooting by now and I need to reassure everyone that I'm fine and in control."

"The Middle East peace conference is scheduled in the near future, but I'm still working on a few of the countries. I know they'll buckle and be there, but the last thing I can do is show any type of weakness right now."

"I'm sure they'll release you today, Jane" Teriq says in confidence. "You weren't hurt too seriously. It could have been a terrible thing for sure, but since it hit you in the outer part of your arm, there's really no danger to you. I'd have to say that if you hadn't moved at that exact moment, you probably would've been killed. Whoever shot you was an expert marksman, a very good sniper. No one's come forward with any information and no one's confessed to even seeing anyone with that type of weapon."

"Ah, here's your doctor's now, President Martin.

"Doctor Whiting, Doctor Richmond, I'm so glad you're here. I was just informing General Auliya of how anxious I am to get back to my work. I have a full plate right now and can't afford to miss more time."

"Are you sure you feel up to it President Martin? You were shot and you did lose some blood, but I must say you're healing pretty rapidly. I can release you today but only if you promise to rest more than usual. It's going to take a while to recover completely but you are definitely on the right road. Just a little more rest than normal and I think you'll look back at this in a week or two and be surprised that it actually happened."

"Oh, I'm ready Doctor, like I told the General I'm a busy person. I really don't have time to lie around in bed all day, but I do promise to rest more for awhile. Just until I feel a hundred percent, which isn't far from what I'm feeling now" she adds after seeing the determined glint in the Doctors eyes.

"Alright, President Martin, I'll discharge you but you'll need to see me in seven to ten days to have the stitches removed from your injury. It will only take a few minutes to remove the sutures and inspect the injury. Just be sure to keep the stitches dry, cover them with plastic when you shower and I'll remove them in a little over a week as long as everything looks good at that time. Please promise to call me if your arm starts to hurt more, it get's red or hot or you start feeling a little sick, those would be emergency calls."

"Absolutely Doctor, I promise to call should any of those things occur. Thank you Doctor Whiting, thank you. Teriq, get me transportation, I'll be ready to leave momentarily."

"Yes President Martin, it will be my pleasure."

"This is Jim Cochran, WELT News Channel 3, Washington, standing outside of the Georgetown Hospital where the President of the United States is being released today after the shooting the other day in which injured her in the upper right arm. We are so lucky that whoever shot her wasn't a very good shot and missed killing or even seriously injuring her. She only spent three days in the hospital as a precautionary measure and is being released today. I'm hoping that she'll come out these side doors where we may be able to see how well she's doing and possibly talk her into making a statement, live."

Chapter Twenty-Three

"How much further are you planning on traveling today Snake, it's been a long day and I could use a break."

"I wanted to keep going, put more distance between D.C. and us. I'm still good; can you go for a little longer?"

"I guess" Kat says tiredly. "I've been going for close to twenty eight hours now. I can't keep up if I collapse. I need some food and some sleep if you're going to keep up with a pace like this tomorrow."

'Alright, alright, I'll look for somewhere that we can take a break" he says angrily.

"There's a hotel not far from here. We may be able to stop there and get a decent meal and a clean bed, all hopefully anonymously" Kat says quietly understanding his anger left by the emotional toll today took on him.

"Here we are" Snake says. "I don't think this place is open, it looks deserted."

"That's alright, we can still get some sleep, and if it's closed, no one will be the wiser. Hopefully the rooms still have beds in them and maybe there's running water. I could use a shower."

"Let's go to the back and park near the trees. We'll take a room that's close to the car so that if we have to leave fast we can. The doors locked, give me a second" he says a he removes his tools from his belt. "I always carry these; you never know when I'll need access to a locked door."

"Here you go" he says as he jimmies open the lock and throws open the door.

"Awesome" Kat cries when she finds a bed, still made up, a small room with a chair and a dresser and a bathroom to the side. As she wanders the room looking inside drawers, he goes into the bathroom and finds running water.

"The waters on, let's see if there's any hot water.

"Shoot, looks like the powers out, so no hot water but at least we have some water. It's better than nothing. Besides, there's no one here that we have to hide from at the moment."

"Do you think there's any food around the area? I need something to eat, my energy levels down to nothing now" she says.

"I suppose there is. Usually when you find a hotel you find some kind of food. You shower and I'll go in search of the food."

"I found a burger joint a couple of miles down the road. I bought us both loaded burgers with chips and a few colas. That should hold us for the night."

"Thanks Snake, you're my hero" she tells him with a smile and a hug.

"I'm sorry Kitten, for the lousy mood I've been in all day, there's just so much emotional baggage that I'm carrying right now."

"I know Snake, believe me, I know. It'll get easier, but for now, it's going to take a toll. So many bad things have happened, it's hard not to focus on them and forget all the rest. I wonder how Eli and

Mal are doing. Do you think we should call them?"

"No, I'm trying to stay away from communications. We're deep undercover right now. No one knows that we're even alive. I like it that way. It's takes a little of the pressure off."

"About that Snake; I was thinking while we were traveling, if we let everyone know that you died back there at Mike's old place, not Devon, you could assume Devon's persona. That may enable us to do more and get more done undercover. After all you're the one that Jane wants in the worst way, not Devon. So if you are assumed dead then you should be able to go anywhere and do pretty much anything."

"I had thought about that and discounted it. I'm just not sure if I can take on his persona. After all, he was my brother and he just died today. I still can't believe that he's gone. It's always been the four of us, and being quadruplets, it makes us all linked in some strange way. There's always been a connection. I realize that I was out of their lives for a long time, but the connection was always there. I really believe that I would have known had something happened to any one of them. I'll think on it and make that decision later."

"First, I need a shower and some food, not necessarily in that order. Let's eat while it's somewhat hot and then I'll shower and we need to sleep as soon as possible. We don't have time to waste right now. We have to get out west. I need to see Captain Hall and Lucas, see what went on out there and how many deaths occurred because of the bombing."

"Scoot over Kitten. I'm not sleeping on the floor.

Besides, I could use someone to cuddle with. But don't worry, because that's all I'm after right now."

"I know and I love you for that Snake, thanks."

"Eli, do you think Kat and Jacob are doing okay" Mallory asks quietly.

"I'm sure they're fine, probably making good time by putting as many miles as possible between us. I'm headed towards the underground, I want to see what's left and see if anyone's seen Mom and Dad. How about you? What are you going to do?"

"I'm thinking of heading into the office, just to make sure that what I did to the chip hasn't been discovered and changed. If it has, it's going to make my life a whole lot more difficult."

"How about if we meet somewhere later today? I'd like to go over what I find and I'll want to hear from you on the chip and its security."

"Fine with me, until we find Mom and Dad, it's just the two of us for now" she says then bursts into tears.

"I know Mal, I know" Eli says as he hugs her and tries to comfort her. "This is going to be a hard day, maybe a week or so. I mean, we lost a part of us today. We had a real connection, one only quadruplet's have. I'm really not sure if it will ever get any better but I do know we'll get used to it, but that's going to take a while, too."

"Yeah, it is" she murmurs gratefully. "Alright, let's head out. You look for Mom and Dad and I'll go check on the chip. How about we meet back here in say six hours or so?"

"Deal" he says and after a squeeze he lets her go.

"Hey Mongoose, what's going on?" Eli asks as soon as he finds him. "Any word on my parents yet" Eli asks, his face gray, looking ten years older than when he saw him last. Something's wrong, Mongoose thinks.

"What happened Eli, what's wrong?"

"Jacob and Kat left a few hours ago, headed west. Unfortunately, there was a fire fight at Mike's old place and Devon was killed."

"What, when, how....." Mongoose cries, his face a picture of horror.

"Jacob and Kat were making a run for it, we all got caught at Mike's old place and they headed out the door, but there was a sniper somewhere out there and he took a pot shot at a window, unfortunately Devon was just looking out that window to see where Jacob had gotten to when a bullet found him, he died instantly" he says quietly, tears running down his face. "We're all tore up about it, so if you could not say anything when Mal gets here later, I'd appreciate it. She's having a real tough time. We were pretty close. That's why I was looking for Mom and Dad, they haven't heard about Devon yet. I kinda wanted to be the one to tell them, if you get my drift."

"Man, I'm sorry, so sorry, that sucks damn it."

"Yeah, it sucks, I know. We at least gave him a small funeral, buried him ourselves on a farm in Virginia, but we can move him later on if my parents want us to. We just wanted to take care of it right away, before the Presidents men found him."

"Wow, I can't believe it. That's such a shock."

"Yeah, I know. We were all shocked when it

happened, it was so damn fast. Faster than you can process it, that's for sure."

"There's Rand, maybe he had some luck finding your parents. We've been looking for them the whole time, since the evacuation and the bombing the other day."

"Rand, how's it going" Eli asks "any sign of my parents yet?"

"Not a thing. It's just weird, I mean, everyone that was underground is now wandering around out here, they all knew your parents but not one person has seen either one of them since the evacuation."

"Shit" Eli says with a sinking sensation in his stomach.

"That's really not good news, man. Has anyone been underground to look for survivors?"

"Actually we just sent a couple of guys down about an hour ago, it took us that long to get the proper protective gear. They're going to look for a couple of hours and then come back up and switch out with some of the other guys. They're doing this in shifts."

"Good, then when the first two come back up, find me. I want to ask them some questions."

"Sure thing Eli, we'll find you" they promise as he walks away. Rand looks at Mongoose with a question in his eyes "what happened?"

"It's Devon; he was killed in a fire fight at Mike's old place, the coffee shop. It was a freak shot."

"Man……damn it…unbelievable…how's Mal taking it?"

"Bad, but she'll be out here later, so you can see

her then."

"Hey Mal, how's it going" Eli asks when she finally answers her phone.

"So far, so good; I just got into my office, about five minutes ago and the computer's finally up. I've also been catching up on the office gossip. Because President Martin's being released today, that's going to be the big news for the day, at least I think anyway."

"Yep, I'm sure that'll take up most of the office gossip. What about that Callander guy, what's everyone saying about him?"

"That he was killed in a shoot out today with the President's Special Ops Unit. They haven't found his body yet, but they're sure he was killed. One of the snipers swore he had a clear shot and took it, but without his body they can't prove anything. It's all supposition for now."

"Well, that's interesting. What do you say about it" he asks.

"I just think it's possible but there's no proof without a body so I don't have any idea what their new plan is."

"Well, keep your ears open and let me know what's going on, when you know something. There's still no sign of Mom and Dad but there's a couple of guys looking for them right now. I expect to hear from them in the next hour or so, so as soon as I know anything, I'll let you know. I promise"

"Thanks Eli. I'm waiting anxiously for that news, so please call me as soon as you know anything."

"You bet I will. I'll talk to you soon, Mal, Bye."

"Snake, where's our end today, when are we stopping?"

"I'm actually taking the long way. I want to stop at my Bike Shop and see what we can find in the transportation area. I don't want to keep moving with the same vehicle for too long, someone might figure that out. We'll be close in about an hour. I used to have a couple of cars and a truck and of course my motorcycle, but I won't be taking that. It's too unique and someone's bound to recognize it, besides, we can't carry the supplies we may need on the bike, so I'm thinking the truck probably."

"Yeah, that's probably the right choice as long as it's not personalized."

"Nope, it's just a plain old truck. Once we trade transportation we should have no more than about an hour to travel. We'll be at our destination today, it may be late but it will be today."

"Awesome, thanks Snake, I need a break. It's been a long hellish day."

"It sure has" he says, flashing back to Devon, the brother he loved who both loved and hated him, now dead.

"Once we reach the underground area, I want to see who I can find around the eastern part of it. There's actually an area that the underground people used, where they snuck off to when they were above ground, where no one could see them, which I'm sure they still go to. I've been thinking about it and I think that's where we may just find Captain Hall. It would be the smart place to put your family until something better could be found."

"Eli, what are you doing here" Mal asks in surprise.

"I wanted to see you, I thought maybe we could go to dinner" he says with a long face, fatigue in the way he's holding his body. "It's been a rough day and I just needed to get away from it all, so how about dinner?"

"Sure, I'm a little hungry. I need to eat for the energy, anyway. Let's find a little sandwich shop, that's about all I can deal with today."

"Sounds good to me, Mal" he says as they climb into his car.

"How about we take a ride to Mom and Dad's, maybe we can figure something out if we're in their house."

"Sure, I'm game. They don't live too far and it would be nice to be able to go to their house, even if they aren't there."

"That was a nice ride, Eli, thanks" Mallory says as they get out of his car to go into the house.

"Here, I've got a key, so we won't have to break anything to get in" she says as they get to the front door. "It smells a little musty in here and look at the dust. Mom would never have stood for that" she admits longingly.

"Yeah, I know" he answers quietly, sadly.

"Eli, what is it" she asks nervously. "What is it that you aren't telling me?"

"Well, Mal, we sent some of the unit into the underground later today after the special suits and breathing apparatus showed up. They found Mom and

Dad. They never actually left the underground. They were found in the hallway just outside of the dining area. It looked like they might have been leaving since they'd gathered a bunch of stuff that I guess they didn't want to leave behind. They never stood a chance once the first Ricin bomb went off. At least they looked peaceful, Mal" he admits choked up, tears threatening, waiting for the denial, the anger that Mal was holding back to blow through him, standing strong for Mal.

"N O . . ." she screams "Oh please Eli, please tell me that it's not true. Please . . ."

"I'm sorry Mal, I'm so sorry" he says as he grabs her and holds on tight.

"I can't lose Mom and Dad, please Eli, I can't lose them too" she sobs, unbearable pain bringing her down, soul absorbing emptiness screaming through her body, shocking her, ripping her apart.

"I know Mal, God how I know" he admits, his voice empty, devoid of any emotions. It's hard to feel emotions when there are none left. "A day from Hell" he murmurs quietly, holding his sister close, comforting and protecting his quickly dwindling family.

"What are we going to do now" she cries in a lonely keening voice. "How can we go on, first Devon and now Mom and Dad, please, please let me wake up from this nightmare" she sobs quietly and hauntingly.

"Mal, I'm sorry, so sorry" he keeps repeating as he slowly leads her to the couch. "Here, sit down for a few minutes, we have plenty of time, we can stay here as long as you need. I'm going to go and put the car in the garage so no one knows that there's anyone here. I promise I'll be right back" he says gently.

Chapter Twenty-Four

"Good evening, I'm Jim Cochran of WELT News Channel 3, Washington, live outside of the White House awaiting President Martin."

"The President was released earlier today from the hospital after having been shot by a sniper three days ago. Fortunately for us, she obtained only a minor injury from that incident. This evening she plans on informing the public what happened the other day and how the military are going to repair the problems that have occurred. We, as United States citizens, can't sit back and allow our President to be harmed like this. Just prior to this news conference, the military have gone to every area within sniper capability and planted their own snipers. There is no way another such incident can or will take place. Here she comes, out of the front of the White House to the podium, looking as if nothing ever happened. You have to give her credit for the strength of character that she's demonstrated repeatedly to the American public. Here she is, Jane Martin, the President of the United States:"

"I want to thank you, ladies and gentlemen of this great country, for tuning in tonight for this impromptu news briefing. I appreciate your support of me and my office and promise you that your safety and care are of the utmost importance to me. What happened to me the other day was done carelessly by someone who wishes me out of office. I refuse to bow to their command and refuse to fear them for I know that we as the American public are right and I stand true and strong knowing that I have your appreciation and your devotion. You know that I am and will do everything in my power to maintain your safety and lives."

"I also know without a doubt who to hold responsible for the atrocity that was committed three days ago. I have received many well wishes from everywhere, from not only this country but throughout the world."

"I believe it was divine intervention that saved my life so that I may keep you, the American public, moving in the right direction. The person responsible for the sniper that shot me whether he himself or someone he ordered is Lieutenant Jacob Callander. He has been trying, for the past few months, to find a way to get rid of me, so that he can assume control of this great country."

"I want to apologize to him in advance for the knowledge that he will never become the head of this country. For that to happen, I would have to leave and I will not leave until I have finished what I have started. For me to do that would leave you, the citizens, in great danger. I will never do that."

"I have been assured by General Auliya, that the capture of Lieutenant Callander is imminent. He has been tracking him since the incident and is close to capturing him. I promise you now that you will be notified of when he is in custody and will also be responsible for deciding how to handle him. We will hear everything that he has to say and you will be the judge on how to repay him for all he has done."

"I still have had no news on my parents. They've been missing since the explosion at the church in Texas. I know that they never worked at the time the explosion happened yet there's been no sign of them near the site or at their home. I have been informed to assume them dead, yet because they are my parents, I cannot. I believe they are still alive out there somewhere, possibly being held as hostages. I promise them this. I will never stop looking for them. If they are being held hostage, I will find them and the person responsible for holding them shall be punished. I can do nothing else.

"I'm going to keep this news conference brief since I promised my doctors that I would rest more than usual for the next few days. Don't worry though; there's nothing wrong with me that rest won't cure. I sustained no serious injuries from that sniper fire. Just a small wound in my upper arm, which is almost totally healed already, thanks to the top care that I received from my doctor's. I also want to let you know how easy it was for my health care givers to access my health report via the chip. They never had to slow down to treat me. All of my health information was immediate when they scanned my chip."

"I didn't need to worry if they would medicate me with the wrong medications for they had all of that information in front of them by the time they needed it. The chip worked beautifully. This has been an exciting thing to witness, the chip in action. Please, feel confident now that you will no longer have any problems when you require life saving medical care."

"It looks like we made it. This has been quite a long day" Snake says in fatigue, dark shadows beneath his eyes after another hour and a half of travel since they changed transportation "I think if we just wander around, talk to the people that are pretty much homeless now, we might get some leads on Captain Hall, telling us who's in charge, who's left, and how many died from the Ricin."

"After we get some information we can meet back here, say an hour from now and bunk out in the back of the truck. I need some sleep soon and you look like you could use some too."

"Yeah, I'm exhausted, but I need to walk a little to get the blood flowing. I spent too much time sitting today. Once I walk off the stiffness, and get some information I'll be ready for some sleep too. I'll see you in an hour, Snake" Kat promises.

"Jacob, it's Eli. I'm sitting here with Mal and we have some bad news."

"What news" Jacob demands. "Now what?"

"It's about Mom and Dad. They didn't make it out of the underground. I hate to give you this information over the phone, but I doubt you'll be back here anytime soon so I have no choice."

"What do you mean, they didn't make it out" Jacob demands, all the air sucked out of him.

"They were in the underground when the Ricin bombs were used. They hadn't had a chance to get out. They'd packed up a bunch of stuff that I guess they thought they'd need. We found them near the dining hall. If it's any consolation, they didn't look like they suffered and at least they were together."

"NO, fucking No" he yells in disbelief. "Shit, shit, Mom and Dad gone too, it's a little too much to take Eli" Jacob says in a choked up voice, trying to maintain his strength for his brother. "I can't seem to take it in. How are you and Mal?"

"I'm okay right now but Mallory's taking it real bad. I haven't been able to calm her down yet, but she'll be okay."

Jacob wanders over to his truck, blind to anyone and everyone around him. "I don't know what to say or do" he murmurs to Eli. "We just got here, about twenty minutes ago. It would take us a good day to get back to D.C., but we'll come back if you need us to."

"No Jacob, I'm going to handle this end of things. We'll do the same thing with Mom and Dad that we did for Devon. We can change things later on if we need to."

"Thanks man, that helps a lot. We can talk about this later, when reality's sunk in more. Right now, I don't feel capable of making any decisions."

"I hear you Jacob. Don't worry about anything. Mal and I will handle things here, once I can get her to calm down. Stay safe out there Bro, the President was just on the TV and blamed the sniper shooting on you, or someone you gave orders to. I know the General's got a unit tailing you, so watch out. I can't lose anyone else."

"I promise to take care. I need to find Kat and let her know what's happened. She's going to take this hard, too. She got pretty close to mom in the past few months. Damn it, I can't believe it" he groans in despair. "I just got my family back after fifteen long years and now a brother's gone and then Mom and Dad. This sucks" he says tears streaming down his face.

"I know Jacob, it really does suck. Look, I gotta go. Mal needs me, but you take care and take care of Kat."

"Yeah, I'll talk to you soon, I promise" Jacob ads before he hangs up. Kat finds him walking aimlessly around the truck with an absent look in his eyes, face paler than she's ever seen it.

"Hey, what's up Snake, you okay?"

"Um, yeah, sorry Kitten, I didn't see you come up."

"I know, I've been here a couple of minutes but you looked like you were thinking. Your mind was certainly not here and I didn't want to interrupt. So what happened?"

"Shit, shit shit" he says in a moan.

"What Snake, what is it, tell me."

"It's Mom and Dad. Eli called a little bit ago and told me that they didn't make it out of the underground before the first Ricin bomb was thrown in. They both died, right outside of the dining hall."

"What" she screams in denial. "You're not serious, you can't be" she yells as the shaking sets in. "Please, tell me you're kidding. It's not funny! You have a sick sense of humor" she accuses.

"Now hold on, I'm not making this up, I couldn't" he exclaims in anger. "How could you accuse me of something like that" he demands.

"You're serious" she answers, tears choking her

voice.

"Oh NO Snake" she cries and grabs him close, sobbing in anger and pain. "I can't believe it" she says into his neck "I just saw them last night. They were happy, like always" she cries in great hiccupping sobs. "Sandy even teased me about you, like she always did" she groans in pain and denial.

"How can we accept this" she questions in a broken tone, disbelief trying to take over.

"What can we do, we're fifteen hundred miles from them and how can we accept this, never

to see them or talk to them again. Why Snake, why are all these bad things happening to us, why" she cries desolate.

"Shhh, I know Kitten, I know" he says as he holds her tight, absorbing some of her pain while allowing her to absorb some of his.

"Eli's taking care of everything back east. He says they'll treat them the same way that we did with Devon and later on, if we want to move them, we will. Something we can think about later on, after all the problems going on right now are gone; after things have quieted down some."

"Snake" she moans in unbelief and pain, a burning pain that radiates throughout her body, only now realizing that it's the pain of death. "Let's go somewhere alone, move the truck so that we're not surrounded by people. I just want to be alone. It may help me absorb this easier, I don't know. I just want to be alone."

'Me too, get in, we'll take off and find a secluded place, there has to be one somewhere close. Here, this should be a good place, he says as he pulls the truck to a stop beneath a large pine tree. "I don't see anyone around, it looks pretty deserted. Hopefully, it'll remain that way for the night. I just need to sleep, think and eat. Not necessarily in that order."

"Yeah, I feel the same way" Kat says, fatigue weighing down her voice.

"Let's eat something. I've got apples, crackers, some cheese and water. I found it all earlier and put it on ice, which I borrowed from someone. Anyway, it's cold and fresh."

"Thanks Snake, I appreciate it. If I would have had my head on right earlier, I would have done the same thing."

"I know, Kitten. It's all good. I took care of it this time. It'll be your turn, next time."

"Deal" she says around a yawn. After a peaceful few minute's taking care of problem one, hunger and nourishment, Kat's eyes start to drift closed.

"Come on Kitten, you lay down here, and I'll lie next to you, and we'll catch a quick nap."

"Sooooo okkkkay" she mumbles as she lays down, asleep within microseconds, a small gentle snore coming out of her mouth.

"I'm so glad for you" Snake says to Kat quietly as he lays down next to her and gently turns her so he can hold her while he sleeps, pictures of his brother, mother and father running through his head, memories of an easier time, a time with no problems. A time of peace and happiness he thinks, a sadness enveloping him as sleep overtakes him.

"Teriq, what's the news. Have you found them, yet? I'm getting a little annoyed by how long this is taking" Jane says, anger in her voice.

"I promise Jane, we're close, within hours of finding them, I believe. We've made it to the outskirts of the encampments that the West underground is using. They had to have made it this far. All we have to do is narrow it down a little. I'm sure I can get someone here to tell us what we need to know" he promises a wicked glint in his eyes that transfers to his voice.

"Fine, but this had better be it" she warns. "If you can't handle this then I have a problem. I obviously put the wrong person in your position. This is a small task that you seem to be having trouble dealing with. I want results, today, Teriq. No longer" she orders just prior to hanging up.

"I will find them" he says out loud in anger, to anyone listening. You will never control me completely, he thinks as he starts snapping out orders to his elite group of ex-special ops. I'll do this job and then you will learn to respect me, you will learn your place, he decides.

"What" Kat gasps a question when a scream startles her awake.

"Shhh, it's alright" Snake says as he keeps his hand over her mouth so that she can make no more noises.

"Someone's gotten into the camp" he whispers near her ear. "I'm taking my hand away, don't make a sound, okay?" he asks quietly in her ear and with a small shake of her head in understanding, he lets go.

"We need to get out of here before whoever made it to the encampment finds us. I know they're after us, not these poor people. I don't want to be responsible for anyone coming to harm because of me."

With a vigorous shake of her head in agreement, they both creep to the tailgate of the pickup and glance outside looking for strangers. "Do not use your gun, save it for when we can make some noise. Knives only for now, okay?"

"Yeah, no guns . . ."

"It's probably the special team that works for the President and the General. We'll have to be extra careful. If they are who I think, they're professional trackers, ex-special ops."

"Great" she murmurs with a wicked glint in her eyes "no problem."

"All clear for now, move, move" he orders quietly but urgently. "Head to the south, the woods, I'll meet you there in just a minute or so." With an affirmative shake of her head, she slinks out of the truck and quickly heads to the southern area of woods.

"Come on Snake, where the hell are you?" she murmurs to herself when he fails to make it to the woods within five minutes of her arrival. "Don't make me come back there after you" she mumbles in worry. What the hell happened, she wonders? I never should have gone ahead of him. I knew better but he was so damn insistent. Hearing a kitten meow she spins around, recognizing the noise that only Snake makes.

"What took you so long" she whispers urgently. "Did something happen" she asks worriedly.

"Not really" he replies, a spark in his eyes.

"Yes, something happened, I can see it on your face. So what was it" she demands quietly before he has a chance to stop her.

"Shhh, quiet; they're close, very close. It's going to take all of our abilities to keep them an arm's length away" he says quickly. "Let's head farther west. We'll have to come back later for the truck. I don't want to lose the truck, it's a handy place to sleep and for transportation, things we need."

"Today we lose this tail, and find Captain Hall, if it's at all possible. We need to get the defenses set up again for the United States. Jane won't stay quiet long. I'm sure she's closing in pretty fast right now. We need something that will stop her cold. There's no way I want her involved in the Middle East Peace talks, which is scheduled to happen in the next few weeks. She'll destroy that quickly and smoothly, and take control of all the countries that show up and participate. Before they know it, every country will be bearing a chip and she'll have charge of them, the capability to kill at whim, her whim."

"This just keeps getting better" Kat murmurs in fear and disgust.

"Don't I know it" he replies back. "I think I see a group
of people to the left up there. It's too dark to really see who they are, but I'm guessing they're part of the underground. Let's take this really slow, just in case they belong to her. The last thing we need is to be caught unawares. I will never surrender to them. I like my neck just the way it is."

"Hey, that looks like Captain Hall" Kat whispers to Snake.

"Yeah, it looks like him and if it is, we just hit pay dirt. Let's wander over there and make sure that there's no one suspicious nearby. I'm not taking any chances. These poor people escaped from the underground, survived the Ricin bombs and managed to keep out of harm's way. I'm not leading anyone to them. I don't want to be responsible for anything happening to them."

A loud gasp is heard when one of the people in the group see who's joining them, "Lieutenant, is that you? I'd heard that you were dead" Captain Hall exclaims quietly and furtively.

"Yeah, it's me and Kat. Can we talk somewhere private but nearby?"

"Absolutely, follow me" he offers as he walks quickly to the south. "This is as private as it gets" he assures them after stopping in a small copse of trees. "It's a good spot, no one can sneak up on it since it's open all the way around except for these eight or ten tree's. It's a handy spot. Now if you don't mind me asking, Lieutenant, what the hell happened? Who bombed us and why?"

"It looks like the bombing came from the President's own troops. She wants everyone out in the open, no one underground. The underground poses too much of a threat to her and her office. She won't tolerate any opposition" he replies in disgust. "How heavy were your casualties?"

"We were hit pretty hard. At first I thought that we might have gotten most of the people out, but the bombing started hours before we expected it. Unfortunately, evacuating is never fast since some people move slower than others. We've lost close to five hundred men, women and children" Captain Hall explains.

"Man, that sucks, I'm sorry. We've taken some huge losses in the past few weeks, too. We need to find some way to stop her before she takes over the world."

"Actually, I've got a surprise. One I think you'll like. We just happen to have her parents. We picked them up after the church was bombed, and took them underground with us. They're being treated very well but I don't think she's aware of them still being alive. As far as she knows, they disappeared after the church explosion. I know she was informed of their disappearance and was told to treat it as if they were dead. She's not happy about that and still insists that they're alive out there somewhere, so we might be able to use them to our benefit."

"That's the best news that I've heard in a while, you're awesome man. I know we'll be able to use them in some way" Jacob answers thoughtfully but finally with hope.

"I think we should keep this under rap as long as possible" Kat exclaims. "We've already been through a great deal. If we can buffer some of the next waves, then we may be home free. Who knows what she has planned next. I do know that Mal fixed the chip. Jane will think that all is the same as it has been when in reality, it's totally different. Anyone that was in the underground will be able to receive a pretend chip. In actuality, they'll get the ink that's used just prior to implantation, along with a fake chip. That way, they'll be able to get away without receiving the real one, they just won't be able to allow anyone to scan the chip since it's a fake and it won't scan. So we're informing anyone that's receiving the fake to stay away from the scanners or it could cost them their lives."

"We had very heavy casualties back east from the Ricin bombs. I lost my parents because they didn't evacuate fast enough and got caught underground when the first wave of bombs began."

"Shit Lieutenant, that's terrible. I'm sorry for your loss, so sorry" Captain Hall exclaims softly, appalled.

"Thank you Captain, it's been hard but we have to help the country so I'm putting work first. I can't afford to take any down time right now. I know this will all catch up with me later on, but for now, we have work to do. Now, you stated that you have Jane's parents, detained after the church bombing. Were they hurt at all and where and how are you keeping them?"

"They weren't hurt; they never made it to the church that day, because we intercepted them. I knew in advance who they were. We'd had them staked out for awhile and since I'm always looking for something to help the cause, I thought they'd do nicely" Captain Hall admits sheepishly.

"Trust me, they will do very nicely. I'll definitely work on that at the earliest opportunity. Unfortunately, right now we have Jane's special-ops on our tails. Any thoughts on where we can disappear to for a few days, just until they get tired of looking for us and move on."

"Actually, I have the perfect place. Back a couple of hundred years ago this was Arapahoe territory.

They used the rocks and made caves in the sides of the mountains for shelter. There are quite a few caves still maintained, that we were offered. The Indians don't like what's happening to this country and they came to us to offer their help."

"That's awesome" Kat exclaims with a grin. "You see, we're not the only ones that understand exactly what she's doing" she remarks to Captain Hall and Snake.

"That's the truth, Lieutenant" Captain Hall agrees. "It's good to see you recovered and doing well" he admits with a quick smile and a look of understanding in his eyes.

"I'm doing great right now, thanks to Snake" she admits with a smile. "If we don't head out pretty soon, that could change quickly" she adds.

"Right, let's go. Give me the general direction, and we'll head that way. We're leaving our truck; just try to make sure it doesn't get damaged or stolen while we're gone. I'd hate to come back to nothing again. It seems to be happening with regular frequency any more. Unfortunately, I'm running out of options rather quickly" Jacob adds in disgust.

'No problem, Lieutenant, your truck will be awaiting your return. If I was you, I'd give them a couple of days to clear out of here, then it should be good to go" Captain Hall offers.

"Snake, did you see that?" Kat asks quietly but with excitement.

"Yeah, I did. Looks like we found some cave dwellers." He adds with a grin. "If we head in further, we may find some of those caves, empty. I don't want to stay with anyone else right now. I prefer privacy, at lease for a little while. I want to be able to make some plans for back east."

"There must be something close here. We've been traveling for hours. Shit, did you hear that?" Kat cries in astonishment. "It sounded like an explosion, the ground just moved too. Check out the dust coming out of the caves. I wonder what the hell just happened," she says, the smile leaving her mouth. "Look at all the people gathering outside the caves. Let's go and see if we can find out what just happened."

"What happened? Was it an explosion?" Snake asks a man of about thirty, standing a few hundred yards from the entrance to one of the caves scattered throughout the area, dust still settling.

"I'm not sure, but it sure did feel like an earthquake. That's about the only thing that would shake the caves like they just shook. I hope none of them collapsed."

"Let's start going from cave to cave. Just to make sure no one's trapped inside. Then we can figure out what the hell's going on" Snake decides as he heads to the nearest cave.

"Anyone in there?" he yells after reaching the cave opening.

"Help us, help, we're stuck, help" he hears quietly.

"There's someone in there" he yells as he heads inside, waving the dust aside that still hanging in the air making visibility tough. Through the dust, he makes out rocks lying towards the back of a small cave. "Where are you" he yells, trying to decide where to start moving the debris from.

"We're back, towards the left side" he hears faintly.

"Kat, to the left, start moving whatever rocks you can" he says as he grabs the closest one and throws it to the other side of the cave. After a good ten minutes he hears exclaiming.

"I can see the light, you're getting close" a voice says.

"Thanks man. I thought we were goners, for sure" remarks a teenager, between coughs, after wiggling through a small opening that Kat and Snake made through the pile of rocks."I need to get out of here, need some air" he says as he stumbles towards the cave opening, holding on to a younger girl.

"Is there anyone else in there?" Snake asks as he walks with them to the opening.

"No, it's just the two of us. That's all that's left of my family now" the male teenager says angrily.

"Sorry man" Snake says sadly. So many people affected, he thinks, so many lives changed. After a long, hard day of searching for trapped individuals in most of the caves, Kat and Snake take a break.

"God, I'm beat" Kat says tiredly as she sits with her back to a stone, a hundred feet from an empty cave that they located during their search and rescue mission. "The one good thing, we found a cave of our very own. As soon as I'm not as exhausted, I'll show some excitement about that" she adds tiredly.

"Yeah, me too, at least we have somewhere to stay out of the weather, and that no-one knows about. Now all we need to do is make it more comfortable."

"I wonder what actually happened. Do we have

any way to hear the news?" Kat asks.

"Yeah, I've got the radio, but I've been trying to conserve the battery life, for emergency situations" Snake admits. "If this works out, we'll head back to the truck and see if we can maneuver it here. I'll be able to charge the battery on a regular basis, that way. Since this is so far out of the way, I doubt we'll have any problem hiding it. Once your rested, we'll get back to the truck, bring it here and set up our sleeping quarters in the cave. We can even cook, since I brought a camping kit with a Coleman burner. All the amenities of a good camping trip" he adds with a grin.

"Snake, you're awesome, you think of everything" Kat says with a big smile.

"Yeah, I try to" he admits with a wink.

"Okay, I'm good, let's head back for the truck. I'm curious as to what happened, but don't want to waste the battery unless we can recharge."

Chapter Twenty-Five

"Good afternoon, I'm Gerry Partell with World Vision

Now out of New York, with breaking news. We've just been informed that there's been an eruption at Yellowstone National Park. We have crews on the way there to bring you live video. In the meantime, I repeat, there's been an eruption at Yellowstone National Park. I understand that the top volcanic experts in the world have been looking at this area for the last ten years, monitoring the pressure increase that's been occurring. None of them has said anything about an imminent eruption. We're trying to reach one of them to bring you information about this emergency. It doesn't look as if it was a huge eruption, but any eruption at Yellowstone National Park is big, since this area has been known as the sleeping giant, being one of the few Supervolcano's in the world. It sounds as if they have reached Dr. Richard Montgomery of the US Geological survey. Dr. Montgomery; thanks for joining us. We were just informed of an eruption that's occurred at Yellowstone National Park. Can you fill us in on the severity of this eruption and what the American people can expect because of this eruption?

Sure, Gerry, I'd be happy to. I contacted one our US Geological professionals that are stationed near the eruption site to get exact details on the problems that we are now facing. There has been an eruption, but the severity of it has not reached a life threatening magnitude for anyone outside of the twenty five mile emergency planning zone. We believe that the eruption was caused by a strong earthquake, a 9.1 on the open ended Richter scale, that occurred in the Denali fault area near Alaska, around two thousand miles from Yellowstone. There were multiple earthquakes in that same area nearly ten years ago that altered the activity of many of Yellowstone's hot springs. Unfortunately, since Yellowstone is such a travel hot spot for many vacationing Americans, and it is vacation time, it may be days before we have a sound figure on how many lives may have been lost from the most recent activity. The eruption has covered an area that is sparsely populated during normal times of the year, but at this time, the middle of vacation time, there's definitely going to be fall out. We're in the process of estimating the force of the ash filled blast, which will help in determining the size of the fall-out area. The National Weather Service is monitoring wind speed and direction so that we can initiate emergency plans to prevent loss of anymore life from this event. We will be evacuating more areas around Yellowstone in preparedness of more quakes."

"I'm sorry to interrupt, but we have more breaking news" Gerry Partell informs Dr. Montgomery and the listeners, in an agitated voice. "I have just been informed that the Alaska earthquake has triggered a tsunami that has hit the coast with a twenty foot wall of water rushing at about five-hundred miles per hour. There is tremendous devastation on the coast. There was no warning for the tsunami. Those poor people had no knowledge of the tsunami that was headed in their direction. We'll bring you the latest video as soon as they send it." Gerry promises the audience and requests video to patch him back with Dr. Montgomery. "What's your feeling on this disaster, Dr. Montgomery? Are these two events linked? What are the long term effects that we're facing from these disasters?

"Absolutely Gerry, the earthquake, being of such a high magnitude no doubt not only created the tsunami, but also aggravated Yellowstone National Park to the point of eruption. Whether this earthquake is the only one, will be something that the US Geological Survey will be watching. With the equipment that we have in that area to monitor these things, we should be able to bring you that information before it occurs, saving lives if possible. Long term effects, everything from the sun visibility to the air purity will be affected by the eruptions. This is a first for this to happen in the middle of the United States. Many areas will have poor air quality with a darker than normal period while the ash is driven by the wind. Anyone in those areas are going to be asked to stay indoors, keeping all windows and doors closed, not using air conditioning that could bring the ash particles into the home. Anyone with breathing difficulties is going to have problems and will probably be asked to evacuate the areas until things have cleared up. This is three natural disasters that have happened to the United States in a matter of hours. The United States will have a hard time recovering from these problems."

"Shit, I can't believe this. How the hell did all these things happen all at the same time? What the hell is going on with this world" Jane screams at Quinton. "How am I supposed to manage all of this on top of the China issue's that I'm dealing with on a daily basis, the chip issues that never seem to totally leave and now this? This is un-fucking-believable" she says loudly. "I will not break down now" she promises, near tears. "They will not win! We're going to need to re-call some of our troops. There's no way we have enough on our soil to deal with these stupid disasters. And you can be sure that the people will be watching everything that I do now. Judging everything, like they do; those space wasters."

"What do you want me to do, Jane? How can I help you?" Quinton asks after Jane calms down a little.

"You can get me the General. I need to talk to him, share some information. It's impossible to keep up with it all when you're out in the middle of no-where."

"Right away, Jane."

"Thanks Quinton. I wasn't yelling at you, I was just yelling, it's what happens to me when I get mad."

"I know. I wasn't taking any of it personally. You got hit with a lot all at once. Anyone would have had problems with that information, if they had gotten it the way you did." Quinton says reassuringly.

"Thanks Quinton."

"I have the General on the line, Jane" Martha informs her over the intercom.

"Teriq, I'm so glad you were available. Have you

heard the news?" Jane asks quickly.

"I had heard about an earthquake that happened near Alaska. It was big enough that this area actually felt the rumblings."

"That earthquake created a tsunami that hit the coastline of Alaska with devastating force. I'm sure thousands have died. The earthquake also caused an eruption to occur at Yellowstone National Park." she informs him quickly.

"Jane, what are you saying?"

"We have huge natural disasters that have affected the states, from Alaska to the Midwest. You're going to need to recall our troops. We need them here, now. We've run out of time to look for my parents and now that Callander is dead, there's no need to keep looking. You need to get back to the capitol. You have troops you need to control and the best way to do that is through this office. I expect you to be back here ASAP."

"Mal, has there been any word from Jacob?"

"No" she admits in discouragement. "It's been awfully quiet for the past couple of days, at least from the west. I hope everything's alright out there."

"I'm sure it is. Jacob's quite careful and so is Kat. I doubt we have anything to worry about" Eli tries to reassure her.

"I know, it's just that with everything that's been happening, the earthquake, the tsunami and now the eruption, I hate for anyone I care about to be out of my sight for too long. I guess you can call me paranoid" she admits sheepishly. "It's starting to feel like it's the end of the world, the end times, you know what I mean."

"I hope that the underground out west didn't take any more hit's with this latest disaster" Eli adds. "I don't want any more to happen to our family. I can't take anymore family deaths."

"Yeah, I hear you" Mallory says quietly. "Devon and then Mom and Dad, I've had enough too, Eli."

"I totally understand" he admits with a small hug, grateful to still have a sister around and missing his parent's every day.

"We're going to have to start moving around, Eli. Jane's troops are getting closer every day, with the chip. We're not taking it so we'll need to move to an area of the city that's finished already. That way we don't need to worry about them showing up and forcing us to take it" Mallory says.

"Let's move into Kat's old place. It's on the south end of town. They've already completed that area."

"Good thinking Eli, let's pack up the necessities and head on over there. I want to get there early. The President's having a news conference this evening and I'm curious as to what she's got to say this time."

"I know what you mean. I hate getting caught off guard by her."

"Good evening, I'm Jim Cochran of WELT News Channel 3, Washington, live outside of the White House awaiting President Martin. This is her prescheduled news briefing, her televised information for the public on the newest information. After the natural disasters that have affected our great nation,

I'm sure her briefing will contain much more than originally planned. Here she is, President Jane Martin:"

"Thank you ladies and gentlemen of the United States; I have some information to impart to you. I've just been notified that Lieutenant Jacob Callander is dead. He was killed by a sniper's rifle right here in D.C. sometime within the past three days. Finally, we can all breathe easy knowing that he can no longer wreak havoc with this country as he has done in the past. He has been an arch rival to me and my office since the days leading up to my taking over this country as President, after our beloved President was murdered during the funeral of the Director of Homeland Security."

"Of course, I'm saddened by this loss, however, since he did not support me or mine then he would have had to be detained anyway and I'm sure that he would have chosen death over imprisonment, so I'm thankful that it was accomplished quickly and emotionlessly."

"I no longer need to fear for my life. With Lieutenant Jacob Callander gone, this office will be allowed to run the way it was meant to. I also need to mention that when Lieutenant Callander's body was found, the bodies of his parents were also located. It is with regret that I must notify you that both Sandra and Joe Callander were discovered dead, buried near where Lieutenant Callander had been buried, at a farm miles from anywhere."

"Now that the news has been relayed, I can move on to more important matters. There is a peace conference scheduled in Brussels in four weeks. I will be attending that meeting, sharing the knowledge of the chip and its importance to the future of the world."

"I know that there will be many countries, possibly all that will want to join the chip implantation and of course, why wouldn't they? The chip makes living easier by protecting the people that have them for their medical information and also doesn't give anything to the illegal's, since all must receive the chip from the country of their citizenship."

"With the peace that will now inhabit the United States, I will be able to move things more quickly without fear of reprisal from Lieutenant Callander. The people of the great United States will have a much more harmonious life than in the recent past. Hopefully, with him gone, there will no longer be a threat hanging over all of us."

"Please remember that you will be called to receive your chip, do not be late. It is inappropriate that you not show up for your chip placement since there are many that are waiting for theirs in line behind you."

"We, the United States, are still monitoring China, whom was responsible for the bombing of the Church in Texas. We have retaliated and taken them down to the point that they are now begging for our help."

"We have commandeered North Korea as our staging area and have displaced their citizens in the act. However, I have spoken to their President and we have come to an agreement. Together we will help China regain its footing; however we will NOT rebuild them. They destroyed something of great value here in these United States and we have destroyed much that was great in their country."

"According to the President of China, they've learned their lesson about the United States and have promised never to attack us again, since I promised them that if they attack one more time, they will be annihilated. The history books will tell the story of how there used to be a country called China but it no longer exists because it came up against the world's most powerful force, the United States" she states arrogantly.

"We are the most powerful country, have been in the past and are working towards that title again. The weak ones are no longer in office to bring our country down. I promise to protect you, the people of this great country, and make this a country you will be proud of again" she ends with a steely glint in her eyes.

Chapter Twenty-Six

"Eli, she's freakin scary; it makes me sick that she found Devon and Mom and Dad, and is using that information to reassure the American people. I just want her dead. She doesn't deserve to be spared, for what she's doing."

"That woman knows no bounds" Eli adds in disgust.

"To have found their bodies infuriates me, how dare she dig up those that we laid to rest? What are we going to do" she cries, her voice rising with each emotional word.

"Shh, it's alright Mallory, think about it" he says urgently as he grabs her to quiet her down.

"If you think about all that she said tonight, it might be beneficial for us. She really believes that the dead body is Jacob's and not Devon's. That could work in our favor. If she really believes that Jacob is dead, then she might lighten up on the pressure to the undergrounds. She certainly won't feel as threatened with him out of the picture. We all look enough alike that we could and did pass for each other when we were growing up. Since she hasn't really seen Jacob, it would be easy to keep her in the dark about who really died" he admits, a glimmer of hope lighting his eyes, his first positive emotion in weeks.

"I suppose you're right" she admits begrudgingly. "I hate her" she mutters "She's torn my family apart."

"Yes she has, but look at the world, look at what she's doing to the world. There are only a few of us that are against her. We're definitely in the minority with our decisions. She's got the whole or at least about ninety percent of the people in the states on her side. What we're doing goes against everything we've been taught, against how we've lived our whole lives. If we can handle that then we're strong enough to go up against her. Who knows where this will end but we're in it till the end. It's the only hope that the United States and its people have" he replies with fervor.

"You're right Eli, I'm sorry. I'm a selfish bitch. I want my brother and my parents back. I want my life back, is that too much to ask" she cries, tears running down her cheeks, outraged.

"No it's not. It's just not realistic any more, not with everything that's happened in the past eight months or so. There are some times that wishing and dreaming are fine, but this is reality and we can't change what is. I wish I could wave my hands and we'd wake up a year ago, back to the same world we were in. It just can't be done" he admits tiredly.

"We really need to find a way to reach Jacob and let him know what's going on now. I'm sure he's unaware of the announcement that the President made tonight. I hope he takes the word seriously, it just may be the best thing that's happened for him for awhile" Mal says.

"Have you found a way to contact the west underground? There are no cell's working and the radio's are down for now. I'm not sure how long it's going to take to get things up and running again but until then, we have no way to reach anyone out there" Eli asks.

.   .

Clicks and beeps signal the radio's working, "now let's see if we can get a response" Eli informs Mal, after waiting hours for the radio's to come back into action.

"Delta come in, Delta three-eight-seven, if you read, please come in."

"This is Delta three-eight-seven, we read you, come on."

"Delta three-eight-seven this is Romeo two-four-nine, I'm looking for Delta, come on."

"Romeo two-four-nine, this is Delta three-eight-seven, go."

"Delta, my name's Eli Callander, brother to Lieutenant Jacob Callander. I need to talk with you."

"Go on Romeo two-four-nine, you have my attention."

"Lieutenant Callander is good, at the moment out west and I was hoping that you were able to contact him from your base. I am unable to from here plus it wouldn't be safe."

"Copy Romeo, that's an affirmative. What message do you want relayed?"

"Just tell him to contact me; it's the safest way to relay information that's imperative to him."

"I copy Romeo; will relay that message, Delta out."

"Now we just play the waiting game. Hopefully Jacob will contact us real soon. I'd hate for this information not to get to him, but I think we're going to make his day once he hears."

"I hope so" Mallory says uncomfortably. "What if we cause trouble for him just by contacting him? I can't lose another sibling, Eli. What if the president's black-ops unit is listening in on us right now? How can we guarantee his safety?"

"We can't, right now all life is a challenge. We have to move forward with this and the only way to do that is by letting him know. We'll have to chance someone else intercepting this information, it's our only option."

"Romeo two-four-nine this is Alpha one-two-one, come on." Jacob says and repeats "Romeo two four nine this is Alpha one-two-one, come on.

"This is Romeo two-four-nine."

"Romeo two-four-nine, I received a message that you needed to contact me?"

"That's affirmative, Alpha. Need you to know about the last news conference, since it pertains to a Lieutenant Jacob Callander, a deceased Jacob Callander. Do you copy Alpha?"

"I copy Romeo two-four-nine, but I don't understand" Jacob says.

"The body of Lieutenant Jacob Callander was located by the Generals special-op's team on a farm just west of D.C. along with the bodies of his parents, Joseph and Sandra Callander. Romeo two-four-nine, out."

Kat looks at Jacob in shock. "How can that be?" she asks quietly. "That was Devon, not you" she says in confusion.

"I know" Snake says quietly after thinking about

what was just said. "Romeo two-four-nine, this is Alpha one-two-one, come on."

"This is Romeo two-four-nine, go" Eli says.

"Thank you for the update, Romeo two-four-nine, this is Alpha one-two-one, out."

"Romeo two-four-nine, out" Eli says and grins at Mallory, who stood by quietly during the information exchange.

"I guess he got it" she murmurs to Eli with a little smile.

"Yep, it only took him a couple of seconds. He picked up on what I said pretty fast."

"So what's up Snake" Kat asks as she enters the cave with him that they've been staying in for the past day.

"You heard the message from Eli. Jane Martin held a press conference last night and informed the world that Lieutenant Jacob Callander was dead, found buried on a farm in Virginia along with his parents."

"WHAT?" Kat says in confusion.

"No, wait, think about it" Snake says with a grin. "If she recognizes that I'm dead, then neither she, nor her General, or his special-op's group will be looking for me any longer. This should make our life a lot easier."

"Wow, that's weird. I tend to forget how much you and your bothers look alike. I can tell the difference so just assume that everyone can tell the difference."

"No, we really do look like identical siblings. We used to pretend we were each other, and no one caught on. We look alike, just not to anyone that has intimate knowledge of us. It came in handy when we were kids" Snake says, a grin etched on his face. "Poor Mallory, she's a part of the four of us, but because she's female, she never had the experience that the three of us did. She missed out."

"What's the next move then?" Kat asks Snake.

"I think it's time to give the President a little taste of how it feels to see a loved one being held prisoner with the possibility of death should things not be done according to the captor's wish."

"Wow, yes, that's awesome. Let's get this thing on the move again. I want to help get the world back to the condition it was pre-Jane Martin. I'm tired of living the life of an outcast."

"Hold on a second, Kat. The hope of the world going back to the way it was is a million to one chance. You'd be luckier buying a lottery ticket. The world will never be the way it was. Too much has changed and in a short amount of time. The only thing we can hope for now is a more peaceful existence. And even in order for that to occur, Jane Martin must go. We need someone in office that's not as destructive and has a different view of how the world should be. This is going to be a problem, since she's guarded by so many. It's going to take some meticulous planning, a lot of hard work, and our *legend* persona, but if we're lucky, we can do this."

"What's first then?" Kat asks.

"First, we talk to David Hall and see what his input is. He's the one with the hostages. Then we start gathering whatever equipment it's going to take. We need to check around and see if the President called off her specials. If not, then we wait for that time to happen. However, if she made the announcement that Eli said she did, then the specials should be well on their way back home by now. If that's the case, then we start scoping out buildings that are abandoned, we're going to need a base to work out of. It's a lot easier when everyone is closer together and we can discuss things. I'd actually prefer an underground facility. It's harder for strangers to breach."

"Didn't Captain Hall say that there was another underground facility that he knew about but didn't believe anyone else knew about? If there is, that would be perfect. A lot better than digging our own underground shelter. Hey, isn't this the area that they did the nuclear testing in back in the fifties? I know that there were underground shelters out here for that. I don't think they were all destroyed. No way, they couldn't have been, our government likes to keep secret things too much. If there is and the government knows, they could be hiding officials there and we could be standing right on top of them and not know it. We need some computers so we can start investigating, and some computer hackers. I wish Mal were out here. She'd be a big help" Kat says wistfully.

"Yep, she would, but she's needed back east. I'll radio them later and see if she can recommend anyone that could come out here, or is already out here, who knows" Snake says thoughtfully. "I wish that Rand and Mongoose were out here, too. It looks like I'll have to start at the beginning and get a new group going. I'd rather work with the ones that I trained, but, what can you do. Everyone back east is needed back east. I don't dare break up that group. I'll talk to Hall. He's been out here for quite a while, and may know people that would fit the bill nicely. That looks like it's the first order of business. I think we should put Jane's parents on the back burner for a little while, they aren't going anywhere. The longer Jane goes thinking they're dead, the happier I am. Besides, there are other things that need to be done first" Snake says.

"I'll contact Mal and see if she can get her hands on some computers and stuff. If she can, we could head in that direction and maybe meet half way to pick the stuff up. We certainly can't trust someone else to bring it, definitely not the mail. It may take longer, but it's safer than trusting it to someone else. I also want to find out when the next press conference is and what's happening at the White House. I don't trust her. We need to keep tabs on everything that she's saying and doing." Kat says.

"We also need to get everyone hiding out here the fake chip. You know that they're heading this way, to complete the project. No way will they forget these people. If, however, they see that the chips are implanted, then they have no reason to linger. I don't want anyone to receive the real one unless they want to and if they do, then they need to go home" Jacob says with finality.

Chapter Twenty-Seven

"Good evening, I'm Jim Cochran of WELT News Channel 3, Washington, live, waiting for the President of the United States. Since the powerful earthquake that happened yesterday in the pacific coast off shore of Alaska, there have been other natural disasters. It almost seems that the world is under attack. Here she is, President Martin:

"Thank you again for joining me for this emergency situation. I want to inform you of the natural disasters that have destroyed a great deal of our country. It's shocking the way things happened, but no matter how you prepare for a natural disaster, they still end up surprising you. We have very few ways of monitoring these types of disasters. The first disaster to affect the United States was the earthquake that rocked Alaska with enough force to destroy many areas. The second disaster that hit the pacific coast of Alaska was the tsunami, and that destroyed even more of the state. Then we had the eruption that occurred at Yellowstone National park, probably created due to the earthquake. Few people realize that Yellowstone National Park is a 'Supervolcano' one that has been relatively quiet in the past. However, there were eruptions many thousands of years ago; according to the USGS. They have studied that area in depth, since its' such a rare phenomenon, and have quietly warned this country of not only the asset that we have, but also the danger inherent that goes along with that asset.

"Today we faced disasters that can and do happen in the blink of an eye. Many people have been killed and many more are missing or severely injured. The most damage that has occurred is in Alaska, due to both the earthquake and the tsunami. The damage that has occurred from the eruption has not even been estimated yet. Too many things are happening all at once. I promise you, that as soon as we have numbers for the eruption, you will be notified. All that I can say is everything possible is being done to help the public. I have informed our General of the Armies that we need to bring home as many of our troops as possible. They are needed here, in the home land, far more than elsewhere. We have many things to help the people with, and it is 'just' that the help comes from our own. As soon as I have anything new, I'll schedule another news conference to inform you. Thank you for listening." Jane says and turns and walks out of view.

"I'm Jim Cochran of WELT News, Channel 3, Washington. We just finished listening to President Martin address the nation regarding the emergencies that this country is now facing. Between China, the terrorist acts and the natural disasters, we've had a multitude of things happen. How she keeps all that's happened straight in her mind, just demonstrates her great capabilities as President. She's promised to continue keeping the citizens of this country informed as things change. Thank you for listening, goodnight.

"More lies, always more lies" Mallory says

quietly to Eli as she turns off the television. "She doesn't care about the people; all she cares about is power, how much power she wields."

"I know" Elis says, "but, we know better, and the ones that have escaped this life for the underground know better. Our numbers are gaining day by day, so if we can just hang on, I'm sure something good can come from this. Don't ask me what, but something good."

"We need to try and contact Jacob. After the eruption at Yellowstone, we have no idea how affected they were. For all we know, they could be gone" Mallory says tearfully.

"No way, Mal, I'm sure they're fine. They aren't staying near Yellowstone; they're further west than that."

"I know, it's just I haven't heard from them for a while, so I'm worried" she admits tiredly. "So many things are wrong, Eli. Is there any hope that the United States can be better? Can we actually plan a future? What about our lives, can we think about more than what we have, with any hope at all? Will I be able to get married, have children, become a grandparent, someday?"

"Mal, I can't answer those questions, no one can. That's the future you're talking about and no one can see the future." Eli reminds her with a quick hug. "Alright, let's try to reach them. We can at least get an idea of what's happening out west."

"Hey Eli, what's up?" Jacob asks after answering the phone. "We're okay. We've been rocked slightly by the earthquake. Portions of some of the caves collapsed. We spent hours digging people out, but no-one was killed. Guess we got lucky. We're just now headed back to the truck, so we can move it. What?" Jacob exclaims. "We had no idea. We haven't had time to listen to any news. It is cloudy here, but I just figured it was from a storm moving through. Wow, yeah, I'll let her know. I'll call you back after we've had time to charge the phone, another reason the truck's important. That and transportation. It takes forever to walk everywhere."

"What's up, Snake, you sounded a little shocked?" Kat asks curiously.

"Yeah, a little, you won't believe what I just heard." Jacob promises.

"Give" Kat says.

"Eli just informed me that Yellowstone National Park erupted. There are fires all over the area from the lava and hot ash. It's the first time in our history that it's erupted. Granted, it is a Supervolcano, but no one really ever expected to see this happen in our lifetime."

"Wow" Kat says. "How bad was it?"

"Eli said it was a moderate eruption. Nothing like Mt. St. Helen's, back in the eighties, but it was definitely an eruption."

"Hmm" Kat murmurs, thinking. "Is there any way to get some national news on?"

"Not until we're back at the truck. The phone's almost dead. I need to recharge it before we try to use it again. Maybe David Hall's got something we can use temporarily. We should be back there within the hour." Snake says with fatigue.

"Does it seem foggy to you, Snake?" Kat asks

after another half hour goes by.

"Yeah, actually it does. It's possibly ash, I guess. We're not that close to Yellowstone, but ash from a volcanic eruption can travel great distances. It's possible we're seeing some of that here.

"Hey Captain Hall, what's going on?   There seems to be some agitation among the people" Jacob says once they locate Hall.

"I was just trying to spread the news. A bunch of us are headed towards Yellowstone. They had an eruption, you know? Well, our darling President refuses to send any troops there to help the people evacuate, she's sending them all to Alaska. Granted, they need them there, but we need some at Yellowstone, too. The eruption's caused hundreds of wildfires to spring up in the area, there are thousands of people in danger, thousands that need help evacuating or they'll die. We're taking every vehicle we can find and as much food and water available. We can't just sit back and not do anything while people are dying."

"I had no idea. We just found out about the eruption about an hour ago. Eli called to let us know what's been happening. Unfortunately, I couldn't talk long, the phones almost dead, so didn't know about the fires or the need for help."

"Yeah, it's a mess" Hall agrees. "This is our chance to help some of our people, let them know that the underground people are just like them, only they don't follow the President. It could be a tide turner. Besides, some of these people have loved ones that live in that area. They could no more let them die, than I could if they were mine."

"We just spent the day digging out some of the cave dwellers. That earthquake in Alaska did some damage to some of the caves. There were rock falls in quite a few of them, but thankfully we were able to get everyone out safely. There's only a few of us that were able to dig, so it took a lot longer than we thought it would. We didn't even know about Yellowstone until we were almost here. It is foggy here, I thought it was my imagination, but it's definitely getting foggier," Jacob admits.

"Yeah, that's part of the problem that Yellowstone's creating. It's not just the ash from the eruption, but all the fires are adding to the smog in the atmosphere. It'll get much worse before it gets better. Unfortunately, some of the people have breathing problems and this will make things real bad for them. I wish there was something that I could do, but not even a hospital would be able to help. There are just too many people and not enough clean air. Needless to say, some of the underground people will be heading farther west, away from the smoke and smog. The rest are joining us and heading towards Yellowstone. How about you two" Hall asks. "Oh, and what do you want me to do with Jane's parents? We still have them hidden, but now that we're headed for Yellowstone, I really don't want to keep guards on them. We'll need every spare hand available."

"Yeah, I was just thinking about them." Jacob murmurs. "I didn't want to tip my hand about them yet. I wanted to save them for something bigger, a time when the only thing that will help would be to bring out that ace in the hole. I'd rather take them with us. We're going to need them, probably soon with all the bullshit that Jane's pulling. I say attach three good guards to them and they can help with the fire victims when not on guard duty."

"Fine, that'll work" Hall says.

"We're going to head for the truck, stock it up with whatever we can find and see who else needs transportation. We could fit a couple of more people in, I believe. Better yet, send Jane's parents and her guards and we'll transport them."

"That will be a big help, Lieutenant. Thanks!" Hall says before turning to leave.

"Have you heard the most recent news update? Mt. St. Helene's erupted at the same time as Yellowstone, only with a much greater magnitude. The ash and smoke are combining with the ash and smoke from Yellowstone and the news is saying that close to a third of the United States is covered with a dense fog/smog type thing. We're gonna need some kind of air filtering system in place way before we get close to Yellowstone. You can't breathe in the ash, it clogs the lungs, not to mention a great deal of the smoke is not only from the fires but also contains sulfer, from the eruptions. That's a toxic chemical. If you see any large towns as we're driving, maybe looking up a fire department would be a smart thing to do. I know they stock breathing apparatus and might be generous enough to loan us some. All the municipalities have fire departments, but seldom are they used constantly, so I'm sure they have spare respirators. Who knows, they might even have some volunteers that would like to join us in Wyoming. It's not like it's that far from where we are now" Jacob says.

"Stop, that's Hall up there to the left. Pull in there and see what he wants. Hey David, what's up?" Jacob asks after the truck stops next to Hall.

"We need something for breathing. Everyone's having some type of breathing difficulty, now that we're within miles of the fires. What do you recommend Lt.?"

"We made some stops on the way here, at the little towns and their fire departments. We were able to pick up a few respirators, but certainly not enough for all those with us now. But, there's a way to make a respirator out of naturals things. I'll show you how and you can pass the information on."

"You just need some charcoal, and up ahead there should be plenty of burned out trees. Then a spare piece of clothing, preferably tee shirt material, something thin enough for air to get through, and then some dried grasses. You lay the grasses on a piece of clothing, add the charcoal on top of that, then some more of the dried grasses. Top it off with another piece of clothing, tie it all together and place it over your nose and mouth. It takes a few minutes to get used to breathing through the cloth, but once you do, it's a relief. The air is marginally cleaner. It's the best we can do, it's better than nothing."

"Thanks Jacob, it's appreciated. I'll give some lessons to the troops we picked up on the way through, some National Guardsmen that were headed our way. At least they were when we picked them up. Unfortunately, they went against orders. They were being deployed to Alaska, but are from around here and didn't want to leave their families in danger, so they took over the lead and moved this way."

"What do you mean they took over the lead?" Jacob asks suspiciously, his military background kicking in.

"They took over the lead by leaving their command officer back about fifty miles. They didn't want to hurt him, but weren't willing to go any further, not for this president. They're a lot like us, Jacob. Wanting to help but not if it means helping the president."

"Good men" Jacob murmurs. "I'm going to head over to the group that were following us. It's always good to keep visible in case anything happens. I'll see you later" Jacob says to Hall.

"That's all there is to it" David says to the troop he was training on air filter systems.

"Where did you learn how to do that Sir, if you don't mind my asking" a young guardsman asks.

"From a friend of mine, Jacob Callander" Hall says.

"THE Jacob Callander, Sir? Wow! It sure would have been nice to meet him, before he was killed. He was a hero to a lot of my unit members. We thought he was awesome. We could use more like him, unfortunately, he was a one of a kind" the young guardsman says out loud.

"Yeah, he was awesome, a hero. That's all people talked about for the last six months or so. Wish he could have been here for this" another guardsman says.

"Wait, I have someone that you'd probably like

to meet. Kat, can you come over here for a minute?" Hall yells.

"What's up Captain?"

"Gentlemen, I want to introduce you to Lt. Kat Thomas. She worked with me in D.C. prior to my heading west. This woman can probably tell you everything you'd want to know about Lt. Jacob Callander. She's been a friend of his, for what, fifteen years or more?" Hall says to Kat in a questioning tone.

"Yeah, we go way back." Kat admits quietly.

"Man, we would have loved to meet him. He was a hero to us, a LEGEND, Ms. It saddens us that he had to die. With everything that's going on we sure could've used his help" the young guardsman says, hero worship in his voice.

"That's really nice of you to say. He was pretty awesome, very loyal and an excellent soldier and officer. He would have liked meeting you. Wait, he would like to meet you" Kat says with a grin. "Hey, Snake, you busy? I need to talk to you." Kat yells.

"What's up?" Jacob asks when he gets to the group.

"This group's been lamenting on how they would have liked to meet their hero before he was killed."

"Who's their hero?" Snake asks suspiciously.

"Jacob Callander" Kat says with a grin.

"Who?" he repeats after he finishes choking.

"Yep, you heard me" she finishes with a smirk. "Gentlemen, let me introduce you to Lieutenant Jacob Callander, also known as Snake."

"But, Sir, we were told you were dead" the young corporeal stammers, red faced. "We heard it on

TV. The President announced you were dead, she even said that they found your body. I don't understand."

"It's hard to kill a legend, boys" Kat admits with a laugh.

"Wait, wait" Jacob says "I'm trying to keep that rumor running. I'm hoping that as long as everyone thinks that I'm dead, the easier I can move around and get things done. What you heard just now, stays here. That's an order, gentlemen."

"Yes Sir!" they all promise.

"We're getting ready to head out. Now that everyone's had the opportunity to produce a filter mask, we can get moving. We have fires to put out and people to rescue, let's move!"

"Don't go too far Kat, the smoke's too dense. I don't want to lose anyone in this area" Jacob yells, between coughs.

"I don't think there's anyone here" Kat yells to the young national guardsman, who's standing close to her while chopping at a house that's burning almost out of control.

"Probably not, this house is pretty much gone" he yells back

"Let's move on to another area. We need to stop this fire from spreading to the next house." Kat yells, sweat running in rivulets through the black soot that covers everything.

"Look out Kat, that tree's ready to hit the ground" Jacob yells as he grabs Kat by the arm and pulls her out of the way. "You need to pay closer attention. This is a pretty dangerous area." Jacob yells before moving to shovel a deeper trench. "The only way we're going to gain any ground is to increase the width of the trenches. As far as I can see, there are no more people trapped in this area. We need to focus on stopping the fire from advancing."

"I need to take a break" Kat says to Snake. "We've been going non-stop since early this morning. It's after seven at night now and all I've had is water. I need to eat something, I've got no energy left.

"Let's move to that area on the left. It looks relatively smoke free, or at least clearer than here" Snake says.

"Here's a protein bar, and some fresh water. It's not much, but it's the best we can do for now.

"Thanks, Snake. I'll take it. I'm so hungry I'd eat anything right now" Kat says exhausted. "I'm not sure how much more I can give today. We've been going at this since we got here this morning, and that was after an eight hour drive and no sleep.

"You're right, it's been a long day, kitten." Snake says tiredly. "I wish there was a creek nearby. I could use a bath to get some of this thick soot off. My skin can't breathe with so much crap on it" Snake says.

"There is one, about a half mile back. I saw it on my way through there. It's not in the fire area, so it should be relatively clean. I'll show you" she promises as they head out.

"We need to go to Wyoming, and see what kind of damage the eruption caused. The troops are all at the Alaska disaster. I don' have enough to go around, unless you want me to send the Iranian troops?" Teriq informs Jane.

"You can't spare any, Teriq? That's not going to endear me to the public, if I don't take this extremely seriously, and send help. I doubt that the people affected by this will care one way or the other, what nationality the help is. Send some. Its way more important for the perception of me than it would be for who I send. As long as help arrives, then the public will be fine, I'm sure."

"Okay, I'll send some of the visiting troops. We should be able to see a little about what's going on out there, the TV crews are planning on covering the ravaged area's in the morning. It'll be good to see firsthand what exactly is going on and how bad it really is" Teriq says.

"By the way Teriq, any word from out west, on my parents? I know I told the public that I'd stop searching for them and have those troops help the people, but I expect you to still be looking for them. They're more important to me than a thousand Americans."

"Of course, I'll make sure of it, Jane, and will keep you updated on where we've looked."

"Thanks Teriq, I knew I could depend on you."

"Do you hear that" Snake yells at Kat the next morning as they begin again, the fight to stop the fire.

"Yeah, it sounds like a helicopter. It's not going to be easy to land something like that around here, but they'll do it, anything for the story." Kat yells back.

"Try to stay out of the limelight. It makes it easier to stay under the wire. See if you can find Hall and put him in charge of the media."

"I saw him not long ago, he's close. I'll find him for you and give him the heads up, Snake" Kat promises.

"Thanks. I'll be right here when you get back" he says while finishing his section of trench.

"Hi, this Jim Cochran of WELT News, Channel 3, Washington, with Carol Littman, live at a scene near Yellowstone National Park. Carol, it's Jim, you're live."

"Thanks Jim. I'm Carol Littman of WELT news, Channel 3, Washington, near Yellowstone National Park. As you can see by the live video feed that we're sending, it's pretty much a disaster. I haven't seen any American troops out here helping, but if you think about it, we are stretched pretty thin, what with China, terrorism and the Alaska disaster. We're either running low or we're out of troops to send here. However, there are people helping. Here's the leader of a rather large group of citizens, David Hall. David, what can you tell me about what's happening here in this area? Who are those people that look to be digging, and trying to put out the fires?

"Carol, these are American citizens, trying to help their fellow man. When disasters strike, the people gather to help. It's part of what makes America such a great place. People from all walks of life, offering anything and everything they have to help. These people are part of the underground forces. They wanted to show everyone that they are no different than anyone else. They're not bad people, they're not out to hurt anyone, they're just misunderstood. They love this country, they love their way of life. They're your mothers, fathers, sisters, brothers, neighbors. They don't like how the country is being run, which is their right. After all, we live in the land of the free and the home of the brave, no matter the leader. This just demonstrates to everyone that the underground citizens are not the ones causing the problems."

"Thanks, David. It's impressive, to see so many people helping, without being told to. Just by helping their neighbors, strangers, it's an excellent demonstration of the American spirit. There seems to be hundreds, maybe thousands that are helping."

"Carol there are thousands helping and the numbers keep getting larger, day by day. There are more people out there then you know that do not believe in the way the country is being led. They would rather protect their freedoms than follow blindly. After all, it's what this country was founded on. If you can't take care of each other, then humanity loses. None of us can afford that loss."

"Teriq, what the hell" Jane says, shocked. "You need to get our damn troops out there. We can't afford this kind of televised bull. I want troops dispatched immediately."

"Jane, there are NO troops to dispatch. We already sent them everywhere else. You wanted them sent to Alaska, remember? You said that the mid west could take care of its self!"

"Yes I did, but now they need to get to Yellowstone. I will not allow anyone to put me in a bad light. I demand that you stop that underground, before more people join. And while you're at it, make sure they take the chips, might as well kill two birds with one stone. We will take over the rescue operations and plant the chips while we're at it. All will follow my lead, or they die, including that damn underground."

"Right away President Martin" Teriq says as he pulls out his phone and prepares to order the troops stateside, again.

"Wait, watch," Jane says anxiously. "Look in the back ground, Teriq. Who do those people look like to you? That's my parents, I know it is. Wait, they might zoom in to that area. That looks like my parents" she says excitedly. "Why would they be working with the underground? They would never choose to do that freely. I'll bet that they're being held hostage. That's the only way they would ever take that side."

"Jane, why would they help if they were hostages? If I were a hostage, I wouldn't do anything that would help my captors. As a matter of fact, I would do everything in my power to hinder my captors. Anything to cause trouble, make things more difficult." Teriq says quietly.

"They look like they chose to participate in the help. I don't see anyone holding a gun to their heads to get them to help."

"How dare you" Jane says as she rounds on Teriq, going nose to nose with him. "You may not speak like that about my parents. Never! Do you understand Teriq? I will not tolerate that from anyone."

"Fine Jane, but I insist that you look closely, make sure that you're right. I would hate to see you open yourself to danger. You already have enough to watch out for. If you think about it, it explains why we've heard nothing from them or from their captors. If they truly are not captives, then they wouldn't contact you, there would be no need."

"Teriq, those are MY parents. They've been captives all this time. They would NEVER betray me or their duty. Now, this discussion is over. You WILL dispatch troops to Yellowstone, and you WILL get my parents back from that group. That's a DIRECT ORDER" Jane yells. "Now get out of my sight."

Chapter Twenty-Eight

"It looks like we've gained ground, finally" Snake says, a week after arriving at the park. "The fires seem to be under control, at least as far as I can see. Everyone we could get out is out. The area's totally devastated, but we've had no more deaths, which is a good thing. Let's take the truck out and see if we can spot anymore problems" he says to Kat.

"Wait, who's that?" Kat asks after spotting a few trucks headed towards them.

"I'm not sure" Snake says as he prepares for the worst, by pulling out his sidearm.

"We come in peace, Sir" a young man says as he jumps out of the first truck, hands high, showing no weapons.

"Where are you from?" Snake asks as he wanders closer.

"We just drove about thirty miles, west of Jackson Corners. That area's totally devastated, Sir. We were looking for a safe place to live. The town we came from is pretty much gone. All the buildings have been burned out. These are the people from Jackson Corners. They've got nowhere else to go, they're hungry, tired and some are wounded. We need help, Sir."

"You've come to the right place, then" Snakes says after scanning the vehicles and seeing the dirty, exhausted faces of men, women and children.

"You're welcome to whatever help we can provide. We have food, it's not much, but it's more than you probably have. There's also a few medic's with the group, so we can help those who are wounded."

"Thanks so much Sir, we all really appreciate it." the young man says, tears running down his cheeks. After he turns around and motions the okay to all the people, a cheering goes up and those that are able jump down from the trucks.

"Kat, get some of the guys and have them help these people. Find a couple of the medics and send them over here. We need to set up a triage area, to see what we're dealing with. I think food is the most important thing right now, especially for the kids. They all look pretty hungry. So what happened? Those injuries look more like war injuries, not fire injuries" Snake says after seeing three men being helped to the triage area with suspicious looking wounds.

"It was the strangest thing, Sir. One minute we were digging trenches to stop the spread of the fire, the next, we had people shooting at us. They looked like the army, but they didn't speak English. I think they were the troops that the President ordered in. You know those Iranian troops. They certainly weren't there to help us, more like to kill us all. We were lucky to get away, unfortunately, not all of us were lucky, it was a massacre. We had to leave some of the people behind, they were mortally wounded."

"How many troops would you say were involved in this?" Snake asks.

"There were way more than us. So, I would guess maybe a hundred, maybe more."

"Did they follow you?" Snake asks.

"They were trying to, but there were fewer of us, so we have a head start. How big of one, I'm not sure. Maybe a half hour, maybe more, they really couldn't follow too quickly. Their vehicles were military issue. Harder to get through some of the areas we went through, besides, we're from around here, so had a general idea of where we wanted to go. We just got really lucky to happen across you, Sir."

"Kat, gather up the troops. We're going on the offensive. I don't want to allow that group to get into our area. These poor people have been through enough for now."

"On it Snake" she says as she hurries out of the area, whistling for the national guardsmen that have been assisting with the fire containment.

"Gather all the men and meet me at the south side of the cleared out area. We've got enemy troops headed this way. You have five minutes to gather everyone, including weapons and anything else that may give us an advantage. We need to be ready before the other troops arrive."

"I can have my troops gathered and headed out Ms, if that would be a help?" the young guardsman offers.

"No, Lt. Callander will be giving the orders. You are to report to the south side of the cleared out area, for further orders."

"Yes, Ms."

"Lt. Callander, all the troops are ready and waiting for further directions." Kat says formally to Snake, since more than a hundred guardsmen are listening to the exchange.

"Thanks, Kitten. I'll be right there."

"Gentlemen, thank you for the speediness. It's appreciated. I'm not sure how much longer we have until the foreign troops find their way here. I do know that they are loaded for war, not rescue. They're also shooting anyone that they feel is a hindrance. We're going to be ready for them. I do not intend to lose anyone to these soldiers." Jacob says firmly. "We're going to stay here and prepare, let them come to us. It's time to teach you a little about special-ops and how it works."

"Kat, I need all snipers spread throughout the area. Make sure they all have good visibility for oncoming troops. Now hustle." Snake demands.

"Alright men, pay attention. We're about to come under attack. When a special-ops unit comes under attack we take over the aggressor mode, shoot first, ask questions later, and take no hostages. Your ability to use silence is of the utmost importance. You never want to give way your positions. I wish I had more time to prepare you, but I don't. I want everyone here to spread out, go about five hundred yards east and watch for the Iranian troops. They should be here momentarily. Do not let them enter this area. This is the protected area. We have men, women and children to protect. Now move, move . . ."

"Keep your men firing; we need to stop these assholes before they get any closer to base." Jacob yells at the young guardsman. After more than an hour of battle, quiet surrounds the area.

"Shit" Jacob says when he comes across the young guardsman that was leading the troops, lying on the ground, blood soaking through his uniform shirt, a glazed look on his face.

"You're going to be okay" Jacob says as he whistles for help. "Stay with me, kid. What's your name?

"Greg, Sir. Greg Landower" he murmurs. "I'm from Casper. Please tell my parents what happened to me" he says quietly, gasping for air.

"Stay with me Greg. You're going to be okay, you can tell them yourself. Just stay with me" Jacob orders as he puts desperate pressure on the worst of the chest wounds covering the young man.

"Yes Sir" Greg mumbles, gasps and dies.

"Damn it" Jacob yells. "I'm sorry Greg. It was an honor to serve with you" Jacob says quietly as he reaches out to close his eyes, anger in his movements. "You have not fought in vain, Greg. You are a hero."

More gunfire erupts in the distance as Jacob moves through the area in search of Captain Hall. "Hey David, how's the casualties here" he asks when he finally finds him.

"We've had light casualties, Jacob" David Hall says. "But any casualty is too many as far as I'm concerned" he says in anger. "We're fighting in our own homeland, against forces that are supposedly helping the President. Maybe they are, but they certainly aren't helping the people of this country. This whole world is freakin backwards. Nothing is what it seems anymore."

"Get ready, the firefight seems to be getting closer" Jacob says as he hears more weapons going off. "Wait, what the hell? Those sounds are too far away. Someone else is attacking the Iranian troops."

It sounds like it's coming from behind them. I haven't seen this since Beirut, where I was part of a special-ops group, and we were pinned down. Mongoose brought some guys in to save our asses. Those have to be special ops, they moved too quickly and quietly. I wonder if it's Mongoose again," Jacob thinks.

"They were back east, but could have decided to head west, see if there was anything they could help with. Or maybe they decided to follow the Presidents troops, since they're foreigners.

"Jacob, how's it going man" Mongoose asks after the fire fight stops, quiet reigns in the area and the special-ops group finds the underground.

"Mongoose, you're an answer to a prayer, man." Jacob says as he slaps him on the back.

"Awww gee, Jacob." Mongoose says with a grin.

"Kats gonna be happy to see you" Jacob admits smiling. "It's been a rough few weeks, but she'll be happy to have her cohorts around again, less pressure" Jacob says just before the sound of a happy scream is heard.

"Mongoose, hey, I'm so glad to see you" Kat says as she grabs him in a big hug.

"Told ya" Jacob adds with a laugh.

"Whoa Kat . . . let go, I'm not going anywhere" Mongoose says after giving her a big hug, his face all smiles while he peels her off of him.

"When did you get here? Are you alone? Who

came with you" Kat asks in a rush.

"I just got here, no and everyone." Mongoose says with a straight face.

"What?" Kat says confused.

"I answered your questions, that's all, and in the order that they were asked" he adds laughing, when she still looks confused.

"Oh, OH, everyone's here? Where?" Kat asks as she spins around to look.

"They'll be here in just a minute. They were tying up some loose ends." Mongoose promises.

"Mal, you're here!" Kat says with a scream and a run for a hug.

"Kat, how are you, you doing okay? I've missed you" Mallory says as she hugs her friend. "Eli's right behind me. We had some Iranian soldiers that needed our attention, so it took us a little longer than Mongoose, but we made it. Rand's with us, and Lucas, and we picked up another twenty of Jacob's special-op's group. Our group just keeps getting bigger."

"That's awesome, Mal. It's been a huge job to get all the fires out, but we did it. Haven't had time for anything else, but at least we accomplished that and we didn't lose anyone. Unfortunately, we lost quite a few just now with that skirmish. Jane's never going to stop the bullshit."

"True. We need to have a meeting about our president. There are some things that have changed and some that are just wrong" Eli says after joining the group and hearing the last part of the sentence.

"Eli, welcome, bro" Jacob says with a man hug and a slap on the back.

"Hey Jacob, it's good to see you" he says with a hug back.

"We need to talk to our people, then we can go somewhere and catch up on what's going on now" Jacob says after greeting everyone that made it through with Mongoose.

Chapter Twenty-Nine

"What the fuck is going on, Teriq? You lost contact with our Iranian troops? All of them? How the hell can that happen, without a bomb going off to take them all out? Just how many did you lose contact with?" she demands, furiously.

"Now hold on Jane. I didn't lose contact with all the troops, just the ones that were headed to Yellowstone. Who knows, maybe Yellowstone erupted again. Maybe because of that, their radios are out. I'm not seeing this as a huge problem nor a loss of troops. Any number of things can happen out in the field to cause silence. I believe they're all fine, unless, like I said, there was another eruption. They were a well trained group. You don't have anything to worry about with these guys."

"What are you going to do to find out, Teriq?" she asks sarcastically. "Wait for them to call you? Tell you everything's fine? You may have faith in them and their abilities, but I don't."

"Actually, I'm dispatching that small special-ops group that we have. They've been waiting for something to do for a few days now. Might as well use them" he says quietly, anger bubbling just below the surface. *How dare she talk to me that way*, he thinks. *Soon Jane, you will find life a little different. Things will be the way they were meant to be.*

411

"President Martin, I have a call on line two for you" Martha says after Jane picks up the phone.

"Put it through Martha." "This is President Martin. What can I do for you?" she asks the voice on the other end of the phone.

"President Martin, my name is John and I happen to be one of the underground leaders. I have some information for you regarding your parents."

"My parents, John? My parents are missing and presumed dead. Can you clarify that for me?" she asks.

"Yes I can. Your parents are not missing but are being held by the underground forces as a safety net. You'll be able to view them at nineteen hundred hours today on channel fourteen, and hear the message that they have to pass on to you. Make sure you tune in, since I will not be responsible for them should you not."

"John, how do I know you're legitimate?" Jane asks sarcastically.

"Tune in and find out, Jane, and you'll have no doubt that I'm legitimate. If you don't, I can't guarantee the safety of your parents for any length of time" he says and hangs up.

"Good job, David. Now we just need to get our "hostages" ready for their fifteen minutes of fame." Jacob says. "Make sure the room is ready with no possible way to identify it. Just the prisoners and their chairs, and the American flag making a statement of no doubt who's taking these actions. And make sure the guards have all black including face masks, goggles, gloves and clothes. I don't want there to be anyway to identify them. We can't take any chances; Jane has some far reaching tentacles, like the bug that she is."

"You got it Jacob. It's close to being ready as we speak. Just about everyone involved volunteered for this job. It was tough picking only a couple" David admits with a laugh.

"It's everyone's dream come true for the moment. Anything to aggravate the president, she's just not as popular as she thinks" he agrees with a chuckle. "I'm not sure how much longer we're going to be able to stay here without discovery. After the broadcast tonight, we'll be shortening our time considerably. Put the word out that everyone needs to be ready to leave with short notice. I'm headed out to start passing on that info now. She's going to get pretty mad tonight and her temper causes her to make some rash decisions. I have no doubt that she's going to throw her special-ops group at us and I'm sure it will be to destroy, not take hostages. She still doesn't know that I'm alive, that's about the only good thing left. I'm not too sure how long that's going to hold, though. She's already suspicious. I just wish I still had a snitch on the inside. It would help keep us not only safer but ready. I'm out of here. I'll be back before the broadcast. See you tonight David."

"See ya Lieutenant."

"There you are" Snake says after locating Kat.

"Hi Snake. What do you mean there you are? Were you looking for me" she asks.

"Yeah, I wondered if you wanted to watch the broadcast with me tonight?"

"Sure, I'd like that. Want to go now? It's only a half hour from now."

"Let's go then. So how was your afternoon Kitten" Snake asks as they start walking towards the safe house, where the Martins are being held.

"Good, busy and slightly productive, so good."

"Mine too, busy, and productive. After this broadcast we may have to do the quick escape thing again. You know Jane. She lives with a very short fuse. Actually she keeps things pretty fun because of that."

"Yeah, she's pretty predictable." Kat agrees with a grin.

"Let's check out the room. The broadcast is scheduled for ten minutes from now."

"Awesome, the whole room is black. The flag stands out nicely against the dark color. The table blends, and the guns are a nice choice, don't you think? I bet Jane get's really pissed when she sees her parents against that back-drop." Kat says gleefully.

"Yeah, I can see her getting really pissed." Snake admits.

"Did you feel that" Kat asks as she grabs on to Jacobs arm. "It felt like a little earthquake, or something."

"Yeah, I felt it. Weird. It could have been a small earthquake. There are fault lines in this area of the country. Hope that's the worst of it. I'd hate to have to move all these people out of here fast. That could pose a problem. We've gathered quite a following, what with all the extra troops and the civilians from neighboring towns."

"The broadcast is starting in just a few more

minutes. There are Jane's parents, and the troops that are representing us. Stay back so that there's no way the camera can pick us up. I'd like to keep our whereabouts secret for as long as possible. I'm getting a lot more things done incognito than if they knew we were still alive."

"Alright, listen."

"We know you can hear us Jane. Do you notice that your parents are alive and healthy looking? They're going to stay that way, as long as you back off with your search. We are working towards a common goal, the goal of the safety of this country. If you can't meet our demands, then you will watch your parents lives snuffed out on television, just like your preferences for the American citizens, that you feel have committed some type of crime. Your parents are guilty of a crime against this country, treason. Their treasonous act, against the true United States of America, has the penalty of death. You . . .

"What happened," Jane screams when she hears screams, sees dust clog the air, the ceiling starts to collapse, and then the walls. The camera starts shaking and falls to the ground recording feet moving quickly around obstacles that suddenly appeared. Something hits the camera and the footage stops. "What happened, where are my parents?" she screams to Quinton, who was watching the video with her and witnessed the same ending.

"It looks like it was an earthquake. We can find out where they were, as soon as we pinpoint where the earthquake occurred, just now. Once we do that, you can dispatch your special-ops troops. Jane, this could be a good thing for you. Without that earthquake, it would have been nearly impossible to find out where they were broadcasting from. I'm sure your parents are fine. They've been kept alive this long and they know that they had a great bargaining chip as long as they were kept safe" Quinton says reassuringly.

"That's true, Quinton. Thanks." Jane murmurs after regaining control of her panic.

"I'll contact the General and set him on the trail of the underground" Quinton offers.

"Thanks, Quinton. I appreciate it. Tell him to contact me as soon as he has any information."

"Of course Jane, I'll let him know."

President Martin, I have a call for you on line two" Martha says.

"This is President Martin, what can I do for you" Jane says after answering the phone.

"Jane, it's Teriq. There was no earthquake in the United State just now."

"What are you talking about? I saw it happen, live on video, and so did Quinton. He was standing next to me when it happened. I have no doubt that it was an earthquake."

"Something did happen a few of minutes ago but it wasn't an earthquake. It was an eruption, out at Yellowstone National Park. It was larger than the last one that occurred nearly a week ago. I'm sorry, Jane. It's highly doubtful that there were any survivors from this latest eruption."

ABOUT THE AUTHORS

Dennis (D) and Cheral (C) live in Northeast Ohio, namely the snow belt area, with their two dogs, a King-Sheppard, (Sasha) and a Golden Lab mix (Buddy). They live near their four wonderful children; Chrystal, Heather, Joshua and Jason and their eight awesome grandchildren, Stephanie, Aaron, Shannon, Kristin, Brandon, Matthew, Sophia and Joe.

They have been blessed with love, happiness and family for more than thirty seven years. You can catch them at their website **www.dcwhite.org** or find them on facebook, twitter, linkedin, tumblr.

Use Capitol Angst in search.